CW00841624

Captive

R.J. Lewis

Copyright © 2020 R.J. Lewis

All rights reserved

The characters and events portrayed in this book are fictitious. Any similarity to
real persons, living or dead, is coincidental and not intended by the author.

No part of this book may be reproduced, or stored in a retrieval system, or
transmitted in any form or by any means, electronic, mechanical, photocopying,
recording, or otherwise, without express written permission of the publisher.

ISBN: 9798612886273
Independantly Published

To my readers, for their unending support.

PART ONE: THE MIDDLE

1.

VIXEN...

The bed dipped and a warm hard body pressed against my back. I felt his hot hand run down the side of my body and under my silky nightgown. His thumb traced along the edge of my panties.

"Baby," he whispered, his voice low. "I missed you."

I squeezed my eyes shut tighter, praying he'd stop if he didn't think I'd woken up. It was foolish thinking, but I kept waiting for the day he'd lose interest in me and leave me deserted on the bed.

He didn't stop his touching. He traced my panties for several moments. I felt him hover over me, watching the side of my face. Always watching me. Always gauging my reaction. I tried to play it cool. Let him think I was still asleep. Maybe, just maybe, he would leave me alone.

But then his finger slipped under the hem of my panties and I felt him at my core, swirling his thumb at the nub of nerves, masterfully triggering a spark of pleasure in me. My body betrayed me as my thighs squeezed around his hand, begging for more.

He laughed deep in his chest.

The show was over.

He knew I was awake.

I hated him.

I hated him.

I hated him.

And yet my thighs parted now, and my hips bucked at his touch, at the rhythm of pleasure he was pulling out of me. I bit my bottom lip, refusing to moan, refusing to let him know how good it felt. Pleasure did that. Fucking messed with your head. The second you were under the spell of pleasure, it didn't matter who was giving it to you. It only mattered that you got fucked to orgasm.

And Nixon...

Nixon knew every inch of my body.

Knew what made me tick.

What made me scream.

What made me beg.

He played me like a fiddle.

And I hated him.

I hated him.

Oh, God.

A whimper escaped my mouth.

"Ah, there she is," he groaned in my ear, biting at my earlobe as he swirled that thumb in circles over my clit. "Did you miss me, Vix?"

I didn't answer, but my eyes parted open. The room was dark still, and I didn't care there was a gun on the nightstand, the end of it pointed in our direction. He was always so sloppy with his firearms. It was like he threw his shit down as fast as he could just so he could slide into bed with me.

His index finger slid into me, and I sucked in a breath. *Oh, God.* He rubbed me as he pumped his finger slowly in and out of me, but it wasn't enough. It was never enough.

"I think you missed me," he went on, amused.

I ground my hips, lost to the feeling, grating out, "No, I didn't."

He chuckled. "I think you're lying. Your body's telling me something different, baby."

"No."

"Yes. Listen to it. You're soaking wet, you can hear me fuck you with my hand."

And he was right. The sloppy sounds of his movements filled the room, and he went quiet just to make his point.

I gritted my teeth, pissed off that he was so fucking cocky and right. "Not wet for *you*, Nixon."

"No?" he questioned lightly. "What then?"

"Could be anyone."

I kept waiting for the day these words would piss him off. I tried so hard to let him know how insignificant he was to me. How little his touches affected me.

But Nixon barked out a laugh and took it all in stride.

He didn't care. Because my body was telling him otherwise, and that was all he minded.

He removed his hand and pushed me on my back. Propped on his elbow, he looked down at me in the dark with the cockiest smile. I looked over his face, annoyed at how gorgeous he was. His dark hair fell inches over his forehead, there was stubble on his cheeks, but it didn't hide how cut his jaw was, or how raised his cheekbones were. His lips were soft and full, though right now his bottom lip was sporting a cut.

Another fight.

Another sucker punch to his face.

He deserved it. I was sure he'd enticed whoever had hit him, and I was sure the other person looked far worse.

Just as I was lapping his face up, he was doing the same. Always that look of utter reverence accompanying him as he looked me over, his smile turning wicked.

I was his toy.

Still fresh and new.

Still unbroken.

"Do you think," he wondered, playfully, "if I sucked your cunt, you wouldn't scream my name?"

My heart thumped hard in my chest. I was never immune to his dirty talk. To his dirty fucking. To his dirty, cut mouth.

I glowered at his arrogance, but I played along, feigning a yawn. "I think it could be anyone's mouth on my cunt."

He groaned deep in his throat as a dark look crossed his expression. "Fuck, when you talk like that, baby, it takes everything inside me not to split your pussy wide open around my cock."

My body warmed. I felt the flush in my cheeks as my body zinged with anticipation. I could let him fuck me, toy with me, suck me to orgasm – it didn't mean I cared for the bastard. It just meant I wasn't a victim in all this mess, and I liked that. I liked that I didn't let him ruin me a long time ago when he fucked me that first time as I cried in his arms, pleading for him not to kill me.

I'd never told him to stop then.

I wouldn't tell him to stop now.

That wasn't how this was going to work.

I wasn't going to walk free from this by playing the victim.

Sometimes I believed so heartily that I would find a way out of this prison.

Other times, it felt like I'd die in it.

And then there were times, times like now, when all that mattered was his cock buried in me. I often forgot who I was, where I was, who *he* was.

Did I mention he could fuck for hours?

Forgetting for hours was sweet bliss.

"I won't scream your name," I told him, defiantly.

His eyes came alive and his lips twisted into a sexy smirk. Nixon loved a challenge. He pulled my night gown up and over my head and then slid my panties down. I stared up at the ceiling, pretending none of this mattered. But my heart was stampeding in my chest, and every inch of me was buzzed with energy. His large body slid down the bed. He pulled apart my legs and kissed along my inner thighs. I swallowed hard, aware he couldn't see me now that he was buried between my legs. My eyes glazed and my mouth parted, tiny little breaths coming in and out as he left tingles behind every kiss.

He blew hot breaths on my pussy, taking his time now. I almost growled at him to just fuck me with his mouth already, but I went through the steps, opting to grit my teeth than to beg.

When I felt his tongue run up my slit, my body jolted, as though I'd been struck by lightning. I felt his laughter vibrate through me, and I didn't care now.

I groaned at his tongue strokes, at his teasing light flicks to my clit.

"Say my name, Vix," he demanded, sucking at my clit.

I shook my head, tears stinging my eyes. "No."

He sucked at my clit harder, adding the perfect pressure to make my eyes roll to the back of my head. My hips quaked and my feet dug into the mattress. My hand almost flew to the back of his head, but I gripped the pillows instead, squeezing them tightly as he brought me to the cusp of pleasure...and then retreated again.

Fuck, I hated him.

Playing me.

Always playing me.

"You want to come?" he asked, sucking at me gently now, leaving me utterly deprived. "Say my name."

When you've been robbed of an orgasm, it leaves behind this nasty, horrid feeling behind. Incompletion and frustration swirled inside me, angering me. It knocked the walls of my pride down, made me insane with desperation.

I was so empty, it hurt.

"Please," I whispered, begging. "Please..."

Please don't make me say it.

He sucked me hard, and I groaned in surprise, nearing that edge again.

Oh, my God, was he going to give me this?

A victory, at last.

My hands flew to his head, and I sank my nails into his scalp, forcing him to stay. He ate me out, groaning along with me, like this was pleasurable to him.

And there it was, that blinding flash of pleasure approaching.

"Nixon," I whimpered, unable to stop. "Nixon!"

I came hard, his hands pinning my hips down so I could ride the wave of pleasure with his mouth never leaving me, his tongue buried inside me.

I could feel his lips spread, feel his smile, and I wanted to claw his eyes out. He'd done it again. He'd won. I'd said his fucking name and he hadn't pried it out of me.

As he moved back over me, his naked body broad and muscled, he settled over me, crashing his mouth against mine. He parted my lips and lapped his tongue against mine, forcing me to taste my juices. He loved this sort of shit.

"Kinky bastard," I murmured into his mouth, biting gently at his bottom lip.

He chuckled, staring into my eyes as he nudged his cock between my legs, prodding my entrance. "How do you want this kinky bastard to fuck you, Vix?"

I clawed my fingernails down his back and grabbed at his ass. "Hard," I demanded, nipping at his jaw. "Real fucking hard, Nixon."

With a smirk, he delivered just that. He thrust into me, hard and punishing. I felt his balls slap against my ass as he delivered blow after painful blow. Between thrusts, he swatted at my breasts, watching them redden beneath him. The sting sent jolts to my belly, dizzying me with need. Sweat trickled down his face, his pants came out hard and scattered. He watched me, his eyes never straying from my face, as he fucked me until I came apart beneath him.

I cried his name out again, and he wore that look of victory.

He came straight after me, tensing over me, the veins in his neck protruding as he groaned through his pleasure.

His body dropped down beside me and he let out a long exhale. We both stared at the ceiling for several quiet moments. His hand went over me, trailing down my body, rubbing gently at my pussy. His finger nudged at my entrance, swirling my come and his lazily around my folds.

"Did you miss me, Vix?" he asked again, curiously this time.

A tear rolled down my face. "Yes," I whispered, hating myself for admitting it.

He grunted in response, satisfied. "We got paid handsomely."

"*You* got paid," I corrected, icily. "I took no part in it."

"I'm ensuring our future."

More tears fell. "When will you set me free?"

His strokes never paused. My question didn't phase him. "You're free already. You got everything here at your disposal."

I scoffed, shaking my head angrily. "I am a prisoner here, Nixon."

"I make sure you're safe."

"Stop lying to me."

"I'm not letting you go." He moved his finger inside me now, pumping me slowly, building the sparks up again. "You belong with me, Vix. I caught you. I killed for you. You're mine."

He said it so casually. Like it wasn't my fucking

life in the palm of his hand that he was slowly squeezing the soul out of.

He distracted me with his touch, swirling that finger until I was raising my hips needily for that orgasm.

"You're a hungry little kitten tonight," he commented, swallowing my mouth as I came undone. He kissed me like I was the air he breathed, and he couldn't get enough of it.

And I kissed him with the same intensity because I was attached to him in a horribly fundamental way.

He fucked me again, harder this time, trying to touch my soul in the process. But I never relented.

My soul belonged to *me*.

The wall I'd built since he locked me in this place never wavered. I fortified that motherfucker so he could never have it.

My soul...

Goddammit.

"Nixon," I groaned as I came again and again.

My soul belonged to me.

2.

TYRONE...

Nixon lived in the penthouse apartment of Hotel Browning. Tyrone thought it was real fucking weird for a dude to live in a hotel, but it made sense after a while.

Hotel Browning was the most luxurious hotel in the Gulf Islands. Located on Grander Island, it was surrounded by nature reserves and frequented by hippy tourists and the super wealthy.

There was so much fucking money on the island, and Nixon had buckets of it. He could afford just about anything.

Including eyes and ears.

Hotel Browning afforded him the best security for him and his hot piece of ass. He worshipped Vixen.

No, for real.

Tyrone had never seen this kind of worship since the Helen of Troy.

He had to shake his head as he sat in Nixon's penthouse living room, listening to the crazy motherfucking fight happening in the bedroom. There was a lot of doors being slammed, a lot of screaming, a lot of shit being broken.

Oh, and none of it was coming from Nixon.

He wondered if the fucker was dead.

He couldn't blame the girl for trying.

Nixon had savagely annihilated his entire crew for her. She was his property, no doubt about it. She lived and breathed in Hotel Browning and had never been allowed to leave it.

So yeah, maybe she killed him, and maybe she was screaming over his dead body.

But then he heard him.

"Shh, baby," he murmured. "Baby, baby, baby..."

As Tyrone cringed, he knew deep down this relationship was going to end in disaster. They were going to wind up killing each other.

And he knew...

He knew who would be the last one standing.

3.

VIXEN...

"**Y**ou're not being yourself," Nixon said in a soothing tone. He stood in the middle of the room, done up in his black leather jacket and jeans, his hair neatly combed back. He looked like a sex god, not ruffled in the slightest he'd fucked me until four in the morning and slept for hardly three hours before starting the day.

I glowered at him, tying the bath robe around my waist as I stormed past him and to the bed. The dress that had been put out for me to wear today was neatly arranged on the mattress, wrinkle free thanks to whatever maid had been in the apartment recently.

They were always changing.

Nixon was paranoid.

Couldn't have the same maid for more than a week.

I was sure he'd employed half the population on the island already.

I grabbed the dress and threw it on the floor before turning to him. His eyes went from the dress on the floor and back to me again.

"I'm not going to your stupid fucking celebratory party," I seethed at him.

"We're not celebrating," he corrected. "We're conglomerating."

"What does that even fucking mean?"

"Means we're going over another job."

"You just finished a job. Who'd you fucking kill this time? Some cartel king in South America?"

"No, baby," he let out a patient breath. "The cartel king I was after was here in *North* America."

I knew he was bullshitting me.

He thought this was so amusing.

I paced around the room, throwing glares his way. "You ever care that you're killing people, Nixon? People with feelings and souls. Fucking human beings!"

"You make it sound like I'm murdering little fucking elves at the North Pole."

"But you would, wouldn't you?"

He shrugged, half-heartedly. "If it paid well. If it put dresses on you like the one you just threw on the ground, sure. Pick it up, baby, and put it on."

"No," I refused. "I'm not going to be your fucking fluff on the side this time. Go find someone else."

"We've been through this," Nixon replied, staring fixedly at me. "I don't want anyone else, Vix."

"Well, you should!"

"Well, I don't."

Frustration bubbled inside me. I raced to the window and flung the curtains wide. I turned to him, screaming, "What if I threw myself out the window? Is that the only way you'll let me go?"

When Nixon didn't answer, I grabbed the lamp on

the table stand beside the television and ripped the cord out of the wall. I flung the lamp against the window and watched it crash into a hundred little pieces.

The window didn't even crack.

"Like I said the last time you did this, the windows are bullet proof, baby," Nixon explained.

I was panting now, trembling everywhere. "You won't even let me kill myself."

Nixon's jaw clenched now, the patience finally leeching out of him. "You're never going to harm yourself, kitten, I'll make sure of that. I had it done so others can't hurt *you*."

Defeated, I flung my arms up in indignation. "I can't keep living like this, Nixon. You have to let me go!"

His face remained steady when he answered simply, "Never."

"Never?!" I fumed. "Are you trying to make me go crazy? Do you like seeing me like this?"

He came to me then, and I shook my head, determined to keep him at arm's length. I grabbed whatever there was on the nightstand and threw it his way. He dodged the comb, the clock, the fucking box of tissues, and he kept moving. I smacked his hands away when he reached out, but he was just a wall that kept on coming. He wrapped his arms around me, and this time I broke. I slammed my fists into his chest, sobbing as he forced me into his embrace. He ran a hand through my wet hair, holding me tightly even as I thrashed at him.

"Shh, baby," he murmured into my hair. "Baby, baby, baby..."

"Stop calling me that!"

But like usual, he shushed me, rocking me back and forth, using that fucking word of endearment. It had never felt generic coming from him. He said it with so much feeling, it almost felt like my name. I began to settle down, sniffing into his chest, breathing his scent in like it was a drug I couldn't get enough of.

I wasn't aware he was leading me back to the bed until he stopped to pick up the dress. I tried to wriggle out of his grip, but he only tightened his hold on me.

"Let me go," I growled.

"I want you to get dressed –"

"I'm not going!"

"Baby, you're coming with me whether you like it or not."

"I'll fucking scream, Nixon," I threatened, glaring up at him. "Everyone in this fucking hotel will hear me!"

He looked down at me, the calm before the storm. "Now you know I had these walls soundproof, too, baby."

I felt suffocated. Anger ripped through me again, churning my insides. I opened my mouth and started to scream when he suddenly pushed me down on the bed and climbed over me, burying his mouth against mine. I bit at him, cutting the wound on his lip open, tasting his blood. He didn't budge, though. He kissed me, tongue against mine, swallowing my sobs whole while stroking my hair like I was a feral animal he was trying to tame.

As expected, it escalated. Nixon knew what placated me. He pulled the knot on my robe and let it fall open. I heard him slide his belt off, all the while he caged me in his grip. I thrashed against him, and he held me down with little effort. I heard his zipper come undone, heard his erratic breathing as he fought to contain me. He spread my legs apart, fighting against our storm, against my limbs fighting him off, and then he slid into me. I gasped as he sheathed himself into me. It didn't hurt. I was wet already. I knew it was coming.

"Yeah, you wanted this, kitten," he growled, his hair unruly now. "You wanted to be punished."

"No..." I groaned.

He slid out of me and then back in, causing me to whimper in the pleasure. He smiled cruelly at me. "Yes, Vix, you did."

He fucked me hard, his strokes strong and punishing. He kept shushing me gently, riding out my tantrum until I had no energy left in me. I sagged, sobbing aloud, gripping my fingers into his shirt to me. No longer pushing him away, I groaned long and deep, fighting now to keep him *to* me.

I ached still from last night. It hurt so much, tears sprang to my eyes. He was swollen and thick, and as wet as I was, it burned every time he pushed into me.

He kept telling me I wanted this. Kept telling me I needed to be punished and used.

"You do, you want to be punished, baby."

Somewhere along the way I conceded. I told him I did, and when he asked how good it felt for him to be inside me, stretching me wide open, I whimpered that I was going to come.

And I did. I came hard around his cock, uttering his name like a curse.

When he came, growling deep in his throat, his forehead plastered to mine, something within me gentled at the sight of his distant eyes looking desperately into mine.

He was searching.

Always searching for that connection.

As I lay panting beneath him, he wrapped his arms around me and scooted me up the bed, resting me in his lap, kissing me softly, his semi-hard cock still inside me.

We'd been through this song and dance too many times now.

And just like before, he forced me back into my cage, held the door wide open and waited patiently for me to climb in.

I climbed in, hating him and myself, though I didn't know which of the two I hated more.

My body trembled and the tears fell endlessly. I buried my face into his chest, nuzzling into his warmth. The beast I was trying to get away from ended up being the one I was using to soothe me.

It was so messed up.

Finally, I calmed down, and he kept on stroking me, lulling me into a light sleep. I didn't know how long I was out for, but when I woke up, he was still there, still holding me, still buried inside me.

My throat hurt from screaming. My eyes ached from crying. I felt...embarrassed for losing my shit.

Why was he enduring my outbursts? How could he remain so cool with me when I saw what he was like with everyone else?

Nixon was awful.

He was cruel and violent.

He had absolutely no issues killing people with his bare hands.

Yet he was using his hands now to calm me.

It was bewildering.

I almost wished he was cruel to me. If I feared him, I might not react so carelessly.

"This is your fault," I found myself saying, stubbornly.

"Is it?" he replied, inertly.

"You let me throw my fits."

"Do I?"

I glowered, turning to look up at him. "You do."

He looked down at me, and my breath stilled for a beat. There was blood all around his mouth and cheek. The gash in his lip looked worse than ever. Below his jaw, there was a trail of red scratch marks, ending just below the collar of his shirt. My fingers flew to the marks and up to his mouth. I tried to wipe the blood away, but he took my hand into his own to stop me.

"Nixon," I breathed out, feeling wretched inside. "I'm so sorry."

For all of Nixon's faults, he never inflicted pain on me to hurt me. He had never been violent or abusive.

It was such a clusterfuck to be humanizing my kidnapper. I knew it didn't make sense. I knew, on some base level, I had lost my marbles. This... this toxic dynamic festering like bad meat between us became our norm. Somewhere along the way I had snapped, had reacted in a similar manner, and he hadn't hurt me for it.

And now it was all I could do when the cage felt too small.

"You can make it up to me later," he said lightly, swallowing my breast in the palm of his big hand. "Right now, I want you to wash up again and get ready."

My eyes dimmed. I let out a defeated sigh. "Why do you drag me to these things, Nixon?"

He pinched my nipple, his cock stiffening inside me. "Because I like when you're near me."

"So you can control me?"

"So I can show the world you're mine."

4.

VIXEN...

I bathed quickly, rinsing off the come between my legs. Nixon simply zipped himself up, even when I told him he stunk of sex. He just smirked at me, not put off at all by it.

I'd spent so much time losing my shit, I didn't have enough time to do my hair. I let it fall in dark wet waves down my back. Then I slipped into the dress Nixon had placed back on the bed.

It was a white, lace, plunge V-neck that ended just above the knee. It hugged me tightly around my waist and hips and left little to the imagination in the cleavage department. Luckily my hair was long enough I could cover the exposing cleavage and not make it so obvious.

I applied a light layer of make-up and then slipped into high-end brand heels. Another purchase from Nixon. Everything in my wardrobe had been chosen specifically by him. I was his doll, something he could dress up and show off.

Because, as I stared at my reflection in the mirror, I was very aware this person looking back at me wasn't *me.*

During my student life, I used to live off ramen noodles and get my hair cut with a coupon at this shady salon. My clothes from the local thrift store had holes in them, and I bought make-up from the drug store next to my home. It wasn't much, and I was on my own, swamped with student debt, employed part-time at a coffee shop a short distance away from the very place Nixon robbed. And while that life sucked in its own way, it was *my* life.

I didn't have that anymore.

I felt as hollow as an eggshell. My insides had been scooped out of me. For two years, I grew my hair out, had my nails done, got my pussy waxed and my clothing picked – all to appease Nixon.

Apathetic, I stepped out of the bedroom and was horrified to find Tyrone spread out on the leather black couch. He looked like he'd been sitting there a very long time, and when his eyes cut to mine, I saw the knowing look in their depths.

Fuck.

My cheeks reddened, and I looked away, unable to meet his gaze.

He'd heard my freak out.

Had probably heard Nixon *conciliating* me.

"Holy hell," Nixon murmured, leaving the kitchen to come to me. There was a look of raw hunger in his expression as his eyes lapped me up and down. "Tyrone, tell me I'm not the luckiest man on the planet."

Tyrone laughed, studying me. "Then I'd be lying, Nixon."

Nixon came to me, his hands grabbing at my hips.

He stood over me, his gaze trapped at the plunge in my dress. Then he kissed me harshly, ruining my lipstick, sticking his tongue in my mouth to taste me. His kiss was quick but thorough. He pulled back, a wild look in his eyes. "I want to run you back into the bedroom and fuck you again in this silly little thing."

"Then we'd be late to your meeting," I replied steadily, though my heart hiccupped in my throat at the idea of being savagely tossed back down again.

I worked hard to appear bored. I didn't want him to know it was a tempting thought. Nixon, in all his fucked-up ways, had mastered the art of dominant fucking. He made it like I needed it to breathe.

I was addicted to fucking.

He could fuck me all day and it wouldn't be enough.

I was sure he liked it that way. I had no other way to spend my days. When he was gone, I was tortured with boredom and long hours trying to quench that aching pulse between my legs.

My kidnapper had turned me into a nymphomaniac.

If it wasn't so fucked up, I would laugh.

"It'd be worth it, wouldn't it?" he asked me, his voice low.

I shrugged one shoulder, appearing unperturbed. He smirked at my expression, no doubt viewing it as a challenge. He didn't like when I acted distant. In fact, it got under his skin more than anything, and even though he hid it well with his arrogant smiles, I knew it dominated his every thought. He wanted my walls down, and he could only do it through fucking.

I wondered just how much that bothered him

right then.

Tyrone cleared his throat. "Ah, well, if you guys are going to have another round, give me a heads-up. I feel like I was part of a threesome, and in reality, you know how those usually go. Two people fuck madly while one stands by doing fucking nothing."

Nixon smiled. "Tyrone, I'd cut your balls off and feed them to you before I'd let you in my bedroom."

"Never stopped you sharing before."

Nixon's jaw tightened. "I'm not sharing Vix." He tried to say it coolly, but I saw the vein in his neck throb. I was strictly off-limits.

Tyrone chuckled and stood up. He was almost as tall as Nixon but nowhere near as filled out. Tyrone was dark and beautiful in his own way. He didn't grouch at everyone, or act aggressive, and he was generally less of an arrogant asshole.

Sometimes I wished he'd kidnapped me instead.

But Tyrone didn't kidnap. He was too normal for that. Plus, his dad worked in parliament, and hiding things like a kidnapped victim in a hotel on an island in the middle of nowhere didn't seem likely to work.

"You know if Hobbs is here?" Nixon asked as we moved to the door.

"No," Tyrone answered, "but everyone arrived the last time I checked."

"Anyone we know?"

"Yeah, the usual crew." Tyrone's eyes flashed back to me, adding with a smirk, "And Doll."

I paused mid-step, groaning inwardly.

I fucking hated Doll.

5.

VIXEN...

There was a conference room on the ground floor of the hotel. It was a huge, opulent room with a long cedar table and twelve chairs. The walls were sandy beige with a few overpriced artisan paintings hanging and a sparkling chandelier dangling over the table that looked ridiculously over the top.

The floor to ceiling window boasted an incredible view of the island coast. No boats anchored on this side of the island. Nixon had once said there was not enough shelter for them, and thus, the ocean looked infinite, with the mountains in the distance adding that extra breathless element to an otherwise spectacular view.

Upon entering, I gravitated to the window first thing. I ignored the faces in the room. Along the way, I scooped up a full glass of champagne on a diamond encrusted tray and took a small sip.

I was very aware I passed Doll. She was sitting in a chair, her eyes already on me as I went. She was wearing some trashy looking red dress, and her legs were on top of the table, completely uncaring of the view she was letting everyone in on.

"I see you haven't gotten tired of your pet, Nixon," she commented, snickering.

I threw a bored look her way. Despite wearing that trashy ass dress, despite choosing the most butch position that left little to the imagination, Doll looked like a bronze goddess. She was a Puerta Rican beauty with a dimpled smile and tits to die for.

Shame she was such a fucking bitch.

"Watch your fucking tongue, Doll," Nixon retorted.

I stopped at the window and hid my smile. Nixon didn't accept anyone talking any kind of shit about me.

"I meant no offense," she replied, delicately. "Actually, I'm thinking of having my own pet too, but I hear they bite, and I wouldn't be keen on putting one down. Has that ever crossed your mind, Nixon? Having to put your pet down if it bites?"

"Doll," a voice said in warning.

I recognized the voice.

Rowan.

He spoke in a business-y tone. I'd heard a lot of their conversations and knew a bit about him. He was a real estate mogul with a lot of enemies. Apparently getting to the top meant getting his hands dirty. You wouldn't think it by looking at him. He was a tall, solid dude in a suit.

"Doll, I will put *you* down if you don't shut the fuck up in the next ten seconds," Nixon told her. "Killing you would be so easy, I think it would be fun, and nobody would miss the ice princess."

"Calm it down, guys," Tiger intervened, sitting across from her. He was another dude I'd run into multiple times in the meeting rooms. He was stocky, short and bald. I knew nothing else about him. He kept to himself, his identity completely shrouded in secrecy. "We need to work with each other, so let's tone it down."

"I'm just making conversation," Doll retorted, defensively. "Asking what to do if a pet bites isn't wrong, and I shouldn't be threatened death for it. I'm going to tell Hobbs about this."

Oh, my God. She was such a child.

"Doll, you instigated this," Rowan said.

"No, that's alright," Nixon replied. "Run to daddy if it makes you feel better, princess."

"He isn't my daddy, asshole," Doll growled.

"You sure about that?"

"Fuck you, Nixon, and fuck your little chihuahua in the corner. You should put it down before she claws your fucking face next."

Was she referring to the claw marks on Nixon's neck? I shut my eyes tightly, cringing. He should have changed into something less obvious, not show them off like little trophies.

"Baby gave these to me in a different sort of fit, Doll," Nixon returned cockily.

My cheeks warmed. Thank God they couldn't see my face.

That seemed to be the ice breaker. Chuckles filled the room. Doll let out a hard laugh, her dark mood diffused. "Touché, Nixon, you sexy bastard."

I took a bigger sip, waiting for my head to swim.

These people were so fucking dysfunctional.

This was my life. Being around people with names like Doll and Tiger.

Jesus.

I was sure there would be another dozen more spats before the meeting was over, but they never took it too seriously. They didn't need to when they had one purpose in mind: to get the job done, get paid and get out.

And they all had their own purpose for being here.

People like Nixon and Rowan weren't driven to get paid – they had more money than they knew what to do with. And Tyrone, who was born in a privileged household and sent off to boarding school while his father immersed himself in his career in politics, didn't have to be here, either. No, Tyrone was driven purely from a place of rebellion – one taste of the fast life and he was hooked, and he probably got a kick out of living a double life.

Others like Doll, on the other hand, took these jobs for an entirely different reason. They couldn't look after their money. I had a feeling all her money went up her nose or in a game of Vegas poker, and when the life of gambling and drugs emptied her pockets, she got hit up with another job.

Glancing swiftly around the room once again, I caught Nixon's cocky grin, Doll's cheeky smile, the humour in Tyrone and Rowan's face and...

My gaze halted for a blink of a moment at a figure I didn't recognize in the corner.

I didn't look at him too long, though I felt his eyes on me when I turned back to the window.

6.

NIXON...

Nixon saw him before Vix, standing at the back of the room instead of sitting at the table. His arms were crossed, his expression clear. He was trying to be a mysterious fuck. Maybe he thought being quiet was going to give him a hard edge. He was surrounded by ruthless criminals and fucker looked like he belonged in a pop band. He had that cute fucking face Nixon knew girls went crazy for. His lips were plump, his eyes blue – the kind of blue someone like Vix would call riveting.

Personally, Nixon would have defined riveting with a punch to the pretty boy's face.

Okay, he knew he wasn't being sensible, and look, it wouldn't have bothered Nixon. At all. Truly, if this pretty boy hadn't been ogling Nixon's girl with the hungriest eyes he ever did see, Nixon would have completely overlooked the baby face's presence. But the fucker was slowly signing his death warrant, looking over Vix inch by precious inch.

Clearly, lines needed to be drawn. Nixon wasn't a complete cunt. He knew the man-boy probably had no idea she was marked permanently. And, to be fair, Nixon liked when his girl turned heads. She was, after all, the most beautiful creature he ever did see.

But something about this guy got under Nixon's skin, and it wasn't the over the top confidence he radiated out of him as he looked about the room, sizing it up. It was something completely different. Something Nixon couldn't quite put his finger on just yet.

As they all waited for Hobbs' arrival, Nixon turned his attention to Tyrone's conversation with Rowan. He was talking about his latest investment, though it was probably circling the drain right that very moment, like all the others. Doll inserted a few jabs along those lines, prompting Rowan to bite her head off.

Returning his focus back to Vixen, Nixon frowned. She was too busy looking out the window, her usual forlorn look accompanying her face. Lately, she as morose and withdrawn. It wasn't a look Nixon liked to see, but the older Vix got, the harder she was to contain.

Nixon wanted to defile her right in front of the pretty boy. He wanted to mark her for everyone to see, make a statement the pretty boy wouldn't forget.

She was his.

His.

Like the sky belonged to the earth, Vix belonged to Nixon.

Mine. He thought with fierce possessiveness.

She's mine.

7.

VIXEN...

Hobbs arrived shortly after I'd caught sight of the guy in the corner.

"I hate this fucking place," was the first thing he'd said as he stormed in, briefcase in hand. "Nixon, you son of a fucking bitch, I'm tired of catching ferries to this cunt of an island."

"Own a boat, boss," Rowan said. "It's smooth sailing, pun intended."

As Hobbs tossed the briefcase down on the table, he slid out of his suit jacket and glared at Rowan. "I don't want to own a fucking *boat*, Rowan. I don't *like* boats. I don't like the fucking *water*, and I have no fucking interest in crawling across the ocean at a snail's pace to get to this *cunt* of a place just to give you *little cunts* your next fucking job." Then he redirected his glare to Nixon and said, "Why the fuck are you sitting on the edge of the fucking table, Nixon? And Doll, unless you're going to give us a pussy show, put your fucking legs down."

Doll dropped her legs and sat up, but Nixon didn't budge. He remained seated on the corner of the table, flicking his thumb in the direction of the corner. "You forgot to scold pretty boy over there."

Hobbs turned to look at the guy in the corner. He rolled his eyes. "Are you trying to be a mysterious fuck, Flynn? Get the fuck outta there."

As the guy left the corner, Doll pointed at me. "What about her, Hobbs?"

Hobbs let out a dramatic sigh. "Leave her alone. I like where she's standing just fine. The room is *elevated* by her presence."

Doll tossed a dirty look my way, and Nixon smirked.

The guy Hobbs called Flynn took a seat on the chair next to Doll. I couldn't help but notice the wary look Nixon tossed him.

"Who the fuck is this kid, Hobbs?" Tyrone demanded, also looking suspicious.

"This is Flynn," Hobbs replied, straight-faced. "Thought I made it clear when I said his fucking name."

Flynn grabbed one of those hotel pens on the table and twisted it around, glimpsing once up at me. I averted my gaze quickly, feeling my pulse jump.

"Okay, well, what is his role in all this?" Rowan enquired, leaning back in his chair.

"Yeah, never seen him before," Tiger chirped.

"He's too pretty," Doll muttered, like it was an insult.

"He's your getaway driver," Hobbs inserted, gritting his teeth. "I would have told you that if you all would just shut the fuck up and let me talk."

"Why do we need a getaway driver?" Nixon asked, a note of disapproval in his tone. "We do things on the quiet. By the time the alarm's raised, we're long gone."

"Good point," Rowan agreed.

Doll's brows shot up. "I guess it's going to get nasty, gentlemen."

"I think Hobbs is going to tell us," Tyrone said. "I think we keep interrupting him."

Exhausted, Hobbs ran a hand down his face. "Do I need to put you bitches in detention just so you'd shut the fuck up and let me talk?"

It was funny hearing Hobbs swear. He looked like a fifth-grade schoolteacher with his thick glasses and clean-shaven face. He dressed like someone from the old railroad days, his suit old-fashioned and proper, and the pocket watch chain hanging along the pocket of his vest was the perfect added touch.

"Sorry, Hobbs," Tiger apologized. "I guess we just have a lot to say."

Hobbs tensed his jaw. "Alright, you turtle looking bald fuck, does anyone else have something to say? Get it out of the fucking open now before I end up shooting somebody."

"I have something to say." That came unexpectedly from the guy Flynn. He was staring at Hobbs. "I've been walking around the hotel for the last couple hours and I noticed there are cameras everywhere. I've never seen a hotel under this much amount of surveillance. What's going on?"

The room was silent for several moments. I noticed a few glances at Nixon and then me.

They know.

"The place is secure," Nixon suddenly said. "The surveillance is under my control. It makes talks like these safe to have."

"Do you own the hotel?" Flynn asked.

"Something like that."

"It's a popular retreat. Can you be certain we're safe to have this conversation?"

Nixon glared at him. "I'm sorry, I didn't think I was under some kind of fucking interrogation right now. If I wanted to be hounded by the likes of you, I'd have crashed a frat party. Hobbs, you never told me you were into recruiting nosy fuckheads."

Flynn crossed his arms, looking right back at Nixon unperturbed. "We've never met. I'm trying to figure things out right now."

"That's Nixon," Hobbs said, like that was all that was needed to explain him.

"Like the president?" Flynn questioned.

"No," Nixon retorted. "Not like the fucking president."

"Nixon has this island covered," Hobbs cut in. "He's got men at every corner under his control. If you farted in the forest, he'd know about it. Talks like these are safe to have."

Flynn nodded. "Okay."

"Okay?" Hobbs repeated. "Have I served my fucking purpose? Anyone else got something to say?"

Nobody said a thing.

"Hallelujah, praise Jesus." Hobbs made the sign of the cross before unlocking the briefcase, uttering curses under his breath.

A second later, the briefcase slammed open and he said, "This is what's happened." He began producing photos and tossing them around the table. "A Hungarian crew ripped off the Irish Gypsies at their central caravan park a few months back in Ireland. They made a run for it, disappearing out of the blue."

"How did they disappear out of the blue?" Doll immediately asked, confused. "Those guys have some serious surveillance."

"I don't fucking know," Hobbs retorted, already looking impatient. "I didn't read their minds, Doll."

"But those guys never get ripped off."

"You don't say." His voice dripped with sarcasm. "Maybe they were hiding under a Harry Potter cloak, who the fuck cares? Point is, the gypsies got blindsided. Had all their lollies in one nest –"

"It's kind of funny," Tiger chuckled. "Cuz they're always ripping people off."

"Yeah, ha-ha," Hobbs deadpanned. "Anyways, the trail went cold and –"

"If they disappeared out of nowhere, there'd be no trail to go cold," Rowan interrupted, shrugging like it was simply not possible.

Hobbs went stiff, glaring daggers around the room. I saw his nostrils flare. "If you bitches don't shut the fuck up, I will give this job to Eman and *his* crew."

That totally shut everyone up.

I met Eman, knew him well. He was this solid Turkish dude – seriously hot, but seriously scary. The crew never liked working with him, said he was too impulsive and always picking a fight. They'd almost blown a couple jobs because of his temper tantrums, and when shit got too tense, Nixon flat out refused to take another job with him, and that created a rift between them. Turned out, Eman was sensitive, and his feelings were hurt. The last time he was here, he blew up at Nixon and smashed one of the table chairs and stomped out, threatening he'd have his own crew and fuck Nixon and Doll and Rowan and everyone else that had been there.

But he had popped his head back in to say, "Except you, Vixen. I have no beef with you."

Hobbs had later informed us that he did indeed put together his own crew of people, and when the stars didn't align for Nixon or the others to take a job together, he'd hand the job over to Eman.

It was all kind of juvenile, but that was the criminal world for you. It wasn't as complicated as the law enforcement and news made them out to be.

"Moving along," Hobbs continued, pointing at the photos spread out before them all, "word on the street is the Hungarians were spotted in Seattle, blowing a shit ton of money. They're shacked up in one of Toby's safehouses."

Toby was another guy I'd heard about but never met. For a lot of money, he provided a safe place for criminals to hide out in when they were under too much heat.

He also dealt drugs. *A lot of it.* The King of Coke, they'd called him.

"How'd you get these pictures?" Flynn wondered, picking up photos of what I assumed were the men.

Hobbs smiled, looking proud now. "Toby is a close acquaintance. We are on good terms with the creepy fuck, thanks to Nixon."

Flynn glanced at Nixon, and a strange expression crossed his features. "What'd you do?"

Nixon, still sitting on the edge of the table, flicked a glance in my direction. "What I always do," he answered, saying nothing more.

Flynn followed Nixon's line of sight to me and seemed curious. "Toby's a huge asset to have. That's... impressive."

Hobbs nodded, careful not to stare at me. "It is."

Nobody wanted to address what Nixon did to gain Toby's approval. Flynn was going to be left in the dark, but he caught the glances in my direction and his curiosity deepened.

I didn't want to think about Toby or what Nixon did. I kept my expression neutral, even though I was distinctly aware of what happened.

"Toby's dropped this golden nugget on us, gifted us with a straightforward job," Hobbs went on, "and he gets a cut, of course, but not as big."

"What about the gypsies? Won't they want their money back?" Doll questioned.

"Fuck the gypsies," Hobbs retorted. "Finders keepers, they should've been more diligent with their dough. Now, Toby's aware these men are armed, and this job will be dangerous. Infiltrating the safe house will require monitoring first. You may be away for a couple weeks. This is not something that can be done impulsively. If this isn't for you, you are free to leave right the fuck now."

He paused and looked about the room, waiting for someone to bow out. But everyone sat still, staring back at Hobbs without a single concern.

They were in.

"Good," he said, looking excited. "This is how we're going to do it."

I tuned out.

I knew better than to listen to the next notch on their belt of crime sprees.

I'd probably hear about it in the news, anyway.

8.

TYRONE...

S hit was going to end badly if this fucking kid didn't stop staring at Vixen.

Nixon had received a call that had him leaving the room. The meeting was over, and everyone was chatting in separate groups.

Vixen was still alone, standing by the window, nursing her champagne. She looked like a picture of misery.

And this Flynn fuck wouldn't stop watching her. No one liked the kid. They'd left him to his devices, and he hadn't minded being cut off from the group.

He was tapping the pen on the table, a bored expression on his face, but Tyrone saw the kid's razor-sharp focus on the girl.

Tyrone knew this kid needed to be warded off.

He took a seat next to him, inching the chair a little too close for the kid's comfort. Flynn glanced at him from the corner of his eye but didn't stop tapping the pen.

Tyrone upped his intimidation. He rested his elbows on the table and leaned in, using his head to block Flynn's view of the girl. Now when Flynn looked up, his eyes met his. The kid kept his expression neutral.

"She's off-limits," Tyrone said in a hard tone. "You'd better look elsewhere right now. You know who she came here with. You heard what Doll said during that little shitstorm at the start."

Staring at the pen, Flynn shrugged. "I wasn't paying attention."

"You weren't paying...?" Tyrone frowned. Was this kid for real? "That's Nixon's property, kid."

"Property?" Flynn repeated, narrowing his eyes at him. "I wasn't aware that was still a thing."

"Nixon's old fashioned," he retorted, dryly. "Stop staring at the girl is all I'm saying. We got handed a job to do at the end of this week. Let's not start it with a cloud over our heads. The last thing we need is for Nixon to beat the shit out of you. We can't have you slumped at the wheel, am I right?"

Flynn didn't respond. The way the kid stared back at Tyrone unsettled him. He wasn't intimidated in the slightest. Fucker had zero fear.

This was worrying.

Tyrone had that whole premonition vibe shit down pat.

Honestly, he would have been a fortune teller in another life. He felt the atmosphere around this guy. The energy was all fucking wrong.

This kid was going to play with fire, and he was going to die for it. Straight up, Nixon was going to kill him and not even blink doing it.

Nixon had a reputation for a reason. He was ruthless, and before Vixen had come along, Tyrone had been certain the guy was a sociopath.

But he had gentled when he stole Vixen from her life, and what a line that was, he had to repeat it to himself. When Nixon *stole* her, he *gentled*. Tyrone would have laughed if he'd been alone to think it.

But he wasn't alone.

He was next to this fucking idiot who had no idea that Nixon would happily pluck his eyeballs from his sockets if he saw the dirty way Flynn was staring at his girl.

What was up with this kid?

Why was he being so brazen?

It didn't make sense.

"You don't know Nixon," Tyrone added, this time softly. "He would go to the ends of the earth for that girl. Please, kid, no trouble."

But when Tyrone leaned back, Flynn's eyes cut straight back to the girl.

Shit.

Shit.

Shit.

Tyrone watched in horror as Flynn stood up and made his way over to her.

This.

Was.

Going.

To.

End.

Badly.

9.

VIXEN...

"We know more about space and planets than we do about the ocean." I blinked out of my daydream and turned to the voice behind me. My heart skipped a beat when my gaze met blue eyes. Flynn came to my side, staring out, his eyes scanning the horizon.

Dark clouds had rolled in, blocking out the sun. Light rain streaked the window; I imagined it would feel cool on my skin. I hadn't felt rain in so long. Hadn't stepped out in close to a year – not since Nixon had taken me to a nearby restaurant the first year I'd been here.

And that night ended badly.

I'd made a run for it, and Nixon had chased me down in the parking lot. My pussy still ached when I remembered the savage way he fucked me later that night.

It was the best fuck of my life.

I looked Flynn over quickly. He was wearing faded jeans and a black and white stripe sleeve sports jacket. His blond hair was cropped short, his face was clean shaven. He didn't look like he belonged amongst criminals, which I supposed was the perfect cover.

He looked...well, he looked downright gorgeous.

I stood up straighter and looked back at the ocean. With a disinterested shrug, I muttered plainly, "Okay."

I wasn't going to open the door for conversation. This guy was like *them*, and he should have known better than to be talking to me. Unless it was Tyrone or the regulars behind Flynn, dialogue was to be kept to a minimum.

From my peripheral, I saw him shuffle closer to me, but his gaze was still fixed to a spot in the sea. With a low voice, he said, "What's your name?"

I felt surprised he didn't know. I'd walked in on Nixon's arm. Wasn't that enough to ward anyone away?

Dangling the glass to my lips, I stated simply, "Vixen."

He took a moment before repeating, "Vixen?" in what sounded like disbelief. "That can't be your real name."

I tossed him a bored look. "Well, it is."

His eyes narrowed curiously at me. His plump lips lifted in a smirk. "What sort of name is Vixen?"

"Like you should be talking," I retorted, giving him a quick once over. "You think Flynn is any better?"

"It means something to me."

"Am I supposed to ask what?"

He smiled and dropped his head to my level, staring at me fully now and I...couldn't look away. "I get a lot done. I persevere when I want something bad enough. I got a sharp tongue, and I'm quick on my feet. Women can't resist my charm, and guys don't think I'm intimidating enough to create trouble. So, I keep to myself, I say sweet things the girls like to hear, drink with the fellas and laugh with them too, and before you know it... I'm in like Flynn."

Okay, it wasn't a response I expected to hear.

And he'd said it in such a way too. The kind of way that made a woman's knees go weak. Yeah, he was charming, just like he'd said. I told myself to toughen the fuck up. I had to remind myself that the strange butterfly sensations in my stomach were driven by a fuckboy that looked like the kind of guy I'd have dated back in College.

And those guys wanted to get in my virgin pussy. Had even made bets on it.

I kind of felt glad Nixon beat them to it.

Man, I was so fucked up.

"Well, your name's shit," I commented rudely. Maybe if I was a snobby bitch, he'd leave me alone, but...he just stood there, glowing at my response.

He smirked and nodded once. "It's shit," he agreed.

I cut my stare short and looked down into my glass, feeling somewhat out of my depth because he was still watching me, and I wasn't used to this sort of attention.

What was he doing talking to me in front of everyone?

Nixon would know about this.

Paranoid, I glanced at the door, half-expecting to see him strolling in. Flynn followed my line of sight, a knowing look on his expression. His lips curved up, an amused smile spreading there. "You're safe," he assured me, softly.

I frowned, glaring at him now with suspicion. "I saw Tyrone talking to you," I abruptly said in an accusing way. "You know you aren't allowed to just come up to me like this. Nixon knows nothing about you, and you're not going to be popular with the crew by disrespecting him like this."

"Tyrone said you were off-limits," he acknowledged. "He also kept calling me 'kid'. I'm twenty-eight years old. I think I know what I'm doing."

I gave him a solemn look. "You don't know Nixon."

He didn't look one bit unsettled. With an easy grin, he replied, "He doesn't know me, either."

I rolled my eyes. "That's cute. Are you implying you're some badass?"

"No."

No. That was all he answered with, and he looked like he genuinely meant it.

"So, you're stupid," I guessed. "Because you have to be to be risking your neck right now."

He laughed confidently. "Actually, I'm safe. This job coming up? They need me. They'll fail if they don't have me."

"Ah," I nodded, understanding. "You're basing your safety on the fact they can't touch you before this job is done."

He smirked. "Exactly."

"And after?"

His eyes glowed now. "I'll be gone. They'll never find me." Then he added under his breath, "I can do that, you know."

"Do what?"

"Make anyone disappear." His gaze cut to mine and lingered longer than necessary, sending his meaning well and clear.

Jesus.

I turned away quickly, feeling my heart catch in my throat. This conversation was dangerous to have, and I didn't trust this guy. I couldn't afford losing what little freedom I was awarded after so many months trapped in my hotel room after simply taking a back exit out of a fucking restaurant.

"You're boring," I stated coolly. "Go away."

I was good at pretending. I dismissed him by staring fixedly out the window. A cold brush off. He couldn't know my heart was thumping wildly in my chest, or how hard I resisted the adrenaline fused shakes at the desperate thought of escaping this stupid island.

He watched me for a few moments, not exiting in haste like he ought to. Instead, he casually nodded at me, a cool smile on his face before he retreated from me.

I let out a long breath, and the anxiety brought on by his presence ebbed away at a slow rate. I resisted the urge to look over my shoulder. I could feel Tyrone's eyes on me. I didn't need him to see me seeking Flynn out to confirm his worries.

He didn't need to worry, anyway.

Like a cow stuck on a farm, I wasn't going anywhere. While the cow was secured behind a fence, I was secured in place by cold ocean water that spanned as far as the eye can see. And with Nixon's surveillance upped like never before, the ferries and boats that entered the marina or anchored not far past the shore were closely monitored.

In laymen terms, I was fucked.

10.

VIXEN...

There was a hidden room in the basement of the hotel. It was heavily guarded by a bunch of Nixon's men who were armed with very illegal guns. They looked like those guys at weight-lifting competitions. Some had that fake bronze tan, too. I wanted to tell Nixon that these guys were obviously strong, but their cardio most likely left much to be desired. I was sure they'd just shoot you if you ran from them, but in the off chance they were disarmed and I had to run from them one day in the future, I kept that information to myself.

Anyway, it was a betting room. A very illegal betting room. A lot of money was blown by very rich, or very corrupt men that came through on their giant yachts. It was past peak season and they kept coming in droves. The services Nixon provided were evidently addictive.

As we approached, the guards practically bowed at Nixon. If his pants were down, I was sure they'd have kissed his ass. Following us was everyone from the meeting sans Hobbs. He never went down to the basement. Get this, he said gambling was against his moral code. That was akin to hearing a murderer condemn thieving, it was just so *what in the fuck?*

The second the doors opened the music flooded out. With his arm possessively wrapped around my hip, Nixon led me in. The room was like a club. There was a bar area, and then a series of tables scattered around the room. There was a stage of exotic dancers, hardly clothed. When I dryly commented once that they might as well have been naked, Nixon explained he didn't allow poles, cages, or strippers; he said that it would "cheapen the ambience."

The betting tables were in the centre of the room, and they were currently filled to the brim with suited men, their eyes downcast at their playing cards. Some of them had a mountain of gambling chips, their expressions smug.

I hoped to God Nixon wouldn't join the next game. I didn't feel like sitting in his lap for hours tonight. Since talking to Flynn, I felt out of sorts. His disappearing comment weighed heavy on my mind. The "what-if" clouded my thoughts. It was dangerous to feel hope, but there it was, already seeding itself.

I couldn't resist glancing over my shoulder at him. I expected him to be staring around the room in awe, his eyes devouring the scene before him. Instead, my breath hitched when my eyes met his. Like I'd been burned, I looked away quickly.

It wasn't bizarre that Nixon invited him down here. Every time they had a job, they'd have their meetings and then unwind in the basement with some drinks. Doll was already knocking back a drink and dancing her way over to one of the betting tables.

She caught the attention of all the men there. She recognized one of them because she descended on him, wrapping her arms around his neck, her teeth grazing at his skin while she looked down at his playing cards. The guy was so clean-cut, he looked like a politician, and he probably was. Too many times to count I'd met or seen people I'd later catch on the television late at night. Oftentimes, Nixon would watch with me, a dry look on his face when whoever it was talked about the greater good. "Funny," he'd said once. "That guy loves his hookers." The guy in question had been some businessman that had made it on television for his charitable nature...and he was running for Mayor in whatever the fuck town he resided in. He'd donated some crazy amount to a kid's hospital and then smiled at the cameras, telling the screen that "every child deserves the best...now vote for me." Or something like that.

It was entertaining, but it was also sad. A lot of these people were married. A lot of them had kids. And their loved ones had no idea they were gambling it up in some hidden room located in the belly of a posh hotel.

I supposed it was nothing compared to the other shit they did.

As we walked, practically everyone greeted Nixon, but they didn't overwhelm him. They gave us space as we strode through the room, stopping for quick chats here and there. Nixon made quick work of cutting every conversation short. He took me to one of the tables in the dining area and snapped his fingers at the nearest waitress. She practically tripped over her feet to accommodate him.

"Get the chef in the kitchen to serve us the usual," he told her. "Tell him pronto. I want our orders at the front of the line."

"Yes, Nixon," she chirped, before hurrying to the backroom.

Pulling a chair out from under the table, Nixon kissed my head and murmured, "Sit down, baby, get comfortable."

I sat down and he took a seat directly across me. His attention was trapped on me. It didn't matter everyone stared. It didn't matter the most beautiful women stopped mid-step just to gawk at him. He didn't even notice them.

I could tell from his expression he was in a good mood. His lips were curved up, his eyes feasting on every inch of my face. It was kind of a fucked-up sight because the claw marks just above the collar of his shirt looked red and angry now...and he still wore them with pride.

"Why are you so happy?" I asked curiously.

"After the meeting, I took a call from my builder," he answered, eyes bright. "My plans were approved. I'm getting our house built on the island, sweetheart. It's happening."

Nixon had been talking about owning the island now forever. He was slowly accomplishing this by buying out everything on it. The nature reserve was strictly off limits from what I heard, but everything else was on the table. He'd said there was the most perfect spot atop the highest mountain on Grander island. He'd bought out the surrounding homes, gave the owners more than they'd ever dreamed of, all because he had this vision in his head of the perfect house.

He said it was for us.

To me, it was just another prison.

To confirm that, I asked, "Do I get to leave this house of ours?"

His expression remained light when he said, "You'll have everything you need there."

"I can't help but feel like I'll be more isolated than I am here."

"I'll make sure that isn't the case."

"Seeing human beings daily helps me, Nixon."

"I know that."

"I can't have a repeat of last year." My voice trembled as memories of that month stuck in my room flooded in. I swallowed the lump in my throat, staring pleadingly at him. "I can just stay here, can't I?"

He leaned over the table and gingerly took my hands into his. He continued watching me intently when he said, "I let you out."

"You nearly broke me."

"You ran from me, Vix."

My eyes stung with tears. "I said I wouldn't do it again, didn't I? And have I once?"

"No, you haven't." He took a deep breath and let it out slowly, looking down at our entwined hands, appearing thoughtful now. "I long for the day I can trust you."

"Trust me now."

"You spent an hour in our room telling me to let you go."

"Because I want to feel like I have a choice in this, Nixon."

"I understand."

Did he? I watched him, waiting for him to dismiss my words, but he stared fixedly back at me, determined not to waver.

The thing with Nixon was I could never tell what his looks meant. I couldn't know if he was looking at me like I was something he owned, or if he was genuinely seeing *me*. Too many times his actions made me feel like it was the former, and that fucking stung.

"What Doll said was right, you know," I told him, bitterly. "I'm practically your pet."

Nixon looked amused. "Is that right?"

"Yes," I icily retorted. "Only, now that I really think about it, I think pets have longer leashes than I do."

"You want a longer leash, Vix?"

"Yeah," I replied, sarcastically. "I want a longer leash, Nixon, and I want you to take me out on walks, too."

He enjoyed playing into my temper. He liked the shit I had to say because it was funny to him, and that just pissed me off some more.

"I'm taking you out now, aren't I?" he said, lightly.

"Oh, for sure." My sarcasm hit tones that even astounded me. "I love to be taken to the basement of your hotel, Nixon. It's so romantic. I love watching married men in here frolic after half-naked women, too. It definitely sets the mood. Do you want to feel how wet I am?"

Nixon was grinning now. "You're so fucking cute, Vix, you know that? When you get angry, it's like watching a puppy have a meltdown."

In a dramatic move, I went to rip my hands out of his grip, but he'd beaten me to it, gripping my hands tighter so I couldn't even do that. He watched my face as it contorted to anger. I seethed and he grinned, never tearing his eyes off me.

"I will scream if you don't let me go," I threatened.

He shrugged with one shoulder. "So, scream."

My face burned with rage. "You want everyone to see your pet have a meltdown?"

"I think my pet is too well-behaved to do that."

My heart sped. I gritted out, "I will embarrass you, Nixon."

Jesus, the smile he gave me now was positively predatory. "Go on, baby, keep me on my toes. Breaking you fills me with purpose."

Was that the trick, I wondered for the first time. Did I need him to shape me into the perfect toy before letting me go? Was that what this was? Taming a bad pet until there was nothing else left to tame?

Was I capable of being so good?

The waitress arrived with our routine drinks, interrupting our stare-down. Wine for me and whiskey for him. He let go of my hands and I rubbed them, pretending he'd hurt me, but he knew he didn't.

"Ease yourself, *pet*," he told me, cheekily. "Have some wine and behave yourself."

Ha-ha. I rolled my eyes and he chuckled. *Asshole.*

He took a strong gulp from his glass, and he scanned the room in the process. I did the same. Tyrone was sitting with the other guys, Doll was still entwined with the suited man at the betting table, and Flynn was at the bar area. He was sitting alone, watching the room. I thought of what he said. How he could make anyone disappear. And the way he'd said it made me feel like he had no reason to lie. My eyes lingered on him longer than they should have. Because when I finally turned away, Nixon was staring at me, his brow furrowed, that amused face fading.

I swallowed hard and glanced around the room again, settling on the stage. I stared longer than necessary, hoping to emphasize it wasn't Flynn that had captured my attention. That it was harmless.

I didn't succeed.

"What do you make of our pretty boy, Vixen?" he asked suddenly, his voice low now.

I shrugged, though my shoulders felt tight. "No idea."

"Should we invite him over and get to know him better?"

I took another sip of my wine, keeping my face neutral. "Do whatever you want, Nixon."

"I think I want to watch you squirm."

My eyes hardened on his. "Why would I squirm?"

"Because you've been staring at that boy every chance you get, and now you look uncomfortable I'm bringing him up."

"I think you're delusional."

"But I think I'm right."

I rolled my eyes, fighting to control my emotions. "Nixon, don't tell me you're the insecure type."

A scary smile spread on his lips and my heart started beating faster. His dark side was inching in. His eyes remained locked on mine as he ground out, "Insecure implies I've got something to lose, and last I checked, you can't lose what you own outright."

"Are you saying you own me?"

There was a wicked gleam in his eye. "Are you saying I don't?"

Jesus.

He was good at this game. At pinning me down with a few simple words, reminding me of my place here. I was his to do as he pleased, and that...grated on me.

"Did you take me down here to fuck with my head, Nixon?" I growled, gripping the stem of my wine glass tight. Not wanting to listen to his answer, I continued, snapping, "If you're going to insult me by insinuating I'm into fuckboys like him, you're wasting your breath."

Nixon didn't laugh in that cocky way I expected. He just watched me carefully, assessing my words. I'd never been a good liar, but I was starting to find ways to bury the truths by believing in the lies. It seemed to work because I'd gotten away with quite a bit recently.

He leaned back in his chair, looking comfortable as ever. There was an imperious expression on his face. He genuinely was unperturbed about Flynn, or about me staring at him. He was fucking with my head. In Nixon's eyes, he was godly. He couldn't fathom a woman might not want him. He wouldn't allow himself to think a lesser looking man like Flynn would capture my special attention.

And, in some ways, he was right. Flynn was nice on the eyes, but he barely held a flame next to Nixon.

Still.

There was something self-assured about Flynn too. He didn't have Nixon's mass, or his muscle, or his thick black hair and wicked gaze, but he held himself well. He was poised and relaxed, and that too was alluring.

And there I was, staring at him again.

Goddammit.

I redirected my gaze to my lap and admonished myself for not keeping my walls up. Just as I thought that, I looked back at Nixon, studying his face. I felt the pulse between my legs quicken. I felt heady with desire as my eyes trailed along his hard jaw and soft lips.

My heart was too hardened to feel any ounce of emotion for the guy, but my body...Jesus, my body betrayed me time and time again. The way it reacted to Nixon was akin to a dangerous drug.

It was one of the things that concerned me about our dynamic.

If I fled, how would my body endure the emptiness he filled?

Or had he just become a way of life for me now? Did I need to break free from him to know just how much control he had over my body?

Maybe it would be easy.

Maybe I would be okay.

The waitress returned in record time. She served a seafood platter in the middle of the table. Then she placed a plate of fish and chips in front of me and a plate of steak and greens in front of Nixon. Standing straight, she clasped her hands and waited for him to dismiss her.

She stared at him with red cheeks and wanting eyes, and he hadn't looked up at her once. These women, they gnawed at the walls for his attention. Unphased by his deplorable nature, his reputation turned them on. They wanted the bad man, because it made their pulses run quicker, their blood run warmer.

I was certain once I would have felt the same way, or at the very least curious. I might have stayed up in the night and felt that pulse between my legs, wondering what it would be like to have someone like him dominating me.

But that was fantasy. You could want the most shameful things in your fantasy, and it was harmless. You knew better than to want it in real life.

At least you could escape from a fantasy.

Where was my escape from this?

Pulling out the steak knife and fork from the napkin sleeve, he began cutting up his steak. I rolled my eyes and gently kicked Nixon's leg from under the table.

He paused and stared at me. I tilted my head in the waitress's direction, and he followed. "That'll be everything," he stated, dismissively.

"Okay, well, I'll be around," she responded, smiling brightly. She inched away from the table, her front still facing him. I watched her from the corner of my eye. When Nixon took a bite of his steak, he paused and turned. She jumped at his stare and took off, disappearing around the corner.

"It seems like most people don't know whether to be enamoured by you, or scared of you," I murmured, taking a bite of my cod.

He smirked. "And what are you, Vix? Are you enamoured, or are you scared?"

"I'm neither," I replied flatly. "You do nothing to me, Nixon."

"Is that another challenge?"

I rolled my eyes. "Believe me, the last thing I want

is to challenge –"

Suddenly, Nixon flipped the table over. I watched in shock as it came crashing to the ground. My mouth parted just as his body slammed into me. The entire chair fell back, his body shielding me. A loud shot sounded, so close my ears were ringing. As I crashed to the ground – Nixon over me – pain rocketed up my spine. I heard him shouting, but I didn't hear what he was saying through the ringing. He sounded angry; his entire body shook over me. Then he covered my body with his, covering every inch of me as another shot sounded out from nearby. Screams erupted, followed by chaos.

"Clear it out!" Nixon screamed. "Out! Everyone the fuck out!"

He held me tight while I heard running amongst frightened voices. It took merely minutes of mayhem before the silence crept in. My heart was beating hard as I tried to absorb just what in the fuck happened. Fear swarmed my insides, seizing me in place.

My brain struggled to catch up. Struggled to piece together what happened. One second, I'd been saying something, and the next...

"N-Nixon?" I whispered, trembling.

He'd buried my face into his chest, holding my head in the palm of his hand. His grip around my hair loosened when he heard me. He pulled away, looking down at me with such concern, his hair falling over parts of his forehead in disarray. "Are you hurt, baby?" he asked gravely. At once, he pulled away, looking over my body frantically.

I remained still, too in shock to move. "Just from the fall."

At once, his face contorted from concern to dark rage. "Shit," he cursed, angry. "Fuck!"

I jolted from his sudden curses, and he immediately stopped, appearing remorseful.

"It's okay," he whispered. "You're okay, I promise."

He stood up, forcing me up with him. I was stiff and shaking. He ran his hands up and down my bare arms, wiping away the goosebumps. He caught the look in my eye as he did it, aware that it took us back to a familiar time. To a moment that was equally traumatic. I saw the change in his eyes. It was like he didn't want to confront it, so he cradled my front to his chest and turned us around. His arm was tightly wrapped around my body when he began to walk, like he was still shielding me from danger. Without moving my head, I looked around the room. It was empty for the most part, except for Tyrone and Doll and... Flynn who was panting heavily feet from where we were. I looked him over, wondering why he looked so winded and...

I gasped at the body at his feet and the pool of blood by what used to be a head.

Oh, my God.

In horror, I spotted a gun in Flynn's shaky hand and tried to make sense of what happened.

He had killed the man who shot at us.

"Thank you," Nixon said solemnly. I stilled at the tone of his voice. I'd never heard him so grateful the entire time I'd known him. I looked up at him, at the pale colour of his face.

"Of course," Flynn replied, eerily calm.

"What in the fuck just happened?" Doll shrieked. "How the fuck did a guy manage a gun in here, Nixon?"

Nixon gritted his teeth. "I'll kill the idiot that let him through."

"Was he aiming the gun at you?"

"No." He held me tighter. "At Vixen."

Doll turned her sights on me, looking concerned. "Are you alright, Vix?"

It was hard to nod through my shakes, but I managed it. My teeth chattered together. If it weren't for Nixon holding me upright, I'd have collapsed to the ground in a heap.

"Can we ID the fucker?" Nixon asked, approaching the body. I buried my face into his chest, not wanting to look at the gruesome sight.

"Hard to know," Flynn muttered. "His head's blown off. His face is covered in blood and brains."

"Check his pockets."

I heard some movement. "His pockets are empty."

"I'll have to check surveillance, see where he came from."

"You got cameras down here?"

Nixon didn't answer. He wouldn't tell someone he hardly knew about something that private. I had a feeling he didn't keep record of anyone coming and going to the basement. What was the point of a private room if it weren't so private?

"We need to check it now," Tyrone said from nearby. "What if this fuck didn't come alone?"

Nixon's chest moved faster. His heart was beating wildly in my ear. He walked us back and tried pushing me away from his body. I felt a chair on the backs of my legs, and my insides seized in fear. He was trying to sit me down? I shook my head wildly and gripped his shirt tightly.

"No," I cried. "Nixon, no!"

I couldn't stand the thought of his body leaving mine. I needed him to act as my shield. I felt safe in his arms, my face hidden from view. I didn't want anyone to see how vulnerable I looked.

"Alright," he whispered down at me. "I won't let you go."

Instead, he sat down on the chair and cradled me in his lap. I kept my face buried in him, inhaling his scent.

"Doll," he said, "I need you to look the body over and tell me what you see."

"I heard your men have left their stations," Tyrone said on a frown. "All of them are scouring the island, looking for possible threats. No one's behind to monitor the hotel."

"Then I'll need you in the surveillance room."

"On it," he said, his footsteps scurrying out.

"What do we do about the body?" Flynn asked suddenly.

"The body's not the issue," Nixon replied all business-like. "It's the intent. I can't figure out why a man wanted to hurt my woman if he's dead. That's where Doll comes in."

It was silent for a few minutes. I heard the heels of Doll moving about, most likely inspecting the body. "Shit clothes, Nixon, but well lived in. He looks like a homeless guy. Flynn, open his mouth for me."

"I'm not opening his mouth," Flynn retorted. "You've got two hands."

"Listen here, you noob cunt –"

"Doll," Nixon cut in sharply, "just do it."

"Are you fucking kidding me?" She huffed. I heard

her shudder and curse under her breath. "Okay, his mouth is fucked right up. I've seen better teeth on a peasant. He was definitely into some heavy drugs."

"Maybe he's a transient," Flynn remarked, eyeing Nixon closely.

Nixon hummed in disagreement. "No, we make sure we don't get the homeless on the island."

"There's a homeless population taking refuge in shoddy boats. He might have come in on one."

"It's too expensive here for them," Nixon explained. "They're usually circling Salt Springs or along the coast of Nanaimo. We're too inconvenient."

"How do you mean inconvenient?"

"I don't allow any drugs to come in. The island's clean."

"Really?" Flynn sounded surprised by that.

"The island's upmarket for a reason," Nixon said. "People feel safe here."

"Good for business."

"No, good for life. There are families here, and all along the mainland it's riddled with crime waves and drug abuse. Kids stand no chance growing up in that."

Flynn was quiet for a few moments before murmuring, "I get it."

I did, too.

Until that very moment, I didn't think Nixon gave a fuck about it.

"So, what the hell then?" Doll questioned. "How does a bum access this room with a gun, and why is he shooting at Vixen?"

"I don't know yet." Nixon's fury was palpable. "But I'm going to find out."

I knew Nixon would.

He would leave no stone unturned.

"No one's hurting my baby," he murmured down at me, pressing a soft kiss in my hair. "Not without dying for it."

As Doll began to question just what happened, I heard Flynn tell the tale. He'd seen the grotty man approach our table with a hand in his pocket. Something about him screamed all wrong, so Flynn had made his way over, his gut telling him something was off.

Luckily – for me – Flynn was close enough to tackle him down the second he withdrew the gun. It happened so fast, he said. He pointed it at me right as Nixon noticed. Nixon lunged for me, shielding me as Flynn tackled the man down and the gun fired at the ceiling. He overpowered him, turning the gun to the man's head in the process. The man ended up shooting himself by accident.

I couldn't stop shaking.

I peeked from Nixon's chest, glancing quickly in the direction of Flynn's voice.

He'd saved me.

Both had reacted.

Flynn caught me looking at him. His expression softened, and I turned away quickly before I felt any warmth for the man.

What would have happened had he not been there? Would Nixon have been shot protecting me?

I closed my eyes tight and tried to remember Nixon as he lunged to me.

I remembered the horror on his face...and his desperate fear of losing me.

11.

NIXON...

She'd fallen asleep amid their talking. It'd been close to an hour after the shooting. She'd shaken so hard in Nixon's arms, her adrenaline firing throughout her little body. She always found a way to sleep through intense emotion. It was her body's way of protecting itself. He'd seen it back when he took her, had seen it every time he was close to cracking into her heart – Vixen simply couldn't process her feelings. Shutting down was her only defence.

They went over the body closely. The man looked to be in his mid-forties and was fucked up from a lifetime of hunger and drugs. Nixon kept his distance as Doll continued to inspect. He'd even called Hobbs down for a second opinion.

Both Doll and Hobbs had extensive history in law and order, though you'd never know it. They had a good eye for piecing shit together. Better than Nixon could.

When Hobbs learned there was a man firing at Nixon's woman, his pissy face turned into that of shock. He adored Vixen, had oftentimes cursed Nixon off for stealing her from the world.

"The world didn't care for her, Hobbs," Nixon had *said once.*

"Who are you to decide that, Nixon?" Hobbs responded, astonished by Nixon's lack of remorse over his actions. "You tore her out of the pages of a life she knew. Her storybook was cut short because of your selfishness."

Nixon coolly responded, "Her storybook would have been cut short with her dead in a shallow grave on that mountain."

That shut Hobbs up.

But, yeah, sure, Nixon accepted playing the part of villain. He had never deluded himself into thinking he'd done right when he yanked the girl out of her world and placed her firmly in the centre of his. It *was* selfish. It *was* wrong. And he felt absolutely *no* remorse doing it. He never would, either. Nixon wasn't that kind of guy. There would never be that glorious moment of reform.

This wasn't that kind of story.

A tiger never changed its stripes, or so the saying went. Nixon would sooner repent for all the crimes he'd committed before ever repenting taking Vixen in the ruthless manner in which he did.

Carpe Diem, he'd learned once.

And he'd Carpe Diem'd the shit out of it the day he decided she was his. And what a fucked up day that was – he'd never spilled so much blood.

"He's a transient," Hobbs said after looking over the body. "I've seen this countless times."

"Flynn said there might be a boat," Nixon replied, thoughtfully.

"What about the ferry I came in on?"

"I'd have heard about him coming through on a ferry or seaplane."

"Then it would have to be a boat."

Thing was, there was no dingy looking boat in the waters around the island. Nixon would have known about it. His men would have sorted that out promptly.

"What was the motive?" Doll asked Hobbs, looking at him like he was the sun in her fucking sky.

Hobbs frowned, looking back at her. "Isn't it obvious?"

"Drugs," Flynn whispered to himself, his arms crossed.

"He would have been sent to do this."

"What the fuck did he think was going to happen, though?" Doll ranted. "You're standing there, aiming a gun at someone's head, and you shoot. You don't just walk away from that when all is said and done."

Hobbs shook his head at Doll. "Haven't you seen it before, Doll? These guys, they're desperate, they're hungry for their next hit, and they're not themselves anymore. The drug's eaten them whole. They are slaves to that hit, and they don't reason the same. They're victims."

"Yeah? Well, no one forced them to take that first hit."

"Don't be black and white," he scolded. "You don't know their reasons, and it doesn't matter right now. This guy got tricked, and now he's dead."

Doll looked shocked by his reaction. Hobbs was fuming for all kinds of reasons. Fuming for the homeless man, fuming for Vixen, and fuming for all the fucked-up drug abuse that wrecked his family during his upbringing.

Nixon understood where the vehemence came from.

But Nixon didn't really care, either. He had tunnel vision, and in the centre of that tunnel was Vixen and the gun that had been aimed at her.

He felt the rage coursing through his veins, igniting the evil nature that lurked not far into his soul. And when Hobbs looked at him, he saw it in Nixon, and it frightened him.

"Steady," Hobbs whispered to him. "Not here. Not now."

After all was said and done, Nixon ordered his clean-up crew to remove the body and dispose of it. Doll had decided to join Tyrone in the surveillance room, and Flynn remained unmoving, like he was unsure of what his role was in this mess.

Nixon noticed the lost look in Flynn's face. Jesus, the vulnerability was startling.

He looked like such a fucking *kid*.

"Get loaded at the bar and unwind," Nixon told him. "Whatever you have is on the house."

It was the very least he could do, and he knew it wasn't enough. Flynn had saved Nixon's girl and Nixon owed him big. For starters, Flynn was promptly removed off his shit list.

Holding her close to his arms, he could bury his nose into her hair, he took Vixen up to their apartment. He settled her into their bed and removed her heels from her feet. He kissed one of her ankles before covering her body with a thin bed sheet.

"Nixon," she groggily whispered in her sleep.

"Shh," he cooed, watching as she slipped back under. He stroked the face he'd memorized every line of. The face he missed every time he went away. "My sweet Victoria."

His little vixen.

He spoke to Tyrone on the phone about what he found on the cameras. Apparently, the bum had made a few appearances, strolling straight through the main entrance of the hotel. He looked groggy and out of it, but his hand had been in his pocket, and he seemed to be in search of something.

The basement, Nixon figured.

"I'll give the tapes a look in the morning," Nixon said. "Thanks, Ty."

"Sure thing, Nixon," Tyrone replied. "I want to catch who's responsible same as you, but it seems this guy came alone. Either he acted out of a drug-fuelled bender, or someone sent him."

Either way, Nixon would find out.

Then he made a call and ordered two of his men to guard their door.

Just in case.

But as Nixon roamed the apartment, a glass of whiskey in the palm of his hand, mulling over the series of events that transpired, he slowly began to realize the men would be standing on guard for nothing.

Something from the past nagged at him.

It nagged.

And it nagged.

Like an itch in his chest, he couldn't suppress it.

It nagged until he stopped pacing.

This had happened before, hadn't it?

He froze at the realization.

Of course.
How could he be so stupid?
There was no real threat.
This whole thing had been orchestrated.
An attack that was doomed to fail.

But who was the culprit?

12.

VIXEN...

I woke up in the middle of the night with my heart in my throat and my body shaking. My hands reached out around me, desperately seeking Nixon. When it touched nothing but air, I gasped in fear.

"Easy, baby," he said from across the room. "I'm right here."

My heart slowed down and I sagged into the mattress. I blinked several times, my sight adjusting to the darkness. Then I searched for him, wondering what he was doing out of bed.

He was standing by the window in the dark, looking out, his phone glowing in his hand. He was in nothing but his black briefs, his broad muscular back was to me. I couldn't see his face from where I lay, but I didn't have to. His body language was relaxed, like he hadn't leapt across a table and saved me from a gunshot merely hours ago.

God, he'd looked so frightened for me.

I'd never seen that look from him before.

I sat up, staring at him, feeling unusually emotional. "Nixon, I'm scared," I admitted, lips trembling.

"You shouldn't be," he simply responded in the most unruffled tone.

I waited for him to turn to me, to come and hold me the way he'd done in the basement. But he just stood there, more attentive to the island below. Cold again. It felt like a smack in the face. There I was, leaking emotion from my voice – an unusual feat by me – and it may as well have fallen on deaf ears.

"I'm not safe here," I told him firmly. "You need to get me off the island."

"You're perfectly safe," he replied. "What happened today was a fluke."

I frowned. "A fluke that may have killed me."

He didn't respond to that. Of course. God forbid he reassure me or anything.

"Do you want me to die?" I asked, desperately. "Is that the only way you'll let me go?"

"You always jump to this," he replied, irritated. "I don't even think you know why you want to go."

I felt a spike of anger. "I can think of a million reasons why."

"The world isn't what you think it is, Vix." He turned his head, glancing at me briefly. "It's cold and dark and it doesn't give a fuck about you."

"I want to learn that the hard way."

"I'm not letting you go."

When he spoke like that – the authoritative tone present – it made me frustrated and want to claw at my face.

He stated he wasn't letting me go like he was talking about a sweater he wanted to wear again. I felt stranded and boxed in. What was the point of living if I had no fucking say?

"You know what this is about?" I snapped, coldly. "This is you enjoying having power over someone helpless. You *like* being in control of me. You *want* me miserable."

"Ah, right, here we go."

"Yeah, here we go," I growled, sarcastically. "Your captive's doing that thing again, begging for her freedom! Oh, the fucking audacity."

"Yeah."

"Yeah, what, Nixon? Yeah, you like the power? You enjoy saving me from gun-wielding men? I think you like it when I'm scared. *Scared* and *miserable* and fucking *powerless*."

"And you want to know what I think?" he retorted, turning fully in my direction. "You *want* to believe I'm all those things because it gives you reasons to hate me."

My eyes widened in disbelief. "I don't need to find reasons. Hating you is easy, Nixon," I argued, feeling the familiar fight in my bones. "You make it very fucking easy to do."

"So, you hate me."

"I do!"

"Go on, keep telling me that."

"I hate you," I repeated, passionately.

He began to move toward the bed, and it made me antsy. I didn't know what his reaction was going to be when he got to me. He was always unpredictable. I felt myself sliding to the other side of the mattress, nearing the edge in case I needed to bolt.

"And there you scurry," he murmured low in his

throat. "Always ready to run from me. You like the chase. This is the game you play, baby. You press my buttons on purpose."

I didn't answer. Half of my body was hanging off the bed. My foot touched the carpeted floor. I stared at him in the dark with my chin up in defiance.

There was nothing pleasant in his expression. Zero amusement clouded his features. Shit, he was pissed. He might hurt me, even. Good. I hoped so. I really wanted him to. Anything to make me loathe him even more.

Instead of climbing the bed, he rounded it, his eyes never leaving me. He was like a lion circling its prey. I brought my foot back up and moved over the mattress, keeping the distance between us.

"Tell me," he ground out quietly, "what would you do with your freedom, Vixen?"

My lips parted, but no words came out. I had no smartass response. I'd never really entertained the thought. What was the point giving myself hope when freedom seemed impossible?

"Do you even know?" he pressed, continuing to circle the bed.

I scurried to the middle of the mattress, keeping my eyes on him. My heart jumped when he stopped moving. He stood still suddenly, staring at me, waiting. The dark look on his face was beginning to frighten me. He looked eerily like the first time I'd been in a room with him.

"What would you do with your freedom?" he demanded slowly. "Tell me."

I sucked in a few breaths, trying to formulate a response quickly. "I...don't know, Nixon."

"You'd find a job, wouldn't you?"

I swallowed, thinking. "Yeah."

"Yeah, and you'd have your own place?"

I nodded slowly. "I guess."

His lips slowly spread into a wicked smirk. "And you'd have a boyfriend, wouldn't you? A guy you'd fuck a couple times a week."

I glared at him. "Yeah," I spat out. "I would, Nixon, but it would be more than a couple times a week."

"Yeah? How many times would you fuck the college boy?"

"Twice a day."

His brows shot up. He feigned surprise. "Is that right?"

"Yeah, and he wouldn't be a college boy. He'd be a lawyer...or a cop, even. The kind of guy that would put people like *you* away."

He barked out a laugh, but it sounded cold and sinister. "Tell me the kind of people you've bunched me into, baby."

"Murderers," I listed off. "Thieves. Rapists."

He made an O with his mouth, again feigning that surprise. "Rapists?"

"Yes."

"I've fucked you against your will, Vixen?"

I balled my hands, boldly replying, "Every time."

I'd hardly finished that sentence when he suddenly moved over the bed, grabbing at my leg. I yelped as he dragged me down the mattress to him. His strength was startling. His biceps flexed, looking massive in the moonlight. I tried to kick him, but he was one step ahead of me. He grabbed both my legs and tossed them over the edge of the bed. Then he

79

trapped them with his own legs and bent over, grabbing at my arms. I went crazy, bucking under him as he forced me down, effortless and quick.

"Let me go, Nixon," I growled, panting.

He gripped both hands in the palm of his large hand and then proceeded to tear my dress off with his free hand.

"This was such a silly fucking dress," he uttered. The fabric tore easily, though I winced and pretended he was hurting me. He barked out another laugh, catching my fake pained face. "You're unbelievable, baby."

"You're hurting me."

"Am I?" He slipped the dress off and proceeded to pull my bra down, freeing my breasts. "Tell me how much I'm hurting you, Vixen. Is it like how I take you against your will?"

I seethed, opening my mouth to form a curse when he suddenly slapped at one of my breasts. I gasped at the pain shooting down my body. He immediately rubbed at the tender flesh he smacked, grinning at the look on my face.

"What's wrong, Vix?" he asked, mockingly. "Don't like what I'm doing?"

Tears sprang to my eyes. I glowered. "Let me go, or I'll spit on you."

"Then spit on me."

I spat on him, a pathetic spat that landed on his chin. He laughed and rubbed at his chin before he smeared my saliva on my pained breast. And then he delivered another sudden slap, this time on my other breast. Another shot of pain travelled down my body, pooling in that aching place, and then he rubbed the pain away again, his touch gentle.

"Oh, sweetheart, if you could see how beautiful your tits look," he murmured, awed. "Pink suits you."

"Fuck you, Nixon." But my voice sounded weak with desire.

"Don't worry, I'll get around to fucking you, Vixen. It'll be forceful, right?"

"Always."

"What about your cunt? Does it feel like I force it open every time?"

Before I could respond, he cupped my pussy, staring down at me now with the most wicked grin on his face. My cheeks burned. I was wetter than I'd ever been, and the victory in his expression both pissed me off and turned me on.

"Baby," he whispered, cockily, "how can you pretend I force you when your body begs for me?"

Suddenly he flipped me over and climbed over me. His front body pressed against my back. He gripped a chunk of my hair and spread my legs apart with his knee. I wasn't fighting it. My body was tense beneath him, every nerve firing with anticipation.

"You think your lawyer boy will fuck you like I do?" he growled, pressing his cock against my entrance. He ran the tip of his cock along my folds, teasing. "You think he'll give a fuck about your needs? You think he'll ever figure out what makes you tick?"

I let out a pained groan as he slowly slid into me. He bit at the back of my shoulder, stinging me before he sucked fiercely at my skin. I closed my eyes, blowing out a ragged breath. Fuck, he was swollen tonight. More so than usual.

"Do you think he'd play along?" he asked before

moving out of me and harshly thrusting back in. We groaned at the same time, and his breaths came out harder. His voice turned lower as he gritted out, "You think you could ever tell him you have a thing for dubious consent? You think these men of law will take your no's and still fuck you like I do?"

"No," I cried out, entirely defeated. "They wouldn't, Nixon."

"No," he agreed. "They wouldn't."

"Just you would."

"Yes, Vix."

"So then shut up and fuck me."

I felt his mouth against my ear. "How do you want it?"

"Dirty."

He groaned with approval. "Anything for what's mine."

And he delivered. He fucked me harshly, moving in and out of me at an animalistic pace. The moment his hand let go of my hair and wrapped around my throat, my eyes rolled to the back of my head. He squeezed just enough to leave an ache, but not enough to cut off the air, and it drove me wild.

Utterly fucking wild.

I buried my mouth into the sheets and moaned into them, lost to the feeling of his punishing thrusts. I liked feeling used. I liked how dirty it made me feel. I liked being Nixon's toy – abused when he wanted to fuck me, and pampered when he wanted to show me off.

But right now, it felt different.

It felt...more personal.

Perhaps it was seeing him leap across the table to

protect me that put a chink in my armour. When he covered his entire body over mine, shielding me from the shot and ready to take the bullet for me, he let his guard down. He pretty much broadcasted to the powerful people in that room what he would die for.

And God, was that true?

Would he truly die for me?

My orgasm hit me in a powerful wave of pleasure, but it died quickly, buried in the pain of my realization. Buried in the need I still had for him after what happened. My emotions surfaced so strongly, and it was physical agony. I sobbed into the sheets, the tears flowing down my face endlessly. He promptly pulled out of me and wrapped his arms around my body, hauling me up the bed and into his lap. He rocked me back and forth, stroking my back, shushing me gently.

"My beauty," he cooed, kissing my temple. "It guts me when you cry."

I buried my face into his bare chest, coating his hard flesh with my tears. "You're breaking me, Nixon."

"Shh."

"I want you to stop."

I couldn't bear the feeling of being cut open. I needed him to just fuck it all away. To dominate me, put me in my place, and make the feelings go away. I couldn't seem to lock them away. They kept surfacing like blood after a bad cut, oozing out of me, making my vulnerability show.

He didn't respond to that. He just held me in his arms, stroking me.

I wished he hadn't tried to save me. Things were less complicated before that moment. If he'd just sat and let it happen, Flynn would have still stopped the man and I would have known where I stood in Nixon's world, and it would have been fine. It would have been what I wanted confirmed all along.

But this...

This fucked things up.

This made me feel like I wasn't his captive and he wasn't my captor.

But he was. He *really* was. He was the bad guy. The guy that deserved to rot in prison for what he'd done.

And I needed to remember that.

I needed to remember my life before him.

He took away my freedom and he threw away my life like they were nothing to him.

My eyes were raw from crying. I held him to me, and there I was, seeking assurance from the very person that was killing me slowly.

It was just so fucked.

But it was fine too. Because it filled my chest with warmth and yearning.

"Are we safe, Nixon?" I asked, worriedly, half-asleep in his arms.

"You're safe, Vix," he assured me, warmly. "As long as I'm breathing, you're safe."

My heart squeezed. "Then don't stop breathing."

"So long as you're mine, I never want to."

He rocked me back and forth, caging me in his arms. After I settled down, I twisted around to face him, wrapping my legs his back. I was very aware we were naked, flesh against flesh, his semi-swollen cock brushing along my pussy. I could smell our arousal in the air, and it was familiar and comforting.

As I watched him, he stared solemnly back at me.

I didn't like the tension between us. It felt personal and awkward. I didn't know how to act when our walls were down. When I viewed him as more human than monster, it made me panic.

"I really do hate you," I whispered, bitterly, clinging on to that tiny shred of rebellion. I used it like a shield.

His lips rose up in a lazy smile. "You never learn your lesson, do you, baby?"

Before I could respond, he flipped us over, placing me flat on my back. He loomed over me, the tendrils of his hair falling over his forehead. When I saw him like that – his black hair gorgeously ruffled, his face roughened and filled with lines, his lips pulled up in a challenging smirk – it did things to me.

"What lesson are you about to teach me?" I asked, acting disinterested even as his hand lazily roamed my body, leaving sparks behind.

He spread my legs wide and plunged into me sharply, filling me whole once again. My eyes rolled to the back of my head as I helplessly groaned.

He kissed along my jaw and pressed his lips to my ear, whispering, "You can't pretend forever."

When he pulled back to look at me, I desperately buried my face into his neck, not wanting to confront his words.

Thank God for small mercies. He didn't push. He simply fucked me the way I needed him to.

"You like this, Vix?" he asked.

"No," I answered through a moan.

"I think you like my cock buried in your little pussy."

"I think you're dreaming."

His chest rumbled against mine. He kissed along my face, capturing my mouth in a deep kiss. "Sometimes I think I'm dreaming, too," he rasped, picking up the pace, driving himself as deep inside me as he can go before he came.

Always he tried to touch my soul.

Always he longed for it in the depths of his eyes.

Always I denied him.

13.

VIXEN...

Sometime in the morning Nixon had left. I slept through it. I curled myself up into a ball of sheets and pillows and surrendered to the darkness. If it weren't for Nixon holding me the entire night, I would not have been able to sleep. I held him like he was my lifeline, and I felt another fissure in my soul.

I was wary when I woke up. It took me forever to get out of bed. My eyes were on the door, and I inched to it, one gruelling step after the next. When I put my hand on the knob, I took a deep breath and turned it.

When it turned freely, a relieved breath escaped me.

I didn't know if the shooting yesterday meant I'd be locked in my room for safety reasons. I was frankly surprised that wasn't the case. It seemed Nixon truly didn't feel threatened at all.

I went to the phone on the night table. Nixon had wired it so I could only call him or the hotel front desk.

He answered after the first ring. "Yeah, baby?"

I took a moment, tapping the table thoughtfully. "The door's unlocked."

"It is."

"So..."

"So?"

"Does that mean there's no danger?"

"There's no danger," he confirmed. "Go through your day like usual. I'm in the meeting room going over some things with the guys. You can see me for dinner when you're done."

My brow furrowed. "Done what?"

"You've got a few appointments. Check the planner."

"Okay."

He hung up and I put the phone down. I grabbed a silk robe hanging in the closet and threw it on. I strolled out of the room and to the kitchen. The planner was on the counter. I flipped it open and grabbed a banana from the fruit basket. As I ate, I looked over my appointments.

Dr. Sullivan 9:45 am
Nail appointment 11:15 am
Hair appointment 12:10 pm

I frowned and grabbed a chunk of my hair and looked it over, catching the infinite number of split ends. I supposed I was due for a haircut. I examined my nails after. They were short and uneven. I'd bitten them off – a stupid habit Nixon had called cute. They looked androgynous, for sure. I wasn't sure how the nail technician was going to salvage them.

I got dressed in a pair of lounge pants and loose shirt. I half-assed my make-up and by then I received a call from the front desk letting me know the doctor was coming up to see me.

Jane Sullivan was a young, pretty doctor. She had red straight hair and blue eyes. She was professional, and while she smiled at me and acted polite, I just never got the warm vibes from her. Like now, when I opened the door to her, she shot me that forced smile, but it didn't reach her eyes. It was like being here annoyed the shit out of her, which was fine. Whatever. Nixon may as well have had a gun dug into the back of her, the way she carried on.

We settled in the lounge room. I took a seat on the couch and waited. She didn't ask me how I was. She simply got down to business, asking me how the birth control was going. I said Fine and Good when necessary. Then she administered the shot in my arm and went through the usual Doctor lingo, letting me know what to watch out for over the next few days.

I zoned out, thinking of yesterday. I swore my ears were still ringing from the sound of those gunshots. I rubbed at the inside of one of my ears, as if that would stop it from making that god-awful sound.

"Are you alright?" Sullivan asked, curiously.

"Yeah," I answered, avoiding her eye. It wasn't like I was going to say, Hey, I got shot at yesterday, someone wanted me dead, but don't worry, the dude missed because he got tackled to the ground by a guy that ended up killing him.

A guy who, I had to add, hinted he could make me disappear.

"How's Nixon been treating you?"

I instantly redirected my gaze to her, shocked by her question. She'd never asked that before. I wasn't even aware she was allowed to discuss him with me.

Noticing my expression, she shrugged weakly. "I heard him lose it in the foyer. He's in a foul mood. Everyone looked scared."

"He treats me fine," I told her, numbly.

She looked dubious. "As you know, I don't work on the island. Nixon has me flown over."

"Okay." Why was she telling me this?

She looked at me long and hard. "So, you know, I've known Nixon a long time, but I'm not on his books or anything. It appears you're pretty isolated and, well, if you ever wanted to talk, I'm here."

It took several moments for my shock to ebb away. I stared at her, trying to gauge how trustworthy she was. It was hard not to be suspicious. I wasn't going to just openly tell her my life story or anything, but...I also felt this desperate need to talk.

So, I asked safe questions first. "Do you see anyone else on the island?"

"Just you."

"Nixon must make it worth your while."

She smiled with ease. It looked real. "He does. He is very generous in the monetary sense. I work at a clinic in an unsavoury area. The extra money helps."

"How'd he find you?"

"He was in rough shape when he came into the clinic. It was after hours. He'd broken in."

"Hurt badly?"

She nodded, solemnly. "Very. He'd been stabbed. Was covered in blood. It was really messy."

I blinked in surprise, envisioning Nixon in bad shape. I'd never seen more than a busted lip on him. "Then what happened?"

"He came to me again a few more times, and we treated him at the clinic the best we could."

"Under the table?"

She laughed lightly, nodding. "Oh, yeah."

I studied her, quietly asking, "Do you know his real name?"

She shook her head, her smile fading. She wouldn't meet my eye when she answered, "No, I don't."

Damn.

It was one of those annoying mysteries about him. I hadn't realized how relevant a name was until I met him. When you interacted with someone who hid their real name, it felt less personal. It drew the boundaries well and clear. As close as I could get to Nixon, I could never get *too* close.

And it wasn't fair.

Because he knew everything about me.

He always had the advantage between us. *Always.*

Relaxing my shoulders, I asked, "How long have you known him?"

She clasped her hands together in her lap, looking thoughtful. "Around five years."

I did the math in my head. He'd known her three years by the time we'd crossed paths. She'd come onto the scene straightaway, tending to me on the island. I'd sort of wondered if he'd just recruited her for the sake of me by how quiet and detached he'd been around her.

"So, he went to you when he needed to get treated?" I asked.

"No. Like now, I was treating a patient he knew."

I went still, mulling that over. It suddenly occurred to me I might not have been the first girl he kidnapped. *Of course.* I was so dumb. With my heart climbing up my throat, I pressed, "Another girl?"

She nodded, swallowing hard as a flash of emotion flashed through her. "Yeah, it was more involved. More than just birth control. She needed medicine for health reasons."

More than birth control.

For some reason, my body went tight and a strange pain – akin to betrayal – shot through my chest. I kept my lips from trembling, though admittedly, every part of me wanted to shake.

Did you think you were special? That all this time it was just you? Stupid girl.

Jesus, my body was acting funny. I cleared my throat to clear away the lump forming there. I wrapped my hand around my neck, aware tears were springing to my eyes. Oh, God, this was so embarrassing.

"Are you okay?" she suddenly asked, all bug-eyed.

"Yeah, I ate something bad last night," I lied, standing up. "Thanks for the shot. I really appreciate it. I definitely don't want a baby. Ever."

"Are we finished?"

"I think we are."

She gathered her things quickly and I shoo-ed her out of the apartment. She looked at me like I had two heads all the way to the door. I slammed the door on her face and then I collapsed to the ground, shaking everywhere.

"Of course, there were others," I scolded myself. "Why the fuck are you surprised, Victoria?"

I shut my eyes, wincing when I said my name. I

hadn't heard it in so long. The tears I suppressed moments ago gave way. They fell down my face in fat drops.

"I just wanna go home," I cried, hugging myself.

It'd been a long time since I'd broken down like this. The last time...God, the last time was in that fucking cabin he took me to. I'd pleaded for my life in that room, and he'd just stared at me the entire time, weighing over what to do with me.

There was no care in him then.

There was no care in him now.

It was all in my fucking head.

You don't spill that much blood and have the capacity to feel.

I kept forgetting how violent he was. How little it mattered to him to take a life or dispose of a fucking body like he effortlessly did last night.

What happened to the last girl he was with? Had he broken her until there was nothing left to break?

I'd been right.

I was just a toy.

Just a toy.

And all toys break eventually.

14.

NIXON...

He was in a cunt of a mood.

He'd spent most of his morning trying to figure out how in the fuck that man found his way to the basement. It wasn't on any of the footage. He'd seen the dead cunt meandering around the foyer, and then he'd disappeared from the cameras.

It just went to show you could have a million cameras lying around, there would always be a blind spot. Someone would always find a way.

Nixon wound up questioning the front desk, and they'd just looked at him with this Bert stare he wanted to savagely rip off.

"I guess the problem is you're all too fucking beautiful to employ," he cursed, glaring at the women with disdain. One of them perked up, and he glowered at her. "That's not a fucking compliment, Janine."

"Jenny," she corrected.

"Whatever your name is. You spent the entire fucking time being chat up while someone that looks like he dumpster dives for a living strolled past you."

"I thought security would take care of unwanted

guests, Nixon."

Yeah, well, security had to be called down to the basement because, get this, there had been a fucking shortage of guards yesterday. Un-fucking-acceptable.

"And," Janine added, "it is discrimination to kick someone out of our facilities because of the way they look."

Nixon blinked slowly, flexing his jaw as he stared at her. "Are you saying from now on you won't be diligent of who comes through the door?"

"No, sir, I'm saying that I didn't think anything of it when he came through."

"You..." Nixon paused, trying to understand. "You remember him coming through."

Janine shook her head. "Well, no."

"I don't understand, Janine."

"Jenny," she corrected again.

Nixon glanced at Tyrone. "What is she talking about?"

Tyrone looked lost for words. "I uh...think she was saying maybe if she had seen him, she wouldn't have thought anything of it because...she doesn't discriminate?"

Janine smiled brightly. "Exactly. Thank you, Tyrone."

Nixon massaged his temples. Fuck, a migraine was coming on. He couldn't take pointless conversation. Who the fuck hired Janine, anyway?

It didn't matter, he told himself.

God, it didn't matter.

Dropping his hand back down, he levelled the girls with a firm stare, and they straightened in response.

"I will feed you all to my dogs if you don't pull your heads out of your asses," he threatened, flaring his nostrils. "No more fucking solitaire on your computer. No more flirting with hotel guests. I pay you to work. Got it?"

The three women nodded at him, wide-eyed with fear.

Good.

He stormed out of the foyer, aware Tyrone followed closely behind.

"Buddy," he said under his breath, "I'm pretty sure that was workplace bullying."

"That was taking care of business," Nixon barked back as he entered the elevator and hit the basement button.

Tyrone stood beside him, shrugging one shoulder as the doors closed. "I mean, I get that you would think that way, but...I'm not sure threatening to feed your employees to dogs is healthy."

"It'll up morale, Tyrone."

"How in the fuck?"

"Don't want to be eaten by a pack of dogs? Then do your fucking work, and that won't be a problem. It builds awareness. They'll have to work harder, and if they work harder, they'll feel confident they're not on the menu."

Tyrone made a face. "That's kind of fucked up."

No, what would happen next would be fucked up.

He was going to round up all his muscle and figure out who the fuck let the man through. And then he was going to kill him.

He didn't care if it was a mistake, either.

In Nixon's world, mistakes cost you your life.

As the saying went, a chain was no stronger than its weakest link.

*

Sometimes, when he wanted to torture himself a little bit, he thought of how life would have played out if he hadn't taken that job.

Two years ago, he had accomplished all he set out for. His account was filled with riches, and he was so close to checking out. Maybe he would have settled somewhere cold, like that mountain had been. He loved the cold. The way it made him feel alive.

He didn't have to take that job.

He didn't need to.

He'd established himself in the underbelly. Was feared and respected and highly sought after.

But he was bored.

Money was tedious after a while.

And he was in mourning.

He grieved in silence, shut out from the world, on the island he had just discovered, shacked up on the top floor of Hotel Browning, drinking himself to sleep, until he couldn't take his own company.

So, when Hobbs made that call, had said, "Hey, in case you're interested, there's a huge lump of treasure in the heart of Surrey. It's dangerous. There's going to be gunfire. One of your men will probably die. Figure you might want a bit of excitement. Better than drinking yourself to death on that lonesome little island. What do you say?"

He wanted to say, Fuck that. No thanks.

He might even toss the phone out the crappy rattling windows and be done with that bullshit.

But he found himself silent instead.

As the seconds ticked by, he began to consider.

He didn't want to feel the heaviness in his heart anymore.

He sort of wanted to die.

And this job...well, he might end up in a shootout. He could see himself going out that way. Fighting to the very bitter end.

Maybe the law would take him out.

Maybe it would be the cunts he was going to rip off.

Fact was, it was better to die that way than to die of a broken heart, perched in a dilapidated hotel room, on an island that needed too much saving to give a shit about.

"Count me in," he'd said.

15.

NIXON...

"When are you gonna let the girl go?" Hobbs asked, settling down next to Nixon at the bar of the basement.

Nixon wiped at the blood spatter he'd missed, ignoring Hobbs. He'd literally just taken a seat a minute ago. The morning had been long and gruelling and – as he got down to piecing the events last night – had resulted in an unexpected chase across the marina and into a waiting ferry.

"Nixon," Hobbs pressed, irritably. "I'm asking you a fucking question."

"Thought my silence was answer enough."

Hobbs took his glasses off and rubbed at his eyes like he had a headache. "How much blood you willing to spill over her?"

Nixon threw the napkin down and lazily dragged his gaze over to him. "Are you going through some mid-life crisis, Hobbs? You're taking a huge interest in my life all of a sudden, and last I checked, we're business partners. We've got a job in the next few days –"

"You're seriously going to leave Vixen behind to

rip off some dickhead for a bit of gold?"

Nixon's gaze narrowed. "She's safe here."

"She'd be safer on her own, did you know that?"

He didn't want to hear it. Jesus, he heard it enough from Vixen lately. The girl had no fear anymore. She was splitting open at the seams, and there was nothing Nixon could do to close her back up again. Long ago, he'd fuck her and it would be enough to silence her for a while. She had enough sense to fear him.

But now...

Now she was harder to tame.

He wanted to go back to the way it was. He wanted her to be afraid. He wanted her to obey and plead for her life and be relieved when he let her live another day. *That* Vixen was easier to gratify. *That* Vixen had accepted her fate. He'd known what he was doing then.

Now he knew fuck-all.

"It's been two years is all," Hobbs added, solemnly. "I didn't want to say anything in front of the others last night, but we both know the attack yesterday deliberately failed. This is...*familiar*, isn't it?"

Nixon tapped his fingers on the bar, contemplating. "It is."

"We know who was responsible before."

"It's not him," he said firmly. "I killed him."

"His body was never recovered."

"*I killed him.*"

"You sure about that?"

Nixon laughed coldly. "Last I heard, you can't live without a heart."

Hobbs stilled. He was the squeamish type. His face paled as he stared dumbly at Nixon. "Okay then."

"Vixen will be okay," Nixon explained, staring down at his untouched glass, deciding it was best to remain clear headed. "I know what I'm doing. I just don't know who to trust."

"Don't insult me."

"Not trying to."

"I brought you into this game. I showed you everything. You were just a punk before, remember? A nobody."

Nixon smirked at Hobbs. "Fucking hell, I hit a nerve."

Hobbs put his glasses back on, glaring at him. "I don't like feeling on the outs with my best man. I've done nothing to you to warrant any mistrust, and I get you're having a vent, but don't ever imply I can't be trusted. You can talk about having no one to turn to, but you can say it by not lumping me with the likes of *them*?" He pointed in the general direction of the people in the room.

"You're being dramatic. I meant it like that, Hobbs. Fucking relax."

But Hobbs wasn't finished. "I'm not just your business partner."

Nixon looked at him, amused. "No, you're not."

"Are you tickling my ear?"

"No."

"We are like brothers, are we not?"

Jesus. "Sure, Hobbs."

"Sure or yes?"

Dear fucking God. "Yeah, Hobbs, we're like brothers."

Hobbs had some serious family issues, man. His shoulders relaxed minimally. "So, what are your plans with the girl then?"

Nixon let out a sigh. He was so tired. His hand was swollen and hurting, and he couldn't stop thinking about the way Vixen held him last night.

She was so fucking feisty.

He loved her bickering mouth; he'd fuck it right this second if he could.

Okay, so he didn't want her to fear him. Not at all. He loved her little insults. Her cute little defiance excited him. But it was escalating rapidly. She was turning a little more vicious than he thought was healthy for her.

He could handle her adorable abuse.

But he was sure *she* couldn't.

"Nixon," Hobbs pressed, impatiently.

"I'm building a house," Nixon responded quickly before he could stop himself. He felt the way Hobbs was staring at him. He didn't have to turn to see his confusion.

"A house?" he repeated, like he needed to taste that word.

"Yeah, a house. A dwelling. A place of residence."

"For you?"

Nixon looked at him this time, raising a brow. "Yeah, I feel like playing house on my own."

Hobbs rolled his eyes. "Okay, and does Vixen have a say in this?"

"She can fill it with her shit, even pick out the colours. I don't give a fuck."

"What's wrong with the hotel?"

Nothing was wrong with the hotel per say. In fact, the security here had never let him down. He always knew where Vixen was. Up until the incident last night, he'd never had to worry about her safety.

The idea with the house had problems. He couldn't control the ins and outs like he did here, but at the same time, he felt this maddening need to possess Vixen in a different manner. Here, she brushed against too many people. The solitary feeling was never all that present. It never felt personal enough. Even the apartment had that hotel air about it. Everything was clinical and detached. She had no way to express herself.

And he wanted a place where he could have her touch everywhere. A place he could walk into and see her small touches on all surfaces. A hairbrush on the counter, a painting she'd picked out, even the colour of the fucking carpets.

He wanted to feel her in the air before he saw her.

His hunger for her was never satiated. He needed more, and then some more.

More, more, more.

His appetite for the girl was gluttonous.

As the silence stretched, Hobbs grew more unsettled. "Nixon," he said, concernedly, "first, it was that fucking cabin, and then when that wasn't good enough, you said the hotel would be better. And now you're talking about a house. This is escalation behaviour. No, no, actually, this...this is...*obsessive.*"

"I don't have her enough here," Nixon replied, shrugging like it was no big deal. "The house ensures –"

"Ensures she's locked away in an even tinier box," Hobbs cut in savagely. "This needs to stop. It needs to end. You can't keep her like she's a fucking *thing* anymore."

Nixon shook his head. Hobbs didn't get it. No one got it. They didn't understand. "She's not a thing. She's...*every*thing."

Hobbs froze, eyeing Nixon peculiarly. "How do you think this is going to play out? In the long term, do you think she will suddenly wake up and want to stay with you?"

"She already does."

"Nixon, she is miserable."

"No, she pretends to be. That's the game, Hobbs."

If Hobbs didn't stop looking at him like he was crazy, he was going to punch the fucker out. Nixon knew how fucked up it sounded. Yeah, this was like material for the mentally insane, and maybe he was crazy – he could accept being crazy, because then it meant Vixen was crazy too.

They were the same.

The complimented each other.

They belonged together.

She was the tit to his tat.

The ying to his yang.

Oh, fuck, whatever cheesy bullshit it was the regular folk droned about, that was them.

And she knew it too. On some base level, she needed him. He had become her world, just like he intended. Just like he had hoped.

"I'm worried for you," Hobbs admitted anxiously, tapping his fingers along the bar. "I came to terms with how things ended two years ago on that mountain. It was hard to digest then, and it took a long time to believe you weren't just trigger-happy, that... you had your reasons for wiping them out, but... I'm concerned that if something goes wrong, that if you...lose her in some way someday, you will destroy everything in your path, and on your bloodthirsty quest to make things right, you will rot the last remnants of your soul because, let's be honest here, you hardly have much of one left."

Nixon nodded slowly, understanding why Hobbs would think that way. "I'm not that far gone."

"You went through a very violent past, and you lost a lot. I think...she is all you have left, and you're trying so hard to keep her, but... the harder you try to contain her, the harder she will resist. You're doing it wrong, Nixon."

Nixon nodded again but said nothing this time. He had already had this talk to himself before. He wasn't totally oblivious of what he was doing, but... he did try to comfort the girl as much as possible. He renovated parts of the hotel just for her. Had put in a library for her to get lost in, had employed a teacher to give her French lessons when she was interested to learn a second language, and he'd even demolished a hotel room on the same level as their apartment and made it into an art studio for her because she loved to paint and craft shit. Last month there'd been a pottery course and she made the silliest looking shit he'd ever seen, but she'd been proud of the ugly looking pots, and they were just collecting dust now in that room.

See, this was why they needed the house. She could decorate it with that ugly shit.

She'd already been outspoken about the holidays, too. She loved to decorate, hang lights up. Last year she was adamant about a Christmas tree, and he fetched the fullest one he could get his hands on. The

way her face bloomed when he put it together in front
of the tall windows was forever seared into his mind,
never to be forgotten.

Vixen and her fucking festive spirit.

Her smile had left him breathless.

Having this house was *imperative.*

It could be their festive nest of paintings, ugly
pottery, French literature and books – she loved her
fucking books.

And, sure, he understood what Hobbs said to a tee.
She was contained, but that was the way Nixon liked
it. He liked to know where she was, what she was
doing, who she was talking to. He liked to know that
she could never be too far from him, that she could
never look too far into the horizon, that she could
never flee without him knowing about it.

He was not going to set her loose.

It was simple as that.

His phone vibrated just then with a text message.
He glanced briefly at the line on the screen from Dr
Sullivan.

*Appointment finished. I tried opening up to her like
you asked me to, but she didn't seem happy about the
things I said. I'll be back in a couple months. The seaplane has been delayed, so I'll be hanging around for a
bit in case you need me.*

He slipped the phone into his pocket and stood
up.

"Where are you going?" Hobbs asked.

Glancing briefly at his bruised palm, Nixon said,
"I was in the middle of gutting one of my guards. You
still the queasy type, Hobbs?"

Hobbs' gaze flickered to his hand and he stiffened. He didn't respond, not that Nixon waited for one.

He returned to one of the backrooms, to the horrified Tyrone who stood waiting in front of the bound guard that had let the bum through. "Still hasn't said anything?" Nixon asked him, kicking the door shut behind him.

Tyrone shook his head slowly. "He doesn't know who paid him off, Nixon. It was done in the dark. He doesn't know a thing."

Nixon saw the pitiful look Tyrone shot the bloodied man as he sat helpless and afraid. Nixon shook his head. "Don't look at him like that, Ty. He doesn't deserve your pity. He let the man walk in with a gun. He knew what he was doing. He put us all at risk for a small bit of cash and then he took off running. Caught him hiding in a ferry."

"I know that," Tyrone whispered, still appearing disturbed. "I just don't know how you do it."

Did what? Hurt people?

Nixon scoffed. He wanted to tell Tyrone hurting people was the easy part. It was the feeling after it was said and done that Nixon couldn't hack.

The...dirtiness of it all.

He felt like his skin was flaying along with the man he was cutting with the blade of his knife. It left him burning, itching, trembling everywhere.

He preferred easier kills.

Ones he could forget about.

"Well, don't you worry," Nixon murmured, rolling his sleeves up. "If you close your eyes tight enough, you can forget monsters like me exist. Seeing is believing, Ty, so get the fuck out before I finish him off."

Tyrone didn't flinch. He left the room, casting his pitiful eyes at Nixon this time.

Right before he left, he said, "Try to keep the darkness out, Nixon. We don't need more bloodshed."

Bloodshed like the mountain?

Bloodshed like the One Percent ravaging one another in the wake of what he and that crew was responsible for?

Bloodshed was all Nixon knew.

16.

VIXEN...

I forgot hair appointments also included hair removal. My pussy was waxed, my brows were touched up, my moustache and sideburns were gone.

I was such a hairy alpaca.

But it felt good. I'd never have tried these services had I never been kidnapped. There was a silver lining to this fucked up mess, I guess.

While Alessa, the hair specialist, had trimmed my hair in that usual awkward silence (she never spoke to me, I was bad juju), I'd stewed over what the doctor had said.

There'd been another girl before me.

With health problems, sure, but she was no longer a captive. Nixon either let her go or she was dead in a ditch somewhere and...Well, Nixon didn't strike me as the kind of guy that killed what he fucked. He'd never laid a finger on me. I just...couldn't believe he had it in him to murder me so far into our fucked-up relationship. If the same M.O. existed before me, I had to assume the girl was let go.

This was purely wishful thinking. I was aware I could be totally wrong. Maybe the girl flung herself out of the window and Nixon knew better with me to have the windows upgraded.

After I changed into the pretty pink dress Nixon had laid out for me before he'd left, I walked to the floor to ceiling windows and stared out. It was mid-afternoon now. I'd decided to stay in the apartment because I couldn't trust myself not to lose my shit at him.

It was becoming a bad habit – no, *he* was the bad habit. My meltdowns were escalating. I was thoroughly reaching the limit of what I could endure. I wasn't just rattling the cage I was in. I was fucking shit up, and I couldn't seem to stop once I'd let go.

At some point, Nixon would need to realize he couldn't keep this up. I couldn't be locked up forever. There had to be an end to this.

I stared out at the endless ocean abyss. If it meant swimming to freedom, I'd do it. I just needed to leave the hotel undetected.

And if the opportunity presented itself, would I? If it meant I might get caught and locked up in this room for a month straight, would I still try?

In that moment, I didn't know. I feared isolation. I couldn't go back there again.

And for some sick Stockholm Syndrome reason, I couldn't bear the look of disappointment on Nixon's face if I tried and failed.

I didn't even know how I could handle it myself.

The phone rang. When I answered, Jenny from the front desk happily chirped, "Good afternoon!

Friendly reminder, Nixon's reserved a table for two at five o'clock in the restaurant on the ground level –"

"I'm aware of its location," I interrupted dryly. "I go there like five times a week, Jenny."

She paused, and then resumed in her chirpy voice. "Wonderful! If you need direction or assistance, let us know and we will do all we can in our power to make sure your stay with us at Hotel Browning is comfortable and worry free –"

I hung up the phone.

Christ, they were getting faker by the day. I didn't know why she was being extra fucking weird all of a sudden. Maybe she was going for Employee of the Month.

I grabbed my clutch for show. There was nothing in it. I didn't have a wallet, didn't have fucking ID, nothing. But it was pink and sparkly, and it matched the dress so...

I left the apartment and trudged to the elevator. Apathy choked me the entire way.

I was just a fucking number.

At least numero deux.

So stupid.

I entered the elevator and avoided staring at myself in the elevator mirrors. I didn't need to see the fake princess staring back at me.

The elevator made a stop two floors down and an old man walked in, smiling brightly at me. "Oh, my luck!" he exclaimed, staring at my tits before finding my eyes. "Good afternoon, darling."

Oh boy. I smiled weakly. "Afternoon."

We went down a few more floors. I could feel the man's eyes checking me out in the mirror. He was smiling in a creepy way.

"Are you part of the basement scenery?" he asked in a hushed tone, like I was special to be privy to such secret information.

"Yeah," I told him. "I am."

His face glowed. "Would I be able to find you?"

"Mhm." I nodded with a cool smile. "You'll find me in Nixon's lap."

His face instantly dropped.

With a toothy smile, I added, "He kidnapped me two years ago. I've been locked in this hotel ever since. If you ever want to let the authorities know, I'd deeply appreciate it."

He quickly reached over to the panel and furiously pressed a button. His face was ten shades redder than it was seconds ago. The elevator stopped and the doors opened. I watched him hurry out on the random level like he was running for his life.

Yeah, this was the reaction I anticipated. Nothing ever changed. Nobody fucked with Nixon.

Oh, the power of fear.

I let out a short laugh. Because it was better than crying.

The doors started to close when a hand shot out, stopping them. My laugh died straightaway as the doors re-opened and my gaze connected to Flynn. He looked just as surprised to see me as I did, but he stepped in without skipping a beat.

"Vixen," he greeted, that voice rich in charm.

My knees wobbled. *What the fuck?*

"Flynn," I returned pleasantly.

The doors closed and this time I was staring at the mirrors like no one's business. He was staring back too, a soft smile on his lips. I looked up at the camera in the top corner, wondering just how crisp the picture was. Would whoever was watching me notice how flushed my cheeks were getting?

Would they report it to Nixon?

Yeah, Sir, our infrared detected strong levels of heat. Her cheeks were apple red. Our analysts determine she was crushing hard.

Fuuuck my life.

"You look beautiful," Flynn said softly.

When I looked back at him, his eyes were on my face, an appreciative expression adorned his.

"Thank you," I said, smiling cordially. "You look... the same."

Clearly, he possessed very little in his closet. His clothes were the exact same as yesterday. I wrinkled my nose, wondering if his hygiene left much to be desired. From this close, he smelled good, and his clothes weren't wrinkled from overuse.

Chuckling, he uttered, "I have a few of the same pair of clothes. I don't like shopping."

"I never did, either."

Cue silence.

I removed an imaginary piece of fluff on my shoulder, that cordial smile wobbling in its falsehood. Meanwhile, he continued looking like an Adonis, unperturbed by the awkward silence.

Why was the elevator still going? How long did it take to get to the ground level? This was unnatural.

"How've you been?" he then asked, breaking the silence as he turned his body to me.

I found myself turning too, until we were face to face. He was tall as Nixon, but God, that was where the similarities ended. Nixon was hard and sexy, and Flynn was soft and beautiful.

I swallowed when I detected the concern in his voice. "I'm okay, Flynn. I want to thank you for saving me."

"I had to," Flynn responded urgently. "I couldn't keep my eyes off you, Vixen. I'm just glad I noticed the man when I did..."

"You did amazing."

"Were you hurt?"

"No."

"I was worried..."

The doors opened to the ground level. Neither of us turned just yet. He looked down at me like he had so much more to say, and I looked up at him like I wanted to hear it.

"You going to the basement?" he asked, extending his arm out to keep the doors from closing. "I can walk you there."

"No," I answered. "I've got a dinner reservation at the Bistro around the corner."

He pressed his lips down hard for a moment. "With Nixon." It wasn't a question, but he looked at me for confirmation.

I nodded. "Yeah."

"Right, well...after you, then." He waved me out, and he even made that look gentlemanly.

I stepped out. We both walked to the end of the hallway. We stepped into the impressive marble foyer and looked at each other as we branched off in different directions.

"See you later, Vixen," he murmured with a heated look.

My steps faltered. *Shit.*

He shouldn't have looked at me like that. There went my knees again, wobbling. I swallowed and looked away from him.

I hurried to the restaurant, my eyes scanning the ceilings, catching notice of the cameras.

*Sir, we noted she did **not** look back at him. I repeat, she did **not** look back at him. Crisis averted.*

I puffed out a breath when I entered the Bistro. The young hostess immediately noticed me and hurried to catch up to my pace.

"Let me show you to your table," she said breathlessly.

I shot her an annoyed look. "I know where it is, Beth. It's the same fucking table."

"I'm just doing my fucking job," she gritted back under her breath, smiling at me in that fake friendly way.

I instantly slowed down and gave her an apologetic look. "You're right. I'm sorry."

"No problem."

"Is he here?"

"He is." She made a tense face.

I frowned, reading her expression. "Mood?"

"Uh, well...let's just say everyone's on their best behaviour."

Oh, dear. I wondered what awaited me. Nixon could be an asshole when he was in a foul mood.

There was a private area with booths in the back of the restaurant. The booths were further apart than the normal placements. Nixon was seated in the far back, in our usual booth. The lights were already down, and a candle was lit in the centre of the table.

Funny that after two years my pulse still jumped when I saw him.

As I approached, I noticed very quickly how wrecked Nixon looked. His face had more lines than usual. He was staring down at the screen of his phone, reading with deep concentration.

Jeez, he looked intimidating. He was dressed in a heavy black sweater and dark denim jeans. His hair looked like it'd been raked through at least a hundred times. The stubble on his cheeks was getting thicker by the day. It was rare he let it grow out.

"You sure you want some company?" I lightly asked, coming to a stop.

He immediately looked up, all attention to the phone instantly lost. His tired eyes looked me over, and his expression morphed to hunger and...relief?

"Baby, you look ravishing," he remarked. He stood up and wrapped his arm around my waist, escorting me to my seat. He liked this shit. It made him feel good to seat me. I didn't get why. Had never asked. But it was sweet and made my stomach warm.

I instantly forgot why I hated him. I was seething just minutes ago, and now I was just so glad to feel that familiarity between us.

This was what I meant when I referred to him as a bad habit.

A crack addict could damn his drug all day long, but the second he took it, he was on cloud nine and didn't fucking care how unhealthy it was.

Nixon was like that.

Not that I ever tried crack or anything.

Okay, so it was a shitty comparison.

He sat down across from me, his focus right on me.

The phone was utterly forgotten. I was all he wanted to look at, and fuck, that did things in my chest I tried my best to ignore. I caught the way his body sagged into his seat and I knew something was up.

Nixon wasn't himself.

"How are you, baby?" he asked warmly.

In an effort to lighten his mood, I smiled brightly and said, "I just told an old man you kidnapped me."

His brows shot up. "Did you?"

"Yeah, I did. I even told him I'd appreciate it if he forwarded the details to the local authorities."

He chuckled deep in his throat. "How are you liking your chances?"

I pretended to think. "Well, he was more fascinated with my tits and, *oh*, he's a secret basement dweller, which means he's probably got a lot of illegal shit to hide as it is. My chances are pretty low."

He smiled broadly. "That's a shame."

I shrugged, nonchalantly. "One day, Nixon, and it might work."

He considered that for a moment. "You'd have to kill me first, baby."

It was funny in the moment, but sad because it was true. Nixon's death was the most certain way I'd ever gain my freedom.

And I wasn't sure I wanted him dead.

"You never worry someone will notice me and know who I am?" I wondered just then, staring at him seriously. "A person just doesn't disappear without a trace."

Nixon's smile turned soft. "It's not that hard, Vix. The world's—"

"Dark and cold and doesn't give a fuck about me," I

finished, rolling my eyes. "I know."

He shook his head. "Not just that, it's...not as hopeful as you think."

What did he mean by that? I tried to discern him, but he was mercurial and impossible to read. But I had a feeling he knew something I didn't. Something that might depress me. Well, that was fine. I had a long list of shit that depressed me, what was another thing to add?

Beth intervened by placing an ice-cold pitcher of water on the table and two cups, and then she promptly disappeared. She knew the drill. Nixon didn't like to be interrupted unless it was to take our orders.

"How were your appointments?" he asked.

"Fine," I answered, though I felt like my insides were being crushed just thinking about them.

"Dr Sullivan give you a check-up?"

I ground my teeth for a fleeting moment, thinking of my wonderful appointment. "Oh, yeah, she gave me a check-up alright."

He narrowed his eyes curiously. "And?"

And she told me about numero uno, Nixon. What happened to her? Did you let her go? Was I your rebound captive?

I smiled coolly. "All good. We aren't making babies anytime soon."

If I was trying to stun him, it didn't work. He just smirked at me, pouring us a glass of water each with this amused expression.

Not.

One.

Fuck.

Given.

"Now you respond," I urged him, tightly. "I just made a comment about babies, Nixon."

"What sort of reaction do you want me to give?" he questioned, picking up on my mood. "I'm happy to oblige."

"Well, you can tell me that babies are not ever on your agenda, and that you'd sooner have me buried in a ditch with all the other girls you've fucked and kidnapped."

I studied him, searching for a hint of these previous women in his expression. But he was looking more amused by the second.

I thought he was in a dick mood. Why was he so fucking chirpy?

"Okay," he replied with ease. "I'd sooner have you buried in a ditch with all the other girls I've fucked and kidnapped."

My mouth parted. *Oh, my God.* Was that an admission? Or was he being a smartass motherfucker by simply repeating what I'd just said?

He was good. Oh, he was real good.

Still smiling in that fake ass way, I nodded, mimicking his – and everyone's – fucking chirpiness today. "Well, you don't have to worry. The birth control's been lodged in my arm. I'll be a moody bitch the next few days. Because that's what us women do, Nixon. We just take on the hormones, we bleed a week every month, we fuck you so you can just explode in our pussies and not have to worry about a damn thing."

"Your sacrifice has not gone unnoticed," he dryly replied.

"Are you ready for my mood swings?"

"Would be cruel not to be when you live through mine."

I leaned over the table a bit, smiling sourly. "What's *your* excuse for being an asshole, Nixon?"

He didn't pause. "I hate people, Vixen."

I narrowed my eyes. "What do you hate about people?"

His smile wavered slightly as he thought about it. And when he thought too hard about things, he usually flicked his tongue out and slid it along his bottom lip. Just like now. It was too fucking sexy to ignore. "I hate the way they look, the way they smell, the utter shit they spew. I hate that they want you when they need you, and they'd gladly watch you drown to save their own skin. I hate people with a fucking passion."

I winced in surprise. The vehemence in his tone was unexpected. "Ouch, Nixon."

The way his eyes glazed over I knew he was thinking about something personal. "The truth ain't pretty. You should know. The world didn't cloak you in sunshine either."

I stiffened, not wanting to think how close to home those words hit. "Not everyone's a user. There are good people out there."

"Good people become victims. They're just prey."

"To predators like you?"

This time he did pause, watching me with a strange expression I couldn't decipher. It was like... he was surprised by my response. "Am I the predator, Vix?" he wondered aloud, searching my eyes. "Is that what you think?"

I laughed bitterly. "Are you suggesting it's the other way around, Nixon?"

He didn't answer that, choosing to respond instead with, "Do you sleep better knowing I'm the villain in your tale?"

"I hardly sleep," I replied with ease. "I get fucked."

"And you like it."

"No."

His smile was sinister. "Oh, baby."

I felt uneasy, like he was calling out my bullshit. "You kidnapped me. You *are* the bad guy in my life. You know there are good people because you prey on them every day. You are *exactly* what you loathe, Nixon, and you should know better."

He continued watching me intently. "Are you about to school me, Vix, about these good people?"

"Well, no, but..."

"But what?"

"Where's your compassion?"

His eyes hardened. "I don't have any. Everyone's got their own agenda, Vix."

I stared at him soberingly. "What's yours?"

With an unyielding look, he said simply, "You."

You. The way he said it. Just straight and to the point. And so blindingly honest. He may as well have said I was his whole focus, his whole purpose.

My body felt like it was heavy with tender emotions. I fought the smile on my lips. I shouldn't have felt warmed by his response, yet I did. Conversing with the jerk made me content. He never drew away from me. He never hid behind vague responses. He answered the hard questions, confronting what he did every time I brought it up. And this attention he was giving me now? It was consistent. It was starting to be the one thing I could always depend on him for.

I looked around the room, at the dark corners, at nothing in particular, because if I looked at him, I would break into that smile I was struggling to suppress. And maybe I'd feel a little more than I was prepared for. Inside my being there were corners I resisted turning into for fear of feeling that achy splinter inside my soul. Curiosity to explore my emotions was gateway behaviour to the truth that lurked inside me.

I resisted.

But some days the temptation drew me closer to the edge.

Some days I wanted to remember how we began.

To remember there were emotions I was unwilling to confront.

"I missed you today, Vix," he said suddenly, his tone low and serious.

I returned my sight to him. He was staring down at the glass of water, a fleeting look of sadness shrouding him. I stilled. I'd never seen that look before in all the time I'd been with him. As my gaze lingered, I watched him effortlessly conceal it. He raised the glass and took a big gulp.

"I have a feeling you'd rather a stiffer drink," I noted softly.

His blue eyes met mine. He looked me over, his gaze lingering around my cleavage and slowly up my neck where my pulse thrummed impossibly quick. "I'd rather be sober tonight."

I resisted squirming, but I felt the heat between my legs. He masterfully reduced me to this speechless mess. My brain went mute. I was all out of wittiness tonight.

"You thinking about it?" he asked, bluntly.

"About what?" I returned, my voice low.

"About fucking me."

I resisted looking away from his eyes. It took so much effort to pretend he had no effect on me. "I'm thinking about a lot of things, Nixon."

There was no amusement in him. "You're thinking about it, I know it."

"I'm also thinking that I've had a long day –"

"You're thinking of how good it felt when I slapped your tits, when I forced you down, when I filled every inch of your pussy with my cock."

I swallowed, feeling my cheeks heat. "Okay, so I have been thinking it. Haven't you?"

His gaze was heavy. "It's the only thing keeping me from the dark."

"The dark?"

"A very bad place."

My brows came together. I felt a flutter of concern as I asked, "How close are you to the edge?"

"One step, baby."

"Pull away."

In a whisper, he said, "Help me."

I blinked rapidly, too stunned to respond. I also felt panicked. I didn't like seeing him look so misplaced. I felt the urge to lean over, to grab his hand, to tell him it was going to be okay.

But I didn't.

I physically couldn't conquer the fight in my bones.

I couldn't confront the pain in my heart, so I buried it.

I buried it and didn't help him.

He was the first to look away, to pretend he didn't just plead for my help. I felt swamped with guilt.

"Nixon..." I whispered.

Just then, Beth returned with a wary stare in Nixon's direction. She must have gulped half a dozen times before building enough courage to say, "What'll we be having tonight, sir?"

Nixon watched me, waiting for my response.

I'd been so caught up in us I hadn't stopped to look over the menu I'd practically memorized. I lifted it up and pretended to read, but my eyes kept flickering up to Nixon and the way he was staring at me. I couldn't decipher him. It was driving me mad.

"You're not very hungry, are you?" he said, cutting through my thoughts.

I shook my head slowly. "Not chomping at the walls or anything."

He stood up, throwing down the napkin I hadn't realized he'd had wrapped around his knuckles. My vision spotted the colour red and I looked back at his dominant hand, at the knuckles that looked split open with cuts. My breathing slowed as I questioned the kind of day he'd had.

"We'll head out," he said, approaching me. He offered his other hand out for me to take. When I did, he pulled me up and wrapped his arm around my waist, leading me past a wide-eyed Beth and out of the restaurant.

"Are you sure?" I asked him. "You could have eaten."

"I have a different appetite," he replied, squeezing my waist.

We strolled to the foyer. By reflex, I began to turn

in the direction of the elevators, but Nixon tightened his hold of me and had us moving in the opposite direction.

To the exit.

17.

VIXEN...

Shocked, I looked up at him, dumbfounded. "Nixon?" I let out, feeling my heart jump out of my chest.

He didn't respond. His jaw was tense, his expression stern and uninviting. He led me to the exit and opened the heavy glass door. We stepped out under the entrance awning. The crisp October air hit my face and I took a huge gulp of it.

Nixon let me go and gently pushed me away from him. I spun around to look at him. He stood still, hands in his pockets, watching me carefully.

"What are you doing?" I asked him quietly.

Truth be told, I was frightened. This wasn't part of the norm. This was all wrong and my gut was telling me something bad was about to happen.

But Nixon just stood there, harmless. "You told me to trust you," he said warily. "So, walk then. Have a bit of fresh air. Then come back to me. I'll be waiting."

I didn't budge for a long minute. Was this a trap? I looked around. The sidewalks were empty. The street had the random car coming and going. It was kind of like sensory overload. The colours were different than when you looked through a glass window. It was brighter, more vibrant. I could smell the flowers in the entrance garden and a delicious doughy scent coming from a bakery down the street. I looked up, mesmerized for a moment at the darkening sky; it felt like it could swallow me whole.

"Is this a trick?" I breathed out in a tiny voice.

He looked inscrutable, but he shook his head, softly replying, "No, Vixen. It's not."

I still hesitated, though. I couldn't be sure if he was telling the truth. My instincts said he was. Nixon wouldn't play around with me in this manner; he wasn't cruel in that way, but then what the hell did I know these days? If someone was capable of surprising me, it was him.

"Go on," he insisted.

I didn't have a choice, and I didn't want to miss this opportunity, either.

I looked down the street and took my first step. I stared down at my heels on the sidewalk, absorbed in the unfamiliar sound of it clacking on the asphalt.

I looked behind me after my second step and into Nixon's eyes. He looked stiff. He slowly removed his hands from his pockets and settled them against his sides. Kind of like he was getting ready to chase me. His fingers twitched when I took another step, and his jaw tensed impossibly.

I suddenly realized what was wrong.

He was watching me leave and it was going against his instincts. He could hardly handle it. The distance grew slowly between us. I looked around, eyeing the streets, looking up at the storefront buildings in search of any cameras.

He was being twitchy for a reason. Like he didn't have the surveillance he did in the hotel.

If I ran from him now, he could chase me down. But if I slowly distanced myself enough to run and have that head start, he might have a harder time finding me.

I wasn't saying he wouldn't ultimately find me. Just that it would be harder for him to, especially as the night crept in.

No, getting away from Nixon needed more planning. More work. I needed to have a network – kinda like the underground railroad – and that just wasn't possible.

But I would take this. The fresh air in my lungs would never be taken for granted again. This was the most pleasing change in my routine.

I kept walking, and after several minutes of being cautious, I finally relaxed and stopped looking back. I didn't need to. I knew Nixon was watching. I could practically feel the heat of his stare. I wondered how fast his heart was beating. If it killed him to see me grow smaller before his eyes.

I took another deep breath and kept going.

The island was so touristy and pretty. I felt like I was walking down a street in Amsterdam than one in the harsh Gulf Islands. I'd heard Nixon on the phone many times, talking through renovations of local stores. I could see where he spent his money. The place was in extraordinary shape. I passed a few restaurants filled to the brim with diners. I even walked through a throng of guys leaving a café. They'd stopped to stare at me, one whistling lightly under his breath.

It made me smile.

I hadn't felt this normal in so long.

I followed the scent of dough all the way to the bakery. It was the very last store at the end of the street, a tiny little place with a cute green awning and the golden lettered name "Doughy Delights" on the front. The streetlights ended just above the store, and beyond it bordered an endless dark forest.

I rubbed my arms from the chill in the air as I approached the entrance door. It was just before closing when I entered. I scanned the empty tables before my eyes connected to the front counter where a chair was filled with...

I paused. "Flynn?"

He had a plate on the counter before him, and he was talking to an older lady from across the counter with that suave smile on his face. When he heard his name, he turned his head to me and instantly straightened up. "Vixen," he said breathlessly.

I approached the counter where he sat. "Hi again."

His smile was hesitant. He looked kind of out of his depth. "I thought you were at dinner."

"I needed some fresh air." Yeah, I made that sound casual. Because I always went out for fresh air, clearly.

"Me too. I got out and followed the smell here. You ever try Robin's blueberry scones?"

I slowly shook my head as I looked across the counter at who I assumed was Robin. The second my eyes landed on her, she looked away from me and disappeared into the backroom.

She knew who I was.

What local didn't?

Nixon owned this shop, and all the others on the street. He'd bought them all out from the owners, rescued some of them from huge debt, while others were more of a...forced sell.

I wondered what group Robin was bunched up in.

"Come have a try," Flynn said, bringing my attention back to him. He slid the plate between us and pulled the next chair out for me to sit down in. I slid in, glancing briefly at the glass display of baked breads and savouries.

"I've never been here," I admitted quietly, more to myself.

"Take a bite," he urged.

There was an assortment of savouries on the plate. I found the small round scone with a blueberry in the centre and picked it up. I could feel Flynn's eyes on me, the way they lingered on my new pink nails before settling on my face. From my peripheral, I noticed him let out a long breath as he watched me. When I took a small bite and looked at him, he spread his lips in a soft, reserved smile.

"Well?" he asked. "What do you think?"

I hated scones. Robin's scones were no better, but I lit up and lied. "It's great."

"You gotta try her Nanaimo bars." His excitement was infectious. He called out Robin's name and she returned, fixing her gaze to him. He pointed to the Nanaimo bars in the glass window and she pulled one out for me to try.

Robin settled it on a new plate and slid it to me, and then she disappeared again. She seriously wanted nothing to do with me. I might as well have been an extension of Nixon.

Now I could guess what group she was bunched in. Before I reached for the bar, Flynn took it between his long fingers – I noticed how smooth his skin was, no bruises or callouses. He raised it to my face instead, surprising me. My eyes were wide as he pressed the square treat to my lips. He watched my mouth, fascinated.

I wasn't sure this was appropriate.

If Nixon caught a man feeding me, he'd shoot his kneecaps out.

"Have a try," Flynn whispered.

I wanted to tell him it wasn't that simple. This action would never be taken as innocent in Nixon's eyes.

And the way I saw Flynn stare at me, his gaze trapped to me like I was some form of savoury he wanted to try, I didn't think he was being innocent either.

But I parted my lips and took a bite anyway, opting not to overthink it. The moment was fleeting and wouldn't matter after it was over.

The explosion of chocolatey/custardy goodness made me close my eyes. I groaned, nodding, this time for real. "Okay, that's really good."

He chuckled, a soft sound, nothing like Nixon's throaty rumble. "I like this place. It reminds me of being a kid again. My mom owned a bakery once."

"Better than here?" I wondered.

He nodded. "Oh, yeah, only because I'm so nostalgic about it."

"Where are you from?"

"San Diego."

My brows shot up. "Long way from home, Dorothy."

He laughed. "It was never home."

"Where is home then?"

His eyes turned soft. "I don't know yet. I don't stay in one spot too long. I get itchy feet."

"Yeah, well, when you're being a criminal, the world's your oyster."

"I'm just the driver."

I looked at him dubiously. "You get your hands dirty, too."

"Not on the job."

"I'm not oblivious, Flynn, to what goes on."

He nodded, agreeing. "I know. Hobbs didn't care you were in the room when we talked business. I have a feeling he's not usually so inviting."

"Hobbs is a softie."

Flynn quickly looked me over, softly muttering, "I can't think of anyone who wouldn't be soft on you."

My cheeks heated, but I played it off. "Except Doll. She called me a chihuahua."

"She did?"

"You were there."

"I wasn't paying attention."

"Well, she did. She called me a chihuahua."

He shrugged, dismissively. "Doll's intimidated by you."

I scoffed in disbelief. "No way. You've seen her."

"Yeah, she's beautiful, but she tries too hard. You...You're kind of effortless."

Okay, this guy was good. Truly, he suckered me in good. He was easy to talk to, he was sweet, and he looked at me like he was trying to figure me out. It was an interesting change of pace.

As I smiled down at the counter, I lightly shook my head. "This isn't me, Flynn."

"How do you mean?"

"What you see, it's...just a pampered, spoiled girl. I wasn't always this way."

His smile was lopsided now as he regarded me deeply. "You think I'm looking at your dress and your pink nails, Vix?" When I didn't answer, he leaned closer to me. "I see *you*."

My heart beat faster, but again, I played it off. "You're smooth, Flynn."

"Not trying to be."

"I'm not complaining about it. It's a nice change. The men that come here are usually over forty, have hit a mid-life crisis, and want a place to dump their cash."

"Can you blame them? This place looks incredible. I heard what Nixon did, turning it around, bringing in the tourists. You must be proud of him." When he said that final line, he stared hard at me, gauging my reaction closely.

I didn't respond straight away. I just looked around, afraid to admit I wouldn't know what the hell Nixon did because I'd been cooped up in that hotel the entire time.

"You *are* proud, aren't you, Vixen?" he prodded.

I pressed my lips together in a frown. "Don't do that, please."

"Don't do what?"

"Be the type that plays with my head. Whatever you're getting at, just get to it, Flynn."

He blinked a couple times and then turned his body to me. His knee touched mine, he was so close. I looked down at it, aware it was yet another boundary crossed.

"I've asked around about you," he admitted furtively. "And everyone I talk to look away the second I mention you. It's like you're completely off-limits, like...like you don't exist, even." I didn't know what he was getting at. Truth be told, I'd stopped breathing because I was nervous at the direction he'd taken abruptly. "I kept thinking, why doesn't anyone talk about Nixon's girl? Then something occurred to me."

I felt anxious. "What?"

He looked at me squarely. "Are you trapped here?"

Oh, God.

I scanned the bakery for cameras. My head turned to the entrance window, but there was no one there. Paranoia felt like a hot itch at the back of my neck. I brought my hand up to scratch it.

"Because I can help you, Vix," he added.

I looked back at him, but he was kind of blurry. Was I crying? I swallowed hard and quickly slid off the chair. This was a trap, I realized. Nixon had sent me here. He wanted to test my trust.

Flynn grabbed my arm, stopping me from leaving. He pulled me to him quickly, until my front pressed against his. He lowered his head, so his eyes were at my level. With a sincere look, he said, "Let me help you."

My chest was moving fast. Fear of being locked back up weighed on my mind. I couldn't do that again. I couldn't handle another room – another cabin – not anymore. I liked the fresh air and Nixon was trusting me all of a sudden. I couldn't blow it ten minutes in.

"Let me go," I pleaded, trying to take back my

arm, but he was gripping me tightly. "Please, Flynn, before he sees us like this."

"Like what? We're just talking."

"You're *touching* me."

"And you're terrified of that."

"Let me go," I pleaded.

But he didn't fucking let go. He held me tighter still, gritting out, "What's he going to do to you, Vixen? Hurt you? You're so beautiful, it hurts. You know Tyrone says you're Nixon's property, right? You like being that?"

"Let go, Flynn."

"You say the word and I'll take you from here."

I let out a harsh laugh. "Impossible."

"No."

"Nixon would find me, and then he'd kill you."

Flynn's eyes darkened. "Not if I killed him first."

I went still at the sudden change in him. The charming man from before now looked like he was capable of something far more sinister than harmless flirting.

See, I knew it. These guys...they were all fucked up.

They all hid behind a mask.

"You shouldn't say those things," I warned, terrified. Nixon had *not* sent him. He would never have made Flynn say these things to me. "You don't know how far his power extends to. Nixon's not to be fucked with."

"He's only powerful because everyone's so fucking scared of crossing him."

"Because he will kill them." I wasn't just saying that. I was speaking truth. Flynn had to understand this. "He is a force of nature. I *saw* what he's capable of."

Now Flynn looked curious. "When?"

I felt suddenly frozen. Memories of snow and blood clouded my mind. Trepidation flooded through me. I spent so much of my time burying our beginning. I couldn't have it resurface now.

My voice weakened. "You can't understand, and if you did, it'd only be because he's killing you."

Flynn didn't look alarmed in the slightest. "Vixen, I'm offering you an escape."

"I don't want to leave Nixon," I told him, firmly. "Now, if you don't let me go, I'll scream for him. He's close-by, Flynn."

That seemed to shake him out of whatever *this* was happening between us.

"You would scream?" Flynn asked, astonished. "After what I did for you last night?"

His look of disappointment was hard to see, for sure, but it still held little weight to the disappointed look Nixon would give me if he saw us right now.

"I appreciate what you did last night," I told him quickly. "If you hadn't –"

"If I hadn't, he would have killed Nixon," he cut in, his mouth flattening. "Maybe I shouldn't have done a damn thing."

With that, Flynn let me go. I'd been pulling back so hard, I stumbled back. Flynn was too much of a gentleman and already had his arm around me to steady me. But then he dropped his arm and let out a long miserable sigh.

"We've got that job to do very soon," he said flatly, turning his back to me. "If you don't come to me before then, I'm not coming back here after the job's done. This is the only chance you'll get, Vixen."

But I was already rushing out of the bakery, shaking like a leaf. I didn't look back once. I ducked into the clear alleyway between the stores and rested my back against the cool brick wall. I sucked in the fresh air, trying to get my heart to calm down.

How come I felt like I'd just betrayed Nixon?

Was this that Stockholm Syndrome shit again?

I rubbed at my chest. "Calm down, Victoria."

I couldn't look like a frightened mess when I got back. Nixon would know something was up and he would not rest until he figured out what.

Blood and snow and the feeling of being cold swamped me again. I shook, my teeth chattering with adrenaline. I worked so hard to push those memories away. Dear God, I didn't need to remember what Nixon was capable of.

"Please, don't kill me." I pleaded.

"Why?" he asked, detached. "What do you have to live for?"

I brushed the tears from my eyes and waited for my heart to slow down. I buried the memories by focusing on my senses. I breathed in the scent of dough, stared up at the blindingly bright streetlight and skimmed my fingertips along the coarse brick wall behind me. Soon, the memories dispersed from my mind, scattering in random directions.

Then I stepped out of the alleyway and made my way back to the hotel. The breeze picked up. I could hear the leaves of trees rustling around me. I stared up at the sky, mesmerized by the stars.

Two years ago, I was a broke twenty-one-year-old student who didn't give a shit about the stars. I used to think I was trapped then. Oh, how strange the world was.

I was slowly becoming detached from my past. I was scared that, as more time went on, I would forget myself entirely.

I shut my eyes briefly, fighting to reclaim my old self.

I'm Victoria Adams.
I'm now twenty-three years old.
I like pie crusts and pizza pockets.
I grew up in Surrey.
My best friend's name is Kimberly Jones.
I want to be a teacher because Mom was a teacher and she loved kids.
I like going to the movies.
I hate going home.
Tom Hardy is my celebrity crush.
~~I cut myself to feel.~~

By the time I got back, I felt composed.

I found Nixon straightaway. I expected him to be pacing and twitching, but I was wrong. He was completely still. His back was to me, his hands were in his pockets again, and he was staring up at the sky too, unmoving.

I wondered what he thought of when he looked up at the heavens.

I thought of the fleeting sadness on his face in the restaurant, thought of him asking for my help, and my heart squeezed before I could stop it.

My body heated as I slowly approached. I felt this

urge to run my hands up his back and kiss the back of his neck, but I resisted.

My heels were loud, and he heard me nearing. He slowly turned around and found me. His expression was clear, but I noticed the way his shoulders relaxed at the sight of me. He let out a long breath, and his chest dipped, like he'd been holding it in for a while.

He didn't ask me how it was. We didn't speak at all. He offered me his hand instead and I took it. His grip was tight – possessive – as he tugged me back to the hotel doors. He didn't relax until we were in the elevators, and even then, I noticed the regret in his eyes as he looked me over in the mirror.

He'd made a mistake.

He shouldn't have done that.

And he looked at me like I was his.

Only his.

And how dare he thrust me into the cold world he loathed so much.

18.

VIXEN...

We stepped into the apartment, and I was bending over to remove my heels when he tossed over his shoulder, "Leave them on."

I watched him disappear into the bedroom, aware he would be waiting for me. I stood up straight and gripped the kitchen counter, trying to regain my balance. My conversation with Flynn was still raw. I hated that talking about Nixon took me back there again, to that horrible day.

I tried to remember how terrified I had been of him, but I couldn't feel it anymore. Because Nixon wasn't punishing. He never wanted me to suffer. He'd never fuelled my terror. He'd watered down the flames until I was this rebellious little bitch.

Everyone feared him but me.

No, I thrived on pushing his buttons. I liked to see him contain himself. It riled me up to watch a monster hold back his claws, and he loved it too. Because he took it out on me when we fucked, and that was all we seemed to do.

Argue, then fuck.

Fuck, then argue.

Argue, then fuck, then argue.

He reappeared in the doorway of the bedroom, looking at me from across the apartment. I felt like he'd caught me doing something I shouldn't. His eyes narrowed as he studied my posture. "Get in here, Vixen," he demanded in a no bullshit tone.

I stood straighter, fixing him with a glare. "I didn't know there was any rush."

He slid his jacket off and tossed it on the nearby couch before levelling me with a firm stare. "I deserve a thank you."

I crossed my arms stubbornly. "Thank you for what? For allowing me to take a walk outside? Wow, how grateful I am. I'm pretty sure corpses breathe more fresh air than I do."

There was nothing playful in his expression. "Get in the bedroom and suck my cock, Vixen. I'm tired of waiting."

He disappeared into the room again, silencing me. Oh, he knew what that did to my temper. Did he want me to rattle the cage I was in? Jailbreak the fucker all so he could open it back up for me to crawl back into?

I strode to the bedroom, fury in my veins. He was already naked in the centre of the unlit room. His face was tight when he turned to watch me come in.

"Are you removing my voice, Nixon?" I seethed. "Do you want –"

"Shut up," he cut in harshly with a dark look. "Now I love your smart mouth, but I just want to fuck it tonight. No more talking. Give me some fucking respite, baby."

My mouth screwed shut. He looked tense when he sat down on the edge of the bed, waiting for me to service him. He wouldn't even look at me. There was no amusement, no anger, nothing but a tense man that looked like he was at the end of his rope.

I dropped my arms to my sides, aware as ever he needed me.

Tonight wasn't about the push and pull.

Tonight he needed me to make him forget something.

I rubbed at my chest, irritated at myself for feeling warmth there. I had this desire to help him, to remove whatever tormented him, and that made me feel weak.

Here was a man who controlled every part of my life, right down to what I wore and where I went.

And here I was, falling into the emotional trap of wanting to care for him when he was down.

I wished I was strong enough to stomp away. A lesser feeling person would. Maybe the key to my freedom was not giving him respite when he needed it. He'd get sick of that, surely, and cast me out. I was happy enough never to turn him in; I was prepared to make up some bullshit excuse for my disappearance. Anything if it meant he left me the fuck alone.

Yet despite all that, I still found myself moving to him. I was only human, and I reassured myself that it didn't mean anything if I helped him through tonight.

Plus, he was like crack, remember? And I admittedly wanted another hit.

His legs were spread for me, waiting. The position should have insulted me, but all I felt were aching tugs between my legs. Fuck, he looked incredible. All male. He could have been a model in some other life.

A really scary one.

I slowly dropped to my knees before him. My hands journeyed up his huge, muscled thighs. He looked down at me, and I met his gaze, studying the tense lines of his face, wondering what was wrong.

The simple caressing motion to his thighs began to harden him. I took his cock into both my hands, feeling it swell between my fingers. Soon, my fingers wouldn't be able to touch. Soon, the look of his pleasured face would drive me fucking wild.

Leaning down, I spat at the head of his cock and used my saliva as a lubricant. I spread it around his cock and pumped him, riveted by the slippery feel of him.

"Your mouth, baby," he demanded tightly.

I took him into my mouth, and he let out a long breath. His shoulders relaxed as I pumped him and sucked him. I knew the pace he liked. He'd showed me what it took to get him off. He liked the teasing. He liked the eye contact. He liked watching his cock disappear into my mouth.

He gently moved the hair falling over my face and bunched it up over my head. "Deeper now, sweetheart," he groaned.

I took him as deep as I could go, and it wasn't that far in. My mouth ached from how stretched it was trying to accommodate him, but his sounds spurred me on. I felt tingles travel to the pit of my belly. I felt the urge to caress the spot between my legs against his foot – anywhere to relieve the tension.

"Faster now," he demanded. "Squeeze me."

Surprised, I followed his instruction, aware now

he just wanted to be sucked off without any teasing. There was no pleasure in this for him. He needed a weight lifted off his shoulders.

I quickened my pace, closing my eyes as I swirled my tongue along the tip of him. He tasted good and looked good. Everything about him was pleasing. I was not going to delude myself by thinking I'd ever find another godly cock in this life.

He'd ruined it for me, and that was strangely okay.

By how impossibly hard he was getting, I knew he was close to coming. I took him as deep as I could into my throat and massaged his balls. He cursed under his breath and his gaze went distant. He came hard, his fist in my hair tightening, his groans long and pained. His hips went up as he rode it out, pushing deeper still in my mouth, until I was struggling for air.

Then he let go of me and collapsed back onto the mattress. I released him from my mouth and watched his chest rise and fall. His hands ran through his hair, tugging at the ends.

He was still not okay.

"Nixon," I whispered, worriedly.

He made no response.

I climbed up the bed and over him. With my legs bent on either side of him, I sat down on his still hard cock and stared down at him.

He looked back, not a single emotion leaking into his expression. It was peculiar seeing him so vacant. I didn't like it. I wanted our old banter back.

"Talk to me," I urged.

"About what?"

"Well, was that good for you?" I asked, cheekily, desperate to see a smile. "I can rim you next."

His brows shot up. "Feeling kinky, Vix?"

"Yeah, your perversion's been rubbing off on me."

"Well, *that* would be a first for me."

"Me too."

His lips lifted just barely to one side. "I'm pretty sure I took all your firsts."

I tapped my chin, pretending to think about it. "Well, I can think of several guys that I've taken to –"

My breath whooshed out of me as he flipped me over in one big swooping motion, until my back was on the mattress and he was looming over me. There was a wicked glint in his eye and a warning in his expression. "Now, be very careful what you say, Vixen."

I swallowed a laugh, enjoying his reaction. "Oh? Why should I do that?"

"Because I'll hunt down these boys and kill them."

I bit the inside of my lip. "You want to know what's fucked up, Nixon? I actually believe you would."

He dropped his face to my neck and sucked fiercely at my skin. I squirmed, trying to get him to stop. "You're going to mark me."

"Good," he murmured, licking up my throat now.

"Jerk."

"You marked me with your nails. It's only fair I mark you back."

I protested. "Now, I apologized for that."

He paused to look at me. "I'm sorry for leaving a hickey on your throat, baby."

I rolled my eyes. "Oh, I see what you did there."

"Now we're even."

I pretended to look filthy at that. "You hurt me just now, you know."

He let out a hard laugh. "Here we go."

"What?"

"I hurt you again?"

"Yes."

"You're always hurting."

I bit back my smile. "Because you're rough on me."

"Where are these bruises, Vix, that display all your pain?"

"They're too deep to show."

"That sounds like bullshit to me."

"Well, it's true."

"Uh-huh." His chest rumbled with laughter again. "Tell me where else it hurts."

My cheeks heated as I spread my legs and grinded against his front. He looked amused, finally. Seeing his face glow made my heart hiccup in my chest. Like he was still my Nixon.

My saviour. A tiny voice whispered in the black void I'd done so well to ignore.

"Oh, no," he said, playing along. "I hurt you down there, did I?"

I nodded. "I think you need to kiss it better."

He kissed me fiercely, lapping his tongue against mine. He dragged a moan from me before he pulled away and began kissing down my body. I breathed hard, staring up at the ceiling now, awed by what his mouth was capable of. Just his lips on my skin and my body was on fire. He flipped my dress up and slid my panties down. His fingers grazed over my pussy, sending a jolt of pleasure through me.

"Look how wet you are," he murmured, awed.

"Not wet for *you*, Nixon," I said, panting.

"No?" He trailed his hot tongue up my slit. My

hands shot out to his hair. I tugged fiercely at it as my body began to thrum. *Oh, dear God.*

"You think," he started, his hot breaths at my centre, "if I sucked you hard enough, you'd scream my name?"

Heat bloomed from within me.

We played our roles to a tee. The familiarity of it melted me.

"I won't say your name," I told him with conviction, the challenge in my tone present. "It could be anyone's mouth on my pussy, Nixon. You do nothing for me."

I waited for his usual rebuttal. The tongue in cheek response before he pulled apart my words and proved me wrong, but it was utterly absent. The silence dragged, until I lifted my head and looked down at him. His eyes met mine, and instead of amusement in their depths, there was something else.

Something...warm and delicious.

I swallowed hard, feeling increasingly uncomfortable by my body's response to him.

"Lay your head down, baby," he said gravely, "and allow me to prove you wrong."

I dropped my head and shut my eyes as he began to lick me, pulling sounds out of me that – even after all this time – surprised me.

As expected, he proved me wrong.

19.

TYRONE...

Fury drove him here.

He followed Flynn to his room, feeling rage coursing through his veins.

The second Flynn got to his door, Tyrone hurried from behind him and shoved him against it. He forced his front against the door, grabbed at his hair, and growled, "What the fuck you trying to do, Flynn?"

"Get off me, man," Flynn retorted. "What the fuck are you doing?"

"I'm not getting off you until you give me some answers."

"About what?"

"Why are you fucking with Nixon's girl?"

Flynn let out a surprised laugh. "What are you talking about?"

"I saw you at the bakery. I saw what you did!"

Tyrone had seen Nixon leave the hotel with Vix. It was so shocking, Tyrone had wound up following Vixen, praying to God she wouldn't run. Tyrone didn't need that kind of heartbreak from Nixon, and Vix didn't deserve the punishment that would ensue as a consequence of fleeing.

But she didn't flee.

She'd just wandered, looking stunning in her dress, wind blowing through her hair before she'd disappeared into the bakery.

The last thing Ty had expected to see was the way Flynn interacted with her there. The close proximity, the light touches – THE FEEDING HER FROM HIS HAND – it was shocking.

It made him furious.

"I didn't do anything," Flynn told him, sounding pissed now. "She showed up at the fucking bakery. I talked to her."

"You touched her."

"So what?"

"I saw the way you were looking at her."

"She's fucking beautiful."

Tyrone let go of Flynn and took a giant step back, feeling like he wasn't capable of stopping himself from beating this fucking kid to the ground. "What's your fucking aim, Flynn?"

"I have no aim."

"You said something to her, and she fled."

Fixing his sports jacket, Flynn turned to face Tyrone. He glared at him. "None of your fucking business."

"I warned you, kid, not to mess with her."

"I wasn't," Flynn snapped. "I was minding my own fucking business. She came into the bakery on her own."

"I want to know what you said."

Flynn smirked darkly. "Like I said, none of your fucking business."

Tyrone didn't respond. He studied Flynn, trying to understand why he couldn't stand the sight of him. He'd voiced his concerns to Hobbs after the meeting, but Hobbs had brushed him off, adamant the kid was imperative to the job. Toby had stressed a driver was needed, had even steered Hobbs in the direction of the kid who'd been making news all over San Diego for being a street racer.

"If you're fucking around, you're messing with the wrong people," Tyrone warned.

"I went to a fucking bakery," Flynn retorted, slowly, "I was eating from there when she walked through the door and said my name. She sat down next to me, and I fed her from my fucking plate. Why is that such a fucking problem?"

Tyrone didn't respond.

Because...well, because technically it wasn't a problem.

And judging by the confusion on Flynn's face, Tyrone started to think he'd overreacted.

But...something, *something* at the pit of him felt uneasy. He couldn't explain it. The shooting in the basement had rocked him. Maybe it was responsible for making him so fucking paranoid.

The incident had brought out a side to Nixon that frankly disturbed the crew. He'd had absolutely no qualms torturing a man, even when he got no answers. Seeing what Nixon was capable of made what happened two years ago all the more real.

Tyrone didn't want a repeat of that madness.

But he had a feeling he had no control over what was going to happen.

Technically, Flynn saved the girl. Technically, he

had absolutely no idea she'd walk into the bakery.

The kid looked so confused, and Tyrone almost felt guilty for being such an irate dick.

But...

Fuck, he couldn't stop that feeling at his core.

He turned around and stormed away from Flynn. He took the elevator back down to the basement and nursed a few drinks at the bar, watching for hours as Doll drank, danced, got undressed and wooed the men. He watched with a smirk as Hobbs showed up, pulled her off the lap of an intoxicated Rowan and dragged her out of the basement.

"Stop thinking," Tiger told him, noticing Tyrone's quiet demeanour. "You do too much of that, Tyrone."

"I can't shut off," Tyrone retorted. "I can't stop thinking of that homeless guy."

"Vixen didn't get hurt. That's all that matters right now."

The crew cared about Vixen.

That girl was infectious when she wasn't acting so miserable. But lately...lately, Tyrone detected something had changed inside her.

It was another worry.

Just another thing on the long list of shit Tyrone had to think about.

20.

VIXEN...

I sat on the floor in front of the window of the living room with the bedsheet wrapped around my naked body. It was close to two in the morning. Nixon had fucked me twice before releasing me from the bed. He didn't clean me up, didn't ask how good it felt for me. Typical Nixon, making me feel like a used tissue. I supposed I made him feel like any other dick.

This tit for tat was getting arduous, but it was us.

And the hard part of it being us was I was beginning to like it – *really* like it.

I tried to quiet my thoughts by looking out into the darkness. If I stared hard enough, I might see the ocean's waves crashing against the rocks below.

It felt like so much had suddenly happened the last couple days. My routine had been shaken. First, with Flynn. Second, with the doctor's disclosure. And now third with Nixon letting me out and looking at me like...

It couldn't have all been a coincidence. My gut was trying to warn me of something, but I didn't know what it was. There was an ominous feeling of encroaching peril. The feeling was akin to the day I'd been kidnapped.

It was unsettling.

"What are you doing out here, Vix?"

I stirred out of my thoughts and glanced at him from over my shoulder. "Just thinking."

Nixon approached me, looking freshly showered in just his black briefs. Drops of water fell from his hair as he slid down to the floor. He wrapped his arms around me and tugged me back. My back moulded into his front, a perfect fit, like a piece to a puzzle. I tried not to dwell on that.

"Thinking about what?" he asked, planting kisses along my shoulder.

My lips quivered. I was overcome with the urge to ask him about numero uno. It was there, at the tip of my tongue, but I didn't know what reaction I'd get.

Instead, I settled with shaking my head. "Nothing."

His finger traced down my bare arm as he made a thoughtful sound. "You can talk to me."

"Why bother? We'll just end up arguing."

"No," he disagreed. "*You* argue. I'm just along for the ride."

I pondered that comment. "Is it wearing you down?"

"No, I like your fire."

"If I put it out, would you be less enchanted by me?"

"No."

I sighed, at my wits end. "You don't care when I act out. You don't care when I embarrass you. You don't care when I throw my fits and tell random guests you kidnapped me. Tell me, Nixon, what would finally get under your skin?"

As expected, he was completely unperturbed. "There isn't anything you can do that'll drive me away."

I brushed his hand away and scooted out of his hold. Holding the bedsheet tight around me, I turned around to look at him. "I don't buy that."

"Okay."

Okay?

I huffed. "Can't you see I'm getting worse? All I do is flip out. I can't hold back anymore, Nixon. You've unwound me all the way. There's nothing timid or innocent left. You've broken me."

"You were broken when I met you," he replied.

"No," I disagreed. "I was hopeful."

"You still are."

"How do you figure that?"

"Because you still think people are looking for you."

I felt like I'd been punched in the stomach. I sucked in a breath, trying to calm my thoughts. "Two years would make many people give up. That's reality. I become a statistic and I get buried under dozens more cases of missing people. That doesn't mean I should stop hoping."

Nixon went quiet. I didn't know what his silence meant, but there was a weight to it.

"People cared about me, you know," I added quietly, holding back the surge of emotion. "Doesn't it bother you?"

"No," he softly answered. "Not at all."

"Do you think that's normal?"

"*I'm* not normal."

To that, I silently agreed.

Jesus, there was no getting through to him. I could paint the rights and wrongs to him in black and white, and it wouldn't phase him. Because he didn't care. He'd done it once before – *at least* – so why would it matter to him the second time around?

This bothered me. I felt bitter and moody. Whatever warm emotions I felt for him before, I quickly cooled. "Just so you know, that blowjob you demanded out of me wasn't a *thank you*."

"No?"

"No."

"Alright."

Ughhhh.

I sucked at picking my moments. I couldn't hold back when he gave me short ass answers like that. It was probably what he hoped for. He knew me well by now, triggering me because I couldn't hold back my thoughts when I was pissed. I fell right into it. With a harsh look, I spat out, "By the way, Dr Sullivan told me some things."

He propped his knee up and wrapped an arm around it, casually staring back at me like that didn't mean anything. "Yeah?"

Fuck his one-word answers. "*Yeah.*" I enunciated rudely.

He waited a few moments before he shrugged. "Well, are you fixing to tell me what she said, Vixen, or are you going to keep me questioning?" He looked so unbothered, like he really didn't give a fuck.

I frowned. "You know what, maybe I will keep you

questioning."

He smirked now. "Okay."

"*Okay*," I repeated mockingly.

He chuckled, amused. "I know you, Vixen. You can't keep shit to yourself. You're like a rabid squirrel when you're pissed. You'll tell me in the next couple minutes what's bothering you."

"No, I won't."

"Yes," he argued, casually, "you will."

"Because I'll be a *rabid squirrel*," I retorted. "Real nice, Nixon. I should start comparing you to animals now."

"Go on."

"Okay, you're a fucking ogre."

"Ogres aren't real."

"Doesn't matter, that's what you are."

"Okay."

"Yeah, *okay*." When he smiled at that, I fumed. "You're trying to get under my skin, aren't you?"

"No."

"If you give me another one-worded response, Nixon, I will find your gun and shoot this place up."

He sucked in a breath. "Jesus, baby, you're in a mood tonight."

"Can't you see why?"

"Yeah, I can." Amused, he added, "Do you want me to fuck the mood out of you?"

"No, I don't."

"Then are we ready to go to bed yet? It's getting late and we have a meeting with the crew in the morning."

I was tired, but I was more stubborn. "You can go. I'm staying here."

He stood up, and my face heated with annoyance. What, he was leaving just like that? He wasn't going to even pry just a little bit more?

"Wow, you really don't even care, do you?" I lashed out, knowing full well how ridiculous this was – how ridiculous I was being. I just couldn't seem to stop.

"You're being unreasonable, Vixen. Come to bed."

As he began to walk away, I hurriedly jumped to my feet and flew in his direction. I cut in front of him, stopping him in his tracks. My cheeks heated as I looked up at his face, at his beautiful blue eyes and hated the way the fissure in my chest warmed.

"You made me this way, you know," I growled, blinking back tears.

His amusement faded as he took in my distress. "Made you what way?"

"This unreasonable, rabid squirrel way!" I hissed. "If you'd just hurt me the first time I did it, I wouldn't have dared done it again."

He was desperate to calm me down because he playfully said, "I thought I always hurt you."

I wasn't in the mood for hysterics right now. "You know what I fucking mean."

"Vixen, you're not yourself –"

"You keep telling me I'm not myself every time I lose my shit. You never stop to wonder what makes me tick. You just fuck the mood outta me. Unless you plan on having your dick inside me 24/7, this is what you're going to keep getting, Nixon."

"Baby –"

"Don't 'baby' me. I hate that fucking word."

"You don't."

"I do."

When he raised a hand to touch me, I took a step back, shaking my head. "Don't do that, either. Don't touch me like you care."

"Of course I care."

My heart squeezed. "Did you care for the girl before me?"

Shit, fuck, I'd said it. It was out there. It happened. I let it slip. He was right – I couldn't hold back if I tried.

My body went stiff as I gauged his reaction, but he...just stared at me, unbothered, kind of like he wasn't surprised at all.

"Yes," he answered gravely. "I cared for the girl before you very much."

That stung. Tears clouded my eyes. "More than me?"

"Equally, but in very different ways."

I wanted to collapse to the ground and sob. I wanted to hit him and scream. So many emotions roared inside me. I didn't know which route to take. All I knew was this fucking hurt. A lot. And he didn't look sympathetic to my emotions at all.

He cocked his head to the side, staring at me intently. "How does your heart feel, Vixen?"

"Fuck you," I snarled at him. "I don't even care."

"You're a liar."

"I'm not lying."

I wasn't.

No, I wasn't.

I didn't fucking care. I didn't.

I just wanted my freedom. I just wanted to be let go.

WHY WOULDN'T HE LET ME GO?

Fuelled by pain and anger, I let go of the bedsheet because I couldn't storm off in it without tripping over it. I hurried into the softly lit bedroom and grabbed the random crap off the night stand. I threw the box of tissues at the doorway where he stood, followed by the comb and box of Q-tips. He didn't flinch as they hit his chest.

I hated him.

I hated him because he made my heart pound and my skin burn.

He made me search for him in the night.

He made me need him like he was the air I breathed.

He made me miss him when he was gone.

And I just wanted to go.

I really did.

I wanted my old life back.

Desperate, I grabbed the new lamp on the nightstand. This would be attempt number 74453432. I pulled it out of the wall and threw it against the window again. I watched it smash into a thousand little pieces, and still, the window remained intact, not a single bit of it cracked or scratched or anything. What the fuck was this glass made of? What kind of fucking sorcery was this?

Angered, I went to the window and pounded on it with my fists. It didn't even rattle. I screamed, tears falling down my face as I bruised my palms with the force of my strikes.

I felt him come up from behind me. I heard him shushing me like he always did, that calm tone of his striking at my heart, at my anger, at the centre of my being.

The second I felt his arms begin to wrap around me, I spun around and pounded into him. I was screaming all kinds of things.

You made me this way.

You won't let me go.

You want me to fight you.

You like this.

You want me miserable and trapped.

I wailed at him, and he took the full brunt of it, staring at me with an expression I'd never seen before. One that looked equally distressed and pained and miserable.

"How did we get here?" I asked him, panting now, so tired my legs were shuddering. My body wavered against him, this time allowing him to wrap his arms around me to steady me. "I used to be so scared of you. I used to think you were going to kill me. Tell me, Nixon, in that cabin, did you think about it? Just a little bit?"

He looked anguished, watching me for a long moment. "You worry me, Vixen."

Confusion filled me. "Why?"

"Because you already know everything. You already know who was before you. You already know what my intentions were in that cabin. You just choose not to remember."

I blinked slowly, considering his words. "I can't think about it, Nixon, without falling apart."

"Ever think you might fall *together* instead?"

I didn't respond because I didn't know what he meant. It was the worst time of my life. I'd never been so petrified. I couldn't unbury that trauma. I resisted.

"You're really never going to let me go, are you?" I whispered shakily, staring into his solemn blue eyes.

"Never," he said, resolutely.

My shoulders sagged. The fight disappeared from me. I felt myself beginning to accept that this was it – this was how my life was going to be.

"You're not enough, Nixon," I croaked. "I need more of a reason to live, you know."

Nixon's gaze shifted to a spot on the ground. "Careful, baby. You feel that way now, but if you lost me, you might not think so."

I didn't think that was true. He wasn't the reason I was living. No way.

"A person should never hold that much power," I said, feeling more tears fall.

"Shame," he replied, equally tormented. "I never got to make that choice when you came into my world."

As I watched him, the way his shoulders slumped, the way he looked at me with such desperate pining, I suddenly wondered.

Maybe Nixon was just as trapped as me.

Maybe he had no way out.

Maybe, while I fought to be let go, he fought to keep me because he needed to.

Maybe... the one held captive was the captor all along.

These thoughts stunned me in my place. I stared at him like it was the first time, like...I could see the cracks in him, though I knew they were there all along.

"Take me to bed," I whispered, my voice scratchy, the fight in me depleted.

He picked me up with zero effort, pressing his forehead to mine, breathing me in with closed eyes. He took me to bed and held me in his lap, stroking my hair and back with a tenderness that made me want to cry all over again. He shushed me, whispering *baby, baby.* I relaxed, buried my head into his chest, closing my eyes.

After I'd settled down, the room filled with silence. I heard his heart beating in my ear, heard his long, steady breaths.

Then he whispered gently, "I let you out, and it went against everything in me. I know, without a shadow of a doubt, if given the chance, you'd leave me. Still, I let you out. Can't you see I'm trying?" Fresh tears fell from my sore eyes as I listened. "My day begins and ends with you. You're mine, Vixen, wherever you are, wherever you go, your home is with me."

After a while of his stroking and tender words, I felt the pain leech from my body. He always did that – made the hurt go away. I used to fight against it, resist believing he was responsible for making me feel better, but I was wrong. So very wrong.

"What happened to you today?" I whispered in a peaceful lull. "Your hand is busted up and you're not yourself."

"Today," he whispered back, his voice tightening, "I had to feel myself rot, had to be my old self again, and I didn't like it."

I tried to interpret what he meant. "Why did you have to be your old self again?"

"Because sometimes it's necessary. Because it protects us – protects you."

"Is this about that homeless man?"

"Yes."

"You found out who sent him?"

"I found out who let him through the door."

And that man was probably dead. His men were probably covering it up as we spoke. This would have been disturbing to me two years ago. Now? Not so much.

"Is that why you needed my mouth?" I asked.

"I needed to take the edge off."

Reflecting on my wig out, I murmured, "I don't think I helped out much."

"I think you did just fine, kitten."

I traced my finger along his vast chest, running over scars I'd always known were there, but now they intrigued me. I thought of what Dr Sullivan said, about him being stabbed, about her nursing him back to health. I tried to think of Nixon disadvantaged and bleeding, and it was so hard to envision because I'd never seen him that way.

"Is it true you got stabbed and almost died?" I asked, looking up at him in the dark.

He peered down at me, looking utterly shattered from today. "Yeah, that happened."

"What happened exactly?"

"I was a street kid. I thieved and couriered drugs. One day a group of thugs decided to rob me halfway to the drop off point, and they didn't want me to live through it."

"So, they stabbed you?"

"I stabbed them first with this rusted knife I carried. I'd stolen that blade from an army surplus store when I was a kid and never could seem to let it go, call it silly superstition. I'd never used it until then. I knew they were going to leave me for dead, and at the time I had a reason to live. I couldn't die. I needed to fight my way out of it or die trying."

"And you fought your way out of it?"

"I tried. I got seriously hurt and I ran bleeding."

"Until you broke into the clinic," I finished for him, trying to piece the events together.

"Now, that's not true," he admonished, lightly. "The clinic was closed but the doors were still open."

I cheekily said, "But it was technically closed."

He smirked. "Then they should have locked the doors."

"But you'd have died."

"Sometimes I think I should have."

My cheekiness died a sudden death. My heart ached at the thought of him dying outside the doors. "Why do you feel you should have died?"

"I had more goodness in me then."

With a heavy heart, I considered that. Better to die with goodness in your heart than to die completely corrupted by the darkness. It was sad the way the world took you into its grip and chewed through your soul, blackening you, hardening you, changing you forever. And to have no choice in it, either. It was cruel.

"Was it cold?" I miserably asked, watching him closely.

"Freezing." Noticing my deflated mood, he added, "Raining too."

Okay, so now I was envisioning him bleeding to death in the cold and rain, and my heart couldn't take it. "Oh, Nixon."

"I ran with a twisted ankle too."

My misery faded as I shot him a wry look. "I think you're trying to make me feel bad for you."

He grinned. "Is it working?"

I held back a laugh. "It was up until the end."

He placed me down on my back and propped himself up on his elbow, looking down at me with a tender look. I covered my face because I couldn't handle that look; it burned me everywhere. He pulled my hands away, though. "I want to see you, Vix."

"Then stop looking at me like that," I said.

"Like what?"

"You know what."

He gently brushed my cheeks. "I'll stop if you kiss me."

I dropped my hands and looked up at him, waiting for that kiss. He dropped his head to me, searing me with one last look – a look wrought with hunger, with need, with affection – and then he kissed me.

His lips moved tenderly over mine and didn't last long. The second my heart started picking up, he pulled away and pulled me to his chest, leaving me wanting.

He always left me wanting.

NIXON...

His little vixen was falling to pieces, and he didn't know how to stop it.

What triggered it?

Was it letting her walk away from him? Did she feel as ruined as he did? Did her heart burst with panic? Did she feel the urge to turn back and run to him the way he felt the urge to chase her?

He instantly regretted it when he couldn't see her anymore. Nixon had paced, scratching at his jaw, rubbing at his face, feeling the maddening impulse to call his men out and chase her down and bring her back to him, where she belonged.

He couldn't take it.

It went against his very nature. He felt like his limb was missing. This sick need to control her, to own her, wanting nothing more in life than to have her feel the same way he did.

And did she?

Behind her defiance, did she care for him?

Ever since he spoke to Hobbs that afternoon, he couldn't think straight. He knew he had to hear the truth. Vixen was going to get worse. She was going to defy him more and push her boundaries and she was going to keep asking that dreaded fucking question: *when will you let me go?*

But how could he let her go when the mere thought of it left him feeling like he was being knifed through the heart repeatedly?

No, he had to do it a different way. He could try and loosen the leash. He might handle watching her venture just out of view, but anymore than that and it was intolerable.

He had calmed down, breathing deeply through his nose as he came to a stop and stared at the night sky, waiting.

She would have to come to him of her own volition.

She must.

If she ran away now, then this was all for nothing.

He was so tarnished, so sullied with death and violence. Vixen was the only bright part of him left.

How did this come to be?

If he hadn't taken that job, she'd be six feet in the ground, and he'd have lived his life untouched by this rampant madness. It was like a disease. No, *she* was the disease. She bore her eyes into him, dug her nails into his flesh, pleaded for her life and he became infected by her. She had infiltrated his system, clawed through layers of monstrosity, until she'd found his soul and re-awakened it.

And Nixon couldn't let her go since.

And she...

She needed to remember their beginning, or he might never be redeemed.

21.

VIXEN...

I had the most vivid dream. I was in a coffee shop in Surrey and I was free. My heart was heavy with sadness and I didn't know why. I saw Kimberly for the first time, and she cried. She said she missed me, that she never stopped looking for me. We embraced and I hugged her to me, breathing her in, missing my dear friend.

Then she vanished and I left the coffee shop alone.

I stood on the sidewalk, searching the crowd of walkers for Nixon.

I spun around in circles, my mind racing. I felt lost, confused. I needed to find him. He must have been close. I searched every face that walked by, growing panicked.

He wasn't there.

And I distinctly knew why that was. I felt it in my bones. I was free for a reason.

I was free because he was dead.

*

I woke up with tears in my eyes. The morning was

early, the sun hadn't come up, and Nixon was still next to me, his arm wrapped possessively around my middle. I turned my head and looked at his sleeping face. His breathing was light. He was never a heavy sleeper. If I stirred the slightest, he'd know about it.

"I had a dream you were dead," I whispered.

He was too asleep to hear me. Oblivious, his eyes remained shut; his peaceful, sleeping form concealed the arrogant, murderous man within.

But was that all he was? I swallowed the ache in my chest. I felt a strong desire to understand all of him. To know the other parts he'd hidden away. To know his former self.

"What's your real name?" I wondered, looking him over, trying to put a name to him.

I stilled when his eyes fluttered open. He looked back at me, saying nothing. I wasn't sure he'd heard my question. He didn't look like he had. But then his hand reached out to my face and his fingers trailed along my cheek, leaving warm tingles behind his touch.

"How'd I die, baby?" he groggily asked, watching me.

He had heard me.

I sucked in a breath and swallowed thickly. "I don't know. I just knew you were gone, and I was free."

When he didn't respond, I let out a sigh. "It was just a dream, I know. It didn't mean anything."

"How did you feel in your dream?" he asked curiously.

I looked away this time, my eyes pinned to the dark ceiling. "I don't know."

But he saw the tears. He knew I'd cried. Thankfully, he didn't pry, but his expression was intense. He turned my face in his direction and swiped away the tears that had slid from the corners of my eyes.

Something strange was happening between us. He was letting his guard down, and it was so sudden and inexplicable, it left me anxious.

It was kind of like he was preparing for something.

A change on the horizon.

But what sort of change?

Cutting my thoughts short, he kissed me tenderly. I couldn't help the way my body responded to his lips. My mouth pressed eagerly against his, the tortured feeling in my dream carrying into the now.

I'd felt it.

The loss.

The sharp pain of realization. That he was gone, and it should have made me happy. It should have but...why didn't it?

To my urging, he moved over me. His breaths were equally as erratic as mine. He hooked my leg over his hip and sank his hard cock into me. I groaned at the feeling and tore my mouth from his. This was so intimate, so real, like we needed more than just our bodies entwined.

I needed this moment to feel more...tangible.

It wasn't just a fuck.

He wasn't just messing with my head, and I wasn't prepared to pretend I didn't need his cock buried in me.

Because I did.

Looking into his eyes, my heart burst as I pleaded, "Can you say my name, Nixon?"

He paused, his lips turning down in disapproval. "You know why I can't do that –"

"Just this once, Nixon, please," I cried, feeling more tears fall. "For me."

He watched them slide down my face, his expression growing tender. He had to give me this. He always gave me what I needed. He was never cruel on purpose. After he delivered a soft kiss, he looked me gravely in the eyes and whispered, "Victoria."

I shut my eyes tightly, crying. It meant so much to hear him say my name. To know it was still real. It was still remembered. He wiped away my tears and kissed me again, fucking me slowly as I breathed through the burst of emotion in me.

"Thank you," I whispered, opening my eyes. He pressed his forehead to mine, moving in and out of me so punishingly slow, watching me come apart beneath him with a riveted look.

My hands travelled down his back, greedily gripping his skin to me, wanting him deeper. Wanting him to taste my soul. My body hummed for his touch, the urge was so great, I wasn't mindful of the words that spilled from my lips.

Do you feel it?

I'm letting go.

It hurts, Nixon.

You're hurting me.

And it was painful, but it felt good.

Nixon, my bad habit, the villain in my tale.

*

After the sun came up and we were properly awake, I showered with him. I was weak and tired. My explosive row last night left me zapped out of energy, and that dream was the cherry on top.

Of course, Nixon looked the same. He helped me wash my hair and soaped my body, kissing me on random parts of my body throughout. He didn't have sex with me, but he was hard and ready. His thirst was never satiated. He continued to want more of me, even after I'd delivered.

I physically couldn't let him inside me if I tried. I sucked a breath in when he slipped his hand between my legs and washed between my folds. "You alright, Vixen?" he asked, tenderly, noticing the way I'd stiffened.

"Just sore," I murmured, resting my back against his front.

"Anything I can do to help?"

"Just what you're doing."

He washed me with lighter touches, being mindful not to slip his fingers inside me. He massaged my clit as he went, aware of the way my breathing changed. I felt him chuckle deep in his chest. He rinsed me off and grabbed the towel off the hook. He turned the water off and towelled me down in the stall. I watched his face as he dried under my breasts and along my belly. He looked concentrated, content, like he was happy to be doing this. Always the little things seemed to bring him joy, I noted.

When he finished, I reached my hand out to him and he looked at me questionably.

"My turn?" I asked.

This time, the surprise was apparent in his eyes. He nodded slowly and handed me the towel. I looked over his mammoth body and felt slightly overwhelmed. Where to begin? I brought the towel to his chest and wiped away the droplets of water. He looked at me curiously as I went, going over his neck and shoulders. He was so big and muscular; the towel was drenched already.

I dried his legs and cock, finding myself completely comfortable doing it. In fact, looking at him in the eyes was more awkward than taking his cock into my towelled hand.

"What're you thinking, little one?" he asked, quietly.

I told him exactly what I'd just thought. "I can't look at you in the eyes as easily as I can grip your dick, Nixon. It's kind of weird, our dynamic."

He nodded, his expression easing. "I can't look at another woman the way I look at you, Vixen."

My movements slowed as I looked up to meet his gaze. "Is that...a bad thing?"

His smile was faint, content. "No, baby, but there are things that are weird for me too."

Bringing the towel up, I ran it through his hair while staring into his eyes for honesty. "When you go away on your trips, have you ever been with anyone?"

It was a hard question to ask because I'd never had the courage before now to do it. If I'd asked him before, he would have known I wondered, and I never wanted to give him the satisfaction of thinking it mattered to me. I'd been stubborn and defiant, treating him like he was just another body that slipped into me.

That was the game we played.

I pretended not to care, and he fought to prove otherwise.

And I was...tired of it.

My soul was weak and craved something deeper.

I understood this was the natural progression of things. You can't live with someone so long and pretend they did not matter. You can lie to yourself all day long, but when the realization hits and you're tired of skirting reality, you find yourself submerged in a sea of truths.

And the truth was apparent.

He'd taken a piece of me, long ago.

I just didn't know the exact moment.

Or, I had never stopped to think it over because that sort of inner reflection frightened me.

Nixon shook his head, solemnly. "No, I've never been with anyone."

My breath went light. "Never?"

"Never."

"You're saying you're never tempted?"

"Never."

I resumed drying his hair, but this time I edged a little nearer. I pressed my breasts against his chest and slowly kissed up his throat, noticing immediately the way his body stilled. I felt the pulse in his neck quicken, and it alarmed me how affected this man was by me.

I thought of the way he looked when he let me walk down the sidewalk, away from him. How hard it was for him to hold himself back.

He didn't view me as a toy, I knew.

I'd known it all along, I supposed.

But confronting that truth had repercussions. It made things complicated. It made him less evil than he really was.

I pulled back to look at him again, and this time his expression seared me. He looked...anguished and needy. It wasn't just lust, there was a desperate sort of longing for my touch.

I saw it, clear as day, and...I thought I'd seen it before between us, and I'd buried that memory away to protect myself.

"The cabin," I whispered, quietly, almost afraid to hear my words, "it was real, wasn't it?"

He nodded once, eyeing me carefully. "Time to look back on it, don't you think?"

"I'm scared."

He shook his head slowly. "Don't be. I'm your villain, isn't that right? Yet I have a feeling, if you stopped and remembered, you might be surprised what you'd find."

Before I could respond, he took the towel from my hand and stepped out of the shower stall, drying himself off before leaving the bathroom. I stood in the stall for a few minutes, rubbing my hand against my chest.

Images flickered before my eyes.

Blood and snow.

Trepidation and tears.

Warmth and fire.

His silhouette in the doorway.

The body beneath him, gurgling.

Shaking, I shook my head, trembling. I couldn't go back there. I buried it away, determined not to waver. I grabbed another towel off the hook behind the door and wrapped it around myself.

When I stepped out of the bathroom, I paused mid-step, my gaze snapping to the latest maid in the room. She was on her hands and knees before the window, cleaning up the lamp shards. I winced, feeling guilty. "I can do that."

She paused and swung her sight to me. I repeated myself, "I can do that."

Her face morphed to confusion and she let out a series of words I didn't understand. I was about to repeat myself again just as Nixon emerged from the closet in nothing but his jeans on.

"What's going on?" he asked.

"I tried to tell her to stop cleaning up the lamp," I explained, watching as she resumed. "But I don't think she understands me."

"Leave her alone. She's doing her job."

I glowered at him. "Nixon, no one should have to clean up after *my* lamp fits."

He grinned. "You wouldn't feel so guilty if you knew how much I'm paying these ladies."

I continued watching her fill up a tiny trash bin with all the big bits. "You keep recycling through maids, Nixon. Do you even know anything about them?"

"This is Maria," he said simply. "She fled Venezuela after the country went tits up. She's got two kids she didn't want to watch starve to death. She isn't totally legal...yet."

My mouth hung open in shock. "Did you make that up?"

He smiled so wide, his whole face lit up. It made me lose my balance just a little. "No, baby, I didn't. Get ready."

"Can I at least help her?" I asked as he disappeared back into the closet.

"You can," he answered.

"Can we also stop buying lamps for the room?" I added.

"And put that lamp company out of business?" he responded in mock dismay. "You're keeping that cheap ass store from going under."

I suppressed a smile as I called out, "Is that store located on the island?"

"Yeah, family owned business, baby. He needs your lamp purchases."

I laughed, surprised by Nixon's knowledge and how excited he sounded. I joined him in the closet and began leafing through my side of it, sneaking glimpses his way.

"Do you know every store here?" I wondered.

He slid a sweater on, hiding that sinful as fuck body. "Every single one."

"Because you bought them out."

He turned to me, his hair still in disarray. "I saved them from going under."

"I was under the impression you wanted to own them all."

"The ones that were swimming in debt, yeah. The owners weren't keen on keeping their place when I gave them the option of either buying them out or loaning them enough to save them from going under. The latter didn't appeal because they didn't want to pay me off."

"Has anyone refused both?"

He nodded. "Yeah."

"And what did you do to them?"

He gave me a strange look. "Nothing, Vixen. It's just business. Sometimes you win big, other times you don't."

I shouldn't have been surprised, but I was. Nixon had never struck me as the kind of guy that would take no for an answer. Then again, business wasn't personal.

"What made you want the hotel?"

He paused to look at me, and God, I wanted to run my hand through his wet hair and tug it down to me. He was hot when he was wet. Who was I kidding, he was hot at everything he did.

"I thought the hotel was right for us," he said, watching my expression carefully, like he was wary how I'd react. "I thought it was the perfect way to keep you."

"You didn't own it already when we met?" I asked, shocked because that wasn't how he had presented it to me back then.

"No," he said in a low tone. "I came here to escape, and then after the job I returned so you would escape the world with me."

I watched him for a few minutes, understanding him a little more. It should have made me feel glum, or even outraged. I should have been defiant, like usual. I could have said a million snarky things, but it seemed pointless now.

He loved this island. Had put all his money into it, from what I could tell. He was making it his home.

Our home, he'd said.

He'd come here to keep me. To escape from mainland life. Probably to hide me from the media.

Guilt swamped me as I thought of last night. Of my conversation with Flynn. He said he could take me away from here, and I believed he could. He was too confident to bullshit it. It didn't seem part of his nature to spew promises he couldn't keep.

But such a thing was dangerous, and...irreversible.

I dreaded having to see him in the conference room.

As I stood for minutes on end, trying to figure out what I wanted to wear, Nixon let out a sigh and pulled out a random blue dress from in front of me. "There, done," he said. "You can't dress yourself, you know that?"

I frowned at him, dismissing my thoughts of Flynn. "When have I had the opportunity? You always put aside what I'm going to wear for the day."

He pulled out his socks from his stack from the top shelf and shot me a look of disbelief. "Kitten, you are the most indecisive woman I have ever met. You can't dress yourself for shit."

I pursed my lips. "That's not true."

Yanking the dress from my hands, he gestured to my clothing. "Then dress yourself."

He left the closet with the dress, shutting the door behind him.

He was challenging me.

Jerk.

As I leafed through my clothing, I heard him nearby, speaking to Maria. Time went on by as I continued searching, questioning what colour I would wear and if I had heels for it, and god, how long was it going to take me to go through my heels? Feeling overwhelmed with my options, I blew out a breath. Before Nixon, I'd had like three changes of clothes. I'd never had to think about what I wanted to wear.

"You ready, Vix?" he called.

My face heated with embarrassment. "I was going to pick out that blue dress, actually," I lied.

"Is that right?" he replied, cockily. "It's hanging on the closet door. And there's a blue pair of heels on the top shelf of your shoe rack."

I pretended like I knew that. "I know, Nixon."

I opened the door and grabbed the dress hanging from the knob and dressed myself quickly. I stared at myself in the mirror, rolling my eyes because the dress hugged my curves perfectly. Of course, my cleavage was spilling out, but Nixon liked that shit and I sort of liked that he had no eyes for anyone but me.

When I stepped out of the closet, Nixon was his on his fucking knees, helping Maria gather up pieces of the lamp. My head swivelled in surprise at the sight of it. She was talking to him in broken English, telling him she liked the island and the rain. She used her fingers to describe the weather, to explain the rain and then she put her hand to her heart, smiling. When Nixon started to answer back, smiling in that sexy as fuck way, I hurried out of the room, like it would somehow chase away the heat running through my veins.

What the fuck was happening to me?

How had he expertly managed to knock down my defences? It was like he'd known the way all along and was using it now.

But why?

What could he see that I couldn't?

Because whatever it was, he was surrendering to it.

Like...whatever was going to happen was inevitable.

22.

VIXEN...

I avoided Flynn when I entered the conference room on Nixon's arm. I could feel his eyes on me, though. I knew he was watching me. I swept my gaze to Tyrone, who was sitting across the table from Flynn with a frown on his face. His eyes were trapped on him with an unsettled expression. Something was very wrong.

Doll was sitting in her usual provocative position next to Tyrone, in tiny little shorts and a revealing top. She was chewing on a piece of gum and twirling it around her finger, all the while smirking at Rowan from across the table. She was sending off sex vibes and Rowan looked uncomfortable – the tie on his suit was loosened, his hair wasn't in its usual impeccable place.

Doll did this often – fucked the guys on the team, much to Hobbs great annoyance. There was nothing he could do about it, though. He glowered at her often, scolded her in private, and she lapped that shit up like she wanted to be punished by him. I speculated there was some weird Daddy fetish going on.

Shame Hobbs wasn't around just yet to admonish her.

When she saw me, she lit up, taking in my blue dress. "Nice dress, Vixen."

"Thanks," I murmured, warily.

"Nice hickey, too."

"Shut the fuck up, Doll," Nixon cut in, but there was a playful lilt in his tone. He seemed relaxed, not at all affected by whatever it was that plagued him last night. Our morning had been strangely intimate.

Doll snickered. "So possessive all the time, Nixon, doesn't it get tiring?"

As Nixon escorted me to the head of the table, he bit back, "I think every lady wants to feel owned... just a little bit." He sat down on the chair and tugged me down with him. I sat on his lap; the position comfortable. It was so natural, yet I felt awkward because I could feel Flynn's glare directed at Nixon.

"You ever ask the girl that, Nixon?" he said suddenly, his voice hard. "Or you give them no choice?"

Funny how quick a room that was already quiet could quieten down even more. The tension rippled through the air. Doll's smile fell, her playfulness was gone as she whipped a shocked glance at Flynn. Tyrone was poker facing it, but I caught the slightest flare in his nostrils. Rowan leaned back in his chair, eyebrows up, and Tiger – who'd been still next to Rowan – beamed excitedly, like all he needed was a bowl of popcorn.

There was a confident ease in Nixon's body language. He didn't stiffen, didn't glare. He stared at Flynn with silent arrogance. "Baby," he then whispered to me, pressing a kiss on my shoulder, "I feel like a kiss."

My cheeks burned as I stiffened in his lap. I couldn't admonish him here, in front of the crew – I would never do that to him – but I was burning with resistance. I had to mute it entirely. It was not a joke to Nixon. He needed to display his dominance, and I had to relent to him, even when our usual dynamic called for my defiance.

In the open, I was Nixon's.

In the open, I did as I was told.

I dropped my head to him and shut my eyes. I knew Flynn was watching as Nixon pressed his lips to mine. It was gentle at first, even sweet, until he flicked his tongue out. I parted my lips for him, and he slipped it inside, swirling his tongue against mine, adding more pressure to the kiss. Excitement jolted through my body, warming my flesh. Even in the open, marking me to prove a point, Nixon could turn me inside-out.

His kiss was deep and thorough and...dirty. So dirty.

Then he pulled away, his lips swollen and red. I blinked hard, wincing as he turned his face in Flynn's direction and said, "Did that look forceful to you, Flynn?"

Chuckles filled the room.

He made his point loud and clear.

I was beginning to relax as the silence stretched, certain Flynn was wise enough not to respond, but then I heard, "I think it's fake."

I studied Nixon and caught the way his eyes narrowed. "You need me to fuck her, too? Is that what you're getting at, Flynn?"

"I think she's with you because she has to be."

Shit. Shit. Shit.

"Hey now," Doll interrupted in warning. "Vixen's been here a long time, Flynn. If she wanted to leave, she would."

She was bullshitting. I knew she was. They all knew that was such utter crap. They were just smart enough to keep to themselves. Didn't matter who it was, crossing Nixon was a death sentence.

"I think you're all just pussies," Flynn boldly retorted. "Scared of a guy in a hotel on some fucking island –"

"Watch yourself!" Tyrone growled, jumping to his feet, knocking the chair back. "You don't disrespect the crew you're in."

Flynn looked completely chill, though. He looked up at Tyrone with a smirk. "And you're so fucking protective of these two. It's kind of fucking sad. You've been threatening me since the second I got here, telling me to stop staring at Vix or else Nixon will have my head."

Nixon looked mildly surprised, glancing at Tyrone. "You have a problem with Flynn?"

Tyrone pointed at Flynn with a filthy glare. "This little fuck's been frothing at your girl, and I've been trying to keep the peace so we can get this fucking job done."

"My *frothing* saved her, did it not?" Flynn bit back as he relaxed back into his chair. Then he looked to Nixon, his confidence mirroring his. "I'm not calling her Vixen because that's not her name, but *your girl* was at a bakery last night, and you want to know what's fucked up? The entire time she's been here, it was her first time stepping foot in that place."

What in the fuck was Flynn doing?

Where in the fuck had this come from?

My heart was beating so fast, I was going to have a heart attack. My eyes never left Nixon's face. I was terrified of his reaction. I stared at him, pleading silently not to do something stupid. Nixon's jaw went tight. I felt his body stiffening. Flynn was successfully getting to him. Darkness pooled in his eyes.

Oh, no.

"Nixon?" I whispered, worriedly.

"Shut your face," Tyrone shouted.

"What're you gonna do?" Flynn challenged, turning his attention to Tyrone. "You gonna show up at my door and threaten me? All because I fed Nixon's girl from the palm of my hand. She really loved that Nanaimo bar, Nixon, you ought to buy her a box –"

Chaos erupted suddenly. Tyrone had rounded the table and lunged at Flynn, tackling him off the chair and to the ground. But just as he prepared to beat on him, Tiger shouted in alarm and immediately intervened.

"Back down, Tyrone," he told him, effortlessly pulling him off Flynn. "This isn't the place, man."

But Tyrone looked rabid. He tried rounding Tiger to get to Flynn, but it was no use. Tiger kept stepping in front of him. Flynn stood up, dusting his pants off with a cool smirk on his face. At this point, Doll and Rowan were standing as well, moving closer to them to stand in their way. Immediately trying to diffuse the tension while casting cautious glances at Nixon.

But Nixon wasn't budging. His face remained clear, but I knew better than to believe he was calm.

He turned his head to me, meeting my eye, quietly asking me among the chaos, "Is that true, baby? Did he feed you from his hand?"

I was so stiff, I knew he felt it. My lips trembled as I whispered, "Please, Nixon, we can talk about it afterwards."

"Is. It. True?" he repeated slowly. He was so quiet, yet he was all I heard, that murderous edge present in his tone. The screaming had become background noise. My heart was in my ears. I felt sick with terror.

He read the answer in my expression. If I thought his eyes couldn't look more dead, I was wrong.

I was in deep shit.

The door of the room slammed open. I turned away from Nixon's frosty gaze.

"What the fuck is going on?" Hobbs suddenly bellowed, stepping into the room with a furious gaze.

"Flynn started it!" Doll shrieked, rushing to Hobbs. "He started saying shit about Nixon's girl –"

"I had to break them apart," Tiger explained, panting. "Tyrone tackled Flynn –"

"He deserved it, though!" Doll cut in. "He was winding Tyrone up –"

"I want him out of here," Tyrone growled, still trying to get past Tiger. "Hobbs, this kid is a fucking snake!"

Doll nodded heartily. "I agree! Hobbs, you should have seen it. If Tyrone hadn't tackled him, I think I would have."

"Doll, shut up," Rowan said, rolling his eyes.

"Fuck you, Rowan," she retorted. "Where the fuck were you, anyway? You all team Flynn now?"

"Fuck no. What the fuck?"

"Would you settle the fuck down?" Hobbs said, approaching them. He glanced briefly at us, eyeing Nixon before turning back. "Everyone needs to back the fuck down."

But it was pandemonium. Tyrone wouldn't stop cursing, pushing aggressively past Tiger as Flynn stood still, smiling haughtily. Rowan had to also step in, grabbing at Tyrone's arm while Hobbs began to threaten to shoot him if he didn't stop. It made little difference. Exhausted, Hobbs looked at Nixon and pleaded, "Would you tell him to stop?"

Nixon didn't say a thing, though. He just watched, eyeing the scene with that dead expression.

"That's it, I've fucking had it," Hobbs yelled. "Everyone needs to take Tyrone out of here and send him on a fucking walk!"

Tiger and Rowan forcefully walked Tyrone out of the room. Hobbs opened the door for them, threatening all kinds of hell if Tyrone returned in the same manner. Just as they left the room, Doll furiously began to lose it at Flynn. "Take that fucking smirk off your face," she seethed. "You're in deep shit, Flynn. Once this job's done, *you're* done."

"Doll," Hobbs warned, impatiently. "Enough. You need to take a walk."

Doll didn't argue. She stormed out of there, leaving the four of us left. Now Hobbs' attention turned to Flynn...and us. Much like me, he looked wary of Nixon's silence.

"Flynn," he started, "you're not winning hearts here."

Flynn crossed his arms. "Thought we were just doing a job, Hobbs. You act like I joined a family."

"When you enter a crew for a job, how everyone gets along is very similar to a family."

"Well, I wouldn't know. I don't have a fucking family anymore, Hobbs." Flynn spoke sourly as his expression tightened. "I made a comment about the girl, and Tyrone flew off the deep end. I didn't touch him –"

"You don't make comments about Vixen," Hobbs interrupted sternly. "It's that simple."

Flynn glanced at Nixon. "Why? Because I'll be stepping on his toes?"

"You'll be stepping on everyone's toes, you little shit."

"Doll can make cruel comments to her –"

"Doll never takes it seriously. She'd take a bullet for Vixen if she had to."

Flynn gritted his teeth and slapped a palm to his chest. "Didn't I do that already? So, don't I get the chance to have a say about her too?"

"You've been here fuck all days –"

"This girl is trapped here, Hobbs. I can't look past that."

Hobbs tightened his jaw. A look of worry crossed his face as he flashed another look at Nixon. "You need to take a walk, too, Flynn."

"Hobbs –"

"I'm not asking," he bit back. "Take a fucking walk."

But Flynn didn't move. He stood taller, determined not to budge. "I'm not going anywhere."

Hobbs was growing red with anger. "You are making enemies fast, kid. I'm starting to think hiring you for this job was a mistake."

"You'll never find a driver like me."

"Used to have one like you, actually."

Flynn's nostrils flared. "Try finding one before to-morrow."

Hobbs gritted his teeth. "Flynn, take a fucking walk!"

"I'll take a walk."

"Good."

Flynn tipped his head in my direction. "With her."

Silence filled the room. Hobbs looked astonished and out of his depth. He didn't know what to do. He looked at Nixon, a plea in his expression to fix this mess, but Nixon was so still, so cold looking, it was worrying.

I began to stammer, my brain searching for words to ease the tension when I felt a light push against my back. "Get up, Vix," Nixon ordered, edgily, "and go to Flynn."

What?

I looked back at him in shock, but there was an ease in his expression now as he looked back at me. "Go on," he said, gesturing with his chin to get off him.

I got up from his lap and took a few uncertain steps in Flynn's direction. I looked back at Nixon, try-ing to determine what the fuck he was doing. He was relaxed though, his hands folded over his chest as he watched me walk away from him.

Hobbs appeared uncertain. "Vix –"

"Shut up," Nixon interrupted, sharply. "Leave her alone, Hobbs. She can go to Flynn. Let him take her back down to that bakery. Let him feed her again from the palm of his hand. Go on, then."

I stopped moving and looked back at him again.

Tears pricked at my eyes. He was pissed. So pissed.

"Nixon—"

"If you don't leave with Flynn, I will shoot him in the fucking head, Vixen," he cut in, and he looked dead serious. "I will not hesitate to do it, either, and it will be your fault."

Before I could respond, I felt a hand grip my arm. Flynn dragged me across the room, his pace brisk. I dragged my feet, resisting. "Let me go, Flynn."

But Flynn didn't. I started to flip out. I smacked at his arm, pleading.

"Nixon," I shouted, panicked. "Nixon!"

Hobbs immediately covered the door before we got to it, locking it behind him. "She doesn't want to go, Flynn," he told him.

Flynn looked at me, pissed. "Admit you do, Vixen. Tell him you want to get out."

I shook my head, glancing behind me as Nixon sat in the chair, watching the scene unfold with that blank expression. "Flynn," I whimpered, "you have to stop this."

"You're just scared," Flynn said. "Because he forced you here. Because you have no other choice."

I shook my head, even though my eyes spoke the truth, and Flynn saw it. He read my face and tugged harder on my arm, making me wince.

"Are you hurting my girl, Flynn?" Nixon's voice boomed edgily from behind us.

Flynn glared at him. "Not trying to hurt her."

"I threatened her I'd blow your head off if she didn't leave with you, and she's still here, begging to stay," he replied sharply. "Does that sound like she's forced to be here, Flynn?"

Flynn shook his head, snarling, "You use everyone's fear like a weapon. She's terrified of you."

"Is that true, baby?" Nixon asked me, swinging his frosty gaze to me.

My shoulders fell. I looked back at Flynn and slowly shook my head. "I'm not afraid of Nixon."

"Tell Flynn what you're afraid of."

My eyes burned with unshed tears as I looked at Flynn and said, "I'm afraid he will kill you."

"And I will," Nixon growled with conviction, "if you don't leave with the boy in ten seconds."

My insides seized as I stared at Nixon in horror.

"Time it, Hobbs," he said, staring straight at me. "10, 9..."

Flynn dragged me to the door and this time Hobbs moved, looking equally shocked. Flynn unlocked the door just as I heard the number 5 and swung it open.

My body went slack as Flynn hurried us out.

Still trying to squirm away, I desperately tried to reason with Flynn. "You don't know what you're doing. You have to stop this!"

He hurried us across the hotel, skirting past a group of guests. At the foyer, the girls at the front desk looked alarmed. Jenny immediately left her station and rushed in our direction, shouting at Nixon's men to stop us.

But Nixon's men weren't budging. They exchanged looks with one another, hesitating. One of them was on the phone and had a hand up, stopping the men from advancing to us.

Nixon had talked them down.

Oh, my God.

This was worse than I thought.

Flynn swung the doors open and we walked outside. He took only a few steps before stopping and letting me go. He turned around to look at me, watching as I shut my eyes and felt the fresh wind against my cheeks.

The sun was out, for once. It was not gloomy, the clouds weren't dimming the skies. Autumn was on the horizon, and with it the air had turned cool. Soon, the ocean would get worse. The brutal storms would come, and with it there would be strong winds and daring waves. The guests would be few, the seaplanes would slow, and the island would go quiet. It was a tough time of the year for me because Nixon took a lot of jobs in the winter, and I would be left to submerge myself in books, in pointless lessons, in the company of myself.

This, being out here under the warmth of the sun, felt good.

When I finally opened my eyes, Flynn was staring at me, his eyes soft. I frowned at him, bitter from what he'd just done. "Why did you do that?"

He didn't take his eyes off me. "Because I wanted to give you this moment."

"You're going to get hurt."

He shrugged, uncaring. "Then I'll get hurt. At least you got to let the sun kiss you."

I swallowed the lump in my throat, attempting to understand him. I was at a loss. I didn't need to tell him he fucked up, because I knew he wouldn't think so. I didn't know what Nixon would do, if the progress we'd made with each other would come undone, and what that would mean for me.

I studied Flynn now, confused by his behaviour and wondering… "What's your agenda, Flynn?" I asked on a shrug. "What do you think you've accomplished by doing this?"

Flynn didn't skip a beat. "I got to defy him, let him realize he isn't so godly after all, not even on his island."

The passionate way he said that surprised me. Nixon had never met Flynn before he'd come to the island, but the burning rage that emanated from Flynn felt like it'd been simmering for a while.

How was that possible?

"You could have defied him by not dragging me into your hate," I said, trying to figure him out. "I'm not a prop to be used. This is my life you're messing with."

"You're not a prop," he replied, gently.

"That's not how I feel."

"Everyone orbits that man, afraid to cross him, and you're this ethereal creature he possesses like a trophy. You're so beautiful, but you're dead inside because he's ruining you. Who gets to stick up for you, Vixen?"

It was harder to breathe now. His words felt like a noose around my throat. I couldn't even swallow. My eyes hurt, they were so raw. I sniffed and turned away from him.

"I don't think I need saving, Flynn," I forced out. "My relationship with Nixon is…complicated."

"What's so complicated about it?" he pressed, impatiently. "He's caged you in this place."

"It's not that black and white."

"Would you rather be here then?"

"There isn't a straightforward answer to that."

"But there should be," he argued, letting out a long breath. "I told you I could take you off this island, and he would never find you."

I looked at him, smiling cruelly because he really didn't understand, and it was finally time for me to admit what I already knew all along. "You don't get it, Flynn. Nixon would spend every *second* of every *minute* of every *hour* of every *day* looking for me. He would burn every inch of this earth, kill all who stood in his path, until he found me. There is no escaping him. He will always find a way. I am...crucial to his existence."

Flynn absorbed my words, shaking his head slightly. "That's a fucked-up way to love, don't you think?"

The doors opened just then, and Nixon's men walked out, one after the other. My lips turned down as I shot Flynn a look of warning. "You won't win," I told him, sternly. "Whatever you're thinking of doing to hurt or defy him, stop. It is suicide."

Flynn stood tall, looking positively feral as the men formed a circle around us. He spun around, looking from face to face, like he was ready to challenge them. His act of rebellion was over. Nixon had sent for me, just like I figured he would.

"You going to hurt me?" Flynn barked at them, clenching his fists.

"We're not here for you," one of them said, tilting his head in my direction. "Time to come back in, Vixen."

The moment was over.

I sucked in another breath of air, staring up momentarily at the sky once again. I didn't know what awaited me when I returned. For the first time in so long, I actually felt afraid.

"It's going to come to an end," Flynn whispered to me. I looked back at him now. He was searching my eyes, smiling softly. "It will be okay, Vixen."

I didn't respond to him.

I turned and made my way back to the doors, willingly stepping back into my cage.

It hurt to leave the sun behind.

23.

VIXEN...

I was told to go back to my room, and I didn't pause to do so. On my way to the elevators, I walked past Doll. She grabbed me by the arm, her grip tight, and forced me close to her. Her face was so close to mine, her big brown eyes were wide and filled with warning. "You better not hurt that man, Vix. He killed for you, went through hell to keep you. If you ever think about leaving, understand you'll never find that kind of devotion from a man again."

Then she let me go and watched me enter the elevator. I swallowed the dizziness I felt. My stomach churned anxiously as I pressed the button, pleading for the doors to close. And when they did, my eyes jumped to the camera in the corner, watching me. It took everything not to fall apart.

When I reached the top floor, I walked on shaky legs to the apartment. I wasn't sure if Nixon was going to be there, but I held my breath, anticipating it.

The apartment was quiet when I stepped in. I looked around the kitchen and then the living room, searching for any sign of him. I took another step in and almost tripped. I looked down, and my chest tightened at the sight of his black Derby shoes.

He was here.

Just as I saw them, I heard his movements and looked up. He was at the bedroom door, staring at me, wearing that same cold expression. The sleeves of his black sweater were rolled up, his hair looked unruly, like he'd run his fingers through it the way he did when he was pissed.

"Into the bedroom, baby," he said, simply.

I began to shake my head, my worst fear coming true. "Please, Nixon. Don't lock me back in."

He just stared at me. "Into the room," he repeated, his tone cold – so cold.

My body shook as I obeyed. I went to him, staring down at my feet the whole way. He was going to lock me back in, I just knew it.

I felt flat as I brushed past him and stepped into the bedroom.

"Nothing happened," I explained quietly, aware he was standing closely behind me. "I don't know why Flynn would react the way he did."

He didn't respond. Oh, my God, this was so unlike him. I turned around, eyes brimming with tears as I looked at him. He stood still, watching me closely with a dead expression. He looked so ominous. He was so big, and I was so small, and God, I'd never seen him turn his monstrous gaze to me before, but it was worse than I ever imagined it would be.

"Nixon," I began to plead, "this isn't you –"

"On the bed, Vix," he ordered, his voice dangerously tight.

Breathing quick, I approached the bed on shaky

legs just as he shut the door and locked it. It wasn't to keep anyone out, I knew. It was to keep me from having a quick escape.

I took a seat on the edge of the bed and placed my hands in my lap. I kept my focus on the carpet. He stepped to me and let out a shocked breath. "Suddenly quiet, Vix?"

"What do you want me to say?" I whispered, deflated.

"Something catty," he retorted. "Something mean."

"I'm really not feeling it right now…"

"Why?" he demanded.

"Because you're scaring me."

The laugh that escaped his lips was fake. He moved to me and I tensed. Stopping in front of me, he ran his fingers down my hair, and then he began to ball it at the top of my head, gripping it tightly, forcing my face up to look at him. His eyes were dark and endless.

"Isn't fear what you begged for?" he asked, edgily. "You spend so much time telling me you're not scared of me anymore." He gripped my hair tighter, making me wince. "Maybe it's time I remind you what I'm capable of."

My eyes misted over. "I know what you're capable of."

"Oh, so you remember?"

"No, but I know. Images come to me, Nixon, reminding me…reminding me why I HATE YOU!" I screamed suddenly as an image of blood and snow ran through me again. "You're a monster."

"I am," he agreed, eyes alive. "Have I ever tried to convince you otherwise?"

"No," I admitted, "but I forget it when you touch me softly, when you kiss me tenderly, when you say sweet things in my ear and make me feel like you care for me –"

"You want me to stop that?"

"Yeah, maybe I do."

"Because you don't like when I'm sweet to you?"

"I hate it," I seethed. "I wish you'd just fuck me like a brute."

His face tightened. "You act like you don't remember, but you say shit like that. You're in denial, baby –"

"I'm not your *baby*!"

He pushed me down. I twisted my body straight away and hurried away from him, but he climbed the bed and grabbed me again, turning me over like I was weightless. I screamed obscenities at him as he forced my arms over my head and moved over me, covering every inch of my body with his. His face dropped to mine, but he didn't kiss me. He just watched with steely eyes as I unleashed my insults.

I hate you.

You're a brute.

You're a monster.

You like me defenceless.

You never cared.

I want to go home.

People are looking for me.

They are, Nixon.

Don't shake your head like that.

They're looking for me.

I mattered out there.

I did.

I really did.

His face twisted. He looked enraged as he seethed in response, "No, baby, no one cared about you. There's no one looking for you."

"LIAR!"

"It's true. You left and no one stopped to ask about you."

"I had family!"

"Your aunt didn't give a shit. She hated you. You were too beautiful. Her sick boyfriend mourned not seeing the hot college girl that lived poorly under his roof."

"Kim would have said something –"

"You erased your life right before you were taken."

"I didn't."

"But you did. No one's looking for you."

"Stop saying that!"

"No one's looking for you."

Tears streamed down my face. I sobbed under him, knowing he was right, knowing it all along.

He let go of me, allowing me to curl up in a ball and sob until my head and eyes ached. I felt raw, like my spirit was finally breaking, and I didn't know how to mend myself. I'd never learned the skills to self-analyse. I just buried it all away, and I'd done so well for so long, but it wasn't working anymore.

Nixon had slid off the bed at some point and was pacing around the room with clenched fists. He kept darting looks my way. At times he'd stop and take a step in my direction, and then he'd stop and go back to pacing, like he had talked himself out of comforting me.

"I can't hear this anymore," he muttered under his breath. "I can't bear it when you cry, Vixen. Stop fucking crying!"

But I cried harder, wailing into the pillow, feeling the veins in my neck protrude. He started wigging out. He dragged his hands over his face, whispering, "Leona cried, she cried all the fucking time..."

What a fucked-up day.

I said that many times.

"This is so fucked up, Nixon. What a fucked-up day."

"Yeah," he panted. "It's a fucked-up day."

"You let Flynn get to you."

"I did."

"You shouldn't have."

"I shouldn't have."

"Exactly."

"But you shouldn't have let him feed you."

"It was so fucking meaningless."

"I don't care. You shouldn't have, Vixen."

"I shouldn't have."

"That's right."

Eventually, my cries petered off and he stopped pacing. We looked at each other from across the room. We were such sad souls, fused together. His chest was moving fast, and mine was moving fast, too. I saw desire in his face, and I let him see the desire in mine.

Was it fucked up I wanted him to fuck away the pain? Was it wrong I wanted to deny him so he could force the pleasure out of me? Did I long for it so much because it made me feel like for once someone was fighting for me?

Finally, he took a step closer to me. "On your knees, baby."

I went on my hands and knees as he approached me from behind. He flipped my dress up and caressed my ass and thighs. His voice was hoarse when he said, "I'm not going to take it easy."

I nodded, knowing. "You're going to fuck me like a brute."

"Yes, baby."

"What am I going to do?"

"You're going to fight me, like you always do."

I shut my eyes, accepting this, *us*. "Okay, Nixon."

NIXON...

Nixon had ordered his men to back down when Flynn was caught dragging Vixen out of the hotel. He'd felt oddly calm doing it, though his skin had prickled with the intense urge to chase after her, to haul her back to him, to cut that kid's hands off for daring to feed her.

But...it was that very reason he remained seated, feeling his brain blaze with thoughts. Scattered pieces began to come together, but the overall picture was still fuzzy. He felt like he was getting close to some kind of revelation.

"What the fuck just happened?" Hobbs had hissed soon after Flynn had taken her out of the room.

"His defiance," Nixon replied, thoughtfully.

"What about it?"

"He just gave himself away."

Hobbs had frowned, confused. "What does that mean?"

"He's refined," Nixon explained. "He has no fear. He is used to control. He's...like me."

Hobbs approached Nixon, shaking his head madly as he tossed his thumb in the direction of the door. "Him? No, Nixon, he was a street kid his whole life. He stole a car, did burnouts for attention, sent the police on a chase across the city, made them look like pansies. It's how Toby found him. He steered me to him."

Nixon didn't answer. Hobbs didn't see it, but that was because he didn't know what to look for, but Nixon did. He saw Flynn for the first time, saw the same possessiveness over Vixen, but it wasn't in the same manner Nixon felt.

No, this was different.

"I don't think you dug hard enough into that guy's life," he said. "There's something about him that's all wrong."

"I don't see it, personally."

"His defiance comes with too much ease, Hobbs."

"That's because he's arrogant."

"That is not arrogance. That is learned behaviour."

Hobbs crossed his arms, shrugging. "So, what do you want to do about this?"

"I want to look into him."

"Go for it, you won't find much. He lost his mom really young, was a foster kid for some time, ran away a bunch of times, just another statistic from a fucked-up system that gave no shits about teenage kids."

Nixon didn't respond straight away. He'd stared at his watch, counting down the minutes. He'd given his men ten minutes to haul his vixen back to him. That was ten minutes of unsupervised interaction. Ten minutes of who the fuck knows, and God, it felt like eating razor blades.

When those ten minutes were up, Nixon stormed to the apartment and waited for her. He needed to mark her. He needed to possess her.

He needed to remind her who she fucking belonged to.

And he did.

*

That evening, Flynn was eating alone at the Bistro on the ground level of the hotel. Nixon had explicitly instructed everyone to leave him the fuck alone.

He would be sorting the cunt out.

As soon as Nixon entered the restaurant, he had to stand down the hostess. "Not now, Becky," he snipped.

"Beth," she quietly corrected.

"I'm looking for Flynn."

Her eyes lit up. She knew exactly who Flynn was because her cheeks went pink and her demeanour changed. This guy was good with the girls. Made their knees all wobbly and shit.

So. Fucking. Refined.

Nixon used to be that kind of refined, too, until he met Vixen and stopped giving a fuck about the pussy. After all, how could he give anymore fucks about pussy when the only pussy he gave a fuck about was hers?

But anyway.

"He's in the backroom," she said, leading Nixon to him. "I've only just served him a drink. He hasn't ordered yet."

Nixon paused mid-step when he found him sitting in the booth he and Vixen usually sat in. He felt his heart beat faster, felt his fingers twitch with incredulity. It was too fucking serendipitous for this boy to be sitting there.

Composing himself, Nixon's jaw went tight as he approached him. Flynn didn't look up once, didn't seem the slightest bit phased when Nixon slid into the booth across from him. Instead, Flynn smirked up at Becky, in that skilled way. "I think I'll have the lobster, Beth."

She went tomato red. "Got it." Then she swung her

gaze to Nixon and straightened. "Anything for you, sir?"

"Ten minutes of peace," Nixon snapped, and she fled not a moment later.

"Is it fun doing that?" Flynn asked, levelling Nixon with a hard look. "You like making people flee from you?"

"Yeah, I do," Nixon replied with ease. "It's really fucking fun. You should try it."

"It doesn't win loyalty."

"Fuck winning shit," he retorted. "You can buy loyalty these days, Flynn boy. People care more about their bank accounts."

"Then all I gotta do is wave a little more money in their faces and turn them against you."

"I don't think your pockets are deep enough."

Now, this wasn't necessarily true. Nixon didn't know how deep Flynn's pockets were. His assumption was only said to spur a reaction out of Flynn, but Flynn kept his face clean.

He knew this game.

Nixon was right.

So. Fucking. Refined.

"I assume you're here to threaten me," Flynn then said, sitting back comfortably as he stared back at Nixon.

"Threaten would imply there's some looming danger if you don't comply," Nixon returned, shaking his head. "But you're not opposed to danger, are you, Flynn?"

"I wouldn't be here if I wasn't ready for it."

"That's what I thought."

"So, what do you want then?"

"I want to talk."

Flynn narrowed his gaze at Nixon, trying to figure him out. "I think you're here to discuss Vixen."

Nixon smirked, feigning surprise. "Now why on earth would I do that?"

"Because you're angry about what I did today. I took her by her arm and we left that room. I took her outside and watched the sun kiss her skin, and she was...so pleased about it."

"Was she?" Nixon pressed, playing along.

"Yeah," Flynn responded, widening his eyes for effect. "She's like a flower you're letting wilt. I gave her some sun and she shined."

Flynn, too, was seeking a reaction, but he wasn't going to get one. "Isn't she something else, Flynn?"

"She is." He didn't say it in a heated way. It was stated simply, but Nixon caught the way Flynn's eyes wandered in thought. Then he cleared his throat and drummed the table with his fingers, redirecting his focus on Nixon. "Are we leaving for the job tomorrow, or have things changed?"

"My understanding is you're one hell of a driver."

"I am."

"Hobbs thinks we're going to be in rocky waters, and that we'll need you."

"You will," Flynn said confidently.

"Then you don't need to ask whether you're still in."

"I'm asking *you*, Nixon. I don't care what Hobbs has to say. I want to hear it from you."

"Hear what from me?"

"That you'll need me on this job."

"I can't do that, Flynn, because I don't think we

need you at all. I think we've done just fine before you showed up."

"You think you'll get away without casualties?"

Nixon shrugged. "We know what we're doing when we walk into these jobs. If we die, we die. It's what we signed up for."

"You're used to it getting messy." It wasn't said in question. Flynn was just addressing it, seeking a response from Nixon.

"You have to walk in prepared for the worst," Nixon explained, noticing the way Flynn's attention to the topic peaked. "You gotta be prepared to spill blood."

"I hear you're good at it."

"I am."

Flynn's finger-drumming on the table quickened. "Ever any regrets?"

"None."

"You stand by every kill?"

"Every one of them."

Flynn's jaw tensed. "And what happens when you leave the island? Does Vixen just stay cooped up in here, waiting for you?"

Nixon chuckled, raising his brows. "You're taking an awful lot of interest in that girl."

"Curious what you do to the things you own."

"I own them, the end."

"The end for them, you mean."

"Until white knights like you come along and try to play the hero. You're wasting your effort, Flynn. You're so busy trying to prove a point, you've lost sight of the big picture."

"What's the big picture?"

"You got to feed her from the palm of your hand," Nixon said, a devilish smirk forming. "I got to feed her my cock and watched her cry my name." When Flynn's eyes dropped and anger sliced through his features, Nixon continued. "At the end of the day, the truth can't be ignored. Vixen chooses to fuck me. She chooses to take my cock into her mouth, to swallow my seed like she's hungry for it. I don't force her to fuck me. She does it, willingly, every single time. And you...you're just a fleeting wonder. You'll make no mark on her, not the one she needs, anyway. And, to be fucking honest, you won't come out on top, not when you're standing next to the likes of me. So, do yourself a favour and put the topic of Vixen to rest."

"She's beautiful, Nixon," Flynn simply responded, lips turning down. "You shouldn't contain a beautiful thing."

"How about you get yourself a girl and worry about her instead?" Nixon retorted.

"I don't want a girl," Flynn replied softly. "She wouldn't like me. I'm no good for anyone."

Flynn let his guard down. His face dropped and a fleeting look of sadness crossed him. It took Nixon by surprise.

Perhaps he wasn't so refined after all.

Perhaps he was just a fucking kid in a man's body. Look at what he wore, for fuck's sake. He dressed like a street kid would. He talked with confidence, but maybe that confidence was learned from having to survive the harsh streets he'd grown up in.

Nixon frowned now. "I understand you have good intentions, Flynn. You're a bit too soft for this sort of life."

Nixon had been soft at this sort of life too once upon a time.

"This life is all I know," Flynn responded, nose flaring. "I can't spend my whole life doing petty crime, man. I'd rather die out here doing a job than die getting caught stealing car parts in the parking lot of a 7/11."

Nixon sighed slowly, feeling an emotion akin to sympathy for the guy.

The lost look in Flynn's eyes? He saw it in his own long ago.

The fight to stick up for what was right the way Flynn had in regard to Vixen? Nixon might have done that, too.

"Alright, Flynn," Nixon finally said. "Let's end this soap dish talk before the violins start playing. We're leaving tomorrow, and we have a job to do. That means we leave our problems at the door. Can we do that?"

Flynn took a moment before nodding slowly. "I can do that."

*

That night, Nixon slid into bed and pulled Vixen against his chest. She stirred awake with a yawn, whispering, "You've been gone a while."

He'd paced for hours, feeling like he was close to figuring out something big, but not knowing what it was. It was maddening.

On top of that, he couldn't remove Vixen from his head.

He wanted to hurt himself for making her look so worried in the bedroom. For looking so *frightened* of him.

It gutted him.

He felt sick with thoughts he shouldn't have been allowing himself to have.

Like perhaps he wasn't good for her.

Perhaps the more he tried to bring her in, the more she was being driven in the opposite direction.

He couldn't contain her.

He couldn't...*keep* her.

Not like this.

Not in this manner.

"Just thinking," he said gruffly, burying his nose into her thick dark hair, inhaling the scent of her in.

"I hope you didn't hurt Flynn," she then said, a note of disapproval in her tone.

"No, baby," he replied. "I didn't."

"I don't believe you."

"It's true. I just had a word with him. We're on the same page now."

This caused Vixen to turn her entire body around to face him. Nixon frowned when he saw her stunned expression. Did she think he was just some ape that went around beating people's faces in?

While the thought was tempting, Nixon had enough self-restraint to hold himself back.

"No violence on my island," he explained simply. "That's my rule."

"But the homeless man and the guard –"

"They were threats, Vix. I had no choice in that. The island is our world. I protect it and in return it protects us."

She actually looked elated. "I like to hear that, Nixon."

"Which part? That I didn't hurt Flynn, or that I care about our home?"

She smiled softly. "Both."

Seeing her this way made him content. The last thing he ever wanted to see was a look of disappointment in her big brown eyes.

He'd avoid violence at all costs.

He'd leave the fucking boy alone.

Besides, the kid had issues – big issues.

Nixon replayed his conversation with him at the restaurant. He caught the vulnerable look in Flynn's eye, caught the moment of self-loathing when he'd said no one would want him.

He caught...

Nixon frowned suddenly, remembering another thing he'd said. It took him back to a time in the past. To a moment...What moment was it though?

He wracked his head trying to remember, and when the fragments of that memory began to slide into place, one after the next, he felt...confused.

Because it couldn't be right.

It was just a coincidence.

But... that wasn't right, was it?

Nixon shook his head at himself; it didn't make sense.

It wasn't possible.

TYRONE...

The crew had just left the hotel, bags packed, heading to the seaplane terminal.

"We need to talk," Nixon said, coming up behind him.

Tyrone slowed until they were side by side. "What's up?"

Nixon looked fucking wrecked. The bags under his eyes were raccoon-ish. He looked solemn as he glanced around them, making sure no one was close enough to hear.

"I have a problem," Nixon said furtively. "A big problem, Tyrone."

He felt a dip in his chest. "What's the problem?"

"Something very bad is going to happen. I don't know what it is, but I know it's going to go down sometime after we leave."

Tyrone's footsteps slowed. "How do you know this, Nixon?"

Nixon flexed his jaw, looking wretched. "I realized something last night. The past...it doesn't die, Tyrone. It catches up to you."

"What?"

"If something were to happen to me, I need you to make sure Vixen makes it out."

Tyrone felt like he'd been struck by a wrecking ball. "Nothing will happen to you."

But Nixon looked manic. "I need to know how loyal the crew is to me."

"We kept the mountain a secret, Nixon. You know we're loyal. We'd do anything for one another."

"Then...I need your help. I need all their help. I need all the help I can get with this."

Tyrone didn't blink.

Didn't take a moment to respond.

Didn't hesitate in the slightest.

"What do you want us to do?"

24.

VIXEN...

Nixon left in the afternoon, carrying a packed bag, looking...disoriented.

That morning I had tried to impress him by wearing his favourite white dress, but he hadn't noticed.

I stayed behind in the apartment because I never liked to watch him go with the crew, but a half hour after he'd left the room, I heard the two seaplanes in the distance. I looked out the window and saw them soaring in the sky.

Goddammit, I missed him already.

I spent most of the day reading books. What was originally a party room on the ground level of the hotel was now a converted library. Made for me, Nixon had said, but it came to good use for guests at the hotel.

Secluded on an armchair in the corner of the room, I tried to read, tried to get lost in fantasy, but... my thoughts kept drowning out the words. I caught myself numerous times staring off into space. My heart felt heavy in my chest. Maybe it was because I hadn't properly said goodbye to Nixon. He'd left in a hurry, buried in his own thoughts; his kiss had been chaste, that passion absent.

It was why I was feeling out of sorts, I reasoned. Usually he fucked me and left me spent on the bed right before he packed to leave.

"Though you don't like to admit it, I know you don't like to see me go," he would say, kissing the top of my nose. "I don't like it, either. I hate it, baby."

Of course, I never admitted that to him.

I was the one held against her will here.

I couldn't tell the man that imprisoned me in a hotel that I would miss him when he left.

But I did.

I wished I could make the feelings go away. I wished the dependency I felt for him would stop, but they kept growing instead.

I saw a huge stone manor once, a fleeting sight on the bus. It was covered in moss and green vines. I kept thinking it would have taken a long time for those vines to criss-cross over one another. To devour that house took time; it took patience; it took complete neglect from the outside world.

I was that house in a way. My feelings were criss-crossing over one another, one negative thought crossed over by a positive one. I hated Nixon on one vine, but I needed him on another. And so, I was filled with these feelings that contradicted one another; feelings that overlapped and took over and I couldn't do a thing about them because I was here, alone, and no one had cared to save me.

I rested the open book against my chest and slid down the armchair. My sleep had been broken because Nixon had stirred all night. I sensed his anguish. I sensed his troubles. I wish he'd expressed them to me, but then again, he'd pleaded for my help and I'd done nothing.

Feeling drowsy, I closed my eyes and took a deep breath.

Eventually, I fell into a light sleep.

It felt like only seconds had lapsed when I was awoken by an ear-piercing sound. I jolted out of the chair, confused. Judging by how cloudy my head was and how stiff my body felt, I'd been asleep a while.

I hurried out of the library, aware now that it was the fire alarm that was blasting. The lobby was crowded with panicked guests filing out of the doors, their concerned voices talking over one another.

This was serious.

Everyone was clearing out. They practically shoved one another in an effort to get through the doors.

I had to leave. I realized. I had to get in line. I swung my gaze around me, searching for Nixon's men, but I couldn't see them among the dozens of faces around me. I faced forward, heart in my throat.

Was it a drill? I wondered as I listened to the panicked words exchanged.

No, I quickly learned. There was a fire!

There was more than one fire, in fact.

"You can smell the blaze from here," one of the guests said, sounding startled.

"What's going on out there?"

"Hurry and clear out!" someone in the back shouted. "We're waiting!"

The crowd of people pushed to get through.

Shoulders hit mine as bodies forced their way forward, squeezing out of the small doors.

"It's bad!" someone outside screamed. "Oh, my God!"

My heart caught in my throat.

I wouldn't know the extent of it for another few moments. I fought to remain upright, fought against the pushy limbs to keep going.

I finally took a step outside into the crisp cold air and spun around.

Immediately, I was seized with terror.

The entire street was up in flames. I looked up at the hotel, lightheaded by the thick plumes of smoke rising to the sky from its rooftop.

Disoriented, I walked along the middle of the road, eyes bouncing from one burning storefront to the next. I heard the sound of despair, heard sobs and screaming, and there were even people trapped in some of the buildings that were being rescued.

The flames soared, roaring and high.

Like giant cloudy columns, they climbed the skies, one after the other.

Everything...*Everything* Nixon had strived so hard to build was burning.

His island was on fire.

Tears fell from my eyes as I realized the magnitude of his loss.

Poor Nixon. This was going to gut his soul.

People ran. Cars screeched along the roads, headed in the direction of the hills. Sirens sounded, the fire trucks were coming, but the blaze had already done its job.

This was devastating.

Suddenly, as I stood still in the middle of the road, a loud *BOOM* sounded. The earth felt like it was moving beneath my feet. I nearly lost my step as horrified screams followed.

Oh, my God.

It was pandemonium.

Like ants, panicked people scattered in all directions.

I realized I didn't know where to go. I felt lost, confused, spinning around like a top because my home was in that hotel and it was gone now.

It knocked me breathless how much that hurt.

How much, in that moment, I needed Nixon.

I wandered through the cloud of smoke, feeling the heat of the storefronts, knowing I needed to get away. This fire was going to keep spreading.

I'd just begun to follow a group of people when I felt an arm wrap around my waist, and something cold was pressed against the back of my head. I gasped in response, stunned into silence.

"Don't scream," the voice said. "Don't fight. I'll shoot you if you do either."

Pure terror ran through my bones, weakening them. On shaky legs, he led me down the street in the opposite direction of everyone else. We were going toward the dead end, where the bakery was. We stepped into the fog of smoke; it was so thick, I couldn't see beyond the length of my arm.

Then, as we approached, still swallowed by the clouds of smoke, I saw a parked car on the side of the road. By the time we got to it, I was feeling unwell. He told me to stand still while he opened the door and pulled something out. His hand was gripping my arm. I was too frightened to try and run – he'd feel the resistance in me, and I could tell he was a big guy. I stood no chance. Shaking, my teeth chattered. I began to plea.

"Don't," I said. "Please, don't. I'm with Nixon."

"You think that'll save you?" the man asked.

"He will find me."

"It's up to you whether you want him to find you dead or alive."

Tears trailed down my cheeks. "Why are you doing this?"

"Good question," he replied. "I'm doing this because I'm getting a fat load of cash. It isn't personal."

"Nixon will pay you more if you let me go," I tried to say, though I stuttered it.

He didn't respond to that. Instead, he said, "Put your hands behind your back."

I slowly did as I was told. He began to bind my hands together with a cable tie, tightening it until it pressed painfully into my skin. When he stooped down to do the same around my ankles, I bolted.

I ran down the street, toward the screams and chaos. I began to open my mouth and scream help when I felt a body colliding into the back of me. I fell in an awkward way. My hip took the brunt of the fall. The sharp pain exploded through my body, leaving me temporarily breathless. Sweat broke out as I rode through the hurt. The man pulled me up from the ground and this time wrapped his arms around me in a bear hug. He dragged me back to the car, cursing under his breath.

"What you did was stupid," he snapped. "So fucking stupid. I wasn't going to go so tight around your

R.J. LEWIS

ankles, but I'm thinking you're the type that'll just keep running if the opportunity pops up."

I shook my head, feeling hysterical. "No, no, really, I'm not. I've been in this situation before. I was obedient. I swear it."

I wasn't, though, was I?

A lightning bolt of pain shot through my brain as I attempted to reflect on a buried past.

My body writhed, but it wasn't writhing against the man. It was writhing against my mind. It pleaded for me to hold back. To not walk down that path. *You won't like it, Victoria.*

The man shoved my entire body into the backseat of the car. I'd gone numb now, no longer fighting against him. I whipped my head to the side, blinking rapidly as images surfaced.

Bus stops and snow.
Sadness and chaos.
Nails digging into hard flesh.
Gasps and moans.
A voice in my ear.
"You're mine."

I took a panicked breath.

The man tied my ankles tight like he said he would do. Then he climbed over me, and as I turned to look at him, he threw a cloth bag over my head, shrouding me in darkness.

"Where are you taking me?" I asked, breathing heavy now.

He didn't respond.

I'd have preferred he curse at me. The silence was worse.

He slammed the door shut. I couldn't hear anything for several moments except my own heavy breaths. Being so still, I felt cold. My entire body erupted in goose bumps.

This was actually happening. I thought.

It was happening again.

But unlike last time, I couldn't seem to shut down or go numb.

I felt a spark in my body. Felt every emotion. It physically hurt to feel the sadness in my chest.

The driver door opened. The man slid in and the car rocked with his weight. He didn't say a word as he turned the car on and drove slowly through the crowded streets.

As we continued, the screams and cries petered off.

We entered a quiet void.

I lay tense on the leather seats.

It was crazy because the fear brought with it a huge wave of nostalgia. I remembered the cabin and the snow, and suddenly I was hearing Nixon in my ear.

"Time to look back on it, don't you think?"

"I'm scared."

"Don't be. I'm your villain, isn't that right? Yet I have a feeling, if you stopped and remembered, you might be surprised what you'd find."

My breaths slowed.

I couldn't keep running.

I couldn't keep pretending it didn't happen.

Because now I was in the back of a car, bound and frightened, and the opportunity to confront the past was slipping fast.

Taking deep breaths, I told myself to be calm. I told myself it was alright. It was alright to be afraid.

I took deep breaths.
One deep breath.
Two deep breaths.
I shut my eyes.
Shut my eyes and breathed.

And then I remembered.

PART TWO: THE BEGINNING

25.

VICTORIA...

I woke up to the soft patter of rain hitting the roof. The second my eyes flew open, I felt the walls closing in on me. The days were the same and endless.

I threw the covers over my head and shut my eyes, trying to breathe through the tightness in my chest. I wasn't sure I could get up. To face yet another day of the same bullshit. To feel my soul dying.

Sleep was such an escape. It was just...silence. I was finding myself going to bed earlier and earlier every day, longing for the blackness to swallow me.

Depression hit me like a pile of bricks every time I opened my eyes. Every time I had to accept that I needed to get out of bed, I needed to go to school, go to work, pretend to give a shit.

That was the hardest part.

Pretending.

Smiling while you were crying inside.

And for no good reason, either.

People had it harder than me, I knew that. They lost more than I ever would. So, on top of feeling depressed and apathetic, I felt *guilty* for feeling depressed and apathetic.

Everyone liked to remind you to count your blessings. To be aware of how fortunate you were. To just be happy that you're living. Because God forbid you feel like you're hurting on the inside, and God forbid your reasons aren't sufficient enough to warrant these feelings. Because that's wrong – it's *so* wrong to be human, *so* wrong to be stuck in a loop that you can't break. Because, goddammit, *be positive!*

And they wondered why you didn't want to talk about it.

Pfft.

I threw the covers off me and rolled out of bed. I grabbed my phone off the desk on the other side of my room. I kept it far from my bed so I wouldn't be tempted to turn it on in the night and scroll through my many different social media apps.

It...didn't work as well as I'd hoped.

I got only a few heart likes on my Insta post. I thought I'd get more, but whatever. I supposed people weren't interested in selfie pics anymore. I needed to show some more ass or boob. I glanced at my reflection in the mirror and turned side on, looking a little disappointed in my lack of *ass*ets. I snorted at my own pun – this was what my life amounted to at twenty-one years old: depressed and making puns alone in my bedroom at – I glanced at the clock – 6:33am in the morning.

My hair was still damp from last night's shower, so I threw it up in a ponytail – no fucks given. Half-asleep, I quickly grabbed a change of clothes, crept out of my room and tip-toed to the bathroom down the hallway. I held my breath passing Aunt Elayne's room. The last time I'd made a sound, her boyfriend John had lost his shit. His meltdown involved screaming his lungs at me for being a *loud fucking idiot* followed by a series of doors being slammed shut. By doors, I meant one door. He literally opened it and slammed it, over and over again.

It was really fucked up.

I made it safely to the little bathroom with the yellow tiled wall and sticky white floor. Closing the door and locking it, I stripped my clothes off and gave myself a quick body rinse in the shower stall. I was sweating too much in the nights – anxiety and crying until your heart ached was hard business.

I scrubbed my face with the last of the First Aid face wash Kimberly had slipped into my bag when I'd broken out last week. God bless her. Money was tight. Minimum wage was a bitch.

I dried off and slipped into...I paused, glancing horrifically at the change of clothes I'd quickly grabbed from the drawer. A thin white sweater with a yellow stain on the tit area (I'd eaten taco that day and what a fucking mess), and...a black, breezy skirt that ended above the knee.

Shit.

Fuck.

This wasn't going to keep me warm.

It was the start of December. The forecast predicted snow – fucking *snow* in *December* in *Vancouver*. Not that it didn't get cold here or anything, but snow just wasn't that common in the land of rain.

My bus stop was three blocks away.

And I had to be there in...oh, fifteen minutes.

I quickly grabbed my bottle of foundation and brush and nope'd the hell out of the bathroom. Now that I was more alert, I needed to go to my room for a better change of clothes and –

"ARE YOU FUCKING KIDDING ME, VICTORIA?!" John screamed from the bedroom.

My heart seized in my chest.

Change of plans.

I turned swiftly in the direction of the staircase and flew down the steps just as I heard him stomping out of bed. The door whipped open – the tiny house vibrated with the force of it – just as I reached the landing. In a panic, I threw on my gumboots – GUM-BOOTS with a SKIRT on a day that forecasted SNOW – and yanked my backpack and black jacket off the hook.

"You don't have any fucking respect for those sleeping, do you?" John carried on, appearing at the bottom of the stairs just as I had opened the front door. He was still in his too small briefs with his junk practically hanging out, and his brown long hippy hair looked extra fucked this morning. He was so *ew*.

"Well," I quickly said, throwing a salty smile his way, "when it's *all* you do, it's kinda hard to care."

His already dilated eyes widened. "You little bitch–"

I slammed the door on his face and ran for my life. I couldn't miss this bus. I had like two others to catch before making it to campus. I was in the middle of finals and unprepared and these fucking exams were worth 6498342% of my grade.

It was raining a shit ton, and the drops were icy. The sidewalks were slippery, and I was so tired, and my make-up wasn't done, I needed caffeine, and it was just one of *those* fucking days.

I was half a block from the bus stop when the bus came barrelling down the street. Shit. I raised my arms up in the air dramatically, pleading for him to stop. The bus driver didn't slow down, even though he saw me. He drove on by, shrugging at me like, "oh well."

Fucker!

Never mind my lungs were burning like...someone whose lungs were burning from a run like that. I stopped and bent over, sucking in breath after breath. The world went dizzy. I was so out of shape, and I just wanted to sleep and drink caffeine and have caught the bus on time.

He could have stopped.

Why didn't he stop?

Why were there so many assholes in this world?

Feeling dejected, I walked slowly to the stop, crying softly. I missed Mom. She would have dropped me off at school. She would have spent the last of her money making sure I had clothes to wear so I didn't commit fashion suicide. She was such a better person than me. I was such a bitch to her, even by the end I couldn't make up for all the shit I'd put her through.

I stood at the stop for twenty minutes, getting poured on by the icy rain, feeling so cold, I was sure I was starting to feel the first signs of hypothermia.

And, in my typical dramatic fashion, I thought of dying and went, *meh, why not?* I was just hardly skating on by, anyway. I wasn't particularly good at anything. Really, no one would miss me.

I could hear Mom's voice in my head. *You are too*

melodramatic, Victoria. To which, I'd respond with a melodramatic roll of my eyes.

Really, she was right.

But it wasn't like I went off the deep-end or anything. I wasn't the type of person to throw fits or smash things or scream. I just kept it bottled up inside me, and when it got too much, I ate my feelings.

I thought of Aunt Elayne and her screaming matches with John whenever he ticked her off. Once she smashed a lamp against the wall. Jesus, it took months to get the tiny bits out of the frayed carpet. She was so fucking crazy to let someone get to her like that. At least I had enough sense to be composed. I had to give myself credit for that.

The next bus arrived just as I lost all feeling in my fingers. It was literally the slowest braking of all time.

Of.

All.

Time.

I waited a whole minute for the bus to stop dead still and then the doors opened. I stepped on. Thankfully, the bus drivers on my route weren't the cheery type (as evident from the last dude that just fucking drove by). They didn't smile and welcome you on and make you smile back like everything was so rosy peaches. No, they just looked at you with dead eyes that said, "*You're* having a shit day? Try driving through this bullshit. Did you know there's gonna be snow? Try driving through that with a bunch of loud kids your age yammering away about stupid shit. It's always stupid shit you stupid kids talk about."

I scanned my bus pass through the system, but the red light didn't turn green. I swiped it again and... red light again.

The driver let out a long, arduous breath.

"I assure you this works," I said in a cheery voice that was so fucking fake. "I filled it up last week."

She didn't respond.

I scanned it five more times.

Maybe I was doing it too fast?

I scanned *slower*.

Even blew on my card by the third time.

By the fourth time, I blew on the machine.

By the fifth, I just wanted to crawl into a hole.

The bus doors opened again. *Oh, no.*

"I have some coin," I then said, teeth chattering as I began to slide off the backpack. "You can keep going on the route. I'll dig it up."

She didn't keep going on the route, though. She just gave me an impatient look as I hurriedly opened my backpack. My fingers were so numb, it took me forever to get the fucker to open. I knelt down, feeling flushed with embarrassment as the full bus of people began to look at me and, one by one, let out these laboriously long breaths.

Why did I get up this morning?

I could have been in bed.

I could have walked in front of the bus, too, but I didn't want to traumatize anyone.

I also didn't want to be reminded I was a week late on rent and Elayne used my money for cigarettes and alcohol and now it was coming out of her own pocket.

Man, she was going to kick me out if I didn't get on top of that.

I'd have nowhere to go.

Don't cry.

A pair of legs in dark jeans suddenly stopped in front of me. I heard the sound of coins being deposited in the coin slot.

"Bus pass for the girl," said a deep voice.

I heard the sound of the ticket being ripped, and then the large body knelt before me. I looked up, eyes wide as saucers as my gaze collided with deep blue eyes.

"Here you go," he said, extending his hand out to me.

My brain wasn't firing on all cylinders because I stupidly placed my ice-cold hand in his, thinking he was going to help me up, but he was actually just handing me a pass.

His hand was warm, strong, and they immediately closed around mine. I glanced at the large hand before shooting the dude another wide-eyed look. He was really hot, I immediately noted. Full lips, straight nose, a face full of stubble, and...unruly black hair that was damp with strands falling over his forehead. The hair was the clincher, to be honest. It was fuckable hair. Like the kind you ran your fingers through when he went down on you – not that I'd know, or anything, but I watched enough porn to get an idea.

Realizing my mistake, I immediately withdrew my hand. "I'm sorry," I said, turning warm all over. I was so cold just a second ago. Who knew the fix to hypothermia would be a hot dude warming you all over with just one look?

"You mean thanks," he corrected with a smirk, waving that pass in my face.

I grabbed it, smiling softly. "Yes, sorry, thanks. I

can pay you back. I've got the coin here...somewhere, I just need to dig it out."

He glanced at my backpack, filled to the brim with heavy textbooks and tampons and other cringy shit. "No need."

He stood back up and retreated down the bus. I felt a little bummed by that. Not that I expected fireworks to explode between us, but I'd read so many books, I couldn't stop picturing romance scenarios playing out in front of me. What a bad habit to have.

He was just a dude that had paid my bus ticket and –

Why was the bus still stopped?

I looked up just as the fuming driver looked down at me and pointed at the sign above her head. **STOP BEFORE THE RED LINE.** I looked down at my feet. I was so beyond the red line, it wasn't even funny. I shot her an apologetic look and quickly got up and made my way down the bus. Literally, the second I stepped over that red line, she began driving, sending me flying into a random person's chest. I smelled cigarettes and mint before pushing away, muttering apologies as I grabbed the bars and hanging grab handles and searched for a place to sit, or stand, or anything.

I ended up finding an awkward little spot beside the middle doors, which meant getting blasted with icy wind every time someone stepped off.

And someone always stepped off.

This day sucked wrinkly lion ballsacks.

Pulling out my phone, I sent a bunch of scathing messages to Kim.

I hate today.

I'm in a skirt and gumboots and they predicted snow today.

I missed the bus too and had to wait in the cold rain, and now I might be late to my next bus.

I think one of these days I'm just going to throw the towel in and tell the world to go fuck itself. Running away is so tempting, it might be the only escape. Would you run away with me, Kim-Bim?

Her response was immediate.

Jesus, Victoria. That fucking sucks. Doesn't help you live with a raging alcoholic asshole. I don't feel comfortable with you living with him, especially when he stares at you like that. I felt so weirded out when I saw it last week. I'd love to run away. We should go someplace warm because the snow forecast was upgraded to SNOWSTORM.

I groaned inwardly, casting a grimacing look at my bare legs.

When we got to a major stop close to amenities, a shit ton of people filed out. I immediately found a seat and raced to it like my life depended on it. It was one of those horizontal seats, forming a U-shape in the back of the bus. My shoulders sagged with relief as I took a seat and dropped the heavy backpack between my legs. I unzipped it and this time leafed through endless pages of notes. Thankfully, they weren't soaked.

Interrupting me was another message from Kimberly. She had screenshotted a meme that read: I want the students I did group projects with to lower me into the ground when I die so they can let me down one last time.

I let out my first laugh of the day, maybe even the week, and it was so emotionally exhilarating, I felt tears springing to the back of my eyes. I immediately wiped them away, pretending something was in my eye in case anyone looked my way. As I did so, I glanced around the bus, watching as more people piled on and...

Standing by the middle doors was the hot dude with the fuckable hair. He must have just moved there because he certainly wasn't there before. His back was to me, so I was able to gawk without fearing he'd notice. He was wearing a leather jacket with a grey sweater underneath. He was broad, solid, so obviously muscled. His hand gripped the hanging handle above his head and the other was holding a really old looking phone – like those century old Nokia ones that your grandparents used to love – that he periodically glanced down at. His strong jaw was moving, like he was chewing gum, but the bites were hard and slow and...God, he even made that look sexy.

On cue, this really hot girl with fur lined boots stepped on the bus and walked sexily in our direction. She had black leggings and a giant ass and a cute white beanie and her face was just wow. She was the kind of girl I got make-up lessons from on YouTube in the mornings when I was certain John was too passed out to wake-up to, "Now apply your mascara to the other side of your lashes too, ladies, before we finish with a matte setting spray, and there are a few I love that do the job just right. I'll add the links below. Be sure to check them out and don't forget to subscribe."

I subscribed.

To like 100.

And I still never looked like them.

Turning on my camera phone to selfie-mode, I quickly removed my foundation and brush from my pocket and decided I would have to guerrilla do this. I wouldn't look like her, not when I was applying this foundation cold turkey, but it was about the principle of it. I had to at least give some kind of shit. The Youtube Make-up Community would flay my ass if they knew, but sometimes you just gotta do what you gotta do.

"Oh, sorry," Hot Girl said as she elegantly collided into Fuckable Hair's chest.

Smooth move, girl. I commended her.

I watched her, saw the radiant smile she gave him, and I waited for him to respond back with a warm smile of his own. They were probably going to chat it up. He'd ask for her number, and she'd give it to him, and they'd make out and all would be right in the world because beautiful people always got to fuck each other while the rest of us watched with envy.

Instead, he moved aside real quick and sent her flying into the empty seat behind him. She made an *oof* sound and quickly collected herself, hiding her embarrassment by casually digging out her phone and pretending she hadn't made a fool of herself.

My jaw dropped. Dude was savage.

Averting my attention back to the brush, I ran my fingers through it and cringed. Brush was soaked. I would have to use my fingers. I pocketed the brush and began twisting the foundation open. A rough stop on the bus from the laborious breathing driver sent the foundation flying from my hands – I blamed it on my numb fingers – and rolling in the direction of Fuckable Hair's boots.

Oh, shit.

I got up quickly and raced to grab it. It rolled to his boot just as I got knocked to my knees in front of him from laborious breathing driver's LEAD fucking foot.

On my hands and knees, it was my turn to *oof*. I grabbed the foundation and happened to glance up at Mr Fuckable and felt my skin prickle. He was looking down at me, his jaw slowing down as I backed the fuck away and returned to my seat (though at the back of my mind I was thinking, *if I gave him a blowjob, that was the angle I'd be given*). My ponytail had loosened, hair had fallen all over my face, and I wanted to give Hot Girl a look that said, "You think *you* made an ass out of yourself? Giiiirl, at least I got to beat you at something."

This was exhausting.

Admitting defeat, I pocketed the foundation and pulled the ponytail out of my hair, wincing as a chunk of it ripped from my scalp. I ran my fingers through my dark roots, glancing briefly at Mr Fuckable.

He was staring right at me.

My heart lurched. I looked down at my three-year-old gumboots that had stress lines all over the place. The rainbow patterns had long faded, and it looked really fucking sad, but that was my life today – a sad, fucking disaster.

After several minutes of removing pilling from my skirt, I snuck another look at Fuckable. He was staring down at his phone screen, seeming concentrated, although I could only see a sliver of his face because he would glance around occasionally, like he was checking to see where he was.

He didn't look like he often rode the bus, if at all. He looked like the kind of guy that should be riding on the back of a Harley instead.

In fact, he probably crashed his Harley and was taking the bus to a motorcycle shop to purchase a new one.

Yes, my mind ran away from me often.

My eyes fell to his ass now because he was the kind of guy that could make ass in jeans look good.

I was right.

His ass looked good in them. Guy squatted like a beast.

I checked him out slowly, taking my time. My gaze lingered on the black duffle bag between his feet I hadn't noticed. Over the zipper bit there was what looked like a black beanie, but it looked a little long for a beanie. I twisted my head, trying to make out what it was exactly. Maybe it was the kind that went over your face too? I'd seen a bunch of dudes wear them lately, although they couldn't have been older than ten; it was a bizarre choice of outdoor wear, but what did I know? I was currently sporting some serious fashion hell-nos.

Unfortunately, my ogling was nearing its end. I was approaching my stop. I leaned over to press the button when I saw him reach for one closest to him. I paused, watching as he pressed it.

This was too serendipitous.

It was...sort of meant to be.

Once again, I played out a series of romance scenarios in my head – but I made them a little raunchy this time. Like, I would step out of the bus and he'd grab my arm and drag me to the nearest alleyway to suck my tongue. Even though the alleyways were filled with dumpsters and sketchy people shooting up, it was still an acceptable fantasy, and that was beside the point. He'd fuck my mouth and declare he had to pay for my bus pass because he needed to rescue me from spending 2.85.

As the bus came to a crawling halt, I threw the backpack on and rushed to the door in the front of the bus. I had to be ahead of him for him to stop me. It was just the way it had to be. The driver shot me a puzzled look as I dashed over the red line and waited, heart beating furiously in my chest. She opened the doors and I stepped out, tossing my hair over my shoulder because dudes liked that, I thought. My hair caught in the slightly opened zipper from my bag, but it was fine, whatever. I walked slow, hearing his heavy footsteps behind me as I moved, ignoring the icy rain as it slid across my skin.

I held my breath, waiting for him to come nearer and...

He walked past me, moving at a brisk pace in a focused direction.

He didn't even look back at me.

Well...

Fuck.

26.

VICTORIA...

I ended up grabbing a coffee from the coffee shop I worked at three days a week. I literally walked in and out, not wanting to stop to make conversation – or even eye contact – with my co-workers. I didn't have time to anyway, and besides, we weren't that friendly – they were bitchy assholes.

I was sipping on my coffee as I waited for my next bus. It was due to come in ten minutes, but the roads were hell-ish, so I anticipated a bit of a delay.

At least this bus stop had a glass shelter to hide in and a bench to sit on.

The cold snap was mind numbing. *Arctic blast* they'd called it. I saw clouds of my breath as I shakily scrolled through my phone. I saw the latest posts from Amber and Christina and Lauren and Emily and a bunch of other girls I knew from high school that I never talked to. I wasn't even sure I talked to them then, either.

Honestly, why did I even have people from high school on here? Well, I kinda knew why already. At least half of my list were high school peers. And I got a lot of likes from them, so...

I let out a long breath, feeling that sinking feeling in my chest again. The feeling of utter loneliness. I glanced around the streets, watching the cars go by, feeling almost like I was in a dream. Reality sometimes didn't feel so palpable. I'd been sensing myself drifting from the world more since Mom passed. I couldn't seem to come to terms with her being gone.

I put my phone to my ear and listened to the last voicemail I got from her.

Her speech had begun to slur at this point, and she sounded weak and tired. She would cough and breathe with difficulty, but she never gave up.

"Hey Vicks – I know you hate when I call you that, but I miss you. They changed my room at the hospital. You'll have to ask the front desk where I am. It's a better room, angel. I have it all to myself. The nurse put the flowers you got me on the table right here beside me and I can smell them from where I sleep. Thank you for that, Victoria. It was so beautiful to wake up to. I feel better now. I do. I think...I think I'm okay now."

I didn't know what she meant by that.

I'm okay now.

Did she mean she was okay at that very moment?

Or did she mean she was okay with the direction her life was taking her? Straight to death. Had she accepted it and said, "I'm okay" in the face of it?

I listened to the message again, closing my eyes this time to savour her voice.

After, when I turned voicemail off and scrolled through my social apps, I felt...angry at myself for all these pointless distractions. For throwing pictures up of myself like it would attract people who cared for me. It seemed obvious what I was doing.

I wanted someone to care.

Reacting purely on impulse, I went through every app and removed my profile. One by one, I deleted them permanently. Not a deactivation – a *deletion*.

It felt so final.

I didn't realize what I'd done until I'd finished, and then I felt a blast of regret. What had I done? All those years, all those cyber memories, all those pictures I hadn't even stored in my phone…

I started grieving.

Gone, all of it.

But it needed to happen, I told myself. I'd missed out on the final weeks of my mother's life because of these stupid distractions, and then when she died, I'd buried myself in them even more.

At some point, you need to wake up and look around you and *feel* yourself. These distractions dulled the pain, made you feel less alone, but then when you shut them off and sat in the silence, all you had was your own company because they weren't real. Nothing about the internet was real or tangible. It was one fake smiling face after the next.

And a lot of booty pictures.

So many booty pictures.

Jesus.

I pocketed the phone because there was no reason to go on it anymore.

I was still grieving what I'd done.

God, what *had* I done?

I heard the familiar sound of the bus exhaust and looked down the street. The bus had just stopped before the red light. I heaved the backpack over my shoulder and stood up. The chill in the air went straight up my skirt. My vagina was ice cold. I never thought I would say that to myself.

I stepped out of the bus shelter, staring down the street, waiting for the light to turn green and for the bus to come roaring to me.

Then I blinked a few times, realizing very quickly I wasn't being poured on anymore. I looked up at the sky, at the white dreamy snowflakes coming down around me. I shut my eyes, feeling my heart burst. My mom's voice sat in my ears, the voicemail returning to me, every word memorized, every gasping breath heard.

I felt her right then.

I felt her all around me.

My mom, here, coating me in snowflakes, rescuing me from the rain, commending me for deleting that rubbish from my phone.

I smiled.

And just as I smiled, a loud *boom* erupted from behind me.

I whipped around, gasping at the plume of smoking rising from a nondescript building situated on the corner of the street not far from me. It was an adult store from what the vague signs had read. I'd never gone in it, but there'd always been a few random cars parked behind it. Drivers poked their heads out of their cars, staring in the direction of the little building. Pedestrians further from me to the building began running toward it. Screams were heard from inside. My chest tightened as I heard cries of help.

My legs moved before I could stop myself.

My backpack pounded into my back as I ran to the building. A man was already at the front door, beating me by seconds. He tried opening it, but it was locked. He peered through the glass, but it was blacked out. Adult stores hid that kinky shit, I figured.

"It won't open," he said, looking concerned. "Did you see the smoke?"

"It sounded like an explosion went off inside," I replied, feeling jumpy.

"Have you called the police?"

"No, I..." I immediately removed the phone from my pocket and began dialling. He said something about going around the back of the building and checking for a door there. I followed him, phone to my ear as others made it to the front of the building and began pounding on the front door.

"911, what's your emergency," said the operator.

I began to tell her about the explosion, about the black smoke coming from the top of the building, maybe out of a window from the back, I didn't know.

I hurried after the man as he rounded the building. He seemed to know what he was doing. No one else had thought yet to follow us.

The back of the building opened up to a large parking lot, and behind it were train tracks and then an industrial street with tons of car mechanic shops. The parking lot was covered in rubbish and there was a random white cargo van parked, its engine on, sitting idle. The windshield looked tinted, and I couldn't see the driver, but I found it bizarre he wasn't leaping out and seeing what was going on.

I couldn't even be sure he was in it.

The area felt hidden, like a blind spot right there from a busy intersection. It was quieter, too. The helping man was at the backdoor, opening it, just as the operator said to me, "The police are on the way. Don't go in."

I began moving to the man, telling him, "She said don't go –"

The second he opened the door, loud popping sounds erupted. The man fell back in a heap. Voice lost, I dropped the phone and stumbled back as a group of men burst out of the building, faces covered in balaclavas, dressed head to toe in black, armed with long assault rifles.

One collided into me, knocking me to the ground. I fell on my ass, and pain skyrocketed up my tailbone. I looked fearfully at the man that had been blasted with bullets. He was on the ground, unmoving, blood already pooling around him.

I wanted to go to him, but I was too stunned.

"Get it in the van," one of them shouted. "All of it, we're going to get some heat."

My face snapped to the cargo van where they all were rushing around, doors open, throwing in duffel bag after duffel bag in the back. I counted five of them, and they jumped in, one after the other. I held my breath, frozen in place, unmoving – they seemed to have completely overlooked me – as they got ready to leave in record time.

I grabbed the phone, already pressing it to my ear, but the call had gone dead.

The man closest to the sliding door began to close it, but then his head shot up and his dark eyes bore into me. My heart jumped as he paused midway through closing the door.

"Hurry up!" a man shouted.

It happened so fast – all of it – the man slamming the door back open, the man leaping out of the van, running to me. I crab walked away, trying my hardest to scream, but nothing was coming out. It was a nightmare I couldn't wake from.

I couldn't get up to run.

I couldn't scream.

And though it happened so fast, time slowed down all at once. I saw everything play out in slow motion. I had lost all function of my senses as his arms wrapped around me. I flailed, but even my limbs felt weak and weighed down with terror. He dragged me effortlessly, and I kicked into the air, my boots skidding along the ground. He jumped into the back of the van, holding me to him, wrapping me in his iron grip, like a predator pulling its prey into a black hole.

He slammed the door shut, and I was trapped.

27.

VICTORIA...

Shouts of protests erupted all around me as the van took off, speeding. We were on the floor of the van. The man had me sitting in his lap, his arms caged around me. I shook, terrified, a sobbing mess, my shaky vision spotting guns thrown like straw around the interior of the van.

"What the fuck did you just do, Beckett?"

"She was there," the man holding me retorted. "She saw the whole thing. She was calling the cops too. Weren't you, honey?"

He yanked the phone out of my loose grip and threw it behind us. Then he removed the backpack and held me to him. I shut my eyes tightly as his hand skid down my back, flipping up my skirt. Bile rose up my throat and I heaved. He cursed, forcing my head away from him and in the direction of the door.

"She saw nothing," another person said, coming from the front seat. "Throw her out the door, man."

"Fuck off, Roz, I ain't throwing her out the door."

"We don't need any more complications!" another shrieked.

"Shut up, Mills."

"No, you shut it –"

"We got heat!" the man called Roz yelled. "Hang tight, it's going to get bumpy."

"Cops?" one asked.

"I wish."

I jumped as popping sounds hit the van. Bullets, I quickly realized. The man called Beckett threw me off him like I was a bag of potatoes. I fell to the ground, hands over my head as more sharp sounds tore through the van. A bullet seared a hole through the floor of the van, inches from my head. My heart dropped as I broke out in shakes.

"Get alongside him!" Beckett screamed.

A moment later the van door slid open. I looked up, eyes wide as another van came alongside us. We were on the backroads, taking the industrial route passed car shops and quiet garages. The black van careened close to ours, their van door open, a man with a big gun pointed at us. The man Beckett leaned out, his knee painfully pressing into the middle of my back as he sprayed bullets. The noise burst through my eardrums. I covered my ears, crying into the carpeted floor.

"Nixon, would you help me the fuck out!" Beckett screamed.

In response, I felt another body come over. "Get off the girl," the man demanded.

The pained pressure on my back eased. I felt the man's rough hand grip my arm and haul me back, away from the door. My back slammed into the other side of the van. I kept my hands wrapped around my ears and curled into a ball. Gunshots sounded out all around us, the van took a nasty turn, and I screamed as I slammed into a body behind me. The person threw me back down like I was a ragdoll and shouted, "Another car coming up behind us."

Then the other door slid open.

Oh, my fucking God.

More shots fired, and I was in the midst of it, the perfect target.

Someone shouted, "The girl is in the fucking way."

Bullets tore into the van. More holes burned into the metal body, somehow missing me.

"Throw her the fuck out!"

OH, MY FUCKING GOD!!!

A hand gripped my arm. I gasped as I was dragged to the opened door. We were going so fast. Everything whizzed on by, too blurry to see. I was going to hit the pavement and die. I tried wriggling out of the man's grip, but it was no use. He was too strong, and I was too weak, and FUCK THIS SKIRT I was so cold.

"Toss her out now!" came from another just as the guy began to push me over the edge. I shut my eyes, waiting for my life to flash before my eyes, but nothing flashed before my eyes. It was just me and this immobilizing fear all the way to my imminent death.

"No," a voice suddenly retorted. Another hand grabbed my other arm, hauling me back into the van.

"Nixon, let her the fuck go!"

"No."

"She's dead weight!"

"I'll take care of her."

The hand that had tried pulling me to my death let go. The other hand pulled me into a solid chest. "Hold on," he shouted down at me. I dug my fingers into his sweater and felt him leaning out of the van. My stomach dropped. Wind whipped around us. I cracked an eye open, watching as he raised his other hand up, a smaller gun in his grip this time, and fired a series of bullets.

We were leaning out too far. I was sure he was going to drop me. I gripped him so hard, I felt my nails penetrating the skin of his chest. He fired more rounds as I screamed, burying my face into his neck, enveloped in the strong scent of him.

"Got the wheels," he yelled. "He's done!"

A few moments later, Beckett screamed, "Hit the driver! Van's just flipped to its side."

"Inside, everyone!" the driver Roz ordered.

I clung to the man they called Nixon as he retreated back, slamming the door closed. The other slammed shut at the same time. He sat down and I fell into him, gripping his sweater still like I was going to be thrown out any second. I was shaking all over. My hair was in my face. My teeth were chattering, and I could hardly get a breath in. I felt his arms moving, heard him saying, "We're not far from the next vehicle, are we, Roz?"

"No, buddy, we'll be there in no time."

"Anyone behind us?"

"No," Beckett said, his voice making my skin crawl. "They won't be far though."

"Hear anything on the police scanner, Tucker?"

"Oh, they're looking," Tucker said. "Witnesses caught the van, but no licence plate. They're going to be not far behind us if we don't shake tail."

"We'll torch the car and dump the girl. Then we'll take the backroads all the way to the highway."

Relief ballooned inside me, along with sheer terror. I dug my fingers into the man's shirt, aware I was clawing at his chest. He didn't wrap his arms around me like the other man did, but he didn't push me away either.

"Not long now," he whispered so only I could hear. "Hold on."

*

I held on, quite literally.

My mind had hushed the entire time. I couldn't bring myself to think of what had happened. It was like my emotions had shut down, and I was an apathetic ball of nothingness.

Shouldn't I have been screaming? Crying? Begging for my life?

I just sat there, in a random guy's lap, clinging to him because he had kept me from eating the pavement.

Never mind an innocent man had died. Hell, maybe this guy I was sitting on shot him to death. It didn't even matter. What mattered was he had stopped the dickhead that had grabbed my arm and been willing to obey orders to throw me out the fucking door.

And because of that, I was tethered to him. Amongst the evil, he was...well, less evil than the rest.

The silence in the car was tense. Everyone was on high alert, their adrenaline through the roof. I could feel it strongly, though I couldn't feel it in the man who was holding me.

No, he was totally relaxed.

It couldn't have been ten minutes before the van

took a few turns and stopped. The engine went off and the silence didn't last long. My heart sped in my chest as everyone began moving quickly. The man I was sitting on didn't move so fast. He sat there a few moments longer, his breathing calm; I felt his eyes on me, but I couldn't bring myself to look up at him. In a sudden move, I felt his nose press against the back of my head, heard him inhale the scent of me quickly before he pulled away.

It was so quick, I almost missed it.

Then he shuffled down the van and grabbed at the door. He slid it open and nudged me off him. I stepped out into the cold, snowy day. The sky was overcast, and the light had lessened. The storm was coming, I knew, and I was going to be left in the middle of nowhere. Which was fine, I thought, as I spun around, in the wide open, spotting another black van nearby, but it was a normal family van, totally inconspicuous.

The man that had saved me took me by the arm and walked quickly away from the van and from the group of men. The roads here were dirt, and the fields on both sides looked neglected, not a single resident or business close-by.

"Follow this road out," he told me. "You'll find a farm a few miles from here. I saw cars out the front. Someone will be there to help you."

I didn't even wait for him to finish. I pulled my arm from his grip and began running, which was fucking tough to do in these boots. I didn't have my backpack or phone on me, but I didn't give a fuck about that.

I wasn't much of an athlete. I already felt cramps

in my side, and the cold air was hard to breathe in. My hair fell over my face as the snowfall grew thicker. I couldn't feel my legs. They were so numb and stiff and fuck this skirt, but I was sure I'd damned it enough already.

I didn't glance back once, but I smelled smoke in the air. I knew that van was getting torched. They would hop into their other van and leave, and I would go home and drink more coffee and cry to Kim and this would all be over.

If I'd still had social media, I could have written a post about it. People would share it. Maybe I'd be inspirational.

I'd harp on about never taking life for granted again, and God, I wouldn't.

From here on out, I would pay more attention to school, make more friends and lose my virginity.

Yes, I told myself. When this was over, I was going to be a new me.

I hadn't run far, my heart was beating in my ears, but I heard something louder coming up from behind me. I didn't turn to look, but my chest tightened as fear took over once again.

"Stop!" a yell sounded out. Beckett's voice.

Tears sprang to my eyes. *No, no, no.*

"Or I'll shoot you."

Out of breath, I immediately stopped, though maybe I should have kept going. Maybe it would have been easier to die from a gunshot wound than whatever else this guy had in store for me. Because, I was certain, if he took me again, I was not going to make it out of this.

"Please," I begged, turning around slowly, my

hands up.

He stood, feet from me, a gun pointed at me. It was terrifying to look into the end of a gun barrel. It was not a good way to go.

Behind him the white van was being swallowed by giant flames. The black van was moving in our direction, and I knew, straight away, this was over.

I wanted to fall into a heap and sob.

The van stopped beside us, and the door slid open. The tall man I'd been clinging to jumped out, his movements furious. I couldn't see his face, but I knew he was pissed.

"Beckett, let the girl go," he demanded, his voice harsh. "She's seen nothing."

"Are you fucking serious, Nixon?" Beckett retorted. "She's seen us. She knows what our car looks like, and you just let her know where we're going –"

"I won't say anything," I interrupted, hysterically. "I swear it! I won't. I really won't."

"Shut up," Beckett barked at me. "She's seen too much."

"This is your fault!" Nixon gritted out.

"Don't point the finger at me –"

"You took the girl to start with –"

"Try serving ten years in prison and not feeling your dick burst at the sight of *that!*" He pointed the gun at my bare legs. Then, to my horror, he pulled the balaclava off, revealing his face to me. Blonde shaggy hair, deep brown eyes, an angry looking man damning me with his eyes like I was to blame for all of this. "There, she saw me now, it's too late, anyway."

The man driving slammed a fist into the steering wheel. "We don't have fucking time for this, Beckett

_"

"I want the girl to come with us, Roz."

"Then fucking take her, or have her eat a bullet, I don't give a fuck. We gotta go *now* before this storm gets worse."

"Tell Nixon to back down."

But Roz didn't have to say a word. The man called Nixon slid into the seat next to the driver and slammed the door so hard, the whole van shook.

Beckett looked at me now and gestured for me to move.

I had no choice. I looked around, hoping for some miracle, but there was nothing.

I must have moved too slow because the guy suddenly came at me, grabbing me harshly on the arm and pulling me to the van. I winced as he painfully deposited me in the middle aisle seat. Then he slid in next to me and slammed the door shut.

"She's your responsibility, Beckett," the driver Roz said, shaking his head. "No one's gonna be cleaning up after your mess."

"I got it," Beckett retorted, hand still gripping the gun. "Let's just go."

And we went.

28.
VICTORIA...

We were on the road for hours. The first hour was filled with backroads and quiet streets. As more populated streets came into view, Beckett said he needed to cover my eyes.

"In case she sees where we're going," he explained.

"We're not covering shit," the guy behind us said. Tucker, they'd called him. "She's seen your face, Beckett."

And that was all that was needed to be said. My fate was sealed. I was going to die because this fucker had taken his mask off.

No, I admonished myself. I was going to die because I'd chosen to wear this fucking thrift store bought skirt in the wintertime.

I was so stupid.

Stupid, stupid, stupid.

I shut my eyes tightly, fighting the tears. The apathy was kind of fading now. Replacing it was dread and terror and sadness; a swirling tonic of depressive emotions that was going to shut me down very soon if I accepted defeat.

"You don't need to do this," I found myself saying. "I...I have a shit memory. I don't even know what you look like, honest. I haven't looked at your face since you threw me in here."

"Shut up," Beckett simply retorted. "You're a fucking liar. Bitches like you always lie."

"I'm not lying—"

He gripped my hair and pulled suddenly, screaming, "I said shut the fuck up!"

I shut the fuck up. My scalp burned from pain as he tugged a few moments longer before finally letting me go.

Okay, this time I couldn't fight the tears. They slid down my face rapidly, one streak after the next, trailing down my neck and to my collar bone. I was so fucked, and scared, and just *fucked*. I sobbed quietly, clasping my hands tightly, digging my nails into my skin. I flinched every time Beckett moved beside me, but I didn't dare move. I kept myself still, only trailing my eyes around me, taking in my surroundings.

We were speeding along the highway now, leaving the city behind.

"We gotta take our masks off, man," the guy Mills said. He, too, was sitting in the seats behind us with Tucker. "We're going to be spotted otherwise."

The driver immediately grabbed at his mask and tore it off. *Oh, God.* I shut my eyes quickly and covered my face with my hands.

"What the fuck are you doing?" Beckett barked at me, a smile in his voice.

"I don't wanna see," I cried, pressing my palms into my eyes. "Honest, I won't say anything—"

"Leave her alone," Roz said to Beckett. "If she

wants to cover her face, who are we to stop her?"

"Pointless," Beckett muttered.

"Cover her eyes," a deep voice said. Nixon. "In case something happens, we can't have her see us."

Suddenly, no one argued that.

"I'll do it," he said, and I heard his movements from the front seat. Hands grabbed at mine and gently pulled them away from my face. "Keep your eyes shut. I'm going to tie a piece of cloth around your head, alright?"

I nodded, taking in deep breaths as he wrapped the light material around my eyes, tying it at the back of my head. I felt his breaths, he was so close. His gentleness eased me, just a tad.

"Please, don't let me die," I whispered, unable to stop myself. "Please, Nixon."

Oh, God, this was going to sound so stupid, but I'd watched a documentary once about abductions. I heard a girl who'd managed to escape say she'd gotten through to the kidnapper when she made him realize she was a person and not a thing.

Maybe saying this guy's name would make him realize that.

But he didn't respond as he pulled back. I heard him adjusting himself in the front seat, and my heart beat harder now as the car blazed by, hitting soft bumps along the way.

*

I wished I could say I'd fallen asleep, just so I could have been spared a minute of fear, but that wasn't the case.

I was aware of everything around me. Wide

awake, listening to everything they said, just in case I did somehow get away.

"How much gold you think we snatched?" Tucker asked curiously.

"Six duffle bags worth," Roz answered. "Heavy fucking bags, too."

"Sucks to be the bikers today," Mills snickered in the backseat.

"Who operates a stash house in the open like that?" Beckett scoffed, his fingers occasionally skimming along my bare leg. I shuddered every time he did it, and I didn't doubt he liked my reaction. "Those idiots were asking for it. Just gotta ride out the heat now."

"This'll get buried in a week's time," Roz said. "Cops have too many drug operations to worry about a bunch of bikers getting ripped off at one location. The One Percent will have other bases. Hobbs was right. It was the perfect set-up for us with the war on the streets escalating lately. They won't know who hit 'em."

"I disagree," Mills muttered. "This is going to wipe the One Percent out. Think about it...all that dough sitting pretty in one spot. Who does that? An act of desperation. They were going to move all of it at once."

"You saying they have nothing left?"

"Maybe."

"They would have protected their nest hell of a lot more, then."

"Think of the attention that would have brought on them if they were suddenly hanging around a random adult shop. The only competition they've been facing off with is the Vipers. They cracked into a bunch of their nests, made the One Percent paranoid as fuck."

"The Vipers are small time."

"Not after this." Mill let out a laugh. "This...this is going to rile the nest up, guys."

"That's why we're laying low."

They didn't talk for a while after that.

The drive felt endless.

At some point, the radio went on and a count-down of the hottest tracks blasted out of the speakers. But the speakers kept making this scratchy sound and the driver kept banging the roof of the dashboard.

"Could've made sure the speakers were working before you stole this fucker, Mills," Roz said in annoyance.

"Oh, I'm sorry," Mills retorted, "I didn't think to consider your entertainment when I was robbing this thing in the dead of night in front of a house with four fucking dogs yapping every two minutes."

The radio went off.

More silence.

Another hour went by.

Maybe two.

Maybe it was ten fucking minutes.

I felt Beckett's body close in on me. His thigh pressed against mine. Emboldened now, his entire hand wrapped around my bare knee, squeezing it. I felt his head come close to me, felt his nose brush against my shoulder as he inhaled sharply. I swallowed hard, trying not to let my fear show, but I just wanted to cry and push him away.

"Curious where you came from, beauty," he murmured in my ear. "Where were you thinking of going in this little skirt?"

It was so quiet in the car, I knew they all heard him.

I swallowed again, my throat felt so dry. I hesitantly replied in a tiny voice, "I was going to class."

"Oh, right," he said, his face pressing closer to my neck now. I felt his hot breaths, and I shivered in disgust. "Planning on driving those boys wild, honey?"

It took everything to shake my head no.

"No?" he asked, his lips pressing against my throat. "So, you were just gonna tease the boys with your bare legs, then." It wasn't a question, so I didn't respond, and he didn't wait for one as he went on with, "What's your name?"

I didn't answer. It turned my stomach to think he might say my name. For some reason, I couldn't bring myself to say it. He pressed more kisses, this time along my jaw. The second I felt his breath blowing at my mouth, I whipped my face away from him, turning it in the other direction.

It was a cold rejection. I didn't have to see his face to know he was pissed. His entire body tensed beside me. I squeezed my eyes tight, already anticipating another hair pulling, and I wasn't wrong.

He balled my hair into a fist and yanked me back to him, forcing my face in his direction. Hot tears fell down my cheeks. I clenched my teeth, pulling my face away from him, uncaring that he was tearing out thick strands of my hair. The blood was rushing to my ears. I heard him mutter something, like I was feisty or something to that effect before he slammed his filthy mouth against mine. Two seconds into the kiss, I bit his bottom lip hard and he hissed, tearing his face away from me.

"Bitch made me bleed," he laughed in shock. "Fucking skank likes it rough, don't you, honey?"

"Ever looked at your face in the mirror, man?" Mills chuckled. "You are fucking nasty."

"And you're such a flower, huh, Mills?" Beckett retorted.

"I think she wouldn't resist me so hard."

"I think we'll have to find out, then. Won't we, honey?" He ran his hand up my leg and beneath my skirt, cupping my sex suddenly. The violation sent hot pulses of rage throughout my body. "We're gonna have fun with you, I think."

"Fuck you," I hissed, grabbing at his arm and clawing. He immediately grabbed at my hands, cursing, and demanded something to bind my hands together. Moments later, someone delivered. He shoved me face first on the seat and painfully brought my hands behind my back, tying them up with a cable tie. He tightened it so hard, it dug into my skin.

"Play nice, bitch," he told me. "Maybe we'll be easy on you. But keep this up, and I'll make sure I fuck you watching you take your last breaths."

29.

VICTORIA...

I was long past the point of shock.

My tears had dried.

I sat dejected; my fight gone as the sick fuck occasionally touched me. Chatter had long died, and it was straight silence the entire way.

Three quarters of the way there, I felt my ears beginning to pop. The car was driving on an angle, going up, and up.

We were climbing a mountain.

Fuck.

My wrists felt sore from the cable tie, and I needed to pee. My sob-fest had clogged my nose up bad, so I was breathing through my mouth, taking in quick, uneven breaths.

It was hard to say where my thoughts were.

Most of them involved my mother.

I kept talking to her inside my head. I told her I was coming home. I was going to see her, to get ready for me because I wasn't going to make it out of this.

These men were bad.

Even the guy that didn't want me to eat the pavement hadn't said a single word since he'd blindfolded my eyes.

Because he didn't give a fuck.

I tried not to think of what they were going to do to me, but I knew it was going to be rape, and a lot of it. Even blindfolded, I could feel their stares clinging to my skin.

They'd blown that man to the ground without batting an eye, stepped over his dying body without a single fuck given. They were prepared to toss me out of a speeding van where my death was imminent and, again, zero fucks given.

These were evil men.

Still, I couldn't prepare myself for what was to come.

I wanted the ride to never end.

So, when the car began to slow down and the van shook violently as we drove over crunchy snow, I knew the end was coming and I began to have a panic attack.

"You're not going to go far like this," Tucker said. "Roads are too bad, man."

"I'll go until I can't go anymore," Roz replied. "The closer we are, the less of a distance we gotta trek."

We were off road somewhere. The van wasn't equipped to drive through feet of snow. I wondered then how bad it must be out there.

"Should've stolen an off roader," Mills grunted. "Something with big fucking tires."

"The trail has to be taken on foot," Roz said. "It's too narrow for a car."

"How much walking we gotta do?"

"According to Hobbs' instructions, a lot of it,

man."

A few more minutes passed with us bouncing around. My throat felt tight as I struggled to take breaths in. It was coming any second. He was going –

The engine turned off and I could faintly hear the keys jingling.

"Alright, guys, this is it," Roz declared. "Can't go anymore. File out, let's get these bags out and move."

All the doors opened up and the icy breeze whipped into the car. Shivering, I listened tensely as they stepped out and opened the trunk. I heard footsteps crunching into the snow and the heavy sounds of the bags being thrown to the ground.

"Six big bags, fellas. Let's try doing this in one go."

"What about the girl?" Tucker asked.

"Just leave my bag near the car," Beckett replied. "I'll be in the car with the girl for a while first."

"Are you serious?"

"I'm not going to bust a nut in front of you assholes up there."

Laughs erupted.

Ha-ha.

"I think I'll wait around then," Mills said.

Roz chuckled as the trunk slammed shut. "You fuckers and your pussy, I swear. I'm going then. Nixon can carry two because he's the biggest fucker here. Don't be long, or this fresh snow fall will cover our trail."

I heard the sounds of footsteps crunching away. Then a body entered the van and I could smell Beckett's scent in the air as he fiddled around. The back of my seat fell away, landing hard behind me.

My lips trembled, a plea was about to form but

I swallowed it down. The blindfold was pulled from my eyes suddenly, and blinding white light replaced the darkness. I blinked rapidly, trying to adjust. I saw his face close to mine, and his eyes ventured down my body. He pulled my boots and socks off, tossing them randomly behind him. Then he grabbed at my jacket and unzipped it, pulling it down my arms.

"I need these off," he told me, his voice taking on a different edge. "Been a long while for me. honey."

I didn't take the jacket off. Instead, he pulled the sleeves down as I shook violently. But then there was a problem.

"Shit," he whispered, and then poked his head out of the van. "You got a knife or something, Mills? I gotta get this cable tie off her."

Footsteps approached and I looked up to see another face without a mask poke his head in. It was a round face, middle-aged, a light beard on his cheeks. He glanced at me, his eyes lingering around my chest before he stuck a hand into the pocket of his dark pants and removed a switchblade. "Here you go."

Beckett took it and slammed the door shut on him. "Turn around for me."

I didn't move. He grabbed my arm and pulled, making me bend over enough that he could reach the tie. I heard the knife switch open and felt him cut at the tie.

My heart was beating so hard, I felt my stomach turn.

My vision spotted.

I was going to pass out.

Weak all over, I was barely drawing a breath in now.

He slid the jacket off me and grabbed at my sweater next. He removed it quickly. I felt his eyes all over my chest, felt his fingers along my bra strap.

"I think I'll have this on," he murmured, heatedly. "And the skirt too. It's fucking hot."

I didn't respond. The shock was clinging to me like armour.

"Lean back for me," he then directed. I felt his palm press against my chest, pushing me back. I didn't even resist. Maybe this was me giving up. I didn't know, but something had shut off inside me.

I wasn't sure how he was going to do this. There was barely any room in here. My head was dangling off the make-shift rape bed he'd made. But then he adjusted me by spinning me around so I was lying on the seat horizontally.

He mumbled something about it being too cold, so he turned the engine back on and had the heaters blasting. He didn't return his attention to me until the van was warm.

Minutes passed.

He breathed heavily.

I could hear my heart thumping in my ears.

He cleared his throat.

I felt dead inside.

More minutes went on.

The warmth filled the van.

Then he looked back at me.

It only started to dawn on me when he began to undo his belt quickly, like he couldn't hold back any longer, that this was going to fucking happen.

I looked at his grotty face, at the heat in his brown eyes. I looked past him, at the round face peering into the side window. Watching us, waiting for his turn.

Tears fell from my eyes and a surge of fear tore through my shock.

I was surprised right then because...I preferred to feel it, even now, even before he was about to take me.

His body climbed over me and I began to shake my head. My hands shot up, pushing him away when he tried to lean into me. He grabbed them and threw them over my head. I bucked under him, my legs going crazy now. Nausea consumed me. I needed to vomit. I needed to scream. I needed to fight him off me.

"Too late for that," he grunted, forcing my legs down with his.

I spat on his face and he swiftly let go of one of my hands and punched me so hard in the face, I saw white flashes. I gasped from the shock of pain as it shot up my nose and tore through my skull. Weakened by it, I could hardly see straight. He flipped my skirt up and settled back over me. I felt him grabbing at my underwear. I tried to twist and turn but he wasn't moving. I screamed at the top of my lungs, but he told me he liked when I did that. I felt his hard length through his pants as it rested against my hip and I dry heaved. The bile spilled from the corners of my mouth and I felt *so angry*.

I didn't stop fighting, even when he slapped me across the face again, when he grabbed at my hair and pulled. He was going to take me whether I liked it or not, but I wasn't going to make it easy, either.

"Fuck you!" I screamed.

"Look at the fire in you!" he laughed.

I could tell he was struggling to contain me. He

was pissed about it, too. He pulled my hair so hard, I felt like my scalp was burning. I was dizzy with pain, with the slaps he kept striking me with, but I didn't stop twisting.

The trunk of the door opened just then, amidst the fighting.

"Hey, Beckett," said a deep voice.

Beckett looked up in the direction of the trunk. "Yeah, Nixon—"

A loud gunshot ripped through the air.

Beckett's head...popped before my eyes.

Blood spattered in all directions.

And I screamed.

30.

VICTORIA...

I bucked wildly, forcing the lifeless body off me as shots continued around the van and Mills screamed. I gripped the door, slid it open and fell out. My hands sank into a foot of snow. Cold wind and falling snow whipped around me as I crawled out in nothing but my bra and skirt and no boots.

I didn't make it two feet before a hand grabbed at my arm and hauled me back into the van.

"You stay," Nixon growled, slamming the door shut on my face before I could see him.

I was sitting in brains and blood and a man whose head popped from his body. I looked out the window, panting as I saw the back of Nixon rounding the van and firing at Mills.

Mills had been running and suddenly fell to his knees and began crawling away in the other direction. Nixon fired the gun again, but nothing happened, so he threw the gun down and trailed after the wounded man.

Mills begged. I could hear the muffled pleas. Could see his hands in the air.

Pulling something out of his pocket – a knife I quickly realized – Nixon caught up to Mills and stabbed the knife into the top of his skull in one single motion.

The man collapsed to the ground, dead.

The sight was so jarring, I keeled over and vomited more bile.

The smell of blood was in my nose. I was coated in it. I saw it when I closed my eyes. I saw it when I opened them. I groaned in the disgust as I took in the head that was no longer a head, at the oozing flesh and brains and it was so fucked up.

I vomited and vomited some more.

Trembling, I saw Nixon approach the van again. I saw his black hair, and the side of his face. No mask, either. Oh, fuck, I was going to fucking die.

The van door slid open and he bent over to peer in at me. I looked back and this time I really did feel like I was going to pass out.

Nixon was Mr Fuckable from the bus.

Of course he was.

How could he not be, with the duffle bag, with the mask on the duffle bag, with him getting off at the same stop and moving in the direction of the porn store.

He'd changed his clothes though.

It wasn't really my fault.

I had poor attention to detail.

I blamed social media for my lack of attentiveness.

He was in black pants instead and his black leather jacket was replaced by a thick black sweater. He'd smirked at me in that bus and I'd held his hand...

"You paid for my bus fare," I said stupidly, numbly, because I couldn't wrap my head around the fucked-up direction my life had taken. Beginning to shake my head, I pleaded, "Please, don't kill me."

"Why?" he asked, detached. "What do you have to live for?"

My lips trembled and my mind went blank.

I had nothing.

I had nothing to live for.

He stared at me for a beat longer, his face completely still, then said, "Put your clothes back on and get out."

I couldn't move though. The situation was traumatic, didn't he know that? I was all weak and shit. My bones felt like jelly, and everywhere I looked I only saw blood and brains and, *ohmyfuckinggod*, was that bits of bone on my arm?

"Please, help me," I whispered, distraught.

He looked at me, two beats longer now, his face still clear of emotion. Then he leaned into the van, pushing me aside as he dug up my thin white sweater and black jacket – both utterly covered in blood and brains. I whimpered as he threw them at me. With shaky fingers, I picked them up and dry heaved some more.

He watched me as I attempted to put the sweater on, but it was inside-out and I had my hands through the neck hole, which wasn't right.

I was so confused and pathetic. I sobbed aloud, unsure of how to fix my sweater up. I'd forgotten how to put it on and there were brains all over it.

I dry heaved again.

My body was not reacting kindly to any of this.

Everything was monumentally more difficult than a few minutes ago; even breathing took enormous effort.

He snatched the sweater out of my wobbly hands and put it on me. His movements weren't gentle. In fact, he looked pissed off. He grabbed my hand and shoved it into the sleeve, and then again to the other. Grabbing my jacket next, he dressed me in that in two swift movements before shoving me out of the van. My bare feet sank into the snow and I gasped as the cold shot up my legs. When I turned to look at him, he was inside the van, digging under the body and grabbing at my gumboots. He threw one at me, then the other. I quickly slid my feet into them, but my toes were already numb, and I wasn't about to ask a man who'd effortlessly murdered two men for my fucking socks.

I looked around quickly, my eyes darting all over the place. We were stopped on the mountain side, close to a cliff. The snow was coming down heavy, and the dirt roads were mostly covered, except for random patches under giant Douglas Fir trees. Legit, we were in the middle of nowhere, going up some mountain I didn't know. I couldn't see signs from where I stood, didn't know how far we had driven up here.

I started to panic again.

Nixon slammed the door shut and began to approach me. I turned to him, eyes filled with tears, begging, "Can I go now?"

His movements slowed as he watched me carefully, his head tilting to the side. "Where will you go?" he questioned simply.

I pointed in the direction we'd driven up. "There."

He didn't look where I pointed. "You'll die."

"That's fine. I just want to go. Can you let me go?"

He didn't answer straightaway. He glanced around us, at the road we'd taken, at the road we were meant to keep trailing. Then he took a step closer and peered down at me. The snow was in his hair, caught in his eyelashes, piled up on his shoulders.

"You'll die," he then repeated, his voice harder than before. "You have to come with me."

"I'll die either way," I said.

He turned and moved to the stack of duffle bags by the wheel of the car. "Then pick which way you'd rather die. Down there is certain death. Up here" – he gestured his cut jaw to where he was headed – "you might still have a chance."

I watched in awe as he picked up four giant duffle bags, two in each hand. His entire body went taut with the weight, but he looked capable. Even in his sweater, I could see the muscles in his arms and chest flex as he began trudging away from me.

He didn't look back.

I stared at him as he went, and then I looked down at the mountain road we'd come up. Chills wracked my body. I couldn't feel my legs anymore. I considered racing down the mountain, but the sun had moved along the sky and we only had a couple hours left of sunlight. The temperatures would drop and where would I be when night-time crept in?

I would die from the cold.

It would be a sad way to go.

Who was going to find me? Who would bury me? Who would even attend my funeral?

My internet friends might send some cyber flowers my way, but I deleted those accounts, so they were never going to know, and where would the cyber flowers go even if they did know?

My life was so fucking empty.

I'm so lonely.

I looked back at Nixon, carrying an impressive amount of weight in each hand, as he grew further and further away.

The problem was...if I followed him, something in my gut was telling me I was never going to be the same again.

It might have been silly intuition.

But I just knew it, dammit. I really did.

Only, I didn't have much of a choice, did I?

It was either go his way or go down the mountain and maybe have cyber flowers in remembrance of me.

I looked up at the snowflakes as they fell around me, whispering, "Mom, don't leave me. I need you right now."

I tried to feel her in the air. I tried my hardest to think of what she'd do.

Go to him.

They were my thoughts, but they were said in my mother's soft voice.

A gentle calm eased into my heart when I looked up the mountain. *Go to him.* I followed the feeling past the dead fat guy Mills – I dry heaved at the blood all around him – and did my best to catch up to Nixon.

Because he was right.

Going up the mountain might mean death, but it wasn't as certain as the death I'd face if I went down.

And I fucking hated flowers.

31.

NIXON...

There was only so much bullshit he could take. The day, right from the get-go, was utter fucking bullshit.

Hobbs had given him a crew filled with fuckheads. He'd worked with them previous times before and should have known it wouldn't go to plan, that someone as fucking smallminded as Beckett would fuck shit up.

Hobbs had promised him a reprieve from his mourning.

An exciting last-minute job, but this was more than he bargained for.

He didn't look back at the girl as he trudged up the road, but he heard her following feet behind him. She shivered loudly, her teeth chattering as the wind blasted all around, howling like a beast. The cold snap had been expected. You had to have been deaf, blind and dumb all at once not to have known the warnings.

His peripheral caught the bare skin of her legs as she struggled not far from him. Why in the fuck was she in a skirt? And gumboots? She had no socks either. He couldn't find them in that van, and he wasn't keen on poking around that mess.

Every step he took, he saw her in the rearview mirror, blindfolded, being touched by that feral fucking idiot.

Every step he took, he thought of her in that van. Saw the fuckhead over her, saw her fight, that spark in her alive.

Every step he took, he saw her in nothing but her bra, her tits swollen and covered in goosebumps and blood.

This was a complication.

On the ride to the minivan, he'd leafed through her backpack and phone. He couldn't access her actual phone because he didn't know her passcode, but he was able to click a little symbol on the bottom corner of the screen that went straight to her gallery. He was able to go through a handful of her photos, all selfies.

She was pretty.

Really, really pretty.

Unable to hold back, he'd pocketed her phone. He had to throw her backpack in the blaze when he'd spotted Beckett chasing after her. He was a fool to think they'd let her get away. He couldn't leave any sign of her behind.

He didn't know how this was going to play out. How Roz would react when he got to the cabin minus the two men. What Tucker would do when he caught whiff of the girl in their midst for a whole week straight.

Tucker was known for his impulses.

These men...they wouldn't think twice before raping the girl and dumping her in some hole when it was time to go. They'd keep her alive until they bled her dry and then they'd move right along.

And Nixon didn't think he had it in him to watch that happen. He didn't want to be haunted by more fucked up shit than he already was. He didn't need to close his eyes and see the bus girl in his head, bending down to fetch the coin from her backpack as the troll driver breathed heavily over her.

The way she'd looked up at him, startled to find him there, her giant brown eyes scorching him – he couldn't get that image out of his fucking head.

Yeah, this was a very serious complication.

"Fuck," he cursed under his breath, glaring at her over his shoulder because she was so fucking pitiful now, crossing her arms to her chest, her hair covered in wet snow, her skin so pale, he thought she could pass as an ice sculpture.

She reminded him of a defenceless fucking puppy.

But puppies were smarter than her.

Jesus, his chest went tight at the pathetic sight.

This fucking idiot girl in her idiot skirt showing up at the wrong place and at the wrong time and now he had to endure this bullshit.

Such a bullshit day.

He threw his duffle bags down and moved to her. She looked up, brown eyes wide as he picked her up in one swift move. She didn't even object. Her arms immediately wrapped around his neck and she buried her face just under his chin. She was so cold, he had to run his hand up and down her legs in an attempt to warm her.

"Relax," he murmured. "We don't have a long way to go."

That was a lie, though.

They had a long way to fucking go.

VICTORIA...

My shivers weren't so bad in his arms. Our breaths clouded around us as the sun continued to move across the sky. The snow hadn't let up once. It just kept falling and falling.

It almost felt like we would never stop walking. The path was endless and winding. I closed my eyes after a while, feeling myself lulled by the rhythmic movements of his footsteps. His skin was cold, and I could feel the pulse in his neck against my forehead thrumming at a strong, steady rate. I felt how deep his steps were in the snow; the amount of energy exerted without carrying me would have been enough to dizzy any man of his stature. I must not have been easy to carry, but he didn't seem like he was struggling at all.

I should not have felt at ease in this man's arms. I had to remind myself what he was capable of. He'd blown a man's head off and then stabbed the other guy without breaking a sweat. All in under a minute. He had done it without blinking because he must have done it so many times before.

Whatever his purpose was keeping me alive, it must not have a happy ending.

"You don't tell them anything," he suddenly said to me, his tone solemn. "You just stay quiet, got it?"

I had to take a moment to understand what he was referring to, but when I poked my head out from under his chin and saw us turning into a gated path of sorts, I knew.

Don't talk to the other guys. I nodded in response.

The gate was already open when he swung it from us and continued down a narrow path. Clumps of snow fell from the trees overhead, their branches hanging so far over the road, it obstructed us from the snowfall for some time. I saw the footsteps of the other two in the snow, but they were already halfway buried as we trudged up the path to a small looking cabin ahead. It was the most random cabin in the middle of the forest; you wouldn't even see it from the sky if you flew overhead.

The cabin door was wide open. I saw one of them standing there, looking out at us. He seemed confused, leaning against the doorway with his arms crossed.

"I heard gunshots," he said, his voice familiar from the ride. The driver Roz. "What the fuck happened?"

"I'll tell you in a minute," Nixon replied as we approached. He gestured his chin to the cabin. "Tucker in there already?"

Roz nodded, swinging his gaze to me. "Yeah."

He moved aside, letting us through. We stepped into one large room. I immediately spotted a tiny kitchenette with a few cabinets and a deep sink. Beside that were sealed boxes on the floor. Past that, against the wall, was a wood fire stove and a small wooden table with four chairs. In the corner closest to that was a stack of firewood hardly covered in a tarp. And on the other side of that was a single bed against the wall. As Nixon scanned the room also, I spotted another single bed on the other side, behind us, against the wall and window. Seated on it was Tucker, staring at us with a strange expression.

Nixon put me down on my feet straightaway and

nudged me in the direction of the bed furthest from us. I went to it quickly; my stiff feet felt like ice blocks the entire way. I sat down on the edge of the bed and grabbed at the thin wool blanket that covered it. I immediately covered my legs, praying for some warmth.

"Where's Mills and Beckett?" Tucker asked.

As Nixon glanced around the room, he casually responded, "Dead."

Tucker's spine straightened. "What?"

"They were fighting over the girl when I showed up. Beckett had pulled a gun on Mills, and Mills took off running. He shot him a couple times, dropped him to the ground. He was rabid, so I shot him in the head before he turned the gun on me."

Tucker blew out a breath, looking shocked. "What the fuck, man?"

"I saw it coming," Roz muttered, though his eyes were on me as he spoke. "The second he took the girl, I figured he was nothing but trouble."

"Do we need to go back for Mills?" Tucker questioned.

Nixon shook his head. "He got shot in the spine and chest and was bleeding out. I finished him off."

They took a few minutes absorbing that. It startled me a little how easy it was for Nixon to lie. He didn't seem the slightest bit affected. Actually, none of them looked like their hearts went out for the two dead men.

Tucker looked at me for some time before shooting Nixon a peculiar look. "Why'd you go back, Nixon? You were ahead of us."

Nixon removed a knife from his pocket – the same

knife he'd killed Mills with – and bent over, slicing open the top of one of the boxes. "I wanted a turn," he simply said as he opened the flaps and peered in.

Roz looked at me too, running his hand over his light beard. "Did you get to have one?"

Nixon pulled out blankets and pots and various other items I couldn't see, throwing them down feet from where he stood. "No."

Silence.

They watched as Nixon sliced open the other box and emptied it out on the floor. From what I could see, there were cans, pots, a kettle, lots of camping food, soaps, toothbrushes and toothpastes, and more blankets. He sorted it out on the counter of the kitchenette, and Roz helped, leafing through the camping food, reading the meals aloud.

"Butter chicken and rice," he muttered. "Eggs and bacon. Blueberry oats. Just add boiling water. Jesus. They've come a long fucking way, hey?"

Nixon didn't reply. He hardly spoke, I gathered. I hadn't heard a single word from him the entire ride. He appeared reserved, a sore thumb among the others.

As I studied Roz, I noticed he didn't appear like he belonged either.

He was very groomed. His hair was cut fashionably in a short style and his beard looked even. He had the brightest blue eyes I'd ever seen, and they glowed in contrast to the snow and dark cabin walls. He was definitely in shape. I could see his muscles bulge against his black sweater, and he was tall too. Tall as Nixon, but Nixon was definitely broader and more muscular. They seemed close in age, him and Nixon.

They couldn't have been pushing more than a couple years past 30.

Tucker, on the other hand, was young. He must have been close to my age or maybe even younger with black short hair and dark eyes. He wasn't all that muscly, but he wasn't all that skinny, either; he was in the middle, looking the weakest physically amongst the others.

But something about him made my stomach turn. Whenever he looked at me, his gaze lingering, I felt uneasy. He made his intentions known when his eyes slid down my face and to my body. It made me gather the blanket and cover my chest.

He noticed.

"You should take that blanket off," he told me. "You're getting it dirty."

I looked to Nixon, hoping he'd say something, but he wasn't paying attention. He was still sorting out the contents of the boxes on the counter with Roz, but Roz was watching the interaction, staring at me also.

"Did you hear me?" Tucker asked, his voice hardening. "Take the blanket off, girl."

My face burned and my heart sped as I slowly peeled the blanket off and set it beside me. I stared down at it, unable to look at him. My body fell into a fit of tremors – fear and cold hitting me at once.

"Jesus, that's a lot of blood," he noted. "You might have to take that top off, too."

Again, no intervention from Nixon. Why did I expect anything more from him? I remained still, staring at the coarse blanket, praying this guy would leave me the fuck alone.

"You do have a lot of blood on you," Roz agreed, taking steps in my direction. "Fuck, how close was she to the shooting?"

Nixon didn't answer. He made Roz connect the dots on his own as he approached me, blocking Tucker's view of me. I turned my sight to him, staring up at his handsome face, pleading with my eyes for him not to touch me.

He smiled softly. "You really do need to get out of that sweater, sweetheart."

I shut my eyes tight, trying to keep the tears from falling.

"But it's too cold for that," he added. "Let's get the fire going first before you get to clean yourself up."

I let out a breath I didn't know I was holding as I heard him turn and walk back to Nixon. When I opened my eyes again, sight blurry with tears of relief, I caught the look of contempt on Tucker's face.

My hours were numbered.

32.

NIXON...

There was something about her brown eyes. Something about the way she smelled. Something in the way she moved.

Fate had dropped the ultimate temptation in the midst of savages. And the men were hungry. Even Nixon felt drawn in a way he shouldn't.

He didn't like the way Tucker was talking to her. He clenched his teeth, feeling the rage roll off his shoulders as he stood there, silent, his mind playing out scenarios.

He couldn't react impulsively. When you reacted out of anger, chances were you were going to fuck up. He'd seen it one too many times. You had to be in control of your faculties. You had to strike when the opportunity was right.

When Roz rescued the girl from having to strip down to her bra, Nixon looked at Tucker from his peripheral. Pure disdain clouded the kid's face. He wanted to touch her badly. He cast a look of irritation at Roz before he stood up abruptly and stomped out of the cabin.

"This is going to be a long week," Roz muttered.

After the meals were organized, Nixon went to the wood pile in the corner. As he tore the tarp off, noting how poorly it had been used as a cover, he thought it was unusually cold in this part of the room. He stared up at the ceiling, frowning when he felt a gust of wind come through the top.

"Hobbs fucked up," he said, his gaze returning to the firewood. He kicked at the large pile, watching as some of them fell to the ground at his feet. Then he bent over and grabbed at a handful of the cut wood, his worries realized.

Roz joined him. "How? He had the cabin ready for us a few weeks ago."

Nixon pointed to the ceiling. "There's a leak in the roof."

Roz looked up at the gap in the ceiling, his face falling as he returned his sight to the pieces of wood in Nixon's hands. "Fuck, it's wet, isn't it?"

Nixon nodded. "Yeah, it's drenched."

"Can we get the fire started at all?"

"We'll have to go over the whole pile."

The problem was the tarp hadn't been properly secured over the pile. The wind gusting from the roof would have blown the tarp so it was exposed to the elements.

And all of last week it had been raining.

Because that was all it did here.

Just rained and fucking rained.

Stooping down, Roz began rifling through the pile, shaking his head as he went. "The floorboards are rotted through, man, all around this spot. I don't like our chances finding a dry bit."

"We'll have to cut them up, find dry spots in the middle. I think there's some fat wood in here, too."

"Fat wood?"

"It burns regardless of how wet it is."

"Still going to take a while. We might not be warm tonight."

Nixon glanced at the girl on the bed as she shivered in her bloodied top, looking dejectedly at the blanket she wasn't allowed to use. He wanted to tell her to wrap herself in it, blood and all, but he didn't want to make his concerns known with Roz present. As far as him and Tucker were concerned, she was just a dead girl walking.

But if she didn't get warm anytime soon, she wasn't going to last the night. Even Nixon was feeling the effects of the cold. This sort of weather consumed you from the inside-out.

And she was so fucking little.

Interrupting them, Tucker returned to the room, glaring at him. "Where are your bags, man? You didn't come with any, too busy carrying the fucking girl. Is she made of gold to you, Nixon?"

Nixon just stared at him. Roz stood up and shot a look of warning in Tucker's direction. "Don't talk to him like that, man."

"Why?" Tucker retorted. "Because I'm talking to him like I ain't fucking scared?"

"He's killed people for lesser reasons, Tucker."

Tucker looked at Nixon, trying to get a reading on him, but Nixon just stared back at him, his expression straight. Obviously feeling the heat, Tucker played it off with a shrug. "I just don't see the bags, is all."

"I know where they are," Nixon said. "On the trail

still."

"They'll be buried in snow. We should have them here, man..." Tucker shrugged again, playing it off. "Right?"

Walking past Tucker, Nixon stuck his head out of the door and stared out. The weather was only going to get worse. The snowfall was growing thicker, and visibility was lessening. They had maybe another hour of daylight, and even still, it was dim already.

He tried to remember where he dumped the bags. He knew the spot, but he couldn't be all that certain. The last thing he needed was for them to be buried in feet of snow and have to dig around for them, especially if at some point the snow began to harden.

Fuck.

He stepped out to see how much colder it'd gotten. He heard Roz and Tucker following. All of them stood under the snowfall, staring around.

"The bags can be found," he heard Roz tell Tucker in a hushed tone. "He got the girl because what else will we have to do over the next week?"

Nixon glanced at Tucker, noticing his temper had weaned now in response to Roz.

"Sorry, Nixon," Tucker said quietly. "I didn't realize."

Roz crossed his arms. "What's the plan then? You going to get the bags tomorrow morning, or what?"

Nixon shook his head slowly. "This storm's going to get worse. I need to go now."

It felt wrong to go, but he couldn't keep idling around, worrying about the girl. Only...his chest constricted at the thought of her being left alone with these guys. And Tucker was reacting erratically. He had no self-control.

Fuck.

Fuck.

He clenched his teeth, trying to figure out what to do.

"I'll go back for the bags," he found himself saying. "Tucker will come with me."

Tucker seemed confused. "Me? And carry *two* bags? Roz is bigger than me."

"I gotta split the wood," Roz inserted, shrugging. "That's just the way it is, man." Then he smirked at Tucker, and Nixon caught it – he caught the message behind it; he was going to be left with the girl, to do as he pleased.

No, no, no.

A sharp knifelike feeling stabbed into Nixon's side, the anger so acute it was punishing. But he bit his tongue and stormed into the cabin. He didn't need to grab anything. He didn't need to do anything but leave, but he found himself pacing quickly, casting a quick glance in the girl's direction.

So fucking little.

She looked back at him, her eyes following him as he turned his back to her and clenched the edge of the kitchen counter, digging his fingernails into the fucking wood.

So fucking tempting.

He didn't understand what was happening to him. Why was he so fucking twisted up about this shit? He couldn't bear to look at the girl again.

He didn't know her fucking name.

He didn't know a single thing about her.

She was ordinary and helpless.

She meant *nothing* to him.

Yet…something just didn't sit right with him to leave her in the hands of Roz to do as he liked. Maybe it was the way she looked at him on that fucking bus: those fucking brown eyes, that fucking innocent look, that fucking shy smile – *this was so fucked.*

Maybe it was the way she'd unexpectedly said "please, Nixon" when he'd wrapped that blindfold around her eyes – it went straight to a spot in his chest he hadn't felt stir in so long – that gave him the sinking feeling in the pit of his stomach.

Whatever it was, whatever the reason, his emotions were fucked. A simple job had turned into an emotionally draining situation he hadn't anticipated.

And, to think, he'd taken the job to run *away* from his emotions.

Now, he couldn't have a moment's thought without her in it, and when he thought of her, he felt a heavy pull in his gut. He was aching for something he did not even understand. But the intensity of it robbed him of his senses. From the second he'd seen her being pushed out of the speeding car, he felt panic.

And the panic hadn't lessened since.

In such a short amount of time somehow, she'd claimed him.

But this was not possible.

He wasn't that kind of guy.

Without glancing back at her, he strode out of the cabin before he could stop himself from leaving. The guys were smoking when he'd pointed in the other direction and told Tucker, "Get moving. Let's get this done with."

Tucker began to walk as Nixon turned to Roz. He couldn't stop himself from saying, "Leave the girl untouched. I got dibs on her first."

Roz took a slow puff of his cigarette, studying Nixon's face slowly. "That's right. You're not fond of sloppy seconds."

"I'm not fond of fucking a girl covered in bruises, either," he retorted, edgily, staring straight at Roz. He knew what Roz liked to do with women because he'd been open about it one too many times. "Don't touch her, Roz."

Don't make me kill you.

Roz smiled with ease, though Nixon saw straight through it. "You have my word. I'll be too busy splitting wood, anyway."

Nixon was gone before Roz finished his sentence.

VICTORIA...

Roz returned alone. I kept staring at the door, waiting for Nixon, but then Roz shut the door and started opening the kitchenette cabinets in search of something.

My heart started to pound with unease. Nixon's presence had provided me with a kind of comfort – false, perhaps, but the way my body responded right now, I knew I was having a hard time not being in a room with him.

"Just you and me for a while," Roz said just then, pulling out a few flashlights from the drawer. He checked to see if they were all working one by one, and then he grabbed two and came to me. My body tensed as he approached. I watched him warily as he stopped and tossed a flashlight on the bed next to me. "It's going to get dark soon."

Then he left me and strode to the corner of the room. I watched as he stooped down and began scattering the firewood in all directions. He made a triumphant sound and leaned over, flicking the tarp away to grab at an axe. "Fucking score," he murmured to himself, using the axe to chop through the wood.

I knew it was in my best interest to make conversation. That documentary still sat in the forefront of my mind. Talk to your kidnapper. Make him realize you're not a thing. You're human. Let his guard down.

But…Jesus, it was totally different in real life.

I wanted to talk, but I was too scared to. I was scared he'd turn his attention to me and remember I was there and then off my clothes went. There would be no Nixon to come saving me this time, I knew, as I glanced at the closed door.

"Some wild day you're having, huh?"

I turned my head in his direction and found him staring back at me, a soft smile on his lips. He was sitting down on the hard floor now, one leg splayed in front of him, the other tucked in. A piece of wood sat on his lap as he chopped away at it slowly, splitting it down the middle.

"You weren't part of the plan," he told me, softly. "Honest to God, I had no fucking clue I'd be riding through a week in this dilapidated cabin sharing my company with someone as fucking gorgeous as you."

I didn't respond. I just looked back at him, listening.

"I never would have wished this on anyone," he continued with a troubled expression. "But rest assured, we're not complete monsters, alright?"

A tear fell from my eye as I managed a nod. He smiled pleasantly at that, pausing in the middle of his cutting to give me a long look. "God, you are...stunning. What's your name?"

My voice was gone. I opened my mouth but nothing was coming out. My pulse was still in my ears, *swoosh, swoosh, swoosh.*

"You don't have to say anything, sweetheart. I know you're scared."

My shoulders sagged in response. I watched him continue to cut the wood, noticing how slow he was going. It wasn't a methodical kind of slowness, either. He was hardly putting any effort in. He ran a hand down his face often, shaking his head.

Finally, he seemed to have had enough and threw the axe down completely.

"Too tired," he mumbled. "Long day for me."

He stood up and went to the window beside the bed. The sky had begun to really darken now, and with it the cold was getting worse. "I can't even see much of anything out there." Then he glanced over his shoulder at me and his body went still. "You're shaking."

I was.

I hadn't stopped, actually.

The cold was in my veins now. I would die of it, I knew.

Roz came to me, purposely moving slow, like he didn't want to startle me. He stopped before me, his eyes going over my upper body. I thought, *God, here we go, he's going to touch me.* But instead, he took off his black sweater and handed it to me. I gaped at him, not understanding. My brain was fuzzy. I was delirious with tiredness. He came closer and knelt down to my level. His blue eyes looked wrought with sympathy. He whispered, "Sweetheart, you're going to freeze like that. Take your sweater off, wear mine, and then get under the covers."

I immediately did as I was told. I wanted nothing more than to be under the blanket and warm. The sweater was hard to take off. My fingers were numb and I wasn't myself. My movements were slow and awkward, and he caught on quick because he helped me take it off. I felt his gaze on my chest, but it didn't linger there long. With gentle touches, he helped me put on his sweater, and then he pushed me back so I was lying on the bed and threw the blanket over me.

"Try to get warm," he told me. "I'll get another blanket for you."

I brought the blanket up to my chin and pressed my knees to my chest. I wrapped my arms around my legs and took deep breaths, shutting my eyes, searching for warmth. I heard Roz come up from behind me, and I saw another blanket fall all around me, adding another layer against the cold.

"Breathe under the covers," he instructed. "Tell me if it doesn't get better in ten minutes."

He left me huddled under the blankets.

My soul was bursting with gratitude. I cried softly; my emotions were all over the place. I kept thinking maybe he was on my side. Maybe he was being sweet and he genuinely hadn't intended for this to happen.

But at the same time, my guard was up. It seemed too good to be true. Not even Nixon had been nice to me like that. I would have preferred the silence and the straight face because then I wouldn't be filled with this kind of hope that I'd make it out of here unscathed.

"You feel warmer, sweetheart?" he asked, approaching me again.

I was still shaking like an earthquake. I felt so weak and desperate for warmth. Maybe he'd spare me another blanket.

Unable to hold back, I shook my head, crying. "I'm so cold."

I felt him come closer. I was aware he was bending over me, staring at what little he could see of my face. I saw the worry lines around his eyes. "Let me into bed with you," he said. "I'll only touch you to keep you warm, I promise."

I resisted at first. It seemed like a trap.

But I tried to reason with myself...if he'd wanted to have his way with me, he would have by now.

I tried moving over on the bed. When he saw that, he immediately kicked his boots off, slid under the covers and helped shuffle me over. He had to lay on his side with his back against the wall because he was so broad, and the bed was only little.

He wrapped his arm around my waist and pulled me into his chest, and the first thing I noticed when he did that was how warm his hand was. I felt like ice being thawed by his touch. I shut my eyes in relief and buried my head into his chest covered only by a thin undershirt.

"How's that?" he asked me, his tone low.

I nodded, breathing out, "Thank you."

He didn't stroke my back or let his hand wander. He did exactly as he promised. "Try to get some rest," he murmured to me. "You need it."

It startled me how quickly my body relaxed, and my mind switched off.

I fell asleep feeling warm for the first time today.

*

It was dark when I heard the door of the cabin open and felt a sharp gust of wind blast into the room. I opened my eyes and slowly turned my body around. Roz's arm was still wrapped around me, and he was dead asleep, not even stirring at my movement.

I saw one large figure enter the dark room, followed by a smaller one. Both were carrying giant duffle bags.

Nixon and Tucker.

"Shut the door," Nixon ordered quietly.

The door shut and Tucker stumbled ahead of Nixon, looking around the room. "I can't see shit."

Somewhere on the bed was the flashlight Roz had given me. My hand immediately swept around me. I'd vaguely felt it against my back as I'd slept. As I searched, I was aware Nixon had taken a few steps in my direction. I could feel his eyes on me just as I'd found the flashlight and turned it on. I aimed it in his direction, making sure the light didn't hit his eyes.

"Here," I said quietly.

He came to me then, stopping just before the bed, his giant frame looming over me. His face was red and wet. His hair was everywhere, drenched. He looked miserable from the cold.

He took the flashlight from my hand and aimed it at me, no shits given. I winced as the light flashed in my eyes and then down my body and then at the body behind me. The light shook just then, like maybe he was shivering... or maybe it was something else.

"He touch you?" he asked in a whisper, his tone indecipherable.

"Only to keep me warm," I answered, gathering myself under the blankets again.

The bottom half of his face was more visible than the upper. I saw his jaw clench, like he was angry about this.

"Can I crash on the bed?" Tucker asked, shuffling around behind him. "I'm wrecked, man."

Nixon's eyes were still on me as he said, "I'm going to try and get a fire going."

Tucker collapsed into the bed and Nixon stomped away. I heard him at the pile of firewood and looked down my feet in his direction. As he dropped to his knees, he placed the flashlight beside him. I could see him better now. He looked concentrated as he pulled his knife back out and cut at the wood.

"There's an axe," I whispered to him.

He looked up, meeting my gaze. He had a way of making me feel like he could see straight into me. My heart skipped a beat as he mumbled, "Don't need it."

I was wrecked, could have slept the second I shut my eyes, but something about his presence had my focus directly on him. I raised myself up on my elbow to watch him.

Tucker was snoring within minutes, and Roz's arm reached out for me, pulling me back to him. I resisted, though, and his arm stopped around my hip as he fell back asleep.

"You warm?" Nixon asked me, his eyes never straying from the wood he was cutting. He knew I was watching him.

"Yes," I answered.

"I'll have the fire on within the hour."

"You don't need to do that. You should sleep." Although, to be fair, where the fuck was he going to sleep?

"I want the fire on," he murmured instead, determined. "No one will need to warm you up if it's on."

"Thank you," I whispered with gratitude.

His eyes found mine again. He stopped what he was doing to stare at me for a few tense moments. I didn't miss the way his chest slowed – mine slowed too.

Then he turned away.

He was so shattered, his cuts were sloppy, and some came a little too close for comfort to his body, but he didn't stop until he'd shredded every single wood piece in the pile, sorting through the dry bits and putting them in a separate pile. He would occasionally look up and meet my gaze, his eyes cutting into my own, but he would say nothing.

I was half-asleep, swaying from my elbow position when he finally got up with the dry bits gathered in his hands. He moved to the woodfire stove and opened the firebox. In the dark, he shuffled around, tearing at pieces of the cardboard box he'd opened earlier. I watched him gather a pile of it. Then he was back at the firebox, filling it with the wood and kindling he'd made.

Unable to keep my eyes open, I blacked out and then jolted myself awake, watching through bleary eyes as a light fire began to glow. His movements were slow and tired, but he stood there, for so long, getting it going.

I passed out hard somewhere along the way.

Sometime in the night, I thought I felt a feather-light caress on my cheek.

But there was nothing but darkness when I opened my eyes.

33.

NIXON...

After he'd managed starting the fire up, he'd hovered over the bed, staring at the girl in Roz's black sweater, Roz's arm wrapped lazily around her as they both slept. Nixon felt like he'd swallowed fire. He felt his fingers twitch something awful, the urge to remove her out of that fucking sweater and out of that bed so great, he wanted to punch his head to stop it.

Stop it. He chastised himself.

It wasn't like him to feel this way.

Maybe being in mourning had softened him up a bit.

It didn't help the area around the girl's eye was swelling profusely and she looked extra miserable.

That Beckett fuck deserved the bullet he ate.

He loomed over her at some point, unable to resist himself. He traced his finger around the bruise before brushing his hand along her cheek. His pulse jumped at how soft her skin felt.

If God existed, He was punishing Nixon with this girl.

He ended up sleeping on the floor with his back against the wall directly across from the bed she was in. He was fucked. The trek had killed him, and he had purposely worked Tucker to the bone so he was too shattered to foam at the girl when he returned.

By morning, Nixon was awake before the others, his mind a hurricane of volatile thoughts, his eyes darting every minute at the girl he still didn't know the fucking name of. He put snow in a pot and boiled it over a stove. He was removing the box of tea – typical of fucking Hobbs to put tea and not coffee in the supplies – when he turned and saw her sitting up. He eyed her crazed dark hair and tired eyes – something about tired eyes on a beautiful girl was so sexy – and then Roz's black sweater over her curvy upper body before he whipped his head away and returned to tearing the box of tea open with a little more force than necessary.

This – her, them, all of them here – was a ticking time bomb waiting to happen. And he still hadn't figured out what he was going to do about it – or better yet, *if* he was even going to do something about it.

Of course *you're going to do something about it.*

She sat, uncertain, watching his every move. Then she slipped out of bed – still in that fucking skirt – and went to him. He glanced at her briefly as he removed a dusty mug out of the cabinet.

"I need the toilet," she said, face flushed.

"There's an outhouse around the back," he replied.

She stared at him, uneasily. "Do I just go?"

"Yeah, go."

She pulled on her gumboots and opened the door.

Crossing her arms, she stepped out into windy hell. The storm was worse than he'd expected it to be. The entire cabin had shaken furiously all night long with the force of the winds. He'd been up often feeding the fire, listening as the wind skinned the cabin alive with its bare teeth.

You did not fuck with the weather here.

"Should we be okay with her leaving like that?" Roz said suddenly from the bed, his body relaxed on that thin mattress, his undershirt tight and revealing. She'd been pressed against his chest all night, buried in that undershirt. She probably smelled like him, or maybe he smelled like her, and Nixon would find out which one of the two it was.

Nixon kept his face neutral. "Where else is she going to go?"

"Nowhere, I guess." Roz yawned just then, stretching his limbs out. "Nice to see you got the fire going."

No help from this fuckhead.

Nixon plopped his teabag in the mug, noting idly that Hobbs hadn't even provided sugar or artificial sweetener or any of that bullshit that made shit tasting tea like – he peered at the name – Orange Pekoe taste better.

Roz got out of bed and meandered over to him. Fucker had a suave walk and glowing blue eyes. He wondered how much of his charm he'd used on the girl, and if she genuinely fell into it.

"We should get some food ready."

In response to that, Nixon gestured to the mountainous food pouches sorted in the corner of the counter. He said nothing, but he watched Roz closely as he sifted through some of the meals.

"Remind me why the fuck we're in this rundown cabin having to survive off fucking camping food?" he murmured, petulantly.

"We're invisible up here," Nixon replied simply. "The most barren looking hovel of a cabin, the better. No one would think we'd make it up here with all that gold."

Roz nodded. "No, they'd think we're checking into some posh inn. Still would have been nice. We could have taken turns guarding the door. Could have been balls deep in some beauties right now, too."

Always, *always* thinking with their dicks.

It astounded Nixon the extent of it.

When he immersed himself into this world, he learned a thing or two about the type of man that got hooked.

People like Roz, they were insatiable. They needed the best of everything. The best hotel, the best food, the best hookers, the best ladies, the best drugs and alcohol and company money could buy. They indulged in the best life had to offer, and as a result, they turned into greedy fucks who couldn't handle a week in a shitty cabin without a hole to stick their dicks into. Why? Because they felt *entitled*. They needed that pussy to feel like they were winning. They needed that high-end food to feel like kings. And this sort of living – this barren looking room with cabin food and squalor furniture – it wasn't going to sit right for them; they couldn't hack it. They *deserved* more.

Nixon hated working with people like that.

Other people were purely money-driven, like him. They hoarded their money, took job after job, seeking that rush that money satisfied. It was a temporary rush that had them back at it again. Nixon knew his rush wasn't at all to do with money anymore. It was natural to progress to that realization. When money became an empty goal, life started to feel blank and meaningless. You started taking these jobs because your day to day held no purpose. Nixon was hurting, and he was burying that hurt with a splash of excitement, a rush of adrenaline – but the goal was already reached, he'd taken the gold and now the feeling was hollow.

And anyway, the job turned sour when Beckett abducted the girl.

Nixon didn't feel victorious.

He felt out of sorts.

The girl returned minutes later, her eyes flaring up at the sight of Roz. She felt familiar with him already. One night in bed under the covers and she had let her guard down. He smiled at her and raised a random bag up for her. "You hungry, sweetheart?"

Sweetheart.

Nixon grinded his teeth. This guy was prepared to let this girl eat a bullet just yesterday. Had even urged Nixon to throw her out the van during the gunfire.

She nodded, looking at Nixon briefly. "Yes, thank you."

Nixon drank his Orange Pekoe shit watching Roz set a kettle to boil, talking quietly to the girl as she stood next to him, nodding to this and that. She was still terrified, gulping every time he moved too fast. And when Tucker finally woke up, she shrank back in the direction of the bed, trying not to capture his attention.

Nixon wanted to laugh.

Was she honestly afraid of *Tucker*?

Really?

Tucker, beta little fucker with his sick girl fetishes.

Tucker, who weighed a hundred and fifty pounds soaking wet.

Tucker, who looked like he was the sad result of a goth orgy.

Nixon could kill him with one hand.

Tucker was the least of his worries.

No, it was Roz.

Roz, with his snaky eyes and sweetheart smiles.

Roz, with his sick reputation and smooth words.

Roz, with his ability to woo a woman into a false sense of comfort.

Roz troubled Nixon the most.

VICTORIA...

We sat at the table. I was eating teriyaki chicken and rice from the pouch with a plastic fork, even though my stomach was completely closed to food. I'd had a migraine waking up and knew I needed it. I probably needed caffeine more, though.

I was staying quiet, trying not to step on anyone's toes. There was a strangled tension in the air between the men. They all skirted around each other, barely making conversation.

I didn't feel like your regular hostage.

I felt more like an uncomfortable guest than anything.

So far, only Roz had been nice to me. He was sitting across from me, eating from a pouch of his own. Nixon was feeding the fire and Tucker was outside smoking a cigarette.

"You know, these bags aren't bad," Roz said. "We got a lot of selection, too. I saw peach and cream oatmeal in the pile if you're still hungry."

"I'm okay, thank you," I responded sweetly, hardly through a quarter of the pouch.

"Next time, then. I'm sure it won't be heart stopping but..." he shrugged with ease, watching me with his bright blue eyes. "You gotta be careful not to have expectations, especially when you're used to the good thing back home."

I sat up now, my interest peaked. He was being personal. This was good. I could work with that. "Where is home?"

"San Diego," he answered. "This is definitely *not*

San Diego weather."

Nixon walked back to the kitchenette, looking like he was barely paying attention as he poured boiling water into a pouch.

I couldn't get a reading on this guy.

I couldn't stop staring at him, either.

"No, it isn't," I agreed returning my attention to Roz, trying to smile even though it felt all wrong.

Roz looked at my mouth, and his eyes looked distant. "You're really pretty, you know that?"

My chest went tight. *Please, don't say that.* "Thank you."

"Were you warm last night?"

I nodded, forcing another bite into my mouth. I couldn't taste shit. "Yes."

"You got real close to me."

"I'm sorry."

"No, no, don't be. I liked it."

I looked down at the food, trying to relax. His attention was making me uncomfortable. He stared at my mouth for some time before he cleared his throat and stood up. "I'm going for a smoke."

The second he stepped out, I put the pouch down on the table and sucked in deep breaths through my nose. Tears clouded my vision. My panic attack felt like two cold hands wrapped around my throat, squeezing.

A mug slid across the table to me. I saw the large figure that put it there let go and walk away. I watched him from my peripheral as he returned to the kitchenette, taking large bites out of his pouch as he stared out the window at the two men. He looked deep in thought, the corners of his mouth pulled down.

I turned my focus to the mug and brought the steaming tip to my mouth. I took a quick sip, feeling better when the heat settled at the pit of my stomach where the nerves sat.

My brain was surprisingly mute. I should have been thinking of home, of Kim and school and finals and my absence at work, but...I needed to conserve my energy. If I thought of that, I was going to freak the fuck out and start begging to be let go.

And it was too premature to do that.

These guys were stuck up here for a week, waiting for the heat of their crime to die down and for a man to pick them up.

That meant I had a week to figure out a way to either escape or be released.

I looked back at Nixon, wondering what he was thinking. He hadn't taken his eyes off the men. His quiet demeanour unnerved me. Roz was a smooth talker, Tucker made his intentions known every time he looked at me, but Nixon...he wasn't revealing a thing.

He was the biggest of them all, and every time he ordered something, everyone obeyed. I wondered if he was the leader, and if he was, I'd need to work him the hardest.

Clearing my throat quietly, I traced my finger over the rim of the mug. It took a lot of courage to whisper, "Thank you for the tea."

He glanced at me in response, saying nothing. Swallowing, I added, "And for what you did yesterday in the car."

Now, he turned his body to me, eyeing me peculiarly. It was like he could smell my bullshit from a mile away, and I felt suddenly so stupid.

Okay, wrong move.

I shouldn't have said a word to the guy.

Nixon may have seemed like my saviour throughout this ordeal, but he scared me the most. His eyes were loaded with darkness. His expression always tight and unreadable. And he was fucking massive. The kind of massive I could never stand to fight against. Men of his stature intimidated me. They were nice to look at from afar, but never nice enough to come close to. Chalk it up to my insecurities, but Nixon was fling-worthy. You fucked a guy like him and fondly remembered it, but nothing came of it because you did not want to spend your life feeling physically inadequate next to an Adonis.

But, then again, maybe this was years of social media and airbrushing and perfect bodies that fucked my perception up.

Or maybe my perception was severely altered when I realized bus guy whom I'd have done anything to get the attention of turned out to be a stone-cold killer.

Anyway, despite him being jacked, he managed not to look like a complete meathead. He hid his frame by wearing his thick sweater and loose pants, but you could still see the subtle outline of his body.

He was cut.

The others did not come close to his size.

And that was probably why he carried himself with that silent confidence.

He was at ease here.

He was in his element.

He did not let his emotions own him like the others had already.

Simply put, he knew how this was going to end.

He moved to me again, stopping by my chair. I went still, passive, my gaze focused on the mug. He slid something across the table to me, resting it beside the mug, his skin lightly grazing mine. A hot spark shot up my hand as my breaths slowed. "Painkillers," he muttered, "for your face."

Then he shuffled back to the kitchenette, staring back out the window. I looked down at the two tablets beside my mug. I had completely forgotten my face, to be honest. So overwrought with anxiety and fear, the pain around my eye had faded to the background – the least of my worries.

I brought my hand up to feel it. It was definitely sore when I pressed down on it. It felt swollen and hot and I imagined it was probably darkening.

Were they really painkillers? I wanted to ask as I stared at the tablets with suspicion. I tapped my fingers on the table beside them. I picked one up eventually and inspected it. When I glanced furtively in Nixon's direction, I noticed a smirk on his face as he eyed me quickly.

"If I wanted to, I would," he simply said.

I felt the blood drain from my face. He wouldn't need to drug me, he meant. He could hold me down with two fingers if he wanted to.

I took the painkillers and washed it down with my tea, shooting Nixon another curious look as I went, wondering why he was doting on me like this.

On one hand, he treated me like I was meaningless.

On the other, he had protected me more than anyone else had.

"Why do you keep watching them?" I asked, feeling bold.

After several moments of silence, I figured he would ignore me. But then he managed out, "When you're outnumbered, it doesn't matter how big you are, your enemies have the advantage. You gotta be on guard, ready, prepared for anything."

I mulled that over, biting my lip in thought.

He didn't trust them.

He was waiting for something to happen.

That frightened me more than words could express, because it meant I was teetering on another rollercoaster of chaos.

"It would be in your best interest to keep yourself scarce," he added, searing me with a final look. "You don't look them in the eye, you don't talk unless you have to. Got it?"

I nodded keenly, listening to his every word because he was my final hope in all this. "I got it."

"And keep your body hidden." My heart lurched at that. "Victory can make a man...greedy."

*

Tucker was brimming with impatience. He was constantly hopping off the bed and circling the room, and when he sat down, his knee would bop up and down. The occasional glances in my direction were worrying. I wound up curling myself in a ball with the blanket, trying to cover every inch of my body as I sat on my bed, avoiding his eye.

Roz, on the other hand, never went a half hour

without boiling something up and eating. He sat with ease at the table, ignoring Tucker completely. But Tucker stared at him a lot, like he wanted his attention, like he wanted to silently communicate something.

It was bizarre.

Nixon spent his time feeding the fire. The guy never went out to the outhouse once, had never stepped foot out of the cabin since last night. He stood by the woodfire stove, back against the wall, arms crossed. On occasion, when he was deep in thought, he'd brush his thumb across his bottom lip and narrow his eyes.

The room was so silent, you could hear a pin drop.

I kept wondering, was this how it was supposed to go? They were going to be in here, a week straight, silently watching the hours slip by?

It didn't make sense.

When darkness crept in, each of us had our own flashlight turned on.

And finally, conversation emerged.

"Wish Hobbs had put us in a better place than this," Roz spoke, that charming smile flashing again. "I'd do anything for a shower right now."

"There's a portable tub around the back," Tucker replied. "I saw it under a tarp. It was probably tossed out to make room for all of us, but...I guess nobody anticipated casualties."

"Where am I supposed to hook up a tub in here?"

"You fill it," Nixon said.

"Ah," Roz replied with a nod. "Too much effort."

"Hobbs went the full hillbilly mile with this cabin," Tucker mumbled, glancing at me again. "This is the worst set up since the Italy heist."

Roz laughed heartily. "I think that's an insult to the hovel we were in."

Even Nixon's lips curled up. "At least we had a television."

"At least we had women," Tucker hissed, his aggravation bleeding into his voice.

Looks were exchanged, one in particular in Nixon's direction, which prompted Nixon to look at me, that thumb circling his bottom lip again.

The testosterone in the room was palpable.

Tucker had to re-arrange his pants, looking unpleasant. Even Roz appeared affected. He stole glances in my direction, that charming expression now mixed with a heavy emotion.

Nixon didn't blink in my direction once as he pushed off the wall and fed the fire again. I kept my focus on him because he didn't make me feel like a piece of meat. The scary guy ended up being the only one that had the most self-control.

Tucker stood up and left the cabin again – I assumed for another smoke – and Roz began tapping the table.

"You, uh, you remember what you said to me before you left last night, Nixon?" he asked, glancing over his shoulder at him.

"What of it?" Nixon replied evenly.

"Well...we're kind of waiting around, man."

My heart spiked in alarm. I was not privy to what Nixon said before he left, but the way Roz was tossing glances my way, I had a horrible feeling it had something to do with me.

I tightened the blanket around my body as I anxiously stared at Nixon.

"I'll get to it," he simply replied.

Roz was unhappy with this response. His face tightened. "Got a timeline?"

"Shouldn't you be concerned about other things, Roz?" Nixon turned his full attention to him now, appearing perplexed. "Like how the fuck you're going to return to the States unnoticed when our time here is over."

Roz's face eased as he let out a chuckle. "You heard about that?"

"You fucking Toby over? Who didn't?"

"I didn't fuck him over," Roz explained quickly. "I just skimmed the top off every payment. I didn't give him the full amount because it meant it would be eating into my cut, and honestly, he didn't know, and everything was fine."

"Who was the whistle-blower?"

"Fucking Eman," Roz snarled, shaking his head. "That fucking guy isn't an idiot, after all. He's like a mathematician; his head scrambles numbers around like they're fucking nothing. On the spot, as I paid Toby, he calculated the amount. He even went a step further and looked over the books."

"But I thought you and Toby worked it out."

Roz nodded slowly, going quiet for a few moments, mulling it over. "We were getting there, and then...well, you've seen his granddaughter, haven't you?" Nixon didn't respond, and Roz's body went stiff as he forced out, "What happened was a mistake. I... had a lot to drink. Haven't been on the drink since."

There were so many gaps in his sentences, my mind worked frantically to fill them.

I didn't know who Toby was, but he was enough to make even Nixon go stiff. A guy not to be trifled with, clearly.

And whatever happened between Roz and Toby's granddaughter may have been a mistake but...some mistakes were costly and irreversible.

My curiosity was answered when Nixon said, "You got a bounty on top of your fucking head, and it's so big, you're going to be in hiding for the rest of your life."

Roz didn't respond. He looked momentarily forlorn, like he understood the ramifications. But the expression soon disappeared when his eyes found mine, and the need in their depths could be felt.

I was so fucked, I realized just then.

I was in a den of monsters.

I should have gone down the mountain instead.

*

I'd tried to sleep on the edge of the bed as far away from Roz as possible, but there was a keenness in his touches. He wasn't having it. He snaked his arm around my middle and pulled me to him like it was okay, like he had permission to do it.

I realized letting him into bed last night had been a mistake. He'd asked, and I had allowed it. This was the consequence to one moment of weakness, of delirium and desperation for warmth.

I lay shaking the entire time, petrified he would grope me, petrified of my reaction to it because I knew my inner fight would kick in. The defiance in me felt like rockets in my limbs, ready to kick off.

For some bizarre reason he had resisted.

It was unexpected and uncharacteristic.

But it had to do with Nixon. I knew it at my core.

All night Roz had followed me around with his eyes. He had let that charming glow morph into cockiness. He looked at me like he had every right to. His eyes wandered my body when I went to the outhouse. One time he'd offered to walk me through the snowstorm, and Nixon had intervened, telling him he'd take me instead. He left no room for Roz to argue. "I'm taking her," he'd said in a commanding way, and that was all there was to it.

The walk to the outhouse was short, but it took me minutes to get to it. Nixon had to grab me by the arm and haul me through three feet of snow and freezing winds. By the time we'd gotten to it, my eyes were blinded by the snow and I couldn't feel my body. And then he'd waited for me in the dark, his face tense, his gaze trapped on the cabin.

When I stepped back out, he took me by the arm and dragged me back with urgency. The snow was so deep, I'd tripped along the way and fallen into it, my bare legs burning from the icy cold. He looked down at me with a tight face but gentle eyes.

"Come on," he urged me softly, "get up, baby."

I'd spend several hours later that night replaying him saying those words to me.

Get up, baby.

Simple, doting.

To face the possibility of your demise and be called *baby* so unexpectedly...

He hadn't said it in the way Roz had called me sweetheart and Beckett had called me honey. There was such distinction in the tone, in the manner in which he'd looked at me.

Even then, in the snow, I felt my chest heave with indescribable emotion. It didn't make sense to feel it. It was wrong, wasn't it? To feel then a sudden surge of hope invade my chest.

I knew, right then, I was starting to lose sense of reality. Of what was real and what was not. Of what was right and what was wrong. Instead, I just felt and felt, and with it, the fear felt was so grand and permanent, it was a war of insanity inside my mind.

How could you feel perpetual terror and warmth all at once?

Two opposing emotions clashed within me, and I was so...*insane, insane, insane.*

When we returned to the cabin, Nixon's gaze swept the room while Roz and Tucker looked to be doing their own things separately. His demeanour was edgy, though he returned his focus to that woodstove and let me return to bed.

The bed I was now in.

The bed that was more a jail. Roz's arm felt like slimy tentacles. I waited for him to sleep, my eyes solely focused on Nixon as he tended to the fire, as he sat with his back against the wall, watching, readying, preparing.

There was something about him...

I couldn't describe it.

When I was sure Roz was asleep, when I could hear Tucker's snores, I slipped from Roz's hold and crept to Nixon. His eyes zoned in on me as I approached him. He said nothing when I sat down close to the heat... close to him.

For some time, it was just silence, and while it was

tense for me to be so close to him, it was better than the arms of Roz.

I wouldn't go back to Roz.

No way.

I would rather sleep on the dirty floor.

I turned my attention to Nixon, desperately trying to find words to rupture the silence between us. I needed to talk. I needed to make my presence known – to show him I was a human being, not a thing, that I had a life I needed to go back to.

It took so much effort, still.

You rehearse the lines in your head, but in the actual event in which you were to say them, the words abandoned you, left you dumb and desperate.

"You guys keep calling this place a hovel," I murmured, finally doing it. "I'd have come here on a holiday if I had the chance."

Nixon turned his gaze to me. "You're easy to please."

I smiled sadly. Okay, this was my chance. "I grew up in shitty neighbourhoods. You should see the house I'm living in now." I paused, swallowing hard, astonished that I'd do anything to be in that hellhole. "I have to take three buses to get to school. The day you bought my fare, I'd missed the bus earlier by seconds, and the driver just shrugged at me. Just shrugged, like nothing, like 'oh well,' and…to think, if he had just stopped, I would have made it to class yesterday." Tears clouded my vision. I hadn't intended on being so emotional. But saying it out loud, hearing myself damn the driver, made it all the more real. I was really in this mess alone, and no one was going to break the door down to rescue me.

"People disappear all the time," I said through heavy breaths, looking Nixon in the eyes. "But they come back sometimes, they do. And you were trying to let me go before. You took me by the arm, and you told me to take the road to the farmhouse. You didn't want me in this mess. Please, Nixon, I need to go back home."

I hadn't realized he was drinking tea until he lifted the mug to his lips and sipped, his eyes never leaving mine. He settled the mug on his thigh and didn't respond for some time. I watched, waited, hoping he'd run my words through his head.

"It's not up to me," he finally said. "This is complicated now."

"Why?" I implored, desperately.

"You've seen all of us."

"I won't say a word."

"There's a whole other world you don't know about. It's a world you're not supposed to see, and you've glimpsed a sliver of it, but that's more than most know. There are people who would snuff you out just for being alive as long as you have."

Tears continued to fall. "Not if no one knows about it."

He let out a dry laugh. "Look around you. You think these guys are going to keep this – *you* – between us?"

I swallowed the lump in my throat. "If you could understand the helplessness I feel right now, if you could know I'm a human being with a life of my own, maybe I wouldn't be this nameless nothing in your life."

He didn't respond.

I didn't know if I was getting through to him. He literally let nothing slip, and it was aggravating. "Are you always this quiet?" I asked, though it came out like a snarl, but I was past the point of caring.

Now his lips curved up. "No," he answered. "You wouldn't recognize me outside this paradigm, kitten."

"My name isn't kitten," I told him hastily. "I'm twenty-one. I have family. I have friends. I have people who care about me."

He just watched me as I broke down, that soft smile on his face unflinching. He took another sip of his mug and leaned over, stopping when his face was inches from mine. His eyes locked with mine, and he seemed to study me for some time, tilting his head to the side. Then he whispered, "You're lying. You have no one. You have nothing. I know an empty soul when I see one, baby."

He sat back, leaving me quaking.

He saw straight through me, and I didn't have it in me to tell him otherwise. Because I couldn't force that sort of lie out of me, not when I was so emotional and fragile.

Was it so obvious? How could he know something so personal? I eyed him now, watching him in his at-ease state, drinking the tea he flared his nose at, and I wondered.

"Are you empty, Nixon?" I asked him, surprised by how genuine my question was.

He didn't skip a beat responding. "I'm so vacant, I don't think there's any more purpose left in this life for me. I have nothing to lose. Nothing to fight for, either. In this life and the next, I'll be unchained and forsaken. It's the ultimate freedom."

"Sounds like hell instead."

He smiled, baring teeth and all. It startled me how nice he looked. I'd almost forgotten he was beautiful. "When you're desperate to feel anything, hell delivers. The bad feelings are better than no feelings at all."

I shook my head, disagreeing. "I watched my mother slowly die from brain cancer in front of me, and now I live with this emptiness in my heart. The pain's like a worm, wriggling in my chest all the time. I keep deluding myself that she's here, watching me, giving me hints that I'll make it out of this, but it's bullshit. Sometimes I don't think it's her at all. I think she died and that was the end, but I can't accept that. I've lost myself in the grief, and I'd do anything to stop feeling it. I don't want hell. I want to feel nothing at all."

This time his smile slipped. He had an expression I'd never seen from him before. He looked me over, and I was used to it by now, being stared at by these guys – but I noticed how different it was from him. It was heated, but not in a sexual way. It was so strange to sense that. To feel – for the first time since I'd been taken – that I was being looked at as more than just a thing.

"I know what you're doing," he said quietly, breaking the tense silence. His eyes were pinning me in place. "But you need to be careful letting me in too far. It might have the complete opposite effect than what you're hoping for."

His warning was strange. It didn't come with the tone that should accompany one. He'd said it too gently.

"I want some tea," I then said, looking away from the heat of his gaze.

He stood up and poured me a mug. Handing it to me, he fed the fire and sat back down in place. I sipped the tea quietly, loving the heat in my belly.

Then I curiously asked, "What makes you think I have no one?"

He took me by the hand suddenly and pulled me close to him. My heart jumped, but I was strangely unafraid as he leaned into me. So close, I could see my reflection in his eyes. He opened his mouth, and as he answered, he pulled my sleeve up and brushed his finger along my bare arm. "I've seen your scars, little one. They're only just going white. I've imagined what they'd have looked like bleeding. Raw and deep, like your hurt. I know the look of an empty soul. I detected it from you on the bus the very second your big brown eyes met mine. Who was there to help you grieve?"

My voice was small. "No one."

Tears blurred my vision. He frowned when he saw them fall.

"You're alright," he then whispered, easing me with the soft tone of his voice. "You're okay."

I let my tears flow as he hushed me gently.

I almost asked him to call me *baby* again.

Insane, insane, insane.

Finally letting me go, he pulled away.

The silence between us returned. I didn't go back to the bed. I couldn't stomach being close to Roz again. I grabbed a blanket from the pile beside the kitchen and curled myself in a ball beside the heat.

I watched Nixon feed the fire for some time, locking eyes with him often.

There was a… different look in him now.

He appeared…determined.

Too tired to study his expression some more, I shut my eyes and fell asleep.

NIXON...

She was curled up in a ball, asleep not far from him. She would rather the floor than to be in bed with Roz, and Nixon couldn't help how good that made him feel.

He fed the fire, unable to sleep, unable to stop looking at her.

She was so pretty when she slept.

She was pretty when she talked too. Her lips mesmerized him when they moved. She spoke slowly, choosing her words wisely.

She wanted him to see her as a person. He always had. He was sure she'd probably picked up some stupid advice she'd read from a crime magazine or from those infinite documentaries that were spat out of Netflix every month.

She was lumping Nixon in with the barbarians she'd watched, which was understandable, sure.

In fact, it was more than understandable.

Because, in that very moment, as he watched her asleep, looking so fucking beautiful it physically put an ache in his side, he felt a powerful impulse that frightened him.

He could have her for himself.

He could, he thought. He really could.

The thought was so shocking. He wound up pacing the room, watching the men sleep, watching her curled there, wanting to punch a hole in his head to stop the poisonous thoughts from growing.

But they stayed, and they were brewing, and when

he thought about it some more, he saw the obstacles in the way of this sudden compulsive desire.

Had Roz felt this way too? Was that why he watched her, that hunger so apparent in his gaze? And what of Beckett? Did they both think it was only a matter of time before they could have their hands on her?

Nixon couldn't resist the surge of anger that possibility gave him.

He wouldn't allow it.

He couldn't.

He looked at the girl and felt it in his bones she was here for a reason. Mourning had softened him for this purpose. For *her.*

It was so she could come into his world and obliterate the darkness he'd lived in too long.

*

By the next day, he felt like a paranoid fucker.

He didn't like how much time Roz and Tucker were hanging around one another. Their smoke breaks were happening every thirty minutes, and they would stand a good distance away from the cabin. Tucker, being the fucking idiot that he was, would glance occasionally at the cabin as Roz spoke.

Sometimes, Tucker wouldn't even smoke.

When they returned, everything appeared normal, but Nixon wasn't buying that shit. He pulled his knife out of his pocket and was sharpening it against the sharpening stone he'd kept in the other. He never went on a job without his knife and stone.

Because you never knew when you needed it.

The minute he had started to pace, sharpening his

knife, he caught the look Tucker gave Roz.

Nixon and his knife were a complication to whatever plan they were concocting.

Whatever they were planning, it was to get to the girl. Their dicks were pulsing, their bodies strumming with barely bridled testosterone.

Maybe a girl had always been on the table.

Maybe they didn't think Nixon was going to be a problem until now.

Because it was obvious he was blocking them from getting to her. He let them think that; there was simply no way to hide that he was protecting the girl from them.

As he sharpened his knife, Roz and Nixon caught each other's gazes from across the room, and they stared at one another for some time, gauging the situation. Roz knew Nixon knew.

And now they just waited.

34.

VICTORIA...

The tension was getting worse as the next day progressed. By the afternoon, I started to see strange expressions being exchanged. Tucker was twitchy, his sight locked on Nixon every time Nixon turned his back to him.

Roz was quieter than usual, too. He sat next to me on the bed, elbows on his knees, his eyes on Nixon.

And Nixon...well, he was doing a lot of unusual pacing. He sharpened his knife so many times, I started to read it as a power play.

The day dragged. I didn't know what was happening, but it wasn't good.

I excused myself to pee often, and sometimes I'd just stand in the cold to escape the strain of being around those men.

When I returned from my latest non-pee, I walked into a hushed conversation.

"Not sure what you're doing," Roz told Nixon as I quietly stepped in and made my way across the room, gumboots squishing along the floor. "But you gotta step down, or it won't end well, man."

Nixon stopped to feed the woodstove more logs, re-igniting the embers. All day, the cabin had been warm, and he had been the only one to keep the fire going, but he never did it with his back to the men. He always had his eyes on at least one of them. When I kept seeing this happen, I began to understand there was danger brimming under the surface.

Nixon's eyes flashed to me as I reached the bed. "Go back to the door," he ordered me. "If I tell you to run, you run."

What?

My heart jumped. Blood drained from my face as I looked around the room. Roz was still seated on the bed, and Tucker was in his, a hand hidden under the pillow.

"You don't need to do that, sweetheart," Roz told me, gently. "Nixon's a little unhinged right now."

But I didn't think that was true.

My legs trembled as I took a step forward in the direction of the door.

Roz noticed and his face dropped with annoyance. "Don't you move," he told me, nose flaring. I stopped, dead still, uncertain of what to do. "Jesus, Nixon, we're going to be stuck in this fucking cabin for at least a week, maybe even more at this rate, and you just want to do what? Stare at the fucking walls? Hobbs didn't even provide booze. He gave us nothing to do."

"Did you plan it from the start?" Nixon questioned.

"Her?" Roz's eyes flashed to mine before he shook his head. "No, not her."

"Who?"

"The girl from the store. The one that opened the doors for us."

"The one you pretended to save from us."

"Yeah, but Beckett fucked that up, which we should have expected from the fucking idiot."

Nixon glanced briefly at Tucker. "And then what?"

"You didn't see it, but she pressed the alarm, which activated that explosive from the safe and signalled the guys in the cars out front that we were robbing the place. Beckett shot her for it, then he took her" – he gestured to me – "because she practically fell from the fucking sky."

Nixon didn't respond. He shut the firebox and slowly turned to face them both, his knife back out. He flicked it open, then closed, then open, repeatedly.

"Hobbs would never have permitted this," he said.

"Fuck Hobbs," Roz retorted. "The guy is squeamish as fuck."

"He would never have permitted this," Nixon repeated, sternly.

"No, he wouldn't, because the guy's a fucking hypocrite."

"You're snatching people on the job for your own personal pleasure –"

"I wasn't going to snatch her," Roz re-iterated, pointing at me. "It was the shop worker. Beckett had his eye on her while we scoped out the place. She wasn't some innocent fucking college student. Far from it, actually, and you're only opposed to it because you think of Leona." Roz paused just then, softening the tone of his voice. "How is Leona by the way?"

Nixon barely blinked, answering, "Dead."

Roz stilled, and then slowly nodded. "My condolences."

"Sorry to hear that," Tucker murmured.

"Thanks," Nixon replied.

"Look," Roz continued, "I told Beckett to throw her out the door the second he snatched her, did I not? I wanted nothing to do with the girl, but then he took his fucking mask off, and suddenly we were all taking our masks off. What's done is done. It happened. It's too late to play the fucking hero."

Nixon chuckled, dryly. "I'm not a hero."

"No," Tucker agreed. "You really aren't."

"So, what's the harm then?" Roz implored slowly. "I lived most of my life walking the fucking line, and you know where I ended up, man? I ended up homeless, unable to put a roof over my brother's head, and you know what happened to him? He got to watch mommy's head blow off her body because of some punk cunt who wanted to clean out the cash register of a *bakery*." Roz's face went red as he rattled on, growing angrier. "And he was lost in the system somewhere, who knows fucking where, idolizing me for years because I was good behind the wheel of some fucking car. I wasn't there for him. He went through his teens alone, stuck in a community home until the system threw him out the second he turned eighteen, and he wasted his potential for years trying to be like big brother. And I don't want him to be like big brother. You know what I want? I want him to stop fooling around because he's got too good a heart to do what I do. I want little bro to go back to school, have a house over his head, and not have to worry where he's going to get his three square meals a day because it's not going to be from robbing car parts in a random parking lot of a 7/11!"

That was so much to process. Everyone took a moment.

"There's an easy difference between robbing people and rape," Nixon finally said.

Roz shook his head. "No, not rape. I would never do that –"

"Toby's granddaughter –"

"I was drunk. So was she."

"Roz, you're really not selling it."

"I was not going to rape *her*," Roz said, gesturing to me. "She would have consented."

"If it meant death."

"Then it isn't rape."

Nixon just blinked slowly at Roz, looking perplexed. "Are we really having this conversation?"

"I can have anyone," Roz said, defensively. "Women can't resist me."

"Until they do."

"But they don't regret me. I'm gentle about it. I make them come. It isn't all about me."

Nixon stopped to press a hand over his pulsing head. "I need a minute to process the utter fucking bullshit coming out of your mouth, Roz."

"Women like it," Roz continued slowly. "They want to feel used."

"There's a fine line between feeling used because it's a fucking kink, to pushing them down and forcing them –"

"Because you've never tried it."

"I don't think my dick wants to, Roz."

"Stop sitting atop your mole hill," Tucker suddenly cut in, glaring. "You killed Mills and Beckett for a bigger cut. You think we bought your stupid fucking story? We didn't."

Nixon turned his sights to Tucker, an amused smile curling on his lips. "You really need to watch your tone with me, Tucker. You've been an annoying little shit from the start."

"Are you gonna kill me too, Nixon?"

"I've killed people less annoying than you."

"You should be careful who you're threatening."

Nixon shook his head in detest. "Suddenly you're so tough? That's dog mentality. You think you're stronger because you outnumber me two to one? You're so beta, I feel insulted, Tucker. Stop with that false macho shit. I could blow on you and you'd fly away."

Furious, Tucker slipped his hand out of the pillow, and I tensed. He was gripping a handgun and pointing it at Nixon. "It's you who'll be blown away, Nixon."

Nixon stilled, but not from surprise. "You're talking puns at me? Is this how you want to live your final moments, like something out of a B-grade movie?"

"Fuck you."

In spite of it, Nixon let out a laugh. "Cheeky shit, Tucker, pointing that gun at me –"

"This is on you, man. You can't dictate what is done here."

"You trying to prove that by aiming that gun at me?"

"You deserve to die anyway, Nixon, for the shit you've done."

"Go on and shoot me then, but you watch out,

Tucker," Nixon retorted, turning his entire body in his direction. "Because, unless it's bigger than a .38, I'm going to beat your head into the floor while I slowly bleed to death."

"Let's just tone it down," Roz immediately cut in.

"I'm sick of this guy constantly telling us how it's going to go," Tucker seethed. "It ain't right. We're a crew, a fucking team, man. Who put him in charge?"

"Tucker –"

"As if he doesn't fuck around with the girls. He's been trying to keep her for himself. He doesn't share, that's the real problem, Roz."

"Pussy isn't worth this much trouble, Tucker. Put the gun down."

But Tucker was shaking, his anger growing at the goading smile that was spreading on Nixon's face.

"You're right," Tucker gritted out, suddenly aiming the gun in my direction now. *Oh, my God.* "I see the way you look at her. You just want to win, don't you? You want to feel like the big guy. You're so used to getting your way, so used to winning. Well, you can't have her now, Nixon."

Then he pulled the trigger.

I didn't have time to come to grips with what he had done until seconds after he'd fired the gun and nothing happened.

No bullet rang out.

Nothing hit my body.

The only thing I felt were my legs wobbling and me falling down to the ground beside the bed, gasping from shock.

I felt weak all over.

Nixon lunged at him not a beat later, slamming

his fist into Tucker's face and knocking him down cold. "You think I didn't find your gun in the night, Tucker?" he growled, standing over his unconscious body. "You think I didn't know what you fucks were up to?"

I saw Roz move quickly in my peripheral. He was in the wood pile, his hands digging around. Nixon moved to Roz now, pushing his sleeves up his arms. "You looking for that axe you hid, Roz? How were you going to do it, exactly? In the night, when you thought I was asleep?"

Roz turned around, his face glowering with contempt. "You want to be known for killing your whole crew, Nixon? This would ruin you."

"Would it?" Nixon asked evenly, coming at him. "I guess we'll find out."

"You're really going to kill us because of some pussy?" Roz asked, raising his hand out now, as if that would halt Nixon. "If you stop now, we can put this behind us, and no one will know. You can have the girl to yourself. You can let her go or fuck her to death for all I care. I wasn't gonna kill her, anyway –"

Nixon tackled Roz to the ground, cutting him off mid-speech. Nixon's knife fell away from them as he used his fists on Roz.

To my utter surprise, Roz was equally as strong. He managed to throw a punch at Nixon's face that pushed him half off him. Then they were a ball of fists, fighting to subdue the other.

Roz may have thrown a series of surprising punches, landing a few against Nixon's jaw, it still wasn't enough to knock Nixon completely off him. I saw the concentrated look on Nixon's face as he accepted the onslaught and began wrapping his hands around Roz's throat.

Roz's arms flailed around him, his hands searching.

"Nixon," I screamed as he grabbed at Nixon's blade and swung it at him. Nixon let go of his throat as the knife slashed through the side of his neck, blood pouring out of him now. Roz grunted, teeth clenching as he fought to bring the blade back to Nixon's throat. Nixon's hands gripped Roz's wrist, surprisingly leaning into the blade as he twisted Roz's hand, struggling to aim the tip into Roz instead.

"Don't," Roz pleaded in a strained voice as the tip closed in on his chest. "Not like this, Nix...Please. Please, my brother, Nixon. He's waiting for me. Not like this. Please..."

But Nixon only flared his nose and plunged the tip straight into Roz's chest, forcing it all the way in. Roz let out a guttural gasp, his hands letting go of the knife and grabbing at Nixon's face. Nixon pulled the blade out and stabbed it into his chest again...and again. Every time he pulled the blade out, blood spurted out of Roz's chest, pooling around his body. I had to look away, unable to stomach the sight of it, but I heard him rasping, heard the blood gurgling in his lungs, and it would forever haunt me.

Tucker stirred from the ground, slowly regaining consciousness. I didn't have to say anything to Nixon. He heard the movements and got off Roz. With the knife still in his hand, he went to Tucker next.

I pulled the blanket off the bed and buried my face into it. With my hands over my ears, I screamed into the blanket so I wouldn't hear Tucker's cries.

35.

VICTORIA...

I hadn't moved from the floor long after the cries had ended.

I heard Nixon's movements all around the room. Heard the sounds of bodies being dragged. Felt the cold wind on my body when he swung the door open.

My body was wracked with tremors. I was horrified, my brain muted, my body a cold shell.

I couldn't process.

At some point, I'd shaken so hard, my limbs rattling, the blanket had slipped from around me. My eyes cut to the door just as he stood at the threshold. It was mid-afternoon, the sun was hidden, the snow was still falling, the room was dark, and the fire had gone out.

He was a dark silhouette.

Ominous looking.

Terrifying.

Covered head to toe in blood splatter, face wind beaten and red, hair dishevelled and wet. He stepped in, his footsteps slow and heavy on the hardwood floor.

His body looked heavy from exhaustion. His movements were slow as he opened the firebox and began trying to revive the embers.

He hadn't looked at me once.

I was glad for it.

Because I was scared of what I'd find in the depths of his eyes if he did.

His face was flat, cold – it unnerved me to see it. To know I'd been trying to talk to such a man in the hopes he'd let me go. My hope had been nonsensical. This man killed without hesitation, and all I could see and feel in that moment was death, death, death.

I used to think having to watch my mother deteriorating was traumatic enough, but that death – while ugly in its own right – had not come close to this. Mom's passing was a slow and expectant decay. Nothing armed me for the suddenness of the deaths that had occurred in plain sight of me, so close I felt it, the gore and blood and sounds – all of it swirled chaotically inside my mind, making me lose complete sanity.

My brain was scrambled. My thoughts incoherent. My gaze swung to the door, and for some unfathomable reason, my flight response was kicking in. I just wanted to be gone. Away from death and blood and terror. It would get me only to certain death, but I wasn't thinking that far ahead. As far as I was concerned, death was my ultimate fate regardless how this played out.

I was still in my gumboots as I slowly settled on my knees, the urge to run jolting my muscles awake. His back was turned to me, occupied in the dying fire. The door of the cabin was ajar, and I knew all I had to wait for was a sudden slam of wind to have it swinging open the whole way.

I stood up, bracing myself, testing my balance. I expected to fall back again. Surely, I couldn't have full equilibrium of my body with all this chaos inside me.

But I did.

I was standing straight. I felt...determined to flee.

He must have sensed me moving, because he turned his head in my direction. His expression turned wary. He saw me eye the door, he saw the determination in my face, and he whispered tightly, "Don't."

Just as that word left his lips, a heavy breeze slammed into the cabin, and the door swung wide fast.

I bolted

He didn't chase me when I made it out the door. I was going in a linear direction, into the trees. My boots sank miserably into the snow, all the way to my knees. I tripped having to unbury my feet with every strenuous step. The wind and snow swirled around me, slamming into my face, my eyes, my bare legs.

I lost visibility almost straightaway.

I was aware I was sobbing into the air, though I didn't feel the tears running down my face. Every inch of me felt so cold, and as a result, I was quickly stiffening.

I couldn't have been that far from the cabin when I fell, face planting into snow and bush. I stopped moving and bawled in defeat. I couldn't get up if I tried. I shook, my hair wet all around me, the wind dancing a wicked tune as it whipped me, and god, it felt like hot lashes against my skin every time.

Every time I shut my eyes I saw blood pooling on

the floor. I saw brains and Beckett and a head blowing apart over me.

More than that...I felt the immobilizing terror of it all. It couldn't be ignored.

Yet...I couldn't find it in me to give up. I forced my head up, blinking rapidly at the white all around me. I didn't want to die. It scared me to think I was going to, maybe right here, in this place, and I had never amounted to anything and no one was alive to care about me.

There was such an acute pain in that – dying and knowing no one loved you.

I began to crawl aimlessly as my thoughts roared an angry melody.

Maybe I didn't put myself out there enough. Maybe I tried too hard, maybe I was too fake, maybe I'd spent too much time with my head buried in a fake world, envying people I thought lived better than I did.

Maybe my life wasn't so bad. Maybe I had everything I needed all along.

I only missed Mom when I knew she was dying. I never thought she'd leave me. I had always been secure in the knowledge my mother would always be there for me. How were you supposed to live with yourself when you looked back on empty moments that could have been shared with someone you loved but took for granted?

I only cared about my life when I felt I might die. Where was my oomph to get ahead? It seemed all I knew how to do was graze by in life, barely breaking even. My potential was now lost, once again taken for granted.

I crawled and crawled.

Every day I had ballooned the small issues and made them control my feelings, my outlook on life. I had been too negative, too hard on myself, too enveloped in *me* without ever having truly focused on me.

I couldn't recall a single moment of inner reflection.

I couldn't recall ever confronting my faults.

I couldn't recall ever forgiving myself for ignoring Mom when she needed me the most.

I was going to die not ever knowing myself.

I felt like my heart had collapsed in my chest. I buried my face in the snow and cried hard. I stopped crawling. My body was too stiff and so cold, I couldn't even feel the cold anymore.

This was it.

I couldn't go on.

The wind battered all around me, and I shut my eyes, surrendering to the elements.

36.

NIXON...

He found her straightaway. Had followed the tracks in the snow to her body. She'd run, then fallen, then crawled, then...stopped.

Nixon felt his heart tighten in his chest when he came upon her still form in the snow. He stopped over her. A tremor wracked his body at the sight of her frozen body.

She was still like death.

Her skin was white as snow.

Her dark hair was splayed out around her; such a deep contrast it was amongst the white.

Her lips were pale, her face covered in a thin film of fresh snow.

He thought it unnatural to come upon a being so angelic. This land was too beastly, too unfeeling. You could disappear into the trees and never be found again. The land did that; it swallowed you whole, it made you become part of itself.

He thought, even dead, she was the most beautiful woman he had ever seen.

But she wasn't dead.

He'd trudged behind her right after she'd fled the cabin. He'd seen her at a distance. He'd sensed her chaos as she desperately sought an escape.

But it wasn't an escape from *this*, he realized, as he looked down at her.

She was aware he was here, yet she stared ahead, unblinking. She wasn't trying to run from him.

She was trying to run from herself.

This small body had been warring with itself long before her abduction.

Something about that realization stirred him on a deeper level. He looked down at her empty face and felt an overwhelming urge to remove her sadness.

Was she as empty as he felt? He wondered. Did nothing stir in the depths of her? Did she toss and turn every night, lost in apathy? Did she loathe waking up in the mornings because it made her confront how vacant and purposeless her life was?

He'd seen hints of pain in her brown eyes when she'd looked at him the first time. He'd only turned away from it because those sorts of encounters should be fleeting and impersonal. You don't get to touch upon someone's life over one look. Yet he'd stood close to the doors on that bus, feet from where she sat, desperate to look at her again, desperate to feel that stir of something deep inside him. Something he thought he had lost a long time ago. Something he felt was recently killed in its entirety just a short week ago.

Nixon scooped her body out of the snow. She shivered in his arms, which was a good sign. Hypothermia struck wild and fast here. He watched her carefully as he trudged back to the cabin. Saw the fresh tears fall from her eyes, and he wanted to ask her, "Where does it hurt the most, little one? Is it your heart? Does it still beat? Is it your soul – do you still feel it humming beneath your skin?"

He took her into the cabin and slammed the door shut with his foot. He settled her down on the bed and knelt to her level. He grabbed at her wet clothing and removed them one by one. She looked so tired, her body was weak and red in places. Stripped to her bra and underwear, he grabbed at several blankets and wrapped them around her. Five layers later and she was still shivering. She needed more heat.

"Stay awake," he told her.

She watched him through bleary eyes as he returned to the woodstove and reignited the fire. It was such a bitch to do when the fire died out, and because the wood was still moist, the fire was extra smoky.

Nixon was frozen, too. His fingers were stiff and painful. He was covered in dried blood and he still had two bodies not far from the cabin he needed to dispose of much further away. The last thing he needed were predators to come poking around.

No, he'd dump them a good distance away and then he'd tell Hobbs where they were when he came. Hobbs would do a proper job of disappearing them for good, and then...

Nixon glanced over his shoulder at the girl.

Then what?

The girl was a motherfucking complication.

She had tried so hard to capture his attention, to plead her case. And he had tried his hardest to distance himself from her because he didn't want to know. For her sake, he didn't want to explore her layers and feel the pulse within him surge.

Better to let the feelings taper.

To let the moment go.

To not feed into the mad compulsion he felt in his bones.

He couldn't have her.

He couldn't.

But those brown eyes held him captive when she looked back at him.

They made him do stupid things.

They made him demand in a deprived sort of way, "Tell me your name,"

VICTORIA...

"Tell me your name," he snapped at me. His gaze was piercing. He was looking at me like he was trying to figure me out. Or maybe trying to figure out what the fuck to do with me. I couldn't be sure.

"Victoria," I managed out weakly.

"Victoria," he repeated thoughtfully, staring into the flames now. My reaction was immediate – my chest stirred, and my heart raced. "I don't know what to do with you, Victoria," he admitted, closing the firebox door.

He returned to me, this mammoth of a man, covered in blood and cold, kneeling down to my level. He raised a hand to my face and pressed it against my cheeks. I could hardly feel him. Then he grabbed at my blankets and began opening them. Too weak to fend him off, I had no choice but to let him, watching him carefully as he touched at my bare arms with a frown. He began rubbing away my goosebumps, looking into my eyes at the same time.

"You're not warming up," he said. "I need you next to the fire."

I shook my head weakly. "I don't want to move."

"I'll move you."

"Please, don't." I grabbed at the blankets and stubbornly wrapped them around myself again. "I'll be fine. It's just my hands that are cold."

He didn't look pleased by that. "You're irritable because you're experiencing hypothermia."

"I'm irritable for other reasons," I snapped suddenly. "And I think they're obvious reasons."

He watched me for a few moments, blinking slowly. Maybe he was shocked by my tone – I sure was. This guy could so easily snap me in half. He didn't seem the patient type.

"I think I'm irritable," I amended quickly, worried now. "I'm just really cold and tired."

"Give me your hands," he told me.

My heart spiked. "Why?"

"Not going to hurt you," he assured me.

I had no choice, did I?

I was completely at this man's mercy.

I slowly let go of the blankets and offered him my hands. I eyed him warily as he took them gently into his own and tucked them under his black sweater. My heart jumped in my chest as he pressed them flat against his stomach.

"Keep them there," he told me, letting my hands go. I felt his abs flex as he grabbed the blankets and wrapped them tightly around me.

As he waited for my hands to warm up, I kept my eyes directed to his chest. He was too close for comfort, but I didn't mind it when I felt how blazing hot his skin was. My hands felt like they were thawing, and it hurt. A lot. It was almost unbearable.

We didn't speak. I was aware he was watching me, though. Every time I willed myself to look back at him, I caught his expression. He was deep in thought as he studied me. I could have begged for my life now that I had his full attention, but it seemed utterly pointless.

It was apparent at this stage he was in complete control.

I thought of what Beckett had said earlier. *I see the way you look at her. You want her for yourself.* It troubled me to think that might be true.

If he did want me for himself, there would be no one to stop him.

"How do your hands feel?"

I shrugged weakly. "Like they're going to fall off from the pain."

"Okay, keep them there then."

Panic tore through me suddenly. I gave him a bug-eyed look. "Do you think they'll fall off?"

He gave me a blank stare. "What?"

"What if I have frostbite?"

"I think I got to you before that was possible."

"How can you be sure?"

His lips flickered up with amusement. "I'm sure."

I caught the hysteria in my tone and looked away, feeling overcome with embarrassment. "Is paranoia another sign of hypothermia?"

"I think that's just you."

I went quiet for a few minutes. My hands were finally warming up and now I felt stupid.

I let out a slow breath as I reflected on the two men he'd killed. "Were they really going to kill you?" I asked quietly.

"Yeah," he answered. "They had it all figured out."

"When were they going to do it?"

"It would have been soon." He said it so casually, his whole demeanour composed.

"That didn't surprise you?"

"No," he said. "Not when you're living this kind of life."

Of course. How could you pit monsters together and expect them to play nice? They were all, in their own right, horrific.

The blood on his cheeks had dried, some of it flaked off with his movements. The coppery stench of it was in the air around us.

Just above the collar of his sweater was fresh blood oozing from the cut Roz had inflicted on him. The gash looked deep, but the blood didn't seem to be flowing out of it any more than a papercut.

Of course. Only a man like him could make a cut like that look so minor.

It was so shocking to think two souls had died feet from me. Just like that. That the man I was touching was responsible for it.

It was vile.

This man was vile.

He felt my trembling. He watched me as I fell into a bout of despair, and he didn't look sympathetic in the slightest. His blue eyes hardened, and he leaned in a touch to say, "Best to refocus your energy on what would have happened had I been the one dead. What would they have been doing to you right now?"

My breaths thinned as I gaped at him in shock. If he was seeking a reaction, he got one. I couldn't help the jolt of anger coursing through my body. I said, "Beckett, sure, but I'm not sure Roz deserved to go like that."

He shot me a cold smile. "Were you fond of Roz, Victoria?"

It was the third time he'd said my name, and my chest felt strange every time. "He begged for his life at the end. Said he needed to be there for his brother." Fresh tears fell from my eyes as I thought of the plea in his voice. Oh, my God. What was wrong with me?

"Roz was worse than Beckett," Nixon simply said.

I swallowed hard. "Because of what he did to that guy's granddaughter?"

"That was just one instant."

"Is she okay?"

Nixon's lips flattened. "I don't know. You'd have to ask Toby, and I'm not sure he'd like to talk about it."

I felt awful for the woman. "Was she drunk, like Roz said? Is that how he managed to take advantage of her?"

"Maybe," Nixon retorted. "Does it matter?" No, it didn't. Before I could respond, he stood up, forcing my hands to leave the heat of his stomach. Without looking at me, he added, "She was twelve."

He stomped back to the fire and fed it more wood as I came to grips with what he said. There I was trembling again, but not from the cold. I was trembling from how disturbed I felt. I'd slept next to Roz, a predator who had preyed on a child. That poor girl. My stomach turned violently.

Monsters.

I crawled up the bed and settled in the very corner. I wanted to disappear into the wall. I wanted to rip the feelings out of my chest and mutilate them.

This sort of fear was inescapable.

It was life ruining, the extent of it so punishing.

I wondered how anyone made it out of this sort of trauma alive.

Until I realized, they made it out, just not in one piece.

Present

I gasped in shock as the memories surged through me at an alarming rate.

Emotions I had buried for so long surfaced.

It had taken so much mental strength to trek down memory lane, but the second I began the journey, I found myself rooted in the centre of my past, awed by the events.

Awed by my strength.

I remembered the apathy and the pain of losing Mom. I remembered the stark loneliness I'd felt every morning I'd woken up in that bed, dreading the day. I wanted to cry for that girl. I wanted to hug her to me and tell her to be strong because she was so fucking sad.

More than that, I remembered the fear I felt. Such a unique sort of terror most don't feel in a lifetime.

It was fear and...something else.

Something wrong...

Something arousing...
Beneath the thick layer of fear, there were other happenings.

As the car sped along the uneven road, I shut my eyes, remembering the beginning of my deranged relationship with Nixon.

37.

VICTORIA...

There was no reprieve – this day wouldn't end. I sat, my spirits deadened, still cold to the fucking bone.

Nixon had boiled water for hours and thrown it over the dried puddles of blood. He scrubbed it with dishwashing sponges that he'd found in one of the boxes. Then he used Beckett's blanket to soak up the blood before disposing of it outside. I mean, it was a shitty job. The blood was still there, but it did feel better knowing the hardwood wasn't so saturated. I also noticed that there hadn't been a whole lot of blood where Tucker had died. I imagined Nixon had finished him off with his fists instead.

It was all so fucked up.

I'd only gotten up to use the outhouse. However, I needed to drink. I needed to eat something. I felt my body giving out, but I was too weak to move. I moved down the bed and curled into a foetal position. I covered my face and shut my eyes as Nixon moved around, his footsteps a never-ending rhythm.

At one point he'd dragged something heavy across

the floor, but I had mentally checked out and didn't have it in me to turn around to see. I'd used the blankets like barriers to keep him out, even though it was so hot in the room.

The sound of water sloshing followed and went on forever. Then it stopped and I heard Nixon's heavy breaths replace the silence.

When I heard more water splashing, my eyes opened. Curiosity was a bitch. I quietly turned around to look at what he was doing.

He'd dragged the portable tub into the middle of the cabin and filled it up with water. There was a long black hose running across the room and out the door. He'd used his boot to prop the door open just enough to let the hose out.

His solid back was facing me. He looked kind of funny because the tub was so small compared to the width of his body. But he'd managed to just fit in. I watched him dunk his head into the water. He scrubbed at his scalp and face. Then he grabbed at one of the kitchen sponges and rubbed a bar of soap to it before vigorously scrubbing his body.

Just watching him clean himself made me feel grimy. I was so filthy and disgusting. I hadn't brushed my teeth yet, hadn't properly cleaned my girly bits. I felt like I might explode just thinking about it.

He used his blade next to shave his beard. I heard the sound of it sliding across his cheeks from where I lay. It disturbed me to know he'd sharpened that fucker so good, it was probably better than a shaving razor.

It was oddly satisfying watching him get clean. My eyes trailed his broad shoulders, noticing random bruising along his skin. This was not a guy that took it easy, I realized. The bruises were old and nearly faded, for crying out loud. Did this guy love violence?

I thought of the four people he had murdered in front of me.

Yes. I thought. He loved violence just fine.

He made quick work of his body and then he stood up. I tensed at the sudden move. The water spilled over the edges of the tub and sloshed on the floor. My eyes were glued to his body, though, to the endless little scars along his back and sides, to more bruises along his bare thigh and legs.

He was ripped. Of course, he was, I'd known that already, but actually seeing it was a whole other ballgame.

It was a blunt reminder he was all man.

He looked so much bigger without his clothes on.

I guesstimated he was at least two hundred and fifty pounds. That was easily over a hundred pounds heavier than me, and it was all muscle. I could never, ever, *ever* in my wildest dreams overpower him.

Hell, I wouldn't have been able to overpower Beckett who couldn't have weighed more than me by much.

I was so fucked.

Yet, I was still staring at his bare ass as he moved across the room to fetch a blanket from the floor. He used it like a towel, running it over his clean-shaven face. He looked good without the stubble. His fuckable hair fell over his forehead, damp and dripping water to the floor. He turned more in my direction, and I couldn't help the trek my eyes took down his front.

Okay, yeah, he was ripped from the front too, and big...Big, as in, *big*. As in, he had a third fucking leg, if you caught my drift.

When I looked back up to his face, his head was already turned in my direction. His eyes met mine, and my heart jumped from the surprise of it. I threw the blanket over my face before I could think of a better move to make.

And I could have made so many better moves than that.

Oh, God, I wanted to die.

Although, not really.

I didn't want to die at all.

But my cheeks were flaming red.

This wasn't how our dynamic was supposed to play out. I shouldn't be feeling embarrassed under the blankets like this. I should be withdrawn and apathetic and waiting for him to decide what he wanted to do with me.

None of those documentaries touched upon these sorts of moments. Moments when you caught your captor in the nude and ogled him shamelessly.

"Your turn," he said, breaking the silence. "Get up."

With my heart in my throat, I stiffly removed the blanket and slowly slid out of bed. I couldn't meet his eye as I stood up and made my way over to the tub. From my peripheral, I noticed he'd thrown his pants back on, but the zipper was undone the whole way, and he wasn't wearing any briefs. He remained shirtless; the water continued falling from his hair, sliding down his shoulders and giant arms.

"I'm going to drain it out," he told me. "It'll be a

while to fill it. I've melted enough snow, we just have to reheat it. You can wash your clothes in the sink up here. There's a pot inside it with some soapy water."

I nodded when he finished. He threw some large pots over the stove top to heat, and I sort of appreciated I didn't have to do that. I felt so weak and tired. I just stood there the entire time, making him do the work.

He'd used the hose to drain the tub. Then he began to fill it with water. I waited patiently until it was halfway full. I felt awkward, unsure if he expected me to take my clothes off in front of him.

Thankfully, he barely glanced in my direction and strode to the tiny table with four chairs. He took a seat on the chair with his back to me and began sharpening his knife against the stone again.

I quickly undressed. My fingers trembled from exhaustion, but I didn't care how badly I needed food, water and sleep. I needed the heat of the water more than all of that combined.

The clothes were in a pile on the floor when I slowly stepped into the tub. The heat was so amazing, I could have cried. I slowly sank into the tub, feeling the kinks in my muscles loosen. The water wasn't going to be hot for long, so I quickly dunked my head in and soaked my hair. I swirled the bar of soap in my hand until it foamed and used that to wash my hair. I wasn't going to complain that it was scentless. I wasn't going to complain that it didn't help separate the knots in my hair. I didn't give a single fuck. I just wanted to be clean. Wanted to feel the horrors I'd witnessed wash away.

Funny what a simple bathing could do to your

soul.

I felt more put together. The weight of depression eased as I watched the dirt leave my skin.

I didn't take long. When I finished, I glanced around the room, looking for the nearest unused blanket. I had to step out of the tub to get to it. I looked warily in Nixon's direction. He was still seated, back still turned to me, sharpening that knife without a break in between.

I got out of the tub and raced to the blanket. I wrapped it around myself quickly and took my pile of clothes to the sink. I had to use one hand to scrub my clothes otherwise the blanket would fall from me. I half-assed it and then hung my bra and panties next to the heat of the fire. I was lazier with my skirt and sweater; they were in a shitty pile beside the stove.

I returned to my bed and sat down on the edge of the mattress. I kept the blanket tight around me as I glimpsed periodically at Nixon. His face was visible to me from where I sat. His face was flat, expressionless, his concentration enveloped solely on the knife and sharpening stone in his hand.

It didn't seem like he gave a single fuck I'd bathed feet from him, or that I was naked and wet, hidden only beneath a thin layer of wet blanket, on the bed in direct view of him.

I may as well have been invisible.

NIXON...

She was wet, naked, her body hidden beneath the

thinnest layer of blanket to ever grace this fucking earth.

Nixon tightened his jaw as he swiped the blade back and forth.

Back and forth.

Back and forth.

She'd been staring at him when he'd bathed.

She'd stared at his naked body.

She'd stared at his cock for the longest fucking time.

This wasn't normal captive behaviour.

Yet, when he glimpsed at her from time to time, he'd seen the way her shoulders tightened. The fear returned to her eyes.

She was terrified.

So, if she was so fucking terrified of him, why did she keep staring at him? Why did her eyes follow his every move and journey down his body without any effort to be discreet about it?

This shit was mind-fuckery to the extreme. Nixon couldn't play into it. He couldn't pay it any attention. He just needed to make it through the week ignoring that maddening impulse he felt for the girl.

He could do that.

Maybe.

He wasn't entirely sure, if he were being honest with himself.

He'd savagely killed the crew because they wanted to touch her, and god-fucking-dammit, he was adamant they had no right.

But now that he was alone with her, now she was so close to him, so accessible, he felt wrought with the same urges they had.

Only...he felt like he had every right to it.

Which was ludicrous.

Right?

It was ludicrous?

Why didn't his body feel that way, then?

Why didn't his own brain condemn him for his hypocrisy?

Where was his self-fucking-control?

When he was sure his cock wasn't bursting at the seams, he got up and made food. The girl was starving. He'd heard her stomach growling. She was just too scared to move, to capture his attention. She didn't know what he was going to do with her.

Frankly, he didn't know, either.

He boiled a food pouch and made her some tea. He set it on the table, and when she saw that he had made his own pouch and tea, she connected the dots and took a seat at the table, that thin as fuck blanket still wrapped around her.

She was so fucking tempting, it was madness.

They didn't speak while they ate. She didn't look like she had the ability to. She was ravenous, all etiquette from before completely gone as she shoved giant mouthfuls of beef and rice into her mouth. Nixon kept his gaze fixed to his pouch, but he caught the way her blanket slipped. He knew her tits were kind of visible, and suddenly, the rice tasted rancid.

This was hell, wasn't it?

To want something so fucking badly and not be able to have it.

To feel the urges all the way to the tips of his fingers.

This fucking tempting beauty, with her brown

fucking eyes, with her visible tits, with that sad excuse of a blanket...

His appetite disappeared.

His cock stiffened in his pants again, and he felt angry at himself.

This reaction was elementary school shit. He should not have been so effected.

But he was.

He had never wanted a girl so bad in his life. He had never looked at one and gone mad with need.

Not like this.

Never like this.

To have shed so much blood – to have murdered men in cold blood – all because on some base level, at the core of him, he felt...

Oh, fuck...

He felt she was his.

What a horrifyingly fucked up admission.

It didn't come as an unsteady thought like before.

He was resolute about it.

He threw the pouch down on the table and bolted out of the cabin, dragging a hand through his hair, gripping it so tight, he wanted to rip the strands to dispel the aching he felt in his balls. When that didn't work, he scooped a handful of snow from the ground and rubbed it on his heated face.

He needed to be sensible.

He couldn't have the girl. His world demanded she be erased. She was against the fucking rules. No one would allow this. Not even Hobbs would protect him.

This was a complication.

He fucking loathed complications.

*

He had made sure to stay outdoors for several hours in the cold. He simply didn't trust himself.

He might touch her.

Truly.

It was a harsh truth.

Leona would be disgusted by him.

He sat with his back against the cabin, watching the snow fall around him, trying to talk sense.

"If I could make this feeling go away, I would," he whispered aloud, like he was talking to her. "Leona, I would. I'm not that far fucked, angel."

He wasn't.

Right?

But that wasn't true, was it?

It would have been so much easier to have been the bystander. To have let the men do as they pleased. He wouldn't have witnessed it. Really, he could have walked away telling himself that they had outnumbered him, that he had been powerless, that they could do such an abominable act to an innocent girl was completely of their own volition. He would have been able to go on with his life and be untouched by the dirtiness of it.

"Maybe I could have done that once," he murmured, numbly. "I might have walked away."

He might have, true.

Maybe a few years ago, when he was desperate to prove himself. Now that guy, though, he wouldn't have been able to have cleansed an entire crew. *That* Nixon was weaker, not yet hardened or skilled enough to outsmart others.

Now, though, *now* it meant nothing to kill.

He'd thought he was all the way gone. Too far gone to feel any bearing on right and wrong. Even when Leona was alive, his feelings weren't as intense.

"Victoria," he whispered.

Fuck, the name alone made him go mad with lust.

This wasn't normal.

This was something else entirely.

This was a girl he hardly knew that had anchored him back down to the real world after being detached from it for so long. He felt so utterly human, so utterly weak, and what disturbed him the most about that was he liked feeling that way. He liked knowing he might still have something to lose.

Nixon was certain he'd never come across the chance at redemption again if he were to let her go.

The act of saving her from the men wasn't going to outweigh the act of taking her for himself, but he reasoned that if she were to be let go, she would be dead regardless.

His world was filled with people that would not allow her to exist past this point.

It was a problem he would have to sort out when the time came.

He got up just as the sky began to darken. He returned to the cabin, aware as ever that he might have spent too long overthinking it. He might see her and the urge might be gone entirely.

When he stepped into the cabin, he found her asleep on the bed, wrapped tightly in that blanket. He didn't come too close, but he watched her from across the room, unable to shake the feeling she was meant to be here.

She was meant to be his.

38.

VICTORIA...

I couldn't believe I was feeling this, but the silence was maddening. It was a different sort of torture. For two whole days, there had been literally no interaction. We'd sort of fallen into the habit of communicating with little gestures. Like, if it was bath time? A gesture with your chin in the direction of the tub. If it was food time, Nixon placed my plate and drink on the table and took a seat across from me with his own plate and drink.

He didn't even look at me.

I was non-existent.

If I happened to get too close, his nose would flare. Other times, he'd randomly storm out of the room like I'd done something to piss him off.

At this rate, I was certain I would be dead in a ditch by the end of this. I was not winning him over. I had silently accepted this too, because trying to win him over required the balls to break the silence between us, and I didn't have it in me to do that. I was aware of what he was capable of.

What if I pissed him off enough he'd gut me with

the knife he'd been sharpening?

And on that note, he was always sharpening his knife, and it made me shiver at times because he'd sharpened that fucking thing right before he killed Roz and Beckett.

Was this some ominous foreshadowing?

Mentally, my brain had exited the building when it came to confronting I might die at the end of this. Honestly, my body had gotten sick and tired of being afraid. It just went sort of numb, like, "hey, if you're gonna die, we'll get scared again when we finally cross that bridge, Victoria."

Living in fear every second of every minute was so exhausting. I was just going through the motions now. Enduring the long ass days with this tense fucking silence felt like my soul was being grated slowly.

I'd just brushed my teeth and bathed for the third day in a row. I didn't feel uncomfortable stepping out of the tub because Nixon kept his back to me every time I bathed. I wrapped myself up in the blanket and returned to my bed with my bra and panties. My shoddy job of drying my skirt and sweater had been unsuccessful. They ended up smelling from sitting in a pile, and now I preferred to just hide under the blanket.

Just as I went to slide my panties up my legs, Nixon abruptly stood up and began undressing for a bath. I immediately hid under the blanket and threw it over my head. He didn't even drain the water. He just stepped into the tub with the water I'd used and scrubbed.

His movements were louder than usual.

I formed a little hole in my blanket and peeked at

him. He was on his knees in the tub, going over his body so hard, his skin was red. His face was tense, his expression angry as he dragged the sponge over every bit of him.

I should have been wary that he was angry, but my attention was drawn to his body and the way it flexed with his movements. I was entranced by it, had come to know every inch of his body by being the peeping tom that I was.

Plain and simple, he was fucking delightful to look at.

He was losing a bit of weight. His muscles looked more distinct. He'd do a million push ups before bed, so his arms were still bulging. He seemed to try to work himself to the bone until he was so tired, he'd fall into the other bed and pass out within minutes.

When he finished, he stepped out of the tub and didn't bother drying himself off. He paced the room, dragging a frustrated hand over his head. I noticed his dick was harder than I'd ever seen it before. It felt wrong to be looking at it so much.

It was especially wrong for the jolt I felt in my body in response.

Jesus, I was riled up, dizzy with the shot of lust I got every time I saw him like this.

I covered my face again and shut my eyes, breathing deeply. It was fucked up to feel turned on. It was fucking weird to be capable of that after everything. I felt ashamed of myself. I admonished my body. I loathed how wet I felt between my legs. I almost cried because of how helpless it made me feel.

It didn't help I couldn't keep my eyes off the guy.

It didn't help I couldn't seem to stop myself from

keeping my eyes off the guy.

It also didn't help the silence between us was torture. Every time he spoke in that deep voice, it stirred something unfathomable in my chest.

While I knew fear was the right and most appropriate response for me, I also felt warmth when I reflected on how he'd saved me.

Time and time again.

From Beckett.

From Mills.

From Roz and Tucker's sick intentions.

It was possible Nixon had his own agenda. He could have done it for reasons that were selfish. But he hadn't raped me. He hadn't touched me. He hadn't even looked at me.

Which meant...

He didn't have to save me from any of them.

Maybe, on some base level, my brain had rationalized that, and my body responded with some false sense of safety.

Maybe, at the end of the fucking day, he was all man and I was all woman, and we were stuck in a cabin, nude half the time, bathing half the time, filled with a silence that I sensed he might have wanted to break too.

It was quiet for a while now. I slowly removed the blanket from my head and found Nixon seated on the wooden chair. My heart sped in my chest because he was still naked and wet. The chair had been placed facing my bed, and he was sitting there, staring back at me.

What the fuck?

I blinked, shocked.

I blinked again, burning inside.

This was the most attention he'd given me in days.

I didn't know how to react. I lay tense and unmoving, looking back at him, noticing how heavy his gaze was.

I knew a look like that.

Had seen it in the others.

My breathing slowed. I should have felt panicked, but I was too stunned by his attention. My body hadn't caught up yet.

He was holding his knife and stone, but he wasn't sharpening it. As I looked him over rapidly, I noticed his dick was still hard and visible to me now. I squirmed; my cheeks heated at the gush of wetness I felt pooling between my legs.

I swallowed and looked back at him. I swear he knew what I was feeling. I was sure of it. His eyelids drooped lower as he watched me. His expression morphed. He appeared self-assured, a quiet sort of confidence in him now as he said curiously, "Has anyone ever sucked your cunt, Victoria?"

I was shocked.

Mortified.

Gob smacked that he could say that to me after days of zero interaction.

Well, I made sure to *look* that way. It was the appropriate response. To hang my mouth open in dismay. To frown and look disgusted.

Yet my body was as hot as the fire.

"I can't stop wondering what you taste like," he whispered, thoughtfully, his gaze so intense, it left me breathless. "I'm curious if you'd let me near you. Would you, Victoria?"

He didn't wait for my response. I watched him as he slowly set the knife and stone down on the table. He stared at them for a beat longer, a thousand thoughts blazing through his mind, before he redirected his focus to me.

Then he came to me.

Strolled to me in four easy steps.

I felt my body press back into the mattress. I tightened the blanket around me, but my eyes bore into his the whole way.

He didn't give me any time to process what he was going to do.

He simply stopped by the bed and yanked the blanket off me in one quick move. He threw it on the floor behind him and dropped to his knees. He grabbed at my legs and spun me around, yanking me down the mattress so my legs were dangling off the edge.

I was naked and vulnerable and about to have a heart attack. I closed my legs as he gripped my thighs and shook my head at him. "Don't, Nixon." My words were weak. I was crying. I felt the tears fall down the side of my face as I looked down at him.

"Why?" he retorted, his face grim. "You've been looking at me for days. You've been wet and squirming. You want me to make the ache go away, baby?"

Baby.

That word again.

The way he said it.

So gentle. So doting.

More tears fell. I hid my face from him, sobbing

R.J. LEWIS

because the pulse between my legs quickened and I would do anything to satisfy it.

"It's wrong," I cried. "I don't want it. I don't."

"You don't?" he questioned. "Or you keep telling yourself you don't?"

"I shouldn't."

"No, you shouldn't."

"It's wrong," I restated.

"Yeah, it is," he agreed. "So why does that excite you so much?"

I shook my head, more at myself than him, because he was right. For some sick reason, I was so fucking excited. I wanted him to bury his face there. Had imagined it at night. Had wondered what it would feel like since the moment I saw him on that bus.

What if he did it and I hated myself for it?

How could I live with myself for being so weak, for allowing a murderous man to touch me without putting up a fight?

The whole situation was wrong.

I was so fucking confused.

"Do you think you won't be a victim anymore if you let me touch you?" he asked me. When I nodded, I felt his hands grip my thighs tighter. "Tell me no, then, baby, but open your legs for me when you do."

I took a few breaths absorbing his words. I understood his intentions. It sounded like a sick little game. If I told him no, but spread my legs, it was an invitation but not one I would admit out loud to.

I was aware how close he was. I could feel the need in him by the way he gripped my thighs. He'd been hard for me, I realized. Maybe he'd been fighting himself this whole time.

As I let out a long breath of air, I relaxed my legs and whispered, "N-no."

The air sounded like it'd been ripped from his lungs when he uttered, "Thank fuck."

Within seconds, he spread my legs wide and buried his face between them. The moment I felt his mouth at my swollen core, the heat of his tongue along my wet slit, I could have blacked out from pleasure. I gasped as delicious jolts shot up my belly. I buried my fingers into his wet hair as tremors wracked my body.

"Jesus, you're sensitive," he said, awed. "Why are you so fucking sensitive, Victoria?"

I didn't know.

But I could guess.

I didn't care to respond because his tongue was making my body twist and turn with need.

He sucked hard, then slow, then teased around my clit. He drew out sounds that surprised me. I cried for him to stop, even though I held him still to me, my body begging for more of his mouth.

"Say my name when you come, baby," he groaned as he sucked me hard.

I shook my head, moaning, "No," over and over again.

"Yes," he urged. "Say my name while I suck your delicious cunt."

I dug my feet into the mattress as he swirled his tongue around my clit. I yanked at his hair so hard, aware I was going to come. I tried to whisper for him to stop, to tell him no again, but the second the crest of pleasure approached, I began whispering, "Nixon," instead.

I came hard.

All the tension left my bones.

The orgasm ripped through me, intense and more satisfying that I could have ever imagined. Even the aftershocks were heady.

After I came down from the high, he pulled away and I instantly buried myself under the blanket again, forcing a barrier between us.

I couldn't face him.

Not after that.

I could hardly face myself.

NIXON...

No one had ever touched her like that before. He knew it by the way she gasped. She made these surprised little sounds as he sucked that sweet little pussy.

And now he was aching worse than ever before.

She hid herself from him so fast, like she couldn't confront him, or herself for that matter. He felt his heart soften at that. She was so sweet, and he was so...

so...

F

U

C

K

E

D.

He sat back down on the chair and stared at her little form buried under the covers. He wanted to remove them, wanted to run his hand down her soft body and tell her it was okay to feel confused.

He felt confused, too.

That wasn't a game he had ever played.

Frankly, he was shocked his dick hardened for it.

He liked it.

He knew she liked it, too.

As twisted as it was.

As wrong as it was.

It just... was.

VICTORIA...

No words were exchanged for hours. I remained hidden under the blanket, listening to his every move. He wasn't stomping around like usual, which was an okay sign. But I did feel him come near me at times, and I sensed he was staring at me.

For a long while, I was confused with myself.

I expected to feel dirty, but I didn't.

I expected to be dismayed by myself for allowing it, but I wasn't.

I kept replaying the feel of his tongue against my most private part. One could get seriously addicted to that. The stories made sense. Kim's gushing over it had not been exaggerated.

Just as it was nearing bedtime, he did his usual infinite push-ups beside his bed in just his briefs. I peeked at him from under my blanket. The flashlights were all off. The only light was coming from the glow of the fire. I watched his dark silhouette as he moved briskly. Up and down.

Nixon was a devastatingly beautiful guy.

A monster with a face that could attract anyone.

I did have to tell myself that Roz too had been beautiful, and I had felt absolutely nothing for that monstrous man.

Beauty didn't influence my feelings.

So, what was it about Nixon then?

Why did he make my body thrum with unwanted feelings?

It felt primitive to allow your body to have so much control. It seemed like such a cop out, though, to blame my weakness on visceral needs. Because my thoughts weren't condemning me. I was not angry at what I had allowed to happen, or at how aroused I still was.

When he finished, he collapsed into the other bed. I held my breath as I watched him rest a hand under his head. His chest began slowing down as his heart rate returned to normal.

I slowly removed the blanket from my head, feeling like the darkness was a blanket of its own. Resting on my side, I watched him, trying to make out his face, wishing I knew what he was thinking.

He could have touched me when he went down on me.

He'd been bursting for it.

The guy didn't take it by force. It was simple as that. He wasn't like the others. It didn't redeem him, not at all. The idea of him still frightened me, but he wasn't totally emotionless, and he wasn't entirely without morals.

Monsters were supposed to be black and white. They were meant to commit evil deeds and have selfish motivations. Nixon wasn't fitting into the role, and it was impossible not to be curious about it.

As twisted as it was, a part of me hoped he'd come to me, and when he didn't, I felt hollow. My thighs squirmed against each other. Desperation crept in; the urges were too great to ignore.

I... began to shiver. I made my teeth chatter loud enough he could hear. I hiked the blanket up to my chin and shook. I even let out a few short breaths. I played it up, pretending to be so cold, I couldn't get warm.

In all fairness, the room wasn't the warmest it had been.

There *was* a chill, so he couldn't doubt it.

I just happened to exaggerate it. I turned over so my back was to him and scooted to the wall. I made myself into a cocoon and shivered. I heard the shuffling sounds from his bed. I wondered if he was watching me.

Then I heard more movements, and I held my breath.

I was asking for it.

I was being reckless.

I had a longing only he could fill.

Body trumped mind. What a dangerous game to play.

I shivered for barely a minute when the bed dipped with the weight of him. He slid under the covers and wrapped an arm around my middle, pulling me into his chest.

"You cold, baby?" he murmured into my hair. I nodded in response, teeth still chattering the same time I felt my heart quickening with excitement.

It startled me how good this felt, to be in Nixon's

arms and not feel any bit of fear. Arousal dominated my senses, made the lines blur worse than before.

I felt him pressed against my back, felt the hard ridge of his cock against my ass. It was...fuck, it was scrambling my brain.

My nude body squirmed against him. My butt pressed against his length. I was wet again and burning. I wanted that sweet release, wanted him to touch me again.

"Go away," I whispered weakly, cheeks burning.

I was so fucking bold.

I couldn't believe lust triumphed over shame.

When I felt his arm begin to loosen around me, I pressed my back against him. With quick breaths, I repeated, "Go away."

There was a moment of stillness in him.

Then his arm tightened back around me, and I felt another bolt of excitement at the pit of me. I felt his breaths against the back of my shoulder. Felt his mouth skirting along my skin. "Did you like me sucking your clit, Victoria?" he asked huskily. "Is that why I'm back here?"

My eyelids drooped at his words. My mouth parted; the breaths left me faster now as I whispered, "I didn't like it at all."

"Does your pussy feel the same way?" he questioned as he pressed light kisses along the back of my shoulder. "Or is it wet for me right now?"

Jesus.

I was so aroused; it was hard to focus. I blinked slowly, forcing out, "Not wet for *you*, Nixon."

"No?"

I shook my head. "No."

Suddenly, he pulled me up the bed. My heart caught in my throat as he sat up and settled me on his lap, my back pressed against his front. He threw the blankets off us and spread my legs apart on either side of him. Before I could turn to look at him, his hand shot up to my throat. He gripped it, keeping me still. A bolt of fear shot up my spine, stiffening me, until he leaned his head in, mouth pressed to my ear, whispering, "You tell me to stop playing, and I will, baby. That's all you have to say, anytime, however raw with need I am, however lost you are, you just say Stop. But if you don't, I won't hurt you. Trust me."

"Trust a killer?" I let out, my head dizzy with worry.

"Have I hurt you before now?" he replied, his tone gentle.

I felt tears cloud my vision. "No," I admitted.

"I saved you from the bad men, didn't I?"

"All but one."

He chuckled deep in his throat. "Fuck, you got some fight in you, you know that? You can be feisty with me, if you like. I know a little vixen when I see one."

I didn't respond. My chest was moving fast with warring emotions. His hand still gripped my throat. I was aware how we must have looked – me sitting on his lap, his cock hard beneath his briefs, my legs parted, vulnerable and open as ever. His other hand hadn't moved. He waited for me, waited for my lead.

And the seconds passed like this. With me realizing he wouldn't hurt me. The stiffness in me left as I slowly relaxed against him. He noticed it straightaway because his hand slid up my inner thighs...

slowly.

So painfully slow.

"I'm going to finger you," he told me, tightly. "You're going to grab at my arm and try to pull me away from your neck. You're going to plead for me to let you go, but I want your hips to grind against me. Got it, little vixen?"

I was so lost to the feel of his hand running up my thigh, so close to where I needed him to be. All my senses fixated on his touch; my body yearned for it.

"Yes," I panted. "I got it."

He blew out a harsh breath, like he was stunned by my response. "Fucking hell, baby."

NIXON...

Fucking hell.

Was this real?

She threw her hands to his arm, digging her nails into his skin, trying to remove his hand from her neck. He was taken aback by her strength at first. Little beauty was full of surprises. He almost thought to let go...but then his hand reached the tender flesh of her core and her hold on him lessened dramatically.

Her hips bucked up to meet his touch as a soft moan left her mouth. Just the sound of her in the throes of pleasure made Nixon delirious. He shut his eyes, feeling his pulse quicken as his fingers swirled around her slit.

She was drenched.

Wetter than when he took her in his mouth.

Victoria liked this fucked up game more than he'd

imagined. She completely let go of herself, moaning into the air, holding his arm instead of pulling it away. He tightened his grip around her throat and forced her face to his. She gasped in response, enjoying his dominance. He had to see her face. He had to look her in the eyes as he slid his middle finger into her.

Her eyes were glazed back, and her mouth parted when he slid his finger into her wet channel. Her pussy gripped him so tight, it made him tense with surprise.

"Why are you so tight?" he growled, nipping at her jaw. "Anyone ever done this to you, Victoria?"

She was too lost in pleasure to respond, but he felt he knew the answer already.

She was so stunned by the sensations, so utterly sensitive to his every touch, it was obvious why that was.

And it made him angry.

Angry that those fucks might have taken her.

Taken what was his.

She *was* his.

He believed it in his bones because he looked at her and wanted to taste every inch of her soul. He wanted to devour her, claim her, bury his teeth into her skin and leave marks all over her. It was so fucking animalistic the things he wanted to do to this little body.

He watched her writhe in his lap, bucking at every touch, moaning incoherently, and he was awestruck by her beauty. She could pretend she didn't like it with her words, but her body spun a different truth.

He could get used to this game.

He might never tire of the challenge to prove her

words wrong.

But he needed his cock inside her. He needed to feel her pulse around him. Needed it so badly, he was shaking with unrestrained need.

"I like this, Victoria," he grunted into her ear. "I like you writhing in my arms. You're perfect, you know that?"

Her cheeks flushed from his words. He saw a tear escape her eye and as it fell, he lapped it up with his tongue, ridding it from view.

He didn't like to see her cry, but she looked beautiful with glistening eyes. He felt her body tighten, knew the signs of coming release. His hold on her neck tightened and it drove her over the edge. She came hard with his finger inside her pussy, with his thumb circling her clit, with his name whispered in his ear.

And he shut his eyes, savouring every second of it.

39.

VICTORIA...

I was still shaking as I came down from my orgasm, but the throb between my legs hadn't dulled. I turned my head to Nixon and ran my lips along his neck. I felt him tensing beneath me. His hand still gripped my neck and it tightened, as if to admonish me.

"Nixon," I whispered, wantonly. I was writhing in his lap, desperate to quench the need in me.

His chest rose and fell rapidly now. "Be cautious, Victoria," he warned.

But we were past the point of caution. I'd tasted nothing but blood and danger; it was in this room, tainting my senses. "I think we're beyond that."

"No," he snapped, sounding feral. "We'll be beyond that the second I have you beneath me. There'll be no going back, you understand?"

I nodded stiffly, but he remained unmoving. "I gotta hear you say it," he urged tightly.

"I understand."

He inhaled sharply. I could feel how tight his body was beneath me. "Give me your mouth, kitten."

I looked up at him just as he dropped his head down to me. He brushed his full lips against mine; it felt intimate, soft. His other arm went around my waist, tightening around me like a belt as his other hand dropped from my neck and ventured to my breasts. He cupped my breast possessively as he added more pressure to the kiss. It was such a heady feeling, I parted my lips, giving him complete access to my mouth. His tongue clashed with mine, and he let out a soft, approving groan; that sound went straight to the apex of my core, and I writhed again, unable to resist.

"Now, I know you've done *that* before," he murmured, pulling away to catch our breaths. He trembled around me, unreserved and open. "Do you feel your heart about to burst, baby?"

My cheeks warmed, but I responded, "No, I don't."

"Are you sure?" he asked, amused. "Because I can feel it against my hand here."

"I think you're mistaken."

"And I think you're lying."

There was such a fucking rush in this, I couldn't explain it. "Prove it, Nixon."

In a blink of an eye, he had me flat on the bed beneath him. He was over me, propped on his elbows on either side of me. He had the most wicked grin on his face as he peered down at me. "I'll prove it when you scream my name," he told me. "You'll be clawing my back, arching into me, begging my dick to split you in half."

"That's quite a demand," I whispered, trying to keep my voice even. "Anything else you have planned?"

"For now, only this," he said, pressing a hand to my chest. "And because I'm being such a kind man, I'll fuck you missionary just this once because you're a sweet little virgin who deserves a gentleman's touch for your first time. What do you say, little vixen?"

My pulse quickened, and I knew he felt it against his hand. I let out a long breath, shaking beneath him. "What makes you think I need a gentleman right now?"

"Oh?" He swiped his tongue along the seam of my lips. "You want a brute's touch, Victoria? That's so fucking hot."

His hand slid down my body, leaving tingles behind. When he reached my sex, he slid his finger between my folds and rimmed my opening, watching me intently as I bucked beneath him. "Does it make your pussy gush to have a bad man touch you, Victoria?"

"Yes," I admitted, panting, "it does."

He slipped a finger inside me, making me gasp. "So fucking tight. Jesus." His forehead dropped to mine as he shut his eyes, looking awed. "You're soaked, baby. You really do want this ugly all over you."

If he didn't stop talking, I was going to come just from listening to his words. I could barely keep my eyes open. I moaned as he slid his finger in and out of me. Like before, he didn't push into me far, but every time he retreated, he'd swirl his fingers around my clit, working me slowly, always applying the right pressure. His expertise at this hadn't gone unnoticed. This man knew how to please.

And I knew...nothing.

Pulling away, he slid his briefs off him. His hands

gripped my legs and he spread them apart, bending between them to deliver a thorough stroke of his tongue along my core. He ran it up my slit and sucked at my clit. I groaned, my back arching as my hands flew to his head.

He kissed up my body, taking a hardened nipple into his mouth, sucking fiercely before he trailed up further, taking my mouth against his. The kiss was sloppy now, he was busy spreading my legs apart. I felt his length along my pussy, felt his head nudge my entrance. Then he pulled back to look at himself slowly pushing in. My hands grabbed at his arms, my nails dug into his skin. I blinked back tears, the nerves flaying me open.

"You're scared again," he murmured, looking at me now, his eyes studying me. "Is it sinking in what you're allowing to happen? Does it frighten you to be fucked by the likes of me?"

"It frightens me you have complete control of my fate," I answered, honestly, as tears fell.

"Is that why you're crying?"

"I'm crying because I'm giving you this."

He wiped my fallen tears. "And I'm not deserving of it."

"This is all I have to give," I cried, shaking beneath him. "I have nothing else, Nixon."

His brow furrowed. "You say that like you want something in return."

The plea fled my mouth before I could stop myself. "Please don't kill me at the end of this. Please, don't. I'm not ready to go, Nixon. I'm not ready to see my mother."

He stilled over me; his astonishment was palpable. He appeared in disbelief. He slowly shook his head, letting out a puff of air as he spoke. "I don't want to kill you, baby. I want to *keep* you. Don't you understand? I fought for you. I killed for you. All so I can have you." His eyes hardened now as he grabbed a fistful of my hair and dropped his mouth to mine, delivering a chaste kiss, gritting out, "And I *will* have you. You're right, I'm in full control, and I'm not trying to abuse that power. I just feel this is right. I feel it's necessary. We're here, two fucked up spirits, damned in this fucked up wasteland, and I can't bear it anymore. I can't do it alone, and neither can you. We're doing it together, little vixen. Starting now."

I absorbed his words slowly. It would be many nights before I understood the full extent of what he said. To learn the full weight of what he meant to do with me.

In that moment, though, I felt overwhelmed with relief. I sobbed beneath him, gasping for air, feeling grateful that my time wasn't going to come to a violent end.

"Spread for me," he demanded as my breaths calmed. "You can tell me no, but you're going to fuck me with your little hands running down my back. You understand?"

I hadn't realized I'd tensed and brought them back together again. I nodded as I spread my legs apart for him. He settled between me again, his cock pushing into my entrance.

"Like a gentleman," he asked, tightly, "or like a brute, baby? Tell me now."

My heart hammered in my chest. I shut my eyes, bracing myself. "Like a brute, Nixon."

I couldn't bear to be taken gently. It was too unnatural after what transpired in this cabin the last few days. It would have felt fake. And what I had with Nixon, I knew straightaway, was a vicious push and pull. It would not be fitting for us to act like lovers in a passionate tryst.

It was more than that.

Or worse, depending on how you looked at it.

It was savageness. I needed to hide behind a false façade.

To confront the truth would be traumatizing.

I needed this shell. For my sanity.

To hold onto my former self, I had to pretend.

I ran my hands down his back, clawing into his flesh as he pushed into me one inch at a time.

He growled, "You're mine," as he tore through my virginity the same time he touched my soul.

NIXON...

She stopped breathing as he pushed into her.

She was so tight, he had to let out a few breaths to restrain himself from pushing in all the way and just taking her the way he was desperate to.

Victoria felt good.

Unnaturally good.

He felt like she was gripping his cock with the same tightness she'd gripped his soul. It was a punishing pressure. He felt twisted with pleasure, but also tense with fear.

What was he doing opening himself up to her like this?

Giving her the control until he was her captive and she was his captor.

He was giving her the power to destroy him.

In the moment, he did not mind.

He kissed her hungrily, tasting her mouth as she dug her fingernails into his back and dragged them, clawing him. The pain stole his breath; his blood touched the air, cool and stinging.

He wanted to do the same. He wanted to sink himself into her, hold her down so she could not move and brand her with his teeth sinking into her skin.

And that's what he did.

He fucked her, like a brute, like she asked for. She cried from the pain of it, then she cried from pleasure, and then she gripped him, nails dug in his flesh like an anchor as he dropped his mouth to her neck and sucked fiercely, scraping at her skin with his teeth until she tensed and cried out some more.

There was no enjoyment.

This was brutal marking.

This was animalistic fucking.

He was showing her he possessed her.

He showed it by pinning her down and taking what he wanted, spearing his cock in and out of her with long slow thrusts.

She took the full brunt of his force. He stole her cries with his mouth, he lapped at her skin like she was water and he was dying of thirst.

But it was not all *take, take, take.*

He thrust deep and found a spot that contradicted her no's. He asked her gruffly, "Does this spot make your head spin, little vixen?"

She shook her head no, but then gasped as he

found it, time and time again.

But it wasn't enough. It didn't send him over the edge just yet. He needed to see the lost look in her eye.

He demanded it, seething, "Look at me, baby."

And she did.

He looked her in the eyes and watched the tears slide down her face. He saw the fight in their depths. Saw the glowering and the need. Oh, the fucking need. She gave him what she'd given no other. She'd accepted her fate, locked in his arms.

Used.

Abused.

Devoured.

And she couldn't hold back the way that made her feel.

She quaked around his cock, coming hard. He felt her muscles pulsating, and it pushed him over the edge.

He came hard, shocked at the burst of pleasure, at the serenity he felt.

And when that wasn't enough, he dazedly watched his come leave her cunt, and he adamantly used his fingers to draw them back into her again.

*

He had lost, he had mourned, and he had been no closer to figuring out his purpose in this world. He'd had no spiritual awakening, nor a moment of clarity.

Even now, possessing the girl, keeping her for himself, there would be no salvation waiting for him on the other side of this.

Nixon wasn't looking for deliverance.

What surprised him the most about his fixation

with Victoria was that she was intending to bring out the beast in him. She wanted to see him in all his roughness. There wouldn't be sonnets written to honour their relationship; the world liked it better when the woman softened the man, when she tamed the animal from within him and changed him for the better.

That wasn't on the table here.

It. Wasn't. That. Kind. Of. Story.

Their reality wasn't going to offer that kind of happily ever after. Nor would it ever.

It was going to always be this: her writhing beneath him, glaring into his eyes while he undid her, while he pulled her apart.

While he proved her wrong.

He'd fucked her three times tonight. He couldn't seem to stop himself, and her appetite never wavered.

He filled her with his seed, and what hardened his cock the most was how wild her body bent to him while she cried for him to stop.

It was so utterly fucked up.

If she hadn't been digging her fingers into his ass, forcing him into her as deep as he could go, he might have resisted. It was an abnormality he hadn't learned to accept in its entirety. To fuck a girl who found it weak to give verbal consent. To fuck a girl who begged instead with her needy hands and poisonous words.

He fucking *loved* the shit she spewed.

"You like my cock inside you?" he'd asked.

"Any cock will do," she'd answered.

"You're going to scream my name, baby," he'd promised.

"No, I won't," she'd argued.

"You're mine, little vixen."

"I'm nobody's, Nixon."

He'd never felt so alive.

She was insatiable in her lust for him, and when he took her, she fell into this visceral state. She wanted to be conquered; she thrived for it.

And when she lay spent, head buried in the pillow, what they'd done dawned in her pretty brown eyes and she'd hide herself under the blanket. Shame turned her cheeks crimson, and when he neared her, she shrivelled away, reminded of her fear of him.

This was going to end in madness. The voice inside him whispered. This can't go on forever.

But he intended for it to.

When Hobbs returned, when they fled this little cabin, he was going to take Victoria with him.

He'd found a treasure that overshadowed all his previous triumphs.

She would become his greatest victory.

40.

VICTORIA...

I woke up the next day and found him seated at the table, just his briefs on, his hair a tantalizing mess. He was carving something out of a small piece of wood. He was already looking at me when I sat up, but the gaze was fleeting before he returned his focus to the wood.

"What are you making?" I asked him, sleepily.

"Chess pieces," he answered, glancing at me again. Every time his eyes landed on me, my chest stirred something awful. The blues of his eyes were so bewitching. I had to look away to escape the heat of it.

"I'm not good at Chess." I sounded shy. It couldn't be helped. I didn't know how to behave after last night. Every inch of me ached. I was aware I was covered in bruises, in red teeth marks, in his come. The smell of us hung pungent in the air.

"Neither am I." He sounded amused. "It'll be fair play. Unless..."

As his words trailed, I looked at him curiously. "Unless what?"

He watched me, never wavering. "Unless you can

think of a better game."

Heat rushed to my cheeks. Without thinking, I brought my hand to my neck, remembering last night. He caught the movement, and his eyes blazed. "You want to be corrupted today, Victoria?" There was a dangerous edge in his tone. He studied me, waiting for my response.

Suppressing my eagerness, I shot him a weak smile. "I'm just *really* bad at Chess is all."

His expression broke. He let out a surprised laugh and tossed the chess piece down on the table. "A day of depravity it is."

As I made to move off the bed, I grimaced and stilled. There was a sharp pain between my legs. Nixon watched me, catching my discomfort. "Stay still. I'll run you a bath. You'll feel better in the water."

He got up and cleaned the tub before filling it back up with hot water. Steam rose from the tub when he picked me up from the bed and settled me into it. The water felt cathartic on my tender flesh. I shut my eyes, savouring it.

"Is that better, Victoria?" he asked in a low voice. I opened my eyes and looked at him. He was kneeling down at my level, his face close to mine. He cupped handfuls of water and poured them over my breasts, looking captivated by me. I'd never seen someone stare at me with the depth he did, with such extreme need for me echoing from his gaze.

"Yes," I answered quietly.

"I like that you're in pain," he admitted, trailing his wet finger up my throat. "I like that I put it there, and that you begged for it." His finger trailed along my bottom lip, and he stared at it, his eyes growing more distant as he added, "I like that you gave me your body and no one else got to watch you twist beneath them. Those looks are mine now. They belong to me. I can only hope I'm not too tarnished for you. That...maybe you can hold me in the same regard. That you may want me as badly as I want you..." His words faded as he tried to read my expression, searching for...

For what?

I was hardly breathing.

In that moment, I was still tired, my brain still scrambled and stretched apart.

He was asking for assurance and I'd completely missed the point.

I'd missed it and wouldn't know it until...until I looked back on it two years later in the back of a car, bound and frightened.

My poor Nixon. I misunderstood you.

When he saw the empty look on my face, he gave me a sad smile and pulled away, as if he couldn't bear to be vulnerable in front of me. He stood up and walked to the kitchen, his back to me, his strides slow.

As I washed myself, he made food and tea. He fed me while I sat in the tub, soaking. He'd even heated more water up for me when the water I was in began to cool. By the time I stepped out, I'd been fed and cleaned and the soreness between my legs had weaned.

I ran a damp hand down his bare back as he prepared a bath of his own. He turned to me and delivered a rough kiss against my mouth, robbing me of my breath. "Let me wash myself," he said, biting at my lower lip. "Then I want your mouth on me."

I glanced down at his hard cock and my legs quaked.

Weighed down with anticipation, I sat on my bed as he washed himself, taking his sweet old time, dunking his head into the water and emerging out of it like a fucking model. I couldn't look away if I tried.

When he finished, he didn't bother to towel himself off. He simply came to me, sopping wet, hard cock pointed into the air. I held my breath, watching the water run down his muscled torso as he came to a stop before me. I'd been sitting on the edge of the bed, blanket wrapped around me, nervously wondering how he was going to do this.

I should have known by now Nixon was simply unpredictable. He wanted, he took, and he wasn't going to wait until I was comfortable with his cock so close to my face.

He ran a finger down the side of my face, looking down at me with heavy eyes. Then he suddenly gripped a handful of my hair at the top of my head and gritted out, "Suck me, vix."

Vixen.

He kept calling me that.

I was pretty sure I preferred it to baby, but sometimes *baby* was all I wanted to hear coming out of his plump, biteable lips. He seemed to know when to use the terms. I wondered how obvious my expressions were.

He gripped his cock and rubbed the head of it against my lips. I opened my mouth and let him in.

The sharp exhale blowing out of his mouth made me salivate. I sucked him, running my tongue along his shaft, and he cursed under his breath along the way, telling me what he liked.

Tease me.

Lick around my tip.

Take me in all the way. I want to feel the back of your throat. I want to hear you gagging, baby.

He gripped the blanket and made it fall from my body. He pinched my nipples, before gripping each in that possessive way that made my eyes roll to the back of my head. He pulled his cock out of his mouth at random times to smack against my face. I was so wet by the time he pulled back entirely and grabbed at my hips. He turned me around, knees on the edge of the bed and spread my legs apart. He buried his mouth between my ass, running his tongue up the line. I buried my face into the sheets, closing my eyes as he tongue fucked me.

When I couldn't take it anymore, when I was writhing for his cock, he stood back up and slid into me suddenly, burying himself to the hilt. I gasped into the sheets, surprised by how different it felt to be fucked in this position.

"You're already about to come. Do you like when I fuck you from behind?" he asked me, his voice tight with need.

"No," I groaned, weakly. "I hate it, Nixon, you should stop."

His chest rumbled with laughter. When he pulled out of me completely, I felt my entire body deflate. Okay, I didn't actually want that to happen. He was supposed to know that, though, it was part of this fucked up game –

SLAP!

I jumped and yelped, shocked by the smack he'd delivered against my ass. It felt like fire. My fingers gripped the sheets as I seethed, "What the fuck, Nixon?"

He rubbed the cheek he'd smacked as he shoved his dick into me again. He groaned at the easy access. My pussy literally opened for the bastard, welcoming him in.

"You liked that," he breathed, delighted. "You are full of surprises, Victoria. We are going to have a lot of fun, I think."

He gripped my hips then and fucked me hard and fast. He didn't stop to consider I was still aching. He didn't ask if I was hurt. He didn't wonder if I was even enjoying it. He fucked me like he was taking me for his own enjoyment, for his own pleasure, and I came so hard at that, pulsing around his cock over and over again.

He came inside me, groaning through his orgasm, uttering my name. When he pulled out, he flipped me on my back and told me to push his come out of me. I did. He stared at my pussy, his mouth parted, his breaths heavy. His fingers brushed along my tender hole, a look of fascination on his face as he smeared his come all over my folds before pushing it back inside me.

I buried my face into my hands, overwhelmed with emotion.

"Why are you crying?" he asked, soothingly.

"Because I throb," I said in horror. "I don't know why my body is acting this way."

"You want more."

"I shouldn't."

"You feel betrayed."

I nodded, wiping my tears, but they wouldn't stop falling. "I do."

"I'm so loathsome, you feel disgusted for liking my touch." It was stated so calmly, like it was fact and he was just acknowledging it.

I tensed. "I don't know if it's that."

"What else could it be? You lived your whole life being told what's right and what's wrong. Here I am, a murderer, fucking you, my captive, in this hellhole cabin in a place no one will ever find, and you...you pine for it. Your pussy gushes for me. You bend to me like you've always belonged right here, beneath me."

He was right, and I couldn't bear it.

He wrapped his arm around me then and picked my languid body off the bed. He sat down on the edge and settled me into his lap. I cried in his arms as he shushed me gently, making my chest swell with indescribable emotion.

I asked him through sobs, "How am I supposed to put this behind me? How am I supposed to live knowing we did this? Everything is different. The world doesn't feel the same anymore, Nixon."

"Shh, it's okay," he responded every time I let out a string of emotional words. "You're alright, baby."

He stroked me, kissed my forehead and rode out my sadness.

I remembered feeling like...I wasn't so alone anymore.

*

As Nixon began to drain the tub and clean up, I sat on his bed, looking out the window, at the falling snow. I could tell from the swaying branches of the tall trees that the wind was still abhorrent, but the snow itself wasn't blizzard-like.

I didn't bother covering myself with the blanket. There was no such thing as modesty anymore. Nixon had seen every inch of me, tasted places I didn't even know existed.

He'd rode out my breakdown and then I shamelessly wanted more.

He'd delivered. Fucking me to oblivion until there was nothing left of me.

I was burst open, soul scattered in all directions... utterly lost to the cosmos.

And now my mind was quiet, and I was grateful for the silence.

I felt sticky between my legs. He came hard every time. I had to thank God I'd taken my birth control shot last month, because his explosions? They were hitting the bullseye every time.

I glanced at Nixon from over my shoulder, catching the red marks I'd given him today. He looked less bulky than he did just yesterday. I was aware he wasn't consuming as many calories. There couldn't have been much nutrition in the basic camping meals he'd been supplied with, and there was only so much of that crap you could eat without feeling bored to death by the repetitiveness of it.

"I could go for a burger right now," I said longingly.

"We'll get a burger when this is all over," he replied, sounding amused. "What else, baby?"

"I'm craving Cajun fries."

"And for dessert?"

I hummed in thought. "Chocolate. Any kind of chocolate. Big blocks of that cheap Belgium crap you get from Walmart, even."

"I'll get you all the chocolate in the world."

My heart ballooned as I smiled at him. He was in the kitchenette, stuffing the garbage pouches in the box he'd used as a bin. Fucking suited him. It relaxed the stress lines around his eyes and forehead. Made him look youthful.

"How old are you?" I asked him, curiously.

"Thirty-two."

"Is Nixon your real name?"

"No."

"What's your real name?"

He stood up straight and shot me a playful look. "I'd tell you, but then I'd have to kill you."

My laugh was forced. That joke was not cool. "Too soon, Nixon."

"I let my old life go, vixen. Who I was is gone now, erased from the books. I'd have to go back to that life completely if I ever went back."

"You let go of who you were to be part of some underground mafia?"

He smirked now. "I'm not mafia, but that's cute."

"What are you, then? You're part of a gang, right?"

"No. I'm not chained to any side. I'm an opportunist. I take jobs. When a contract is up for dibs, depending how good it is, I take it through my employer."

"Through Hobbs?"

"You're attentive."

"The mortality rate must be very high," I dryly said, hinting at the bloodbath I'd survived.

He laughed and settled his elbows on the counter, facing me. "That's why you have to be good at what you do."

"You're good at killing."

"Among many things."

"You scare me."

"I know."

My smile was faint as I wrung my hands together. "It's surreal being here. My life was so ordinary. People like you existed in the news, removed from me, from my world."

He looked solemn. "You weren't supposed to be dragged into this mess."

"Don't you miss normal life?" I wondered, studying him. "Having to do this all the time, living under a false identity, it sounds... exhausting."

He nodded slowly, the light faded from his eyes. "You have no idea."

I'd stifled the urge to ask him this next question because I was unsure of his reaction, but now I couldn't help myself. I'd never been good at shutting up or picking the right moments. Mom called me a steamroller. She said mystery was never my forte. I couldn't mask my curiosity, even if it killed me.

"Who's Leona?" My question was sudden and out of nowhere, and his eyes flickered to mine briskly. It was the only noticeable reaction I got from him.

With a soft expression, he said quietly, "My twin."

My lips turned down with sympathy. I didn't expect that response. I could hardly keep my eyes on him when I whispered, "What happened to her?"

He swallowed hard, keeping a straight face. "She was sick. She'd been sick her whole life."

"Like cancer?"

"No," he said gruffly. "Cystic Fibrosis. She'd fought it to the end. She didn't tell me she'd worsened...She'd had a lung transplant less than a year ago, I thought...I thought she was okay."

"When did she pass?"

He turned his back to me and grabbed at his sweater. He threw it on, answering numbly, "I buried her three days before I took this job."

I was about to tell him I was sorry for his loss, but he said something about needing to go outside.

I knew he was looking for an excuse to flee.

I'd triggered him.

The second he'd thrown his boots on and exited the room, I buried my face in my hands, damning myself.

It's not my fault. I tried to reason with myself. *How was I supposed to know that happened to him?*

But I'd known he lost someone dear. Even Roz and Tucker – two fucked up psychos – had offered their condolences.

I'd pried and I shouldn't have.

His loss was so fresh. You wouldn't have thought it by how composed he was. It made me realize Nixon wasn't all that he appeared. He hid himself, buried the emotions deep, and yet when he was with me, I felt a spark in him.

Wrapping the blanket tightly around me, I got off the bed and slipped into the gumboots beside the door. I yanked the door open and trudged out into windy hell. I stomped through feet of snow, circling the cabin, searching for him.

I was already numb and shaking when I found

Nixon on the ground, his back against the cabin wall, staring fixedly ahead. He wore a vacant expression, but his face was red and wet from the cold.

"Nixon," I called out to him, standing over him. The wind howled viciously around us, swallowing up my sounds. "Nixon, get up!"

He looked up at me and frowned. "Get inside the cabin, Victoria," he demanded.

I shook, hair whipping around my face and said contritely, "I'm sorry about Leona. I'm sorry I pried."

He chuckled incredulously. "You should never pity a man like me, baby."

"I'm not pitying you. I'm...sad for your loss."

"It doesn't matter." He shrugged his shoulders, looking bitter now. "She died alone, Victoria. She could have wanted me there, and she didn't. She hated me by the end." What he said next was muffled by the wind, but I caught the movement of his lips. *You will too.*

I knelt to his level, already drenched in snow. I rested my hand along his cold cheek and said, "I wasn't there for my mother. I treated her like crap for a few years. I was a teen with her head in the clouds, always dreaming of leaving, and I pushed her away. I blamed her for everything. She'd discipline me and I'd rebel, and we would always butt heads. I thought I knew everything. I thought...no matter where I'd be, I could always return to her. I abused her unconditional love, Nixon." I swallowed hard, fighting back tears. "I understand regret. It takes a toll on you. It makes you grieve for the time wasted rather than the future that was robbed from them. Because, when you face death, you look inwards and accept that your time here is limited, and they did that. My mom and your sister, they already accepted what was going to happen to them. We didn't, did we?" Leaning closer to him, I whispered, "I don't think a sister could ever loathe her brother to her core. He'd have to have done irreparable damage, and I get the impression you're just self-punishing, that...you took this job to avoid confronting her death, that...it's easier for you to believe she didn't want you there at the end. I think...on a deeper level, you know that's not true."

He watched me, his eyes red, his lips parted. His chest rose and fell rapidly as thoughts blazed behind his eyes. "Where did you come from?" he whispered finally, sounding confused. "It's like you fell from heaven and into my lap."

"I told you already," I said, smiling sheepishly. "The bus driver drove on by."

He didn't respond. He just stared at me like I might disappear any second.

And then I saw something else in him.

Something that I'd spend too long recalling and picking apart.

In that moment, a fleeting look of fear crossed his face. It made my body tense because I suspected I knew what he was afraid of.

Nixon, in all his abhorrence, in all his greed, in all his raw pain and mourning and self-punishing, looked at me like I was *his*.

I felt grief for my former life. I felt sadness and horror and a pain I couldn't describe.

At the same time, I felt...relief. I wouldn't have to return to that gruelling life and pretend.

In some ways, I chose to be a captive.

I had relinquished control far too quickly.

I had given in to Nixon within days.

I'd known all along, didn't I?

I cried in the backseat of the car, because I understood the truth I'd fought so hard to ignore.

I belonged to him.

In some ways, I was also the captor.

Because over time, his desperate need for me gave me power.

Power to defy and fight back.

Power to make him battle me, to prove me wrong, to view me as a challenge he had to conquer because he needed to know he was getting to me.

He needed to see me pine for him, and when I didn't – when the power control flipped, when I fought back and spewed venom – he grew more desperate to tame me.

In the end, all he wanted was for me to want him back unequivocally.

My poor Nixon.

I'm sorry I chose to forget.

*

When we returned to the cabin, Nixon had been quiet that evening. He'd stared out the window every so often, his eyes scanning the clearing sky.

I fed the fire for him and we ate at the table, with me turning over the Queen piece he'd been carving out. He'd done a phenomenal job of it.

"Tell me about your life," he said suddenly.

I wasn't aware he'd been watching me this entire

time. Taking slow bites, I said, "There's really not much to tell."

"What were you studying to become?"

"I was going to be a teacher, like Mom." I shrugged. "Seemed like a way I could be close to her."

His smile was warm. "And how was your social life? Did you go out a lot?"

"Not really. I didn't have the money to live it up." With another shrug, I added, "I deleted all my social media right before you guys took me. Funny that."

"Why did you do that?"

"Because I felt like my mother wanted me to be more present with the world happening around me. Who knows, if I'd been buried in my phone, I might have been too distracted to want to document the explosion rather than run toward it like a fucking idiot that I am."

His expression was serious. "Maybe life put you right where you needed to be."

"In the arms of a psycho who dragged me into the back of a van?"

"Into my arms."

I didn't respond. I watched him as he seared me with that soul devouring look. Then he pulled away and got up, cleaning up the table, giving me distance to calm my heart down.

I didn't know until a long time afterwards that Nixon was mining out information from me. That he was getting a better idea of who I was so he could disappear me.

He wouldn't have needed to do much work.

I'd done a good enough job living a lonely life that no one would have noticed me gone.

NIXON...

He spent most of the night seated on the edge of the bed, watching Victoria sleep, naked, red and bruised and fucking beautiful.

She'd entered his life and in such a short amount of time he couldn't remember what it felt like to be without her in it.

He wound up pacing, muttering under his breath, speaking to Leona, asking her what to do.

"Should I let her go?"

He might be able to cover her up. The men were dead, after all, but he didn't know if there had been witnesses to see her being dragged into the car.

If so, he couldn't let her go.

And suddenly he wished the whole world was after her, because that would give him no choice in the matter.

"I don't want to let her go," he said to Leona. "I want to keep her."

Could he do it?

He kept telling himself she was his, but could he physically take the girl for himself and live with it?

It didn't take more than a few seconds to answer that question.

Yes.

Yes, he could do it.

Leona wouldn't have been happy, but Leona should have loved a little before she went. She should have opened her heart up. If she did, she'd learn that one in love was capable of crossing endless boundaries.

He stopped to look down at Victoria, whispering, "Don't hate me for what I'm about to do."

But he already knew what Leona would say.

You'll hate yourself.

He slid into bed and kissed Victoria awake. She was languid and receptive. She was also not her usual defiant self. He made her look him in the eyes as he fucked her, slowly, thoroughly.

She didn't glare.

She didn't fight it.

She held him to her, kissing him everywhere. Mouth and tongue and greedy grips.

When they came, they stared at each other, panting, and spent and it was just perfect.

He sensed her struggle, but he also saw the way her eyes lit up when he leaned in to kiss her, to caress her, to feel the skin he'd marked.

The feelings, they were there inside her, and he would unbury them. He would drag them to the surface, until she was so entwined in him she could never distinguish herself from him.

Nixon was bound to her. He would never be released from these chains, nor did he think he might ever want to be.

He only pleaded he was not alone in this.

41.

NIXON...

Nixon awoke to the sound of heavy pounding on the cabin door. He didn't move straight-away. Victoria was dead asleep in his arms, so used to the loud sounds of howling wind, that this was nothing to her.

He'd known it was time. He'd seen the weather change. The wind had long ended, the blizzard had tapered off, and the sun had been out plenty.

It was time to face the inevitable, and that made him feel...*tired* to his bones. If it were up to him, he'd be locked in this cabin with her forever.

It was time to return to the real world.

Another round of knocks followed, more impa-tient than the last.

He slowly slipped his arm out from under her and covered her nude body with the blanket. Then he stood and slowly walked to the door. He slipped into his briefs and pants along the way. By the time he got to the door, he was decent. With a weary exhale, he opened the door.

Hobbs stood before him, wearing an over the top

ski jacket, beanie, gloves, boots, scarf and sunglasses.

"You look charming," Nixon said first, cracking a smile because this was just too fucking hilarious to ignore.

"Shut up," Hobbs snapped.

"You look like you're going to ski the mountain–"

"I'm not in the mood for giggling, Nixon." Hobbs' glare intensified. "Getting here was not easy. I am cold, I am tired, and this cabin is not what was advertised."

Nixon stepped out, forcing Hobbs to take a step back. He shut the door behind him, saying, "Let me guess, you scrolled through the dark web for this one."

"I bought it, is what I did," Hobbs retorted.

"It's archaic."

"I had to make sure you were all hidden."

"You won't admit you didn't give a fuck with this hovel."

"You're alive, aren't you? It did its job." Hobbs rolled his eyes, adding, "And don't tell me about what I didn't give a fuck about. Coming from the man that stood my driver up and wound up taking the fucking bus, instead."

Nixon chuckled, crossing his arms over his bare chest. "You wanted me to ride in a two hundred-thousand-dollar car to a shithole street. I think you wanted me shot before I even stepped out of the car."

Hobbs tightened the scarf around his neck as a gust of wind slammed into him. "I would never want my best man shot. I needed you on this one. You've seen the guys I pitted you with. I was not impressed, but time was not on my side. The loot had been dropped off at the location, bound to be transported by the next delivery van. These bikers act fast. I felt sick with stress, had the shakes and everything. Wound up in the toilet for hours before you fucks struck, and what a mess you left behind." Hobbs' face twisted in disdain. "Which one of the fucks shot the civilian? Was it Beckett? Why do I have a feeling it was Beckett?"

"It was Beckett," Nixon confirmed.

"Of course it was," he snarled. "What a fuck-up. The bikers are still a mess, all insulted and shit, tearing through the city, not a clue under their nose. They've made contact with Toby. I think that fat fuck may be on to us."

"So, it made it into the news?"

"It did, but it was quickly buried under the shooting that happened two hours later downtown. Bikers lost their shit, pointed their finger elsewhere. It's been a fucking bloodbath."

Nixon resisted smirking. "How are you holding up?"

"I'm not." Hobbs frowned. "I'm queasy, Nixon. I think we hit the wrong fucks on this job."

"They don't know it's us. Relax."

"How can you be sure?"

"This is the One Percent we're talking about here. They have enemies everywhere. They'll think it's personal, and it wasn't."

"I'm concerned about Toby, is all. He's going to hear the details, know Roz had something to do with it straight off the fucking bat. That guy is so obsessed with playing games in the middle of robberies. I already heard through the grapevine he pretended to play hero with the girl at the front desk before he turned the gun on her."

"At least he didn't send a junkie in with a gun," Nixon gritted back.

"If he'd just fucking done what he was supposed to do, it would have been in and out, no casualties."

Nixon nodded, agreeing. "He never thought straight. He was impulsive."

Hobbs immediately stilled and shot Nixon a funny look. "Why'd you do that just now?"

"Do what?"

"You referred to Roz in the past tense."

"Your attention to detail is impressive, Hobbs."

"My attention to bullshit is even better."

Nixon ran a hand down his face, settling it under his chin as he looked back at Hobbs and shrugged. "There were complications along the way."

Hobbs flared his nose. "What sort of complications?"

"Not everyone in the crew made it out."

He raised the scarf up again as another chilly blast of air hit his rosy cheeks. He moved a few steps to the left, peering into the window just as Nixon stepped in front of him, blocking his view. Now Hobbs stood up straighter. "What the fuck is going on? That room looks empty to me."

"There's someone in there," Nixon explained vaguely.

"Some*one*." Hobbs sounded muffled behind the scarf. "Are you telling me only one other from the crew made it out, Nixon?"

Right on cue – at the worst possible moment – a figure appeared behind the window, peering out.

Nixon looked over his shoulder and felt his heart sink to the bottom of his chest. Victoria stood there, in just the blanket, her hair a fucking mess, staring back at him with wide eyes. The second they connected with Hobbs, she retreated quickly, disappearing back into the room.

Hobbs saw her.

He saw her and looked like he was about to have a heart attack.

"Are you fucking kidding me right now?" he growled, pulling down his scarf to reveal his chapped lips.

"They took her," Nixon argued, sharply. "I wanted nothing to do with it."

"Where are the others, Nixon?"

"You pitted me with rapists."

"Nixon, goddammit."

"They wanted *entertainment*."

"Get to the fucking point."

"I didn't let them have her."

Hobbs began pacing, trying to get on his tippy toes to look over Nixon's shoulder and through the window. "Are they *ALL* dead?" he bellowed out suddenly, glaring at him now. When Nixon didn't answer, he stopped and looked grave. "What have you done?"

"What I had to do," Nixon returned simply, no apology behind his gaze. "I need you on my side, Hobbs. Don't ask questions. Don't pry. Just understand that it had to be done. I had no choice."

Hobbs was fuming, but he stood quietly, swallowing his curses down. The only reason he wasn't losing his shit was because Nixon wasn't the kind of guy to fuck up. From the moment he recruited Nixon on his first job those years ago, he had never let him down. He had always acted professionally.

But what in the fuck *was* this?

Hobbs shook his head, trying to regain his composure but he was really pissed the fuck off. The last thing he needed was to deal with a missing persons poster circulating around town with these fucks spotted. "Where was she snatched?" he demanded now.

Nixon gave him a funny look. "Feet from where the man was shot."

Hobbs made a face. "She was behind the shop, right where it happened?"

"Are you telling me she didn't make the news?"

"No," he said icily, "she didn't make the fucking news."

"No witnesses."

"No witnesses with balls enough to talk," Hobbs corrected. "And speaking of balls, mine are going to fall the fuck off if I don't get inside that cabin in the next ten seconds."

Nixon turned to open the door but paused to shoot Hobbs a severe look, warning, "Don't touch her. Don't talk to her. She stays in the corner, and you don't even look at her if it bothers her."

Hobbs was so shocked by the sudden change in Nixon's demeanour, he was momentarily speechless. He had never seen Nixon behave this way. *Why the fuck* was he *behaving this way?* He forced a nod because honestly his balls needed to be out of the cold, and his ass cheeks were so numb he'd do anything to have a seat.

When the door opened, Nixon strode straight in

Victoria's direction. She was curled up on the bed, wrapped in a blanket, face hidden from view. He wrapped an arm around her tiny shoulders and buried his face into her, whispering something Hobbs couldn't hear.

Hobbs stepped into the cabin slowly, his eyes sweeping along the cabin room. It smelled like soap and fire and camp food and...sex. It smelled like sex a whole lot, actually.

He looked down at the floor, at the dried blood stains beneath his high-end hiking shoes that – *deep breath* – he got on special but that dug into the back of his fucking ankles because he wasn't a sporty guy and he fucking hated snow and pretty much everything.

Yeah, Hobbs hated everything.

He especially hated this fucked up surprise.

He was close to hating Nixon, too.

He took a seat on the chair around the cheapest looking wooden table he had ever seen. The photos showed a cosy room with high end furnishings. The table in the ad was "made locally from Douglas Fir and hand carved by a master carpenter with a deep love for rustic furnishings of the highest quality."

This table, before him now, looked like it was snatched from a junkie's shack in the armpits of downtown.

The beds were another sad affair. He eyed the wood; it was...he squinted his eyes...it was like cheap plywood and chipboard shit. Jesus Christ. He got ripped off. Oh, God, he got ripped off good. His cheeks burned. Oh, the shame. He felt like his pride got dick punched.

He would never admit this fuck up out loud.

He returned his attention to Nixon. He plopped down into the chair next to him, directly in front of his view of the girl. Hobbs caught the message loud and clear, but he wasn't about to drop the topic of her just because Nixon was behaving like a fucking weird ass motherfucker.

"Let me get this straight," Hobbs started because he needed to understand this shit-fuckery in its entirety and doing it out loud helped. "You guys robbed the gold at the pickup point, then you fled to the cargo van and shot an innocent man who was trying to play hero. Along the way, the girl was collected. From what I read, there was a shooting along McCleod road, no casualties, and the cars the bikers were in were abandoned. Your cargo van was spotted thirty minutes after the robbery up in flames. You fucks disappeared, and from that point until now, you've wound up murdering your whole crew because, let me get this shit straight, you disagreed with their form of *entertainment*."

"Yeah," Nixon said simply.

"Yeah?" Hobbs repeated with disdain.

"Did you spot the minivan on your drive up?"

"I spotted it under an avalanche of fucking snow."

"Beckett's body is in that van. About ten feet from the van is Mills' body."

"What about Tucker and Roz?"

"They're not far from the cabin," Nixon spoke slowly, looking Hobbs in the eyes. "I dragged them in the bush in case of predators. You may not find them."

"I may not find them?"

"There was a lot of howling that night."

Hobbs glared. "Fucking great."

"I can lead the clean-up crew to them."

"You say that like you're ordering an extra side for your fucking meal at a restaurant," Hobbs snapped. "It isn't that simple, Nixon. Covering up bodies isn't that fucking easy. I don't just tell the clean-up crew, 'hey guys, along with cleaning up the van and torching this cabin, I need you to also get rid of four fucking bodies from existence.'"

"I'll do it myself, then," Nixon retorted. "This is the fucking BC wilderness. People disappear in it every day."

"The only person you need to focus on disappearing is" – Hobbs pointed at the girl from over Nixon's shoulder – "her."

Nixon's eyes narrowed. "You just said she didn't make it in the news."

"Even if no one saw her being taken, she'll be filed under a missing person now."

"Let me take care of that."

"She's seen everything –"

"And she won't say a word."

"Fucking hell, Nixon, you don't know that –"

"I'll take care of it," Nixon hissed, leaning over the table so he was inches from Hobbs' face. He looked so feral, Hobbs had to lean back, disturbed by the expression he saw.

It was the first time ever Hobbs felt unsafe around him.

This was fucking Nixon we were talking about here.

The most composed man, and the hardest motherfucker Hobbs had ever seen.

Hobbs glanced over Nixon's shoulder and at the

girl who was buried under the covers. He wasn't sure how much she could hear – maybe all of it, maybe none. When he looked back at Nixon, he felt his stomach clench at the dangerous look Nixon was giving him. Just for staring at the girl, Hobbs was crossing the line.

This was more serious than he thought.

Hobbs let out a long sigh and straightened himself up on the chair. "Okay," he said in a whisper, nodding to himself. "I see what's happened. The man made of iron and ice has fallen in love." He tapped the table in thought now as Nixon studied him without saying a word. His silence was answer enough. It was true. "Okay," Hobbs repeated again, coming to terms with this fucking crazy development. "I'm not a touchy-feely guy, Nixon, but even I understand the power of love."

"You'll leave her alone," Nixon said, rigidly.

"I'll leave her alone," Hobbs confirmed. "But we don't know that she's safe with you. We don't know what the bikers saw during your gun fire. We don't know if there were witnesses. We don't know if she's ever going to talk about what's happened here. You need to be sure that she says not a fucking word. If anyone ever finds out she's seen all that she has, she will not live long. And with Toby on our backs, I don't know that you'll personally make it out unscathed."

"We can create a cover," Nixon said quickly. "I never worked with these guys all at once. They usually did their own jobs together."

"I fucked up," Hobbs returned, apologetically. "They *were* fiends with the women. I should have known you would not have mixed well with them. I didn't think they'd do something so fucking stupid."

"Which is why, if the bikers are sniffing around, they know I wasn't part of this. I'll tell my own crew to cover for me."

Hobbs gave him a dry look. "You think someone like Doll will keep quiet?"

"She answers to you. She will do anything for Hobbs, her saviour."

Hobbs' lips flickered because he knew that was true. "And you trust Tyrone and Rowan and Tiger?"

Nixon nodded. "They're practically family."

"And what am I in this family?"

Nixon didn't skip a beat. "You're my brother, Hobbs."

Hobbs went all emotional now. His eyes went red and raw. "You fucks are all I have left."

"I know."

"I never liked working with the others. They were dirty fuckers, but I was pressed for time."

"I understand."

"I would never have condoned rape."

Nixon nodded, saying swiftly, "I know, Hobbs. *I know*."

He looked back at the girl in the corner, catching her face now as she turned to look at him with interest. Hobbs smiled softly at her before fixing his stare back at Nixon. "She's pretty."

Nixon smirked. "She is."

"You're sick."

"Yeah."

"You know you should let her go."

"I can't do that."

"If there's no danger for her, if the bikers aren't on

our backs, you should really reconsider that."

Nixon didn't answer that. Instead, he leaned back in his chair, comfortable now. "I need to speak to Toby."

"What the fuck for?"

"I murdered Roz."

"You want the bounty? He'll know about what you've done. He'll make that connection fast."

"No," Nixon disagreed. "He loves his granddaughter, Hobbs. If I tell him he's dead, I'll buy into his good graces. I'll give him my share of the loot. We'll give him Roz's share as well."

Hobbs' face fell. "That's a lot of money you're letting go."

"I know."

"Then all this has been for nothing."

"That's not true."

The girl.

He got to have the girl in the end.

Hobbs wanted to warn him that the girl was too dangerous to have. She was a loose cannon. He didn't trust she'd ever accept captivity. *Who would?*

He knew, deep in his bones, it wasn't going to end well.

But Nixon was so blind with need for her, he didn't see it with clarity the way an outsider would. You can't remove a person from their life and expect them to never want to return to it. You can't make that decision for them.

Hobbs immediately sensed her fidgetiness. She was protecting herself, her own survival. She might not ever love Nixon in the same capacity he did and *would* over time.

This was utterly disastrous.

Hobbs felt crushed at the thought of Nixon broken and emptier than he already was from the passing of his sister.

Leona had been the last string tethering Nixon to the world, and in the last couple years, Nixon's string had frayed and then snapped at Leona's coldness. She'd left him with nothing, with no one, with zero affection to keep his heart from freezing.

She condemned his lifestyle, even though he'd become part of it to give her the best quality of life.

He'd do the same for the girl.

Hobbs knew he would give her everything, and it would never be enough.

He would sell his soul to make her happy. He would drain his sanity one bit at a time, yearning for what might never be his.

Ultimately, the captor would become the captive.

*

"I arranged a ride for you at ten in the morning," Hobbs said as he stepped out of the cabin, slipping into his waterproof, all-purpose gloves – the best 49.99 he ever did spend because fuck this weather and its bullshit. "You'll make your way down the mountain, and where the van is, that's your pick-up point. The van will be gone by tomorrow, though, so don't use it as a marker."

"I'll know," Nixon assured him, stepping out, still bare-chested like this weather did fucking nothing to him. *Fucking mutant.*

"Where will you go with her?" Hobbs asked, wrapping his scarf around his face.

Nixon thought for several moments, but Hobbs sensed he already knew; he'd thought about it already. "I want a seaplane ready."

He eyed him, understanding dawning. "You're going back to the island."

"Yeah."

"Smart."

"The hotel I'm in...it's up for sale."

Hobbs blinked a couple times. "You...you want to buy the hotel?"

"I want to buy the island."

More blinks. "You want to sink all that you've made – all that you've worked for – on this island?"

Nixon smiled at the aghast look on Hobbs' face. "I don't expect you to understand."

"I'm not going to try to. I think I've had enough surprises for one day."

"I need you to lend me some of your men."

"What the fuck for?"

"For protection, in case shit goes wrong."

"You want to make sure the girl doesn't run, is what you mean."

"That too."

"Fucking hell, fine, but you get your own men when you're on your fucking island, alright?"

Nixon chuckled as Hobbs began wading in the snow, cursing under his breath. This was a guy that never did outdoorsy shit. It was too fucking funny to stop watching.

"Think you should hit up a ski resort, Hobbs," Nixon called out to him.

"I'd rather die," Hobbs retorted over his shoulder.

"I'm going to Mexico, Nixon. I'm going to burn in the sun. Fuck this shit."

Nixon didn't feel the same way.

He loved this cold.

He loved the way it made him feel alive.

He didn't return inside until Hobbs had disappeared from view.

And when he did, he found Victoria on the floor, completely nude. She had her knees pressed to her chest; her wild hair was all around her. She was staring at the floor with a numb look on her face.

Nixon stopped before her, staring down at her with concern. "You alright, baby?"

She didn't respond for some time. He felt her throat moving. She was swallowing back emotion. Her lips trembled as she finally looked up at him, her eyes glassy. With a soft voice, she whispered her despair. "You're not going to let me go, are you?"

His chest expanded with his own emotion. "Is that what you want?" he asked flatly.

"I'd like to go back to my life, Nixon."

His lips thinned. "What life is that, Victoria?"

"*My* life."

"You would leave me?" He couldn't hide the note of betrayal in his tone. Was she really so keen to go?

"It isn't that..." she began to say.

"You would forget about me?" he continued, talking over her. "You would put us behind you?"

Why was he so surprised?

He was offering her...*him.*

Of course, it wouldn't be good enough.

What the fuck did a man capable of violence and bloodshed have to give to a woman like her? A woman who deserved warmth and security and love.

"Nixon–"

"I killed for you," he cut in, unable to restrain himself now. "I saved you from an evil fate. Don't I get to keep you?"

Tears fell from her eyes as she stared at him in disbelief. "You're better than that, Nixon."

He gave her a sad smile. "I'm really not, Victoria."

She stood up and began pacing, eyeing him cautiously as he spun around to face her. She wrung her hands together, thoughts blazing. Her chest rose and fell rapidly, her face cracked with fear, then anger. With a tearful expression, she demanded, "How long are you going to keep me here?"

Nixon watched her intently. "We're getting out tomorrow."

"Where are we going?"

"I've got an island."

She stopped dead in her tracks, looking at him horrified. "You're taking me to an island."

"Yes."

"For how long?" she pressed again, breathing harder.

"I don't know." He hadn't thought it through. He wasn't going to lie. "You'll be safe. I'll take care of you."

She shook her head, letting out a soft cry. "I have a life, Nixon," she repeated, her voice rising. "I have a fucking life!"

Nixon stood resolute, unflinching as she began to pace, trembling. "You had a shit life," he corrected, coolly. "You told me about it extensively."

She slapped her chest. "It's still *my* life."

"Well, I want you, Victoria."

"You want me," she said, tone filled with incredulity.

"I want you badly," he admitted fiercely.

"What happens when you take me to this island, lock me up and fuck me until you stop wanting me?" she asked, voice trembling now as she eyed him warily.

"That won't happen."

"You don't know that."

But he did. He knew it deep in his bones. If this was a challenge, he was gladly going to take it. "Allow me to prove you wrong."

"You'll kill me, won't you?"

"No."

"Yes, you will. I'm just a warm hole you slip into. I'm shiny and new –"

"That's not true," he said, hardly above a whisper.

She muttered under her breath as she resumed her pacing. She looked desolate. This wasn't going to be a smooth transition. Nixon knew that already. She wasn't going to fall into him as easily as he had fallen into her. As she sobbed in ruin, he felt his heart thud harder in his chest. She was so beautiful, so gentle and fierce all at once. For a brief moment, he thought of letting her go, and an unbearable agony wreaked havoc within him.

She was his.

She really was.

He looked at her and knew it, goddammit, even now as she paced, as she fought to come to terms with the revelation that she was not going back.

There was no going back.

The second Beckett dragged her into the van, her fate had been sealed.

Nixon hadn't wanted this for her. From the start, he tried to let her go, but it didn't happen, and here she was, and at the end of the day, Nixon was a victim to fate and the emotions fate – that cunt – inflicted on him.

It wasn't his fault.

It really wasn't.

He had no say in this. Didn't she know that? This was pure instinct. To let her go would be like fighting against nature, and in the end, nature always won.

"Let the past go," he told her. "Who you were, it's gone. Don't you feel it? You're not the same person. You told me so. You said, 'how am I supposed to live in this world knowing what we did?' Simple. You live in this world with *me*. Have me, little vixen."

But she wasn't listening.

She was lost in her grief.

She pled to be let go, and he refused.

She said the word please, and he said no.

When the tears dried, and the begging didn't work, she collapsed into bed and turned her back to him. Wrapped in a blanket, she numbly stared at the wall and said nothing for hours.

He paced around her, eyeing her, feeling lost. He tried to feed her, she ignored. He tried to sleep next to her, she went stiff.

He felt her loathing, and it tore at him.

But that's what she was, anyway.

A tear in his being.

She was sweet venom.

And there wasn't an inch of his soul her sweet

venom didn't claim.

He was not going to let her go. Her pouting would end. Her numbness would fade. She would bend to him eventually.

It just took time.

A year from now – maybe two – she'd understand.

As he lay next to her, he ran his fingers through her hair, whispering delicately, "Allow me to touch you."

"No," she rasped, her voice dead.

"I think you want my touch, vixen."

"I don't."

He ran his hand down her body, feeling her smooth flesh, already lost to the feel of her. "I think you'll be screaming my name before the sun comes up," he whispered, pressing kisses on her shoulder blade. "How many times do you think you'll be moaning it in my ear, baby?"

"Zero times," she bitterly retorted.

"This brooding isn't you," he murmured.

"I assure you it is."

He brought his hand between her legs, and she tensed beneath his touch, closing her legs tightly to keep him out. But it didn't work. He parted her thighs in less than a second and ran his fingers along her slit, smiling devilishly. She was slick and yearning. A soft whimper escaped her lips as he worked her clit. "There she is," he whispered, feeling his heart spike at the breathless sounds she was making.

He worked her slowly until she was arching her back, her legs falling open for him. He moved down the bed, yearning to taste her, to take her while her fingers dug into his scalp.

As he predicted, she bucked from his touch and

pulled at his hair. She cried out his name, while also crying out other words. Words he caught between heavy pants.

You won't have my soul.

My soul belongs to me.

*

The One Percent had descended into chaos, turning on themselves as Toby abandoned them in light of Roz's death.

As far as Toby was concerned, he had no idea who wiped them out.

And that...destroyed the unity of the bikers as they began to fight amongst themselves.

Keeping Victoria out of that nest was the wisest decision. Hobbs went from scolding Nixon for taking her to commending him for keeping her out of the fire. At that point, Hobbs didn't know if she'd talk. Her freedom might have her scrambling to the police – and among them, corrupted officers would have passed the knowledge along to the bikers.

Hobbs would have been found out. Both he and Nixon would have been hunted down.

If the girl was alive, she needed to be hidden.

If a threat emerged, she needed to be isolated, her freedom stricken even more than was granted until the threat was purged.

Hobbs wondered if death was better for the girl.

Her name was erased. She was known as Vixen now, the pet name Nixon loved to purr at her.

Over time, Hobbs would find her in the conference rooms and delight in her presence. She was sunshine. He'd catch the hidden smiles – the ones she'd only shoot when Nixon had his back to her. She wouldn't let him know she liked his touches, his stolen glances, his *forced* kisses.

At the same time, the war in her emerged.

One side, clutched to Nixon's side, dependant on his touches.

The other, longing for freedom.

In the end, Hobbs didn't know which of the two would prevail.

PART THREE: THE END

42.

VIXEN...

I remembered everything.

It hurt so badly to open up a scabby wound I'd chosen to bury and forget. Now I was bleeding everywhere. I felt the pain in every part of my body. The wound had never healed properly, but it'd been forgotten. I'd done so well looking ahead; now, looking back, it was like being transported to the past and being forced to re-live the trauma.

Surprisingly, though, I ended up sobbing for different reasons than I'd expected.

I'd demonized Nixon.

I'd made him into a villain, all because I felt so betrayed he'd chosen to abduct me when the time in the cabin came to an end.

But, back then, I hadn't paid close attention to his words. I hadn't stopped to really analyse his expressions and intentions.

He'd fallen in love with me up on that mountain.

He genuinely believed I was meant to be his.

There was such a horrible pain to that realization. I felt like I understood him on a deeper level. I might always have.

The game we had played had become our reality. I pushed him away, watching him fight to re-claim me. I constantly left him feeling short. It was like having eleven holes overflowing with water and watching him close every one of them with his fingers and always being left one short.

He never felt like he was winning.

No matter what he did, I never broke character. I lived playing my part, defiant and cold – and God, he needed my warmth this whole time.

As the tears ran endlessly down my face, the car came to a slow stop. The door opened and the driver stepped out, slamming it shut behind him. I held my breath, straining to hear.

"She's in the car," the man said. "She's not in a good place, been muttering words this whole time."

The backdoor opened just then. The cool air hit my flushed skin. I was sweating everywhere. I felt a hand gently run along the side of my face. Breaths hit my skin and a voice said, "I'm getting you out of here."

I went completely still from shock. "Flynn?"

The blindfold disappeared from my head. I blinked rapidly, looking up in the darkness, my gaze catching his. Flynn was in the car, looking down at me with a soft expression. "Come on, Vixen, let's get you out of this car."

His arms wrapped around me, and he slid me out of the backseat. He set me down on my feet and began untying the rope around my arms. "I had to make this look real," he explained to me. "That way, no one would think you left voluntarily."

I looked around us quickly. We were stopped on a

dirt road in the middle of the bush. I recognized these sorts of trails. Off the road type you find in construction zones or national reserves. I wouldn't know my way back, but Nixon would probe every inch of the island to find me.

Nixon.

He had left for the job. The job Flynn was meant to be present for. But he was here instead, wreaking havoc.

Why?

When the rope fell away from my arms, he bent down and did the same to my ankles. I watched him, my body trembling as the rope loosened. "What have you done, Flynn?" I scolded.

He stood up, towering over me. His face was hard, his eyes narrowed on me. "You wouldn't understand. This was personal, Vixen. Believe me, he deserves it."

"We need to leave," the other man said. "We're running late."

"You go ahead, Jay," Flynn told him. "I'll be right behind you."

Jay disappeared into the woods, leaving Flynn alone with me. I watched him as he went into the car and opened the glovebox compartment. I took a hesitant step back as he pulled out a gun. He caught the movement and gave me a reassuring look, sliding the gun into the waistband of his pants. "Why would I hurt you?" he asked, smiling softly. "I'm saving you, Vix."

"I don't need to be saved," I whispered.

He shut the door, and the lights in the car went dark. He came to me then, cradling my face in the palm of his hand. "I've got a seaplane coming in for us. In a matter of hours, you're going to have your life back."

Too stunned to respond, he took me by the arm and guided me off the trail and into the woods. My heels sank into the wet sloppy ground. Every step took effort removing my heels from the mud. Within minutes, I was panting, unused to walking in these conditions, and Flynn was just blazing by, practically dragging me.

"Slow down," I hissed, trying to pull back my arm. "I'm not cut out for this sort of walk, Flynn."

He slowed down, looking at my feet. "Sorry."

"You're in a hurry."

"I can't afford any delays."

"Then leave me."

Even in the dark, I saw the way his face twisted. "No, I can't leave you. I made myself a promise when I saw you that I would get you out of his clutches."

I shook my head, not understanding any of this. "You saw me days ago, Flynn. Whatever you came here to do, it wouldn't have included me."

His hand tightened. "I saw you a lot longer than that."

What did he mean?

My head ached. I whimpered as a sharp branch whacked into my bare leg, scratching me. He was still going faster than I could keep up, and as I looked around, the darkness in all directions, I didn't know how far from the car we'd made it, or how far we had yet to go.

"I can't come with you," I cried to him, feeling like my throat was closing up. "I'm not leaving him, Flynn."

"Like hell you aren't," he hissed. "You've been brainwashed."

"I really haven't."

"This is Stockholm Syndrome."

"It really isn't."

"Goddammit, Vixen, can you even see yourself outside of this island anymore? He's kept you locked up here for a year straight."

What was he talking about? It wasn't a year – it was almost *two* – but I didn't correct him straight-away because my brain was still mushy, trying to understand.

All I could think about was Nixon returning to find his island in flames.

The devastation when he realized I wouldn't be in the hotel – the hotel would be ashes. He would panic, scrambling to find me, terrified of what had become of me.

I dug my heels into the mud, purposely this time. "You've ruined him," I said, brokenly. "You're burning his island down."

"Good," Flynn retorted.

"People live here. They...They count on him."

"They'll endure. We *all* endure, Vixen."

I shook my head, unable to continue. "Let me go!"

Flynn stopped in his tracks and turned to me, panting. "We aren't far."

"I don't want to go, goddammit."

"Vixen –"

"What has he done to you?"

Flynn dropped his head down to my level, gritting out, "He's stolen from me."

"Stolen..." My mind blazed with thoughts. "What

has he stolen from you? Money?"

"No, not money."

"Gold?"

"No, Vix –"

"What then?" I yelled up at him, frustrated.

Flynn swallowed, struggling to keep his voice steady when he said, "I've been looking for a man who murdered a crew in cold blood after the One Percent were ripped off to the grand tune of twenty million dollars. It was underworld knowledge that a rogue group of guys had broken into one of the bikers' shops and ransacked gold bars just before they were meant to be transported. Since that robbery, the bikers turned on one another and the city descended into the nastiest bloodshed it has ever seen, ultimately annihilating the bikers once and for all.

"Now the man that turned on his crew did it for the money. Stole their share and then paid Toby off to keep him silent. I did a few jobs for Toby. There've been whispers from his men that the man that killed the crew owned an island. I did some digging, threw a lot of money around, asking if there's been anyone coming around selling large chunks of gold. When you steal a pot load like that, you sell it off slowly. A year ago, I got word that a man by the name of Hobbs was selling to a mint dealer – one of Toby's mint dealers. It didn't take much surveillance to see the type of people Hobbs dealt with. One of them...a man who owned an island."

The vehemence in Flynn's tone startled me. I watched him, my body transfixed to his words as he fell apart before me.

"I came to see him for myself," Flynn continued. "I

knew right off the bat, when I saw his smarmy fucking smile, he'd done it."

"How do you know that?" I asked weakly. "You could be wrong."

"Because I'd heard about him before. He'd worked with that crew multiple times. Around the time the robbery struck, he'd left the island on a private plane just before it happened."

"How do you know all this?"

"You'd be surprised who talks for the right price."

My heart slowed. "You came here and saw me?"

"I saw you flee a restaurant. Saw him chase you down."

"Flynn—"

"It happened at the exact time I'd sent men to hack into his surveillance system, so I could keep tabs on him, but he'd found out about them almost right away. I'd overlooked how closely he monitored the waters. He killed a whole boat load of my men that night, and then you were hidden for weeks. It was like...he was paranoid they'd been sent after you. Even now, no matter how much money I throw, it's never enough to get anyone to open up about you. It's like a death sentence. Like...Nixon will know. He's kept your identity locked up, and I know it's because he's so sick in the fucking head, he feels like he owns you."

I ripped my arm from his hand, taking a step back from him. Tears clouded my vision as I looked back on that time in my room last year. A whole month I'd spent loathing him, thinking he'd punished me.

But he'd in fact been protecting me.

Oh, my God.

He'd never once told me because...I shook my head, crying softly into my hands. He didn't want me to know he thought I was in any danger.

He didn't want me scared.

Fear traumatized me, and he knew it.

"So, you did all this..." I choked out, breathing hard. "You did all this to get closer to him..."

"I had word sent out to Hobbs that there was damn good driver outsmarting the cops –"

"You were never going to do the job."

"No."

"You were waiting for him to leave so you could... so you could ruin him."

He smiled, proudly. "Killing him isn't enough. I want him to suffer, Vixen. I want him to come back and see his island in ashes, see his money wasted, find his woman... gone. I want him to feel the emptiness he's made me feel these last two years, and then I'm going to kill him."

When he took a step to me, I took another step back, determined to keep the distance between us. "You lost someone from that crew, didn't you?"

A look of pain flashed in his face. "I did, Vixen."

Tears continued to fall as I remembered Beckett.

Then Mills.

Then Tucker.

Then...

My heart sank slowly. Sadness enveloped me as I whispered, "You lost Roz."

Flynn froze, his face morphing to shock. "How do you know that?" he whispered.

My smile was sad. "Your mom owned a bakery, and she was killed in front of you. You were tossed into the system and then you ran away. You...looked up to him. He was your whole world. You wanted to be him. He predicted you'd be in the back of a car, hoping to be like big brother, but he didn't want that. He wanted you to go to school, to turn your life around..."

Flynn's eyes flared, unshed tears brimming. "How the fuck do you know all this?"

I took another step back. "Because I was there, Flynn. I was there two years ago. Nixon killed them in front of me."

I understood Flynn now.

I understood his motives.

He wasn't the bad guy here.

Neither was Nixon. He'd saved me from a bad fate.

In the real world, among the broken, there were no good guys or bad guys. There were just people with their own agendas, with their own reasons.

Everyone with their own lives to live, their own stories to tell.

Breaking the truth to Flynn was almost impossible. He watched me, his shock inescapable. He wanted me to continue; he held a big breath in his lungs, waiting.

"I was kidnapped right after the robbery," I explained quietly, forcing out the words that would cause him nothing but utter devastation. "Beckett forced me in the car. We drove to a mountain. There was a cabin at the top. They needed to lay low in it, waiting for the heat to die down, but Beckett wanted to rape me. He and Mills stayed back in the car to do it. But...just before Beckett began to take me, Nixon showed up and murdered them both."

I spoke slowly, allowing Flynn the time to digest the words. I needed him to understand the truth, to let it sink in slowly.

"Flynn," my voice quivered, "when Nixon took me to the cabin, he protected me. Tucker and Roz... they were going to do the same to me, and then they were going to kill me."

"Ross would never do that..." Flynn retorted, shaking his head, denying it straight away.

Ross. That was his real name. I frowned. "He was."

"That's bullshit."

"No –"

"You're lying."

I shook my head gravely. "No, Flynn, I'm not. He loved you, but he wasn't a good guy –"

"You misunderstood him."

"I didn't." I gritted my teeth, a flash of anger coursing through me. "If you worked for Toby and you threw money around for hints of the truth, then you missed a giant fucking truth right below your nose."

He was fighting tears now – because he knew I wasn't lying. "What was that?"

"Toby protected Nixon and Hobbs because Nixon killed Roz, and at the time, Roz had fucked Toby over."

"I already know about the bounty and the money, but he set things straight –"

"He raped his granddaughter, Flynn!" I roared. "She was a kid, and you know what Roz said about it? He said he was *drunk*, like that justified it."

Flynn was stunned. He took a stumbling step away from me, his mind scrambling. "I would have known about that," he rasped, tears falling now. "I would have."

"You said yourself no one dared talk about me, no matter the money you offered," I returned firmly. "Wouldn't the same go for Toby and his granddaughter? There are some things you just don't talk about, Flynn."

You never knew who was listening to the whispers.

In a world like theirs, who could be trusted?

If it was an automatic death sentence, what did money matter?

Just then the roar of a plane broke the silence, flying over head of us. I looked up at it as it descended not far above the trees. Flynn wasn't looking. He was staring past me, lost in a trance.

I took a step toward him. "Flynn –"

The sound of gunfire erupted, drowning out my words.

43.

VIXEN...

F lynn snapped out of his trance as gunfire descended not far from us.

My spine straightened in alarm. "Who's firing?"

"I have this place surrounded," Flynn answered
in a hushed tone. "Too many men, outnumbering
Nixon's. Whoever is a threat, they'll be removed
shortly."

Flynn took me by the arm again and we moved
briskly through the bush, toward the gunfire. I tried
to resist at first, too frightened to draw close to it, but
Flynn pushed on, unwavering.

Whoever was there wasn't stopping.

It went on and on.

From one side to the next.

A few minutes later, as more bullets flew, cries
sounded out. Flynn halted, straining to hear. Making
little sound, we waded through, approaching a break
in the trees. I heard the sound of ocean waves crashing, saw the silhouette of a cliff face to one side and
the shoreline up ahead. We were on the shore of the island, in an unprotected bay, too far from town.

"Careful," Flynn whispered, pulling me to a stop. "We wait until the threat is eliminated."

He made me crouch down with him. I didn't protest. My heart was hammering in my chest, my mind blazing, my senses on high alert.

With just the moon and stars to offer light, the seaplane was still circling overhead, its landing approaching. It was a dangerous time to fly. What if it crashed into us? What if there was no way out? What if I got shot in the crossfire just getting to it?

Too many worries hit me at once. I had a hard time trying to quiet my thoughts.

I couldn't see fire, nor the plumes of smoke rising from the town, but I could smell the smoke. I couldn't swallow the hard lump in my throat away.

I prayed for the rain to come.

To put it all out.

I prayed for the island to remain intact, for the homes to still be standing, for no lives costed by one man's need for revenge.

"I'm not going," I whispered, peering at him now. "I'm staying, Flynn."

Flynn's eyes didn't hold the same animosity as before. He looked withered and broken. His words were small, uncertain. "You still need your freedom, Vixen."

"You're scrambling for a cause now," I returned frantically. "You're itching to justify this."

Tears fell from his eyes, an endless stream. "He still killed my brother."

"You know he had to."

He sucked in breaths, the tears fell around him, falling off the tip of his nose. I suddenly realized why they called him *kid*. He looked like a little boy. He was so vulnerable, like a hurt child reacting out of anger. My heart lurched. I took him by the hand and squeezed. He stared at me with pleading eyes, like he was asking me to remove the pain.

"It's alright," I whispered to him. "It's okay to be hurt, Flynn."

"I can't process," he responded in a guttural voice. "I feel like I'm being torn apart."

"There's still time to fix this."

Before he could respond, gunfire – so close my ears ached – broke through the air once more. Another cry sounded out, and this time a girl's shriek erupted in response. "ROWAN!"

Oh, my God.

I gasped. "That's Doll. They're here."

Reacting out of reflex, I ripped my arm from him and sprinted forward. Flynn came from behind me, tackling me back down. I landed hard on my front, the breath ripped from my lungs. "You will get shot!" he hissed. "I don't want you hurt."

"Tell them to stop," I cried.

"Too late for that, Vixen. I'll be dead."

Running could be heard. The firefight was happening so close, we were going to be caught in the middle of it at this rate.

"Doll!" I yelled, just as Flynn covered my mouth with the palm of his hand.

"Stop," he told me. "Please, Vixen."

"Vixen?!" Doll shouted from a distance. "Nixon, she's here!"

Nixon.

My heart surged.

He was here.

The plane engine boomed overhead, finally coming down to touch the water. I saw its blinking lights as the landing gear skimmed over the water, coming to a smooth and lengthy stop.

Flynn watched it with me, his breaths coming faster. "We gotta get to that plane. There's a dinghy on the shore –"

"I'm down!" shouted Rowan from nearby. "Retreat, Doll! Get outta here –"

"I'm not going anywhere!" she roared back.

"Get back –"

Gunfire silenced him.

Everything went quiet again. I panted, tears streaming from my eyes as I realized he might have gotten killed. *Oh, my God.* Flynn stayed over me, forcing me down, breathing quickly over me. Even forced beneath him, I understood what he was doing. He was covering me from head to toe, shielding me from gunfire. *Protecting* me.

Footsteps crunched nearby. I turned my head, eyeing the bush. I caught faint movements. Saw a shadow move from tree to tree. Flynn's head spun in the other direction, catching other sounds from nearby.

"I have a gun pointed at her spine, Nixon," he suddenly said firmly, hiding the vulnerability he'd let slip with me.

I hadn't realized he'd had the gun on me. I didn't feel it at all. But he forced me up now, keeping my back plastered to his front.

I blinked around us, trying to find Nixon, but all I could see were trees and branches swaying with the wind.

A twig breaking from nearby sounded. Flynn turned us in the direction of it, until a crunching sound came in a completely different direction, and Flynn spun back to that.

I held my death, dizzied by the panic I felt.

"Don't be frightened, baby," Nixon called to me from nearby. "You're okay."

My heart jumped in my chest. "Nixon..."

"Shh, baby."

Flynn let out a harsh breath. "I won't hurt her if you retreat."

"You won't hurt her either way."

Suddenly a large figure emerged from the trees in front of us. I knew it was him straight away. I'd memorized the lines of him, could feel him in the air. His arms were raised, his hands gripping tight a gun aimed at us. As he stepped out, treading carefully toward us, the moonlight hit him. His face came into view, and what I saw made my knees weak. His face was bloodied and bruised. The way he walked was all wrong, too. Gritting his teeth, his eyes met mine, and he let out a long breath, like he was relieved to see me.

"Baby," he whispered to me. "You're so strong, my angel. It's okay."

His words made my chest swell. I looked at him, thinking of the past as I merged it with the present.

Nixon, my saviour, my captor.

Even now, doing what he could to save me.

Flynn forced us to take a step back. "Don't push me, Nixon," he warned. "I'm not bluffing."

Nixon's eyes lazily moved to Flynn. "What did I say about playing the hero, Flynn? It's all well and good until you get your hands dirty, and you...you don't know how to do that."

"You really want to test me?"

"Let my girl go." Nixon demanded in a soft voice that was unlike him. "Deal with me personally. Shoot me if you have to. Just...let her go."

"I was already going to let her go," Flynn retorted. "I was going to put her on that plane and set her free."

"She's not going on that plane," Nixon simply said. "But I'll give you this opportunity to leave."

Flynn let out an empty laugh. "Yeah, and I believe that."

"I give you my word."

"The island's surrounded by my men, Nixon, I don't need your word."

"Your men are dead," Nixon said, gravely. "Taken out one by one. You think I haven't been through a gunfight? You think Doll is just a pretty face? You think Rowan, Tyrone and Tiger haven't been through situations like these? I told you before already...we never needed a driver, and this? This was preschool shit, wasn't it, guys?"

"Yes," a voice sounded out. Tiger.

"Absolutely," Tyrone chimed from another direction.

"That's right, gentlemen." Doll.

"You accomplished what you came here for," Nixon explained to Flynn. "You've won."

"You don't know what I came here for," Flynn angrily retorted. "You don't really know anything about me."

"I do," Nixon argued, softly. "The truth was in plain sight. You took advantage of every opportunity you had. You planted that man in the basement, killed him, played the hero, and watched as I panicked, sending my men out, looking for a threat that wasn't there. With no one in the surveillance room, your men planted explosives all over the island. You were never coming for the job. You were going to steal Vixen from under me the second the island began to blow apart. I knew, Flynn."

"What gave it away?"

"What you said to me in the restaurant...You said being here was better than being desperate enough to rob car parts in the parking lot of a 7/11. Your brother said something very similar to me once. A nightmare you both shared, perhaps."

Flynn didn't respond. Still pressed against him, I felt his trembles. I felt his head jerk from left to right as the other figures emerged from the shadows. We were surrounded by the crew.

"Enough bloodshed," Nixon continued, gun still raised. "Enough, Flynn. I can't bear it anymore, not on my island. This was my sacred place, and it's tarnished now. You did it. You took her from me, you breathed fear back into my baby. I've never felt so frightened for her. You've broken me, Flynn. I won't make it past tonight. What more do you want?"

Flynn still didn't respond, but he let me go. He stepped back, dropping his arms to his side. I turned to him, noticing he didn't have a gun on him at all.

"I didn't know Vixen was there," he suddenly said. "I didn't know what my brother intended to do, Nixon..."

"Leave," Nixon demanded, his voice weak. He seemed all wrong. "I'm giving you a chance to go."

"Why?" Flynn asked warily.

"Because I understand what it's like to hate the world."

Flynn's expression broke. The rage dissipated. The pain returned as he looked back at me. "And Vixen?"

"Vixen will be okay," Nixon responded. "I promise."

"I'll be okay," I told Flynn.

My body was tight with anticipation. I pleaded for Flynn to leave, to not do something stupid again. He'd done enough. *No more.*

I didn't know if Nixon was tricking him. I held my breath, expecting the worst, but Nixon just stood there, unflinching.

Flynn took more steps back, keeping his front facing us. Nixon slowly lowered his gun and then raised a hand at the others. One by one they lowered their weapons, though I saw Doll quake, an angry look on her blood sodden face.

The second they were all lowered, Flynn turned his back to us and ran across the beach. In the distance was a small dinghy tied to a log on the rocks. The seaplane still sat in the waters, unmoving, its engine still alive. As Flynn untied the craft, I turned around and hurried to Nixon. He dropped his gun and quickly wrapped his arms around me. I pressed my face against his chest, breathing in his scent mixed with the scent of copper and dirt.

"You okay?" he asked me gruffly.

"Why didn't you kill him?" I asked, staggered.

"I'm tired of killing people, Vix. I've seen his rage...in myself. His road shouldn't come to an end from my hand. He's...got a lot of life left."

"I thought you were tricking him. I thought you were going to kill him."

"And it would have hurt you if I did it. I think you like Flynn's goodness."

"I do."

"I know, baby."

I shut my eyes as he held me. I felt whole being in his arms.

"I remembered." My voice cracked as I pulled away to look up at him. "I remembered everything in that cabin."

He smiled weakly at me. "Now you can heal."

I smiled back, though my heart beat harder because Nixon didn't seem right. There was no glow in his eyes.

"Rowan's on the ground, breathing," Tyrone suddenly said, coming to our side.

"Where was he shot?" Nixon asked.

"Leg. He's moaning like a sissy bitch."

Nixon chuckled. "Drag him to the shore."

Tyrone left our side and Doll replaced it. Her hands were all over me, turning my face from side to side with concerned eyes. "He hurt you?" she asked, teeth clenched.

"No," I answered.

"I would have shot that fucker in the head –"

"Leave him be," Nixon cut in, face pale. "This one goes."

Doll shook her head in disbelief. "I never knew you to be merciful, Nixon."

Nixon's lips quirked up. "I'm feeling a little weak right now."

"He destroyed your island."

"It needed to be done. It's time to move on."

She gave him a sad smile and left our side. Nixon took me by the hand and walked me to the beach. I stopped midway to remove my heels. My feet sank into the wet sand now as we trudged. The sound of the dinghy engine roared in the distance. Flynn took off from the rocks, moving in the direction of the plane. We stopped to watch as the door to the plane opened, letting him on.

I looked back at Nixon, feeling my heart sink now. "Is the island really ruined?"

Nixon nodded slowly. "The hotel's gone. The shops are up in flames."

"All those people..."

"Don't worry," he assured me. "I'll make sure they're taken care of. Whatever the cost. Tyrone promised he would do that for me." Before I could respond, he squeezed my hand. "Come," he urged, walking me down the shore in the direction of the very rocks the dinghy had been tied to.

"We should be going back," I told him. "You look wrecked, Nixon."

"Don't worry about me," he said. "Just come..."

As we moved, I glanced behind me, noticing Tyrone and Tiger in the distance, carrying Rowan along the shore. Doll was all over him, frantically kissing his face. Her soft cries could be heard from the distance.

We reached the rocks just as the seaplane took off. The dinghy was left abandoned, swaying with the current in the beach's direction. I watched as the plane lifted from the waters and flew overhead. As I stared, I noticed how big and bright the moon looked tonight.

"How bad is the cleanup going to be?" I wondered, looking at Nixon. "All those bodies everywhere."

"All Flynn's men," Nixon replied, his body swaying with the breeze.

"This is going to make the news."

"Yes."

"We'll have to leave."

He nodded slowly. "Yes."

I looked at him under the glow of the moon, and he didn't meet my eye. He stared past me and to the ocean. His lips looked cracked, the bags under his eyes worsened. Then...he smiled softly and nodded his head at something.

I followed his gaze, looking into the dark waters.

I heard the soft sound of an engine. I squinted my eyes, concentrating, trying to make out what it was as it grew louder.

I saw a large shape coming in our direction. A motorboat emerged from the darkness, stealing my breath.

"Are we going to motor to the marina?" I asked Nixon, looking confusedly at him.

He slowly shook his head. "No, baby."

"Then what..."

Still holding my hand, he fell to his knees suddenly, knocking me down with him. A soft groan escaped his lips as he forced his head up, staring at the waters. Panicked, I looked him over, noticing now his hand was pressed to the side of his body. I grabbed at his hand, determined to pull it away. I blinked rapidly, noticing his hand was drenched in...

"Nixon!" I cried, panicked. "You're hurt!" I looked

behind us, at the figures still trailing the beach. "He's hurt!" I screamed.

"They know," Nixon breathed out calmly. "Baby, they know."

"Were you shot?" I gripped his arm, desperate to look him over, but he wouldn't let his hand go for me to see.

"I'm okay," he assured me. "Put your hand down."

But I didn't. "Nixon, you need the hospital." I looked at the motorboat now as it slowed down, approaching us. "We need to get you up."

"I'm not going, Vixen," he told me.

I broke out in trembles, feeling utterly lost and terrified. "I don't understand. I don't know what's going on. You're bleeding, Nixon. There's a boat. There's a fucking boat. You'll come on..."

"I'm bleeding out."

"You'll be okay if we get you to the hospital –"

"Victoria, enough," he cut in, looking at me now with desperate eyes. "You need to get up. You need to go to the boat. Hobbs is there."

Tears fell from my eyes. I was bewildered. Stumped. Robbed of all breath and all reason, I cried out, "What are you doing? I don't understand."

His lips trembled as he leaned into me now, eyes focused on mine. I saw the tears brimming in their depths. With a choked voice, he said, "I'm letting you go,"

I fell back in shock, my butt hitting the sand. I looked at him with round eyes. My chest caved in on itself. Everything inside me shook and roared. Dizzied, I felt...*betrayed*. "You're letting me go?" I rasped out, sounding as betrayed as I felt.

"You think I want to?" he asked with a hard laugh, tears falling from his eyes. "I feel like I'm being sawed in half. I'm giving you your freedom. Don't think I'm doing it because I don't want you. Don't think I'm doing it because the light's come to me. I'm only doing it because I have to. Baby, I'm *bleeding out...*"

Blood fell between his fingers. He was surrounded in puddles of it. His sweater was drenched. His skin was ghostly now.

I sobbed, shaking my head. "You're okay –"

"Get your ass up," he admonished me. "Go to the boat."

"I can't leave you."

"You've been begging me to let you go."

"I can't be without you."

"You can."

"I didn't mean any of it," I wept. "I told you I remembered. You saved me, Nixon."

He chuckled now in shock. "*Saved* you? Is that what you think? Poor girl, I took you for myself."

"I let it happen," I quickly said. "I played the game along with you. I forced myself to forget because I didn't want to believe it was real. It was easier to hate you...because it hurt too much to love again. I couldn't stand to be abandoned again. Mom left me and I was so fucking alone, Nixon..."

"Victoria..."

"Don't abandon me, too, Nixon. Get up, *get up* and go to the boat with me."

But he was hardly able to keep his eyes open now. His body sank further into the sand. "My time's over," he forced out. "But I got to have you. I got to have something real in the end. I got to love with all my heart. I got to feel a person capture my soul. Not everyone can say they've loved so whole before. I was your captive, baby, right from the start."

As he lay bent, I wrapped my arms around him, burying my face against his back, sobbing into him. He was dying, fading from the world, finding the light on the other side.

"I love you," I told him sincerely. "You were the only person to ever fight for me, to ever look at me like I was worth something. You killed for me, Nixon."

I settled my face between his shoulder and neck. I kissed his neck and cheek, shutting my eyes to the feeling.

"Nicholas," he whispered to me just then. "That's my name, baby." I shook through my sobs as he dropped his forehead to the sand. "Go to the boat..."

"But I can't leave you here."

"I want to die on my island," he told me calmly. "I want to say goodbye to our home. I want to see you fade into the dark. Then I'm going to see Leona. She'll be on the other side. She's waiting for me, baby. Now go."

A warm hand touched my back. I looked up, wrecked. Tyrone stared down at me with a tender expression. "Get up, Vixen."

Doll came at my side, hugging me from behind, whispering, "We have to go, Vixen."

She forced my arms from Nixon's body and pulled me back. Tyrone took me by the hand and forced me into the water, in the direction of the boat. I resisted at first, shaking my head at him, my voice lost.

"This was how it was always going to be," he told

me gently. "You two were never going to make it. Only one person was going to come out of this."

I stared at Nixon as he fell to his side, his chest moving slowly. "Tyrone, you can't make me leave him like this…"

"He doesn't want you to watch this."

"Tyrone –"

"Time to go back to the real world. Back to your life." His voice toughened. "Do it. For him."

Letting me go, Tyrone stood tall, watching me.

It took everything in me to turn away, to look at the boat not ten feet away. The water was at my knees as I forced myself to move in its direction. I heard splashes behind me. Tiger overtook me, carrying Rowan over his shoulders. Doll came to my side, holding my hand, urging me to move.

I tried to turn around, compelled to go back, but she tugged me, telling me to move.

Every step I drew closer to the boat, I was growing number and number. My heart couldn't bear the weight it felt any longer. My breaths came laborious, my knees buckled. If not for Doll, I'd have fallen into the water and let it submerge me.

I loved him.

I really did.

I loved him so much.

I'd denied him of it.

This was a regret I was never going to move past.

I was empty by the time I reached the boat. I felt Tiger's arms around me, pulling me out of the water. He set me down onto the hard floor, and I crumbled at Hobbs' feet, sobbing.

I kept crying out words I didn't know I was saying

until I'd look back on it.

Don't let me go.

Don't let me leave him like this.

Don't let me go.

Hobbs ran a hand through my hair, saying nothing. Doll climbed in and held me tight as the boat turned.

I never looked up to see the beach fading from view. I never took my final look at him as the boat sped, leaving my heart behind with him.

It was another regret I would never forgive.

NIXON...

He heard the engine fade, taking with it his love.

He fell to his back and stared up at the night sky. He felt like his whole body was being leeched dry. The burn in his side spread, consuming his chest like a raging fire.

Fitting to go like this, feeling the same burn his island did.

Fitting, that of the two, she was the last one standing.

If it were the other way around, he would not have been able to endure that.

"I've never loved so hard," he murmured lifelessly.

Tyrone sank to the ground with him. "Maybe that's why it had to end. Maybe the world couldn't handle that much love."

Tears slid down the side of his face. "Do you think she loved me the same, Tyrone?"

The plea rattled Tyrone to the core. He gripped Nixon's hand and held him tight. "I think she did, buddy."

"Funny," he whispered, shaking his head a little. "I don't think she did..."

"Don't say that."

"She never wanted me, Tyrone."

"She just told you she loved you."

"She would have told me anything seeing me like this..."

The blood wouldn't stop seeping from his body.

It was everywhere.

He was being sucked dry, until the only thing left in his veins was the poison Victoria put there.

Nixon watched the stars twinkle, smiled up at the darkness and felt peace in his heart.

He let the darkness consume him.

Only...it didn't feel dark anymore.

It felt like a bright spark of light all around.

His final thoughts were of Leona.

He whispered, "I love you," to her as she sank down at his side, smiling down at his face.

44.

TWO YEARS LATER...

VICTORIA...

I woke up to the same feeling of pain in my chest every single day. I didn't think much of it, though. I'd gotten used to the pain. I went through the days with a similar aching feeling in my chest I'd felt before I'd been on that island, before I'd met Nixon.

I'd seen so much death, had felt so much fear, I'd stopped going to therapy because my therapist just liked to tell me to hang in there all the fucking time, but she used a lot of pretty verses to disguise it.

When I wasn't stuck in a cubicle answering phone calls for the moving company I worked at, I did a lot of things alone.

Unplugged from the world, I often rode the buses across town and walked the bustling streets of Vancouver feeling like just another face in the crowd.

And I always had my camera at hand.

I took photos of anything that captured my heart.

Be it the rain streaking a window, or a little girl splashing in the puddles – there was so much beauty around when you weren't nose deep in a screen.

Looking up and around made a world of a difference.

It made the pain dull just enough I could smile without tears pricking my eyes.

I was alone before Nixon – I was alone after him – and this time being alone didn't scare me so much.

I learned I was adaptable.

I could blend in just fine.

I could cope.

It also helped I met Brian.

He breathed a bit of life into me.

He was my neighbour in a mediocre building on a mediocre street. A good distraction when I wanted to not think about a certain stubbled face.

It was okay to be distracted, I convinced myself. Two years of healing, it was time to live a little.

We met in the elevator when I moved into the apartment six months ago. Before that I'd been living with Kimberly, but then she'd gotten engaged to her boyfriend and they moved in together. She felt guilty for leaving me to find another place, but it was okay. I liked the thought of living alone, even if it meant being financially strapped.

Man, I was so financially destitute, it wasn't even funny.

In another life, I may have gone back to school, finished my degree and been in a better place. But I couldn't seem to refocus my energies into that. I found myself needing to heal by just learning to be on my own and coming to terms with Nixon's death.

I was learning to survive each and every day, finding myself back to square one.

Unpampered. Crappy clothes from the thrift store – sometimes at Walmart if I wanted to live large. Haircuts from a shitty salon. I never got my vagina waxed anymore – too expensive, so I shaved my snatch instead and had many ingrown hairs to recover from.

This was reality.

I didn't evolve into some beautiful butterfly. I was still the fucking caterpillar, only more damaged and still struggling to make a well-intact cocoon.

A knock sounded.

I looked at myself in the mirror, dressed in a white tank top and black skirt – sans gumboots this time. I brushed my hair before piling it up high. Then I threw the remaining hairpins in my purse – loaded with a whopping fifteen dollars and sixteen cents – and answered the knock on my door.

"Hey, you," Brian said, smiling as he stepped inside with a bag in hand. He dropped his head to my level and gave me a chaste kiss. "I picked a movie."

"What're we watching?" I asked as I pulled away to move to the kitchen. I grabbed the packet of popcorn and threw it in the microwave and took a giant step back.

"War of the Worlds," he answered, already setting it up in the tiny living room. "Why did you move away from the microwave like that?"

"It's been making these weird electrical sounds," I replied. "Landlord won't do anything about it."

He was amused. "You think it'll blow up in your face?"

I laughed weakly. "Yeah."

Not really. I just hated loud noises. Took me back to gun fire and bullets whizzing over my head.

"I'll save you from the microwave," he teased. He wouldn't think he was a such a hero if he knew what I went through. "Come lay with me."

When the popcorn finished, I poured it in a bowl and joined him on the couch. He wrapped an arm around me and pressed me to his side. I shut my eyes momentarily, pretending for a moment it was a larger, more solid frame.

Then I banished that thought entirely.

I wasn't going to move on if I kept revisiting the past.

As the starting credits rolled, I asked Brian, "How was your day?"

"Doing investigative training now," he answered. "Not long before graduation."

"You excited to be a police officer?"

"I am," he said proudly. "I don't think you'll be able to resist me in uniform. Maybe that'll make you crumble."

I laughed lightly. "Maybe."

Maaaaaaybe.

Maaaaaaaaaaaybe.

Maybe as in I definitely did not think so.

We hadn't done more than heated kissing sessions – the heated part was more from his end. Brian had tried to finger me recently, but my thighs pressed shut before his hand got there, deterring his further advances. He respectfully held off and let me go at my own pace.

I should have felt grateful he knew when to stop.

That he didn't push or take.

We may have known each other for six months, but it'd been three months of dating and things weren't heating up at a normal pace. According to Kimberly, I needed to just let it happen, but I couldn't seem to tell my body to do that.

My body was broken, I knew.

It was broken because nothing made it burn.

Unless...

Unless I thought of a man's hard hands prying my legs wide, chuckling at my resistance, telling me I'd be screaming his name as I came.

And Brian...

Well, Brian wasn't going to be doing that any time soon.

I thought of Nixon's words the night that man raised the gun at me. When he circled the bed – when he pounced on me after – gritting those ugly words into my ear when I told him I'd find a man of law to take care of me.

"Do you think he'd play along? You think you could ever tell him you have a thing for dubious consent? You think these men of law will take your no's and still fuck you like I do?"

No, I wanted to say again.

No one would fuck me like he did.

He knew me on a deeper level, beyond physical.

I'd never find that again.

Midway through the movie, when the aliens were checking places out and Dakota Fanning was scream-ing in some looney guy's hidey hole, Brian started to kiss along my neck. Wet, popcorny kisses that I shrugged away from.

"I'm tired," I told him, feigning a yawn.

"I can think of ways to wake you up," he murmured, pressing his mouth to mine.

Tonight, I just wasn't feeling it. I withdrew and gave him an apologetic smile. "I'm sorry, Brian, I'm just feeling funky right now."

He made a sad face before nodding and pulling away. "Alright, I'll give you space, baby." He tensed, realizing his mistake. "Shit, sorry. I didn't mean to call you that."

I was too numb at the moment to care. "No worries."

We stopped the movie and he left, respecting my space, being a nice guy and nice guys were so hard to come by, weren't they?

I paced my apartment, tidied it up, did the dishes and had a quick shower. Under the hot spray, I pleasured myself thinking of Nixon.

I never got to orgasm. The tears always beat me to it.

Stepping out, I dressed in a pair of loose pants and a baggy shirt and peered out the window at the falling snow, wishing for things that would never come true.

I ended up falling into bed, staring up at the dark ceiling for most of the night.

When was I going to be okay? I asked myself. When was I going to wake up and get used to him being gone?

I had dreams of him all the time.

Dreams of him coming into the night, resting at my side, holding me, kissing me, telling me I was going to be okay.

Then I'd wake up – I swear to God I could smell the scent of him in the air – and find the space beside me untouched.

Those were hard dreams to recover from.

45.

VICTORIA...

There was a bird harassing another bird outside the coffee shop window. He wouldn't leave this fucking bird alone, even when his advances were so obviously being rejected.

The most persistent fucking bird in the world.

I took like seventy-five pictures of it on my Nikon.

"Why aren't you a photographer?" Kim suddenly said, sliding into the chair across from me. She took her winter jacket off, smiling at me.

"Not interested in being a photographer," I told her, setting the camera down. "I do it for fun."

"Must be annoying lugging that giant fucker around, though."

The camera was bulky, for sure. "I'm used to it."

"Why don't you just be normal and get a phone that takes pictures?"

I laughed. "I'm not keen on joining the cyber world any time soon."

Kim looked over her shoulder and hollered. "I want the usual, Derek! And add some cinnamon this time. Did you get that? I want some cinnamon in my latte, Derek!" Before turning back to me, replying, "You think if you get a phone with all the bells and whistles, you'll wind up back in the online world?"

"It might tempt me."

"Then maybe that's the world telling you to come back to the dark side."

"Maybe."

She ran her hands up and down her arms, shivering. "It's cold out there. I think there's going to be a blizzard. Hope you're not in a skirt this time."

I smiled weakly. "Definitely not."

She eyed me peculiarly. "You know, I wish you'd tell me what happened to you. You just disappeared off the face of the earth.

I avoided her eye. "I don't want to talk about it."

"At some point, you might have to. You've been walking around with this baggage on your shoulders for like two years now. Ever think you might feel better if you talked to someone about it."

"I can't," I simply said.

When Hobbs had returned me to the city, he gave me an envelope of cash, had asked me, "Are you sure you want to do this?" before I got out of the car.

I'd looked at him and said I was. I had no place in his world now. Nixon was gone and I was free. It was what I'd wanted, wasn't it?

Hobbs told me he'd never see me again from that point on. "This money should see you through a long time. Don't talk about your abduction. Don't tell anyone what happened to you these last couple years. You don't know the kind of attention you'd get, and the last thing I want on my conscience is your death. You left because the pressure got too much. You unplugged and ran, and you didn't want to be found. You took a holiday, you hear? You travelled the country, joined a hippy caravan, whatever the fuck it is people your age do, I don't care. But make it believable."

I told him I would. I promised I'd be fine, and he frowned at me like it was hard for him to watch me go.

"You had a place in my heart from the very beginning, dear one," he told me. "I wanted you dead for only a fleeting moment, but now I'll do anything to keep you alive and healthy. You're one of a kind, with thick skin and a damn strong spirit to have put up with Nixon and his bullshit. You saved him, you know that? You really did. You sparked life into him." He'd paused, leaning toward me. "Speaking of life, you believe in God? Are you a spiritual girl?" I told him I didn't know. "Well, I might hit up some churches, pray to Jesus or some shit. Maybe he'll help me grieve, help me let you go. Only Lazarus will bring us back together again."

I didn't get what he was babbling about, but he was drunk off his ass, recovering from Nixon's death and trying his damned hardest to tell me good-bye.

When I stepped out of the car, that was the last time I saw him.

It was two years of nothingness.

The despair of losing Hobbs and the crew was surprisingly rough. I felt like I lost a family.

"Earth to Victoria," Kim sang.

I blinked out of my thoughts. "Sorry, what?"

"I said did you get around to banging Brian yet?"

"Not yet."

"You getting any closer?"

"No."

She looked sympathetic. "He's a hot guy, I don't get it."

"Me neither."

"He's going to be a cop."

"Yeah, I know."

"Cops are hot."

I nodded numbly. "Yeah, they are."

She narrowed her eyes at me. "You know, sometimes I think a man ruined you or something."

"What makes you think that?" I asked, curiously.

"Because you get a faraway look in your eye. Your cheeks go all red and flushed, and then you look like you're about to cry. I know a look of heartbreak when I see one. I've lived through like a hundred."

I gave her a dry laugh. "I don't think you've gone through one like mine."

She raised a challenging brow. "You want to bet?"

"Not really."

"What did he do to make it different than any other jerk out there?"

"He kidnapped me." I deadpanned.

She stilled, staring at me bug-eyed, and then she laughed because it was so fucking hysterical to even consider that possible. "Can you imagine being kidnapped?"

"I can."

"Did he bind you?" she asked, playfully.

"No, he released the binds, actually."

"Where did he take you?"

"Oh, you know," I murmured, taking a casual sip of my coffee. "He had his own island."

She laughed again, growing redder. "Of course, he

did. I believe you."

"Thank you."

"You're welcome." When her laughter faded, she gave me a playful kick. "I like seeing you joke around. Makes me feel like you're getting back into the swing of things."

"Only took me two years."

"Yeah, well, you were under so much pressure before, especially living with John the cunt head. You been talking to your aunt at all?"

"No," I said with a shake of my head. "Not at all."

"Going back to school?"

"Not yet."

"What about those student loans? Are they taking chunks out of your paycheck yet?"

I hadn't told her they'd been paid off while I'd been on the island. Another loose end that Nixon had made sure to tie off. He'd gone through every bit of my life after we'd left the cabin. Had made sure I wasn't on anyone's radar. "Yeah," I lied. "It's painful, isn't it?"

"Tell me about it."

I redirected the conversation so it was about her. She told me about working as a nurse at the hospital, then she went on about her wedding plans. I tried to listen as much as possible, but my mind was always straying.

When it went quiet, she said she had to go and we said our good-byes. I lingered longer in the coffee shop, staring out the window at the falling snow. I had to press a finger on my wrist to remember my heart was still beating. Sometimes I didn't feel it at all.

Remembering the birds, I turned on my camera

and went through the pictures, smiling softly at the chase between two creatures.

I remembered the rush.

Remembered the feeling of being wrapped around the arms of a possessive man, determined to make me his.

I sniffed back the emotion pooling behind my eyes as I scrolled through more photos. Pictures of the snow fall, of footprints in the snow, of snow angels and Christmas lights and...

I paused, catching a black duffle bag in the corner of one of my shots.

I zoomed in on the picture, focusing on the figure holding it. Strong hands, black jacket, a tall and broad man standing sideways beside a bus stop, a beanie over his head. No face shown. I tapped the screen idly, sighing miserably.

I was seeing him in my pictures now?

Was this how far my inability to move on extended?

Swallowing hard, I turned the camera off and packed it away into the bag. Then I slid out of my seat and left some change in the tip jar before waving good-bye to the baristas.

Stepping out of the coffee shop, I stood on the corner in front of the doors and watched the people bustling all around me. I felt a little lost, unsure of what direction to take.

There was a hole in my heart.

I felt the tears fall.

This was like my dream, wasn't it?

Nixon was gone – I felt his absence – and I was here, alone, facing the world I'd spent so long believing I belonged in.

But this wasn't my world anymore, was it?

I'd been forced to leave it behind. It was never going to be the way it was, and I understood why.

The world hasn't changed. You did.

And I would never move on. Not ever. Two years and I hadn't felt a flutter of hope that I would ever mend.

Maybe a broken heart never healed. Maybe you just learned to live with the cracks. They felt like scars, didn't they? And every time your heart thumped, you could feel the scar tissue, the cracks in the heart that didn't close, raised and inflamed.

*

Brian was at my apartment door waiting for me when I got back. Leaning beside him against the wall was a long box. I unzipped my jacket as I got to him, smiling. "What do you have there?"

He looked down at the box and spun it around so I could see the picture on the front.

A Christmas tree.

I laughed lightly, surprised. My heart warmed. "You got me a Christmas tree? I don't know what to say."

He shook his head. "No, this was here already."

My brow furrowed. "What?"

"Maybe it's from Kim."

"Definitely not."

On the side of the box was my apartment number written in permanent marker along with my name. It was definitely for me. I opened the front door and Brian brought it in. I passed him a pair of scissors and he tore it open, pulling out the pieces. He put it together in the living room in less than ten minutes. It was a full traditional six-foot tree with pretty lights.

My heart bloomed at the sight of it. I had to blink back tears because it reminded me of the tree Nixon had put up for us in our hotel apartment.

"Expensive tree," Brian muttered, stepping back to look at it. I didn't let him see the tears as I approached the tree and unbent the branches. "Who do you think it's from?"

"I'm not sure." I shrugged, but I had a feeling I knew.

Hobbs.

The guy always had a soft spot for me. I was sure Nixon had told him about my love for the holidays. Maybe this was his way of telling me he was still around.

God, I hoped he was.

"Are we still not doing presents this year?" Brian then asked, giving me a pouty look. "It'd be a shame not to have presents under a full tree, don't you think?"

I pondered that over. "Thing is...it can't be expensive."

"Okay."

I aimed a stern finger at him. "As in...less than thirty bucks tops, Brian."

He moved to me, smiling brightly. Dropping his face down to mine, he gave me a tender kiss. "Less than thirty bucks, I promise."

Excitement I hadn't felt in so long burst through me. I kissed him again, this time harder, and he wrapped his arms around my waist. "Wow," he whispered as he pulled away. "You've never kissed me like that before, Victoria."

I grinned, glancing at the tree before I pressed my head against his chest. "I'm just happy."

I knew it was a fleeting sort of happiness, but I savoured every second of it.

46.

VICTORIA...

A few days before Christmas, I went out for dinner with Kim, her fiancé Peter, and Brian. We stood waiting in line at a fancy restaurant Peter had managed to nab seats at – a Christmas gift from his law firm, Kim had explained. We'd booked ahead of time, but the place was so packed, and our table hadn't cleared yet.

As usual with my poor taste in clothing, I wore a black skirt and soft white sweater. I coupled that with heeled boots and a warm black winter jacket. When Brian and I met Kim and Peter out front, Kim gave my bare legs a longer look than necessary before muttering, "You sure you're not gonna freeze in that? I remember the last time you wore a skirt in this weather, there was a blizzard that made it into the records."

"Which blizzard was this?" chuckled Brian, his arm wrapped securely around me.

"It was years ago," I said vaguely.

"It was coincidentally the time she disappeared off the face of the earth," Kim intervened, giving Brian a look of warning. "Be careful, dude. It might happen again."

Brian's eyes widened. "You disappeared, Victoria?"

"She vanished for two years."

My smile felt forced. "Let's not talk about that again, Kim," I said sternly.

"And that's all you'll get from her when you pry the *teensiest* bit," Kim told him, shooting me a playful wink.

Brian gave me a curious look, but I ignored it as we entered the restaurant and stood in the waiting room. I felt a little annoyed at Kim and her incessant need to bring that shit up every fucking time we hung out lately. It was like her practiced patience had run out and she couldn't handle not knowing.

The hostess finally called us up and we were led out of the waiting room and into the bottom floor dining area of the restaurant. As we walked, I looked around, my breath stolen from my lungs at how luxurious this place was. It was two floors, and the staircase that led up to the second floor sparkled under the chandelier lights. I looked up, noticing how opulent it was up there. Not that the ground floor was disappointing or anything, but there was a clear barrier between two worlds: the bottom being the normal folk, the top being the rich as fuck ones. Even the chuckles that drifted down to us sounded elegant as fuck.

I felt grossly under dressed as we sat down at a round table. All the girls wore pretty dresses, fine jewellery, had that whole YouTube make-up tutorial look down pat.

In the meantime, I was still guerrilla styling it.

As I looked over the menu, Brian leaned into my side, whispering in my ear, "I got the cost, Vicky. You get what you want, alright?"

My cheeks flushed. "Thank you, Brian," I said sincerely.

When he pulled back, Kim was smiling at the two of us. "You guys are cute together."

Brian laughed. "Really?"

"Yeah, I wish Peter whispered in my ear like that." She shot Peter a glare. "Why the hell don't you whisper in my ear like that, Pete?"

Peter didn't bat her an eye, he was so used to her shit. "I'm such a robot, you should write a manual on how I ought to act, Kim. I'll study it."

She rolled her eyes dramatically. "He never argues back. He just takes my shit."

"What other choice do I have?"

She shrugged. "I don't know, you can fight back every once in a while."

Peter's lips flinched up as he looked at her, the love in his eyes so blatant. "You fight enough for the two of us, Kimmy."

I noticed the way her cheeks went red. She pretended not to be effected, but I watched her carefully, saw her turn away and glance casually around the room.

I wondered just then…

I wondered if that was how I looked like with him.

Did my cheeks redden? Did he know he'd gotten to me?

My fingers trembled. A huge wave of emotion hit me. I refocused my sight on the menu, but I could hardly read it through the blur of tears.

The waitress appeared and we gave our orders. When she left, Peter said, "Tough time to be an officer, Brian, don't you think?"

Brian grunted indifferently. "It'll blow over."

"What will?" Kim wondered.

"The resurgence of gang violence," Peter explained. "There've been bodies all over the show. Apparently, the bikers are retaliating."

I looked up, curiously. "What bikers?"

"The One Percent, they call themselves. They've been on the down-low for a few years. They just intercepted a drug run from their opponents, stole their huge loot of cocaine. Been hearing from some of my clients that the bikers are working with a bunch of rogue contractors."

"What sort of contractors?" Kim asked, looking enthralled.

Brian shrugged, answering in a bored voice, "These morons take contracts. They do the dirty for a crime boss that doesn't want to get blood on their hands."

"Hitmen?"

"Sometimes. Other times, they'll break into a cash house and clean it out."

"And this resurgence is, what, happening now?"

Peter nodded. "Yeah, came out of nowhere. Makes cases hard to crack when I don't have faces to work with. It's tricky defending a victim who doesn't have a description. Sometimes, it's so obvious what jackass is behind the crime, but you can't do a thing about it. People are getting scared again. No one wants to be a rat."

"They usually sort it out amongst themselves,"

Brian told us, smirking. "They turn on each other, tear one another apart. At the end, they always find a balance."

"The strongest come out on top," Peter added, agreeing with Brian. "Balance will be restored. Just means a lot of bloodshed."

Kim made a thoughtful sound. "Funny you should mention all this. There was a shooting a few days ago, and some guy got rushed into the hospital. He was a big guy, had a ski mask on his face. The cops were really keen to speak to him. They were up our asses the second he got wheeled in."

"And?" Peter prodded when she took a moment.

She threw her arms up in the air. "He vanished before we could treat him."

"Was he hiding some marred as fuck face under the mask or something?" Brian asked, laughing.

"No, the nurse tending to him told me he was gorgeous. Bronze skin, big muscles."

Staring deeply at her, I asked, "Did he give a name?"

"It started with an E, I think."

"Like Eman?" I blurted out without stopping myself.

She went still, shooting me a peculiar face. "I don't know."

Brian and Peter stared at me oddly too, but thankfully the waitress intervened with our food. I decided to stop talking after that, though my mind raced with thoughts.

Contractors.

Ski mask.

Bronze skin and gorgeous face.

It fit Eman to a tee.

I hid my furtive smile. It was insane being on the other side, seeing people that I knew well strike, leaving everyone else dumbfounded.

I felt this sharp desire to be part of it all again. To see sensitive Eman, behind his tough as fuck exterior, whine like a baby the way he used to before his bad blood with Nixon.

Brian held my hand just then, anchoring me back down to the present. He squeezed it dotingly. We smiled at each other just then; his smile was filled with enormous affection, and mine felt...stilted.

It would feel real with time, I told myself.

As they spoke about other things, I looked up at the top floor of the restaurant, eyeing the diners I could see. This was the kind of place Nixon would have taken me to. He'd have had his hand pressed against my back, steering me to the top floor, to a quiet area. He would have pulled the chair out for me to sit down on.

A feeling of melancholy swept through me, and as it ravaged my chest and knocked me breathless, I saw a large figure at the railing of the top floor, his head down, peering at us. The second my eyes found him, his head whipped away, his body twisted to the side, and he stepped away, disappearing from sight.

For a few moments, I sat frozen. Heat rushed to my face as I tried to remember just what he looked like.

Big.

Dark clothing.

Black hair.

I shook my head. *Nonsense.*

I was losing my mind.

But my gaze swept the top floor, and I couldn't remove the niggling feeling in my chest. Without stopping myself, I set my fork down and stood up. Brian asked me where I was going, but I ignored him as I dazedly walked to the staircase and climbed each step.

Every inch of me twitched with anticipation. I couldn't even breathe.

When I reached the top, I stood before a large room, inspecting every single table, searching.

But what was I searching for?

I'd seen him bleed out.

I'd seen the light fade from his eyes.

I'd seen the pool of blood that poured from his side.

It was inconceivable.

Impossible.

Downright ludicrous.

I swayed, hardly able to stand upright when arms suddenly wrapped around me. I gasped, squeezing my eyes shut in yearning as a mouth pressed to my ear. "Victoria, are you alright?"

Brian.

Of course, it was Brian.

I nodded numbly. "I thought I saw someone I know."

This isn't fantasy, Victoria.

This was real life.

He was gone.

*

The rest of the dinner I was distant. I complained about a headache, but I saw the way Kim's gaze narrowed at me. She knew I was full of shit, but the men were clueless.

When we stepped out of the restaurant, the cold air felt cathartic. I breathed the icy air in, hugging my arms across my chest as I gazed at the night sky. You couldn't see many stars, not like you did on the island, or in a cabin on a mountain.

I smiled at the irony.

I felt more like a prisoner out here.

I'd felt more anxiety these past two years of freedom than any other time of my life.

It was so fucked.

Just before we departed ways with Kim and Peter, Brian spoke to them, talking endlessly about something I wasn't paying any attention to.

Overwhelmed with the figure I'd seen over dinner, I turned away to calm down. I walked slowly in the direction of Brian's car, trudging through the crowd, my hand rubbing at my jacket where my chest was. I sucked in a breath, whispered to myself that it was going to be okay, that life kept going, the days kept coming and I would get better.

The snowfall was growing thicker. The wind picked up. People laughed around me, conversations were exchanged. A couple embraced and –

A shoulder slammed into me. I lost my balance and grabbed at the arm belonging to the person that had practically run me down. The first thing I saw was a suit jacket over dark suit pants. I blinked up, sputtering out, "I'm sorry" just as my eyes connected with the face of my past.

He looked down at me, his eyes hard and framed behind a thick set of glasses. His familiar glare cut into me, looking at me with not one ounce of recognition.

My hand immediately dropped, and my vision swam. I shook my head like I was shaking sense into me. "You're not real," I whispered.

He gave me a long look before snapping, "Excuse me, do I know you?"

I took another step back, perfectly aware I was hallucinating. This wasn't real. *He* wasn't real. But... he stood there, on the sidewalk, with a man next to him, watching our exchange with a curious look.

I shook my head, feeling spooked, forcing out a quiet, "No."

He turned away and resumed walking toward the restaurant.

I watched his back as he disappeared in the crowd, his head turned in the direction of the man next to him, chatting away like nothing had happened.

Like I was no one.

Like I wasn't Vixen.

Like he wasn't Hobbs.

Like we were strangers.

47.

VICTORIA...

I didn't know how I got home in one piece. I couldn't remember a single moment of it. I felt like I was in a daze. One second I was on that sidewalk, the next, I'd somehow found my way back to the apartment with Brian.

I wasn't myself.

I paced the apartment, digging out cheap wine from my kitchen cupboard. I drank straight from the bottle and Brian watched me like I was crazy. I got loaded, hoping to grow numb, hoping to forget I'd run into Hobbs on the fucking sidewalk less than an hour ago.

He was real.

It was all real.

Sometimes my time on the island felt like a dream.

Like maybe I'd imagined all of it.

But it was all real. He was real, and the fucker had looked straight through me, like perhaps I wasn't real to him.

I was sure that was what stung the most. I was

invisible now. He played it off so well. You couldn't know he'd had to get drunk just to watch me leave.

I wandered to the lounge room, watching Brian set my perfectly wrapped present under the tree. I took a swig of my bottle, feeling warmth at the sight of him doing that for me. He got me a present. He had it so nicely wrapped; it made my present look like something a four-year-old had wrapped in the dark.

I got him cologne at Hudson Bay. It was on special. It smelled manly. I was sure he'd like it.

But the way Brian held my present made it seem like it was super fragile. Super expensive. *What a nice guy.*

This guy wasn't Nixon, I told myself. The roaring fire I felt for Nixon would never be had again.

In fact, the flame I felt for Brian was akin to a flame from a standard lighter you bought from the local Dollarama.

*But...*it was still a fire at the end of the day.

And who knows? Maybe it would grow. Maybe I could feed it. Maybe I needed to listen to Kim and just let the guy take me. Maybe he would surprise me.

I set the bottle down and stumbled to him as he emerged from under the tree. The second he turned to me, I fell into him, kissing him. He immediately kissed me back, wrapping his arms around me. It was sloppy kissing. It felt pretty good. He led me to the couch and dropped me down on it, coming over me with beaming eyes.

I was so tipsy, my head so cloudy, I felt giddy because maybe – just maybe – I would come. I hadn't felt an orgasm since Nixon. It was too long, and I needed to move on. I needed to realize there were other men out there – good men, nice guys – and they could give it to me just as good.

I was deluding myself.

I was living in complete ignorance.

But I was desperate to prove to myself that perhaps I was still capable of strong emotion.

As Brian kissed me, his hands wandered down my body. His touch was too gentle – too soft. This shit wasn't happening fast enough. "Don't take your clothes off," I hissed at him.

He pulled away to look down at me. "What?"

"Don't take them off."

"Okay, I won't."

I glared. "No, I meant take them off."

Confused, he began taking his clothes off before bringing his lips back down to mine. I brought his hand to my chest, made him cup my boob, but his grip wasn't possessive enough, it wasn't wanting enough. He settled between my legs, hard and ready, his dick still hidden under his briefs. I felt his hand under my skirt. His fingers skirted along the hem of my underwear, and he pulled back to look at me.

"Is this okay?" he asked.

"Don't ask me that," I returned haughtily.

His brows came together. "I'm confused."

"With what?"

"Do you want me to take your underwear off?"

"Why don't you just do what you want to do?"

"But what about you?"

I fumed. "Fuck me, Brian."

He slid my underwear off, his face tense. He looked kind of stressed as he moved back over me. He kissed me again, and then winced when I ran my nails down his back. "That really hurts," he cried out, sounding pained.

"Good," I murmured.

"*Good?*" he returned, shocked. "You want to hurt me?"

"I want you to just fuck me."

"You said that already, and I'm going to, but I don't want you to scratch me, or to tell me not to do something and then mean for me to actually do it."

Jesus Christ. I pulled away. "Don't you have the need to just take me?"

"Of course, I want to make love," he returned. "Maybe you should have told me what you preferred to do before we got in this situation, because I'm fucking confused now."

"I can't tell you what I want, that defeats the purpose," I said, irritated.

"This kind of sounds like a really fucked up game, Victoria."

My eyes brightened. "Exactly, Brian! It's just a game."

Now, he moved off me, looking disturbed. "Is this why you've been avoiding intimacy?" he asked, staring ahead with a blank expression. "Because you've got a weird fucking kink that most people would run the other way from?"

I felt a sharp sting in my chest. "I didn't realize most people would run the other way."

He shot me a look of disbelief. "I'm not comfortable with touching you and you telling me not to. That shit kind of blurs the lines, don't you think?"

"That's why we'd have a code word."

He blinked. "You mean a *safe* word."

"Yeah, sure, call it that."

"I'm not…" he stuttered, shaking his head, looking confused. "I think…I think I should go home. My mom's expecting me to give her a call. She'll want to know how my police training is going and…Yeah, you know, I think I'll give her a call."

Standing up now, he rushed to put his clothes on. I avoided eye contact – he did too – and he took off out of the apartment, saying nothing.

That was the most awkward moment of my life.

Probably his, too.

I blinked slowly into the nothing around me. Then I burst out into giggles, because I was drunk, and this was so fucked it was funny.

I giggled until my giggles turned into fat sobs.

"I'm damaged goods," I said out loud. "Who will want me now?"

No one.

Oh, my God, I was going to die alone.

I slid off the couch and crawled to the tree. I plugged the cord into the wall and watched it light up. I looked up at it, smiling as I cried because it was pretty and I was so sad. And when you see things that are pretty when you were sad it was extra pretty for some reason.

I drank some more wine.

I didn't need Brian, I told myself. I had this tree and this apartment and some money in the bank. Life wasn't so bad.

I stood up and stumbled to the kitchen. I set the bottle down and turned, tripping over the Christmas tree box. I fell dramatically – truly, the slowest, most pathetic fall ever, landing straight on the box, just under the line written in permanent marker. I traced my finger over my address, analysing the penmanship, wondering if I'd ever seen Hobbs' handwriting before.

I had, actually.

He wrote like a calligraphy artist. The curves of his letters were so elegant.

These ones were straight and harsh.

This wasn't from Hobbs.

*

When my head hit the pillow, I fell into a deep sleep.

I had another dream about Nixon. He'd slid into bed and held me to him, and I'd groggily turned and asked him, "How'd you get here?"

"I've always been here," he murmured to me, burying his nose between my neck and shoulder.

"Why don't you visit me more?" I cried, feeling my heart crack.

"I visit you as often as I can."

I relaxed against him as he kissed along my neck, sucking feverishly at my skin. I felt my body heat beneath his touch. Wetness pooled between my legs. I sucked in a breath, admitting, "Brian didn't like our game."

"That game's ours," he growled in my ear.

"I'm starting to realize that."

He held me tighter. "No one will ever get you like I do."

I let out a sad sigh. "I know."

His stubble skimmed my shoulder, his hand slid between my legs, rubbing at my nub of nerves. "You smell like him," he seethed in a low voice. "It's feral. I hate it."

I writhed beneath his touch. "I'm sorry."

"Sorry for what?"

"For smelling like him."

He slipped his finger into me, pumping me slowly. "Tell me you're sorry for kissing that man of law."

"I'm sorry."

"No, tell me what you're sorry for exactly."

He swirled his thumb around my clit, and I groaned, whispering, "I'm sorry for kissing that man of law."

"You can't replace me, you understand?"

I nodded, feeling every inch of me warm. "I understand."

His teeth scraped at my skin, pricking me. "You ever touch a man like him, you wash your skin so I don't have to smell that fuck on you. I'll rise from the dead so fast, he'll be tasting the fist of a ghost."

I nodded eagerly, moaning as he touched me, sucked at my neck, and god, these dreams were always so vivid. They felt so real. I felt like he was truly with me, and if this was all I'd get of him in this lifetime, I'd take it.

I'd take every dream.

Nixon in a dream was better than any man in real life.

But, like every dream, he always left me empty and wanting.

I woke up alone and wet and unfulfilled.

48.

VICTORIA...

T he next morning, I was pacing, unable to quiet my thoughts, unable to stop myself from feeling like odd things were happening in my life.

First, the picture on my camera. I studied the duffle bag, studied the figure holding it. It was too much of a stretch to assume this guy was a contractor, but I couldn't get the thought out of my head.

Next, I saw Hobbs outside Cabochon restaurant, and I was fairly certain he'd been heading inside there. It was the most elite restaurant on that block, it only made sense if that was his destination.

Why was he in town?

Why did Eman – and I had to assume it was Eman – wind up here around the same time?

They were working together. Eman was on a job, and he'd gotten shot up for it. He'd wound up in the hospital and escaped.

Oh, and the bikers were back.

The bikers who, according to Peter, were now working with a bunch of rogue contractors (which was sort of insane, because if this crew belonged to Hobbs, then the bikers certainly didn't know of Hobbs' ties with that robbery that changed my life, the very robbery that destroyed them from within).

See, a lot was happening under the surface, and I was itching to figure out what.

I was tired of this life. I was tired of doing the nine-to-five. I wanted to go back. In that world, I'd be closer to Nixon somehow.

But how do you chase these sort of guys down?

And what the hell was I thinking?

Without Nixon's protection, it was dangerous to be wading into such waters.

Only, I couldn't get the idea out of my head.

Instead of going to work, I called my workplace and coughed dramatically into the phone. "I'm sick," I said, plugging my nose.

"I don't believe you," Cynthia, the receptionist, retorted. "Get a doctor's note."

I scowled but kept my downtrodden voice intact. "I've been calling around. It's not looking like anyone's taking new patients in."

"There are a hundred walk-in clinics, Victoria."

"I don't have a car."

"I don't give a shit."

"Can you tell Justin that I'll be off today?" I replied sweetly, ignoring her demand. This bitch wasn't my boss.

"Why? Because you know he's got a sweet spot for you?"

I dropped my hand from my nose and snarled into the phone. "Yes, Cynthia, because I know he has a sweet spot for me. Because he looks at me like he wants to have my babies. Because, for the first time in one fucking year, I want to take the fucking day off without you guilting me about it, okay? *I'm sick.*"

I hung up before she could respond. I was tired of Cynthia's shit. This was a fucking moving company. They could live without me for one day. Like, relax.

Shoving my old school phone into my pocket, I grabbed my jacket and threw it on. I was out the door, into an elevator and at my bus spot within five minutes.

Destination: Cabochon restaurant.

*

The restaurant was open from 11am onwards. I had to wait around in the cold before it opened, and when it did, I rushed in there, no plan in mind, no idea what the fuck I was looking for, only knowing that Hobbs must have eaten here and that was a good enough start for me.

A hostess by the name of Lori appeared to seat me, smiling kindly. "Upstairs or downstairs?" she asked me, hovering over the two menus in front of her.

Eyeing the menus, I replied, "Upstairs."

"Do you have a reservation?"

Shit. "No."

"One moment. Let me check availability." She flipped through a binder in front of her and skimmed down a page before smiling again. "We have a few tables free at the moment."

She took the menu on the right and led me into the restaurant that was bustling just last night. Right now, it was practically deserted. Right before the staircase, there was a sign that read, "NEW MANAGE-MENT" in bold letters. I couldn't be sure it was there last night.

We walked up the stairs and to a secluded table in the corner.

"Will you be dining alone?" she asked me sweetly as I slid into my chair.

"No," I lied. "I'm actually waiting on someone."

This was the perfect way to ditch my table. I could just say my plus one had bailed on me.

With a pretty smile, she set the menu down on the table before me. "A server will come take your order –"

"Just wondering," I cut in with a smile of my own, "I have a friend that actually frequents this restaurant, but I've lost touch with him."

"I'm not sure I follow," she replied, blinking quickly at me.

"He came here just last night," I said quickly. "I was invited, but I couldn't make it and...I lost his number to let him know. If it's possible, do you think you could pass his number to me?"

She stood up straight, thinking. "I'm not sure we're allowed to do that."

"He's my Uncle," I quickly added.

"You said friend."

I feigned a sad face. "He *was* my uncle, until my aunt divorced him for John, this hipster dude alcoholic who...looked at me in a really fucked-up way."

No, no, *she* was looking at me in a fucked-up way. "I don't think we keep those sort of records."

"He would have made the reservation," I continued urgently. "He's that kind of guy. Always has to be in control of where he goes and what he's up to."

"We really don't keep track of these –"

"His name is Hobbs," I interrupted, staring at her intently.

I saw a hint of recognition in her gaze. She stood up straighter and her face went a little pale. "You know Hobbs?"

My heart jumped in my chest. I leaned over the table, peering deeply at her. "Please, do you know how I can reach him?"

"Who are you?" she asked, like she needed to know first.

"Vic…" I paused, shaking my head slightly. "Vixen. My name is Vixen."

She stood still for several moments, like she was thinking it over. Then she took a step back, telling me, "Let me get the manager for you."

She disappeared from view straight away, her footsteps quick. I sat stiffly in my chair, feeling nervous for the first time in so long.

Life was just so fucking lame.

Nerves like this? It made me feel alive.

Tapping my fingers along the table in anticipation, I glanced around the room, taking in the high ceilings, the large windows and luxury furnishings. Then I looked down at the menu, feeling my soul die at the prices of some of these meals. Meals I couldn't even pronounce.

The sound of footsteps made me look up. A tall, thin man walked in my direction dressed in black fashionable clothing. He was middle-aged, had a groomed white-black beard and sparkling blue eyes. He totally had manager written all over him.

"Good afternoon, I'm Jacques," he told me, standing by the table, looking down at me. "Lori was just telling me you were looking for somebody."

I smiled. "Hobbs."

His smile faltered. "Yes, she said that."

I blinked, waiting for him to continue. "Do you know where I can find him?"

"I'm afraid I can't help you."

My face fell. "Do you know when he'll come back to dine here?"

"I'm afraid I can't help you," he repeated, stiffly.

Goddammit. "He'll want to see me," I urged. "Please."

"We are just a restaurant, my dear," he explained in a friendly way, but his tone was off. "We don't do reunions. We just serve food."

Feeling annoyed, I stiffened a nod. "I understand."

And I did understand. They were afraid of Hobbs, and who wouldn't be? He wasn't the kind of guy you wanted to fuck with.

"But," he added, his voice dropping low, "I've heard the name Vixen thrown around. I've seen the men in power that have said it. I...have heard descriptions of you."

My pulse slowed and my mouth parted as I stared at him with wide eyes. He swallowed and glanced around us, as if making sure we were alone before saying, "You should have a stroll around the restaurant, dear. You might find the answers you're looking for."

He left me straightaway.

I didn't move for minutes on end, feeling a little startled. Then I stood up and looked around the room, taking his words to heart. I didn't see anything out of the ordinary. There were pretty pictures on the wall that didn't mean anything to me. There were a couple diners in the back of the room, but they were old people and they kept looking at me like I was cramping their style.

I went down the stairs of the restaurant, passing Lori who looked at me like she really wanted to tell me something. The bottom floor was equally unimpressive. The restaurant spent a lot of time spewing its history around the walls, telling the diner they'd been around for sixty years, serving the most influential figures over the ages. Its tone was kind of arrogant, but looking over the elite list of diners that had come through, they probably had every right to be.

After a few laps around the room, I stood beside the NEW MANAGEMENT sign and gave Lori – who really, *really* wanted to tell me something – a look of despair.

She looked at me and then the sign, and then she looked at me again.

Then the sign.

Then me.

Then the sign.

Then *I* looked at the sign. It was a pretty average sign for such an arrogant establishment. The board was big, but the actual sign was just a printed piece of paper stuck to it with a blue bit of sticky tack.

A eureka moment struck me as I turned to her and whispered, "Does Hobbs own the restaurant now?"

Lori smiled at me, saying nothing.

Ah, so he did.

I looked around some more, feeling a jolt of excitement now. I wandered to the bar area, glanced briefly at the television screens before my eyes skimmed the empty bar counter. There was a magazine stand in the corner, and on the corner of the bar counter were a bunch of newspapers, but I noticed something odd about the newspapers. They weren't bulky like they usually were. It looked like pages were cut out and piled neatly in a stack. I went to it and picked up the first sheet from the top.

There was an article about the restaurant and the title read: **CABOCHON SAVED.**

My eyes skimmed over it quickly.

Cabochon restaurant, known over the years to be one of the most affluent restaurants in the Pacific Northwest, had struggled the past decade after an architectural renovation turned into one of the costliest blunders in its history. Sending the owners, Tony Holmes and his wife Gloria, into a huge load of debt, the restaurant teetered on the brink of closure.

The Holmes couple describe their moment of relief when two businessmen approached them in their time of need and offered them a deal they couldn't turn away from.

Cabochon was sold for an undisclosed amount.

The new owners, Kyle Shobbs and Nicholas Cooper, aren't new to the city. Having recently bought the Marx Hotel and the popular club Fire-Alive, they've been busy establishing themselves and sure have a lot of money to spare.

My fingers shook.

I quickly folded the paper and pocketed it. I left the bar area, feeling a little weak. Standing by the staircase, I held onto one of the bars as I tried to absorb what I'd just read. It wasn't sinking in. It wasn't making sense...

I hurried out of the restaurant, overwhelmed with the feeling I was being watched.

49.

VICTORIA...

"You've got a hickey on your neck," Kim told me as she stopped by to exchange presents. "Did Brian give you that?"

I handed her present over, frowning. "No, I don't think he did."

Her brows shot up. "Who gave it to you?"

"I don't..." I made a face, confused. "I don't know what you're talking about."

"He must have given it to you. It's really red."

I was too distracted by my thoughts to respond. She set my present down under the tree and turned to look at me. Her soft smile faded a bit as she studied me. "You alright, Victoria?"

"Yeah," I mumbled as I walked around, going in no certain direction. Her eyes flickered down to the article I'd been holding for the past few hours. "What's that?"

"I'm still trying to figure that out," I replied.

"You look like you've been crying."

I had been crying.

My eyes were sore and red. I felt like my emotions

501

had been ripped out of me. So much I'd buried in the wake of Nixon's death now seemed to be resurfacing.

I was devastated. I could hardly swallow without feeling pressure build behind my eyes. And this article was really fucking me up because I didn't understand what I was reading.

Standing still, I looked at Kim seriously. "You know this city better than me, don't you, Kim?"

Looking concerned, she nodded slowly. "Yeah."

"The restaurant we went to, did you know it got bought out?"

She appeared thoughtful for a moment before she nodded. "Yeah, that's why Peter's firm started handing out bookings as presents. The place called them up and told them they were offering seats. I think it was a tactic to build hype around the place because it's under new management. Apparently, the system went down and all the bookings vanished. That's how we were able to snag seats. Pretty lucky, huh? I hear the waiting list before was like two years. The hostess was fully looking appointments over in this giant black binder because the systems weren't up yet. It felt old-school."

"Do you know who bought it?" I asked.

She nodded again. "Yeah, these two guys. They've been buying out a ton of places. They're always in the news now, donating shit. One of them is super hot, but I hear he's not really a nice guy."

I fought the tears swimming behind my eyes as I choked out, "His name is Nicholas?"

Her eyes lit up. "That's right. Nicholas Cooper. He's been kind of everywhere lately. The nurses at the hospital keep gushing about him. You can't really get close to him, from what I hear."

"What do you mean?"

"He's been to a couple functions alone. He rejects every girl's advances. The ladies suspect he's into some kinky shit."

"Why do they suspect that?"

She shrugged weakly. "Because us girls like to fantasize a shit ton, don't we? Rich guy comes into town, rejects every chick that throws herself at him, it just makes him more appealing. More mysterious. Wouldn't you think he's hiding something?"

I didn't answer straightaway.

She eyed me as I paced some more. I knew I was acting out of place. In the two years since my return, I'd never behaved so erratically.

Swallowing hard, I stopped and shakily said, "Are there photos of them?"

She knew something was up, but she didn't say anything about it. Instead, she nodded cautiously and pulled out her phone. "You know, I told you to get one of these and you didn't listen."

I didn't respond as I took the phone from her and pulled up Google. I took a few deep breaths, seeing spots in my vision, before I built up enough courage to type the name in.

I knew what I was going to find.

My heart squeezed tight, and my mind whispered his name.

I knew.

I really did.

But knowing still didn't prepare me.

When the images came up, I wasn't sure what hit the ground first.

The phone...or my body.

*

Kim's arms were wrapped around me as I sat dazedly on the floor, staring straight ahead. I'd completely gone numb. My body had had enough of feeling. It switched off because it was the only way to cope.

"You need to tell me what's going on," she whispered to me, sounding concerned. "You just collapsed."

I glanced down at the phone on the floor, the screen still up, still displaying the photo of Nixon on the street shaking hands with the Holmes couple outside the restaurant.

Thing was, it was a side shot, but I knew his profile, I knew hair like that, I knew every inch of his body by *touch*, by *sight*, by *taste*; it was burned into my memory.

"Do you know Nicholas Cooper?" she prodded, noticing that I was staring at the screen still.

I licked my dry lips, trying to form a response.

"He's got a reputation," she said just then, watching me closely. "I've actually heard Peter talk about him from his office at home. He's got ties with some really bad men."

I didn't respond, and she continued to stare, gauging my reaction. "Victoria, please tell me. Do you know him?"

I blinked away from the screen and looked back at her. "He owns a club and a hotel, right?"

"Marx hotel from memory, but I can't recall the name of the club."

"Do you know if he frequents any of them in particular?"

She shook her head. "No idea. I can try looking it up."

She picked the phone up and started to type away on the screen while I thought it over.

He was alive.

He was in the city.

Hobbs was here, too.

And Eman, I was sure of it.

The crew were probably close behind.

They'd be seeing each other somewhere. Probably a conference room in another...hotel.

Feeling my body jolt, I jumped to my feet. Kim looked up from her phone, asking, "What's going on?"

"I need to go to that hotel," I told her, racing to my room. I opened the drawers of my dresser and started leafing through clothing.

Kim appeared at the doorway, watching me, her blue eyes round. "Why do you need to go there?"

"Because that's where he'll be," I told her. "Or, at least, one of them will be there."

"One of who?"

I made a grunting sound in response. I didn't have it in me to explain. She wouldn't get it and I couldn't waste time. Blowing out a hard breath, I shut my drawer violently and swung my eyes at her. "Do you have anything nice to wear that I can borrow?"

She leaned against the doorway, lips flinching. "What sort of look are you chasing?"

"A dress," I explained. "A form fitting one. I want to show some cleavage, and some leg. I want to feel like..."

Like me.

Because that was me, wasn't it?

The clothes I was wearing now never fit right, never felt right. I missed feeling like a goddess.

"I've got just the right dress," she murmured, smiling at me now. "Do you need me to tag along, Vic?"

I shook my head. "I have to do this alone."

*

Marx hotel was huge, and it was opulent on the inside, but it looked aged on the outside. At night, it almost blended into the rugged street. Its lights were dim, its presence was unremarkable. There was a steady stream of people coming in and out. Some savoury people, others...not so much.

I stepped out of my taxi and stood before the doors, feeling a mixture of nerves and butterflies in the pit of my belly. The only reason I was here was because I had to confront him. He was alive and he'd let me go, and I needed to understand why. Because living like this – feeling like I was breathing only a spoonful of air every few seconds – wasn't going to go away until I had this resolved.

It still hadn't hit me that he was even alive. My body hadn't caught up. My feelings were detached from me. None of it felt real.

I could see my reflection in the glass doors as I approached them. I was in a white, long sleeve, deep plunge, bodycon dress that ended just above my knees. It was a super tight fit, Kim was skinnier than me, but it really showed my curves off and the fabric did well to smooth over the unflattering lumps in certain areas.

The door opened just as I got to them, and a doorman stood before me, smiling kindly as he widened the door to let me through.

"Good evening, Miss," he said.

I walked past him, smiling back. "Good evening."

I stopped in the middle of a large, marbled lobby and looked around. I was immediately out of my depth. This looked nothing like the hotel on the island. It was bigger, fuller, and there were signs everywhere, leading to reception rooms, cocktail rooms, seminars, private meetings and board meetings, and all sorts of functions.

I halted, feeling swamped with shock.

Okay, I didn't know where to go, and now the lobby workers were staring at me curiously.

I moved, my white heels a little tough to walk in because it'd been so long since I'd been this high off the floor – four inches to be exact.

I did full laps around the hotel ground floor. I peeked through doors, walked in on seminars midway through. It was very apparent I was getting absolutely nowhere.

I noticed cameras everywhere I went. Noticed how abnormally monitored this hotel was. For a fleeting moment, I had the most intense fear that maybe there was another girl he called his. Another girl in a pretty dress, trapped inside these walls.

One such girl walked past me in the halls. I stopped moving in the opposite direction and trailed behind her, paranoia eating away at all reason. She was beautiful and tall. Her blonde hair flowed down her back. Her dress was the type he'd have bought and hung in the closet. I wondered, as I followed her, if her pussy was waxed, if my former bitch hairdresser Alessa had worked on her layers because she certainly put more effort in this goddess's hair than mine.

I eyed her bouncy walk. Her hips swayed back and forth like a hypnotic pendulum. So, Nixon had upgraded dramatically, I deduced. He'd found the perfect captive, and she didn't even look miserable.

Because she knew what she had.

I wondered if he fucked her like he did me.

If he forced her down, feeding her his cock. She wouldn't have been stupid to reject him. She wouldn't have spat curses like I did. She would have consented and, how cute, a full-blown consensual affair was transpiring. No lies spewed to hide emotion.

I felt angry at this girl, and so fucking jealous.

My jealousy lasted for a solid ten seconds before the girl let out a beautiful laugh, stopping by the restaurant area to wrap her arms around a man that was so not Nixon.

I almost collapsed with relief.

I'm so fucking crazy.

I changed direction and found myself back in the lobby, back to being gawked at with curiosity by the girls at the front desk.

So, I kept walking.

As I began to turn into a random hallway leading who knows where, I spotted a well-dressed old dude waiting in front of the elevators. I immediately changed direction and joined him. I looked at him from my peripheral, noticed how remarkable his suit was, how expensive his watch looked, how fucking loaded in money he must have been.

This was a long shot.

I was probably wrong to think he was associated with Nixon in any way.

But the old man peered at me from the corner of his eye, too, looking over my body in that hungry way I'd once gotten so used to.

The elevator opened, and he stepped in. I pretended to roll my ankle, gasping in alarm as I fought to regain my balance. He played the hero, stepping out quickly to keep the doors open and to stand me upright again.

"Oh, my God, thank you," I said, flushing.

He smiled. "You're welcome, sweetheart."

I stepped into the elevator, making sure I was a little closer to him than was normal. Of course, these elevators had interior mirrors on every side. Fuck my life. I got to watch him eye my ass before he redirected his gaze ahead.

The elevator doors closed, and he looked at me, waiting expectantly for me to push a button. I smiled kindly. "You first," I said. "The saviour always gets first dibs."

He laughed, louder than was necessary. "I'm afraid you wouldn't like where I'm going."

I tossed my hair back. "And I'm afraid you wouldn't like where *I'm* going, either."

This made him pause as he watched my face carefully now. "Are you one of the girls in the betting room?"

Fucking jackpot.

My smile brightened. "You the gambling type, mister?"

His shoulders relaxed and he looked elated. "My,

my, I can always depend on the gambling room to be frequented by the most beautiful girls."

"You're sweet."

He winked at me – *ew* – and pressed the button to the ground floor.

We rode down and a moment later the elevator doors opened for us. As we stepped out, a cold breeze slammed into me. We were in the underground parking lot. I pretended to adjust my heels so he could overtake me and lead the way. Then I followed as he walked to the end of the huge parking lot and to a door.

This was nothing like the island, either.

It was kind of creepy.

I hurried to his side now, knowing what direction we were going in, aware we would be faced off with some bodyguards, and they would not just let me through without questioning me. Unless, perhaps, I looked like I belonged to this guy.

Taking a deep breath, I slid my arm around the old man's and pressed my shoulder to his, whispering, "I think I need to hold you again, in case I fall."

He turned cherry red. "Hold on to me, honey, and don't let go."

Eww.

We got to the door and he used his cane – I didn't even notice it before, what the fuck – to knock on it.

Moments later, the door opened, and a face poked out. "Yes?"

"Grant here, plus one," old dude replied, smiling up at me with stars in his eyes.

The door shut for a few moments, and then re-opened, this time wide enough to let us through. We squeezed past the bodyguard who'd given us a quick body pat before we went down a narrow staircase to another door.

"Be a darling and open that for me," Grant told me. With a shaky hand, I twisted the knob and turned.

I asked myself what the fuck I'd gotten myself into the second it opened.

50.

VICTORIA...

This place was like an underground club. The lights were dim as we stepped in, music blasted all around. There were people everywhere.

But not normal people.

I could smell the stench of crime in the air. Could see it in the faces of the savages that chatted from every table, from every corner. There was a bar area and a stage filled with dancers. These girls weren't as modest as the ones on the island. They were almost completely nude, dancing provocatively as men salivated from their chairs, tossing money their way.

Still wrapped in my arm, Grant steered me in another direction, moving through the crowd. I felt eyes lap me up. Felt the hands of men casually glide down my back, brushing against my ass, as Grant took me to another door. I felt sick by the time we got to it. This was all wrong. Not what I expected at all.

I'd been too hasty.

I should have just harassed the staff at Cabochon instead.

The bodyguard at this door spoke to Grant, and when he explained who he was, the door opened straight away for us. We stepped into a room almost as large as the one we'd just been in, but instead, this room was bright and quieter. The gentle music was overwhelmed by the sounds of excited voices. There were gambling tables formed on one side, and a small dining area on the other.

Now this, *this* was like the island.

Except...I glanced at the people around the tables, at the black leather jackets, at the cuts on these jackets, and I felt the most intense bolt of fear shoot up my spine.

This room was filled to the brim with bikers, and not just any bikers.

The One Percent.

"Fuck," I whispered under my breath, already detaching from Grant, which was a grave mistake. Grant, my senile hero with the lecherous smile, had been my temporary protection.

The second I let him go, heads swivelled in my direction. I stood alone as the old man trudged to one of the tables, and it had not gone unnoticed.

I stood still, keeping my head held high. I refused to look back at the door, refused to let my emotions slip. I wanted to leave, but I'd been around the block in this kind of world to know that leaving so soon after I'd walked into a room surrounded by these sorts of men was suspicious as fuck.

I looked around, pretended I was searching for a face in the crowd. There were ladies everywhere, some in the laps of bikers, others getting felt up by a man or two, but none – *none* – dressed like I did. They

R.J. LEWIS

were dressed like they were crashing a house party, and I was dressed like I was about to crash a merry-making cocktail event.

"Who the fuck are you?" a gruff voice called out from the corner of the room. I turned to look at him, knowing for sure I was in deep shit. This guy was fucking huge. He sat on this elegant chair, almost like a fucking throne the way he owned it, literally pressed against the corner of the gambling side of the room. He was nursing whiskey from a hand that literally swallowed the glass he was holding. I noticed tattoos on that hand, noticed tattoos on his neck as well, some snaking all the way up to the back of his ear. It was probably all over his skull, too, hidden under inches and inches of ruffled blond hair.

Okay, he looked pretty hot for a bearded biker.

And familiar.

Really familiar.

It didn't mean anything, though, because Roz had looked good, too, and look what a piece of shit he had turned out to be in the end.

It startled me that I was thinking of Roz at a time like this.

Hiding my nerves, I smiled, stating simply, "I'm in the wrong place."

Just as I turned to the door, he said curtly, "Not so fast."

Fuckity-fuck.

I turned back to him, feeling my smile waver now. "Yes?"

"Come here," he demanded.

Heads turned my way, watching me as I made the short trek over. I stopped before him, unable to look him in the eye. He was far too intimidating. "You picked a bad time to come here looking the way you do," he said.

"The Prez will want her," one of the bikers said. "He said he wanted a nice piece of ass."

The biker in front of me looked me over. "Not sure he would like a woman this polished."

"We oughtta just put her in a room and let him decide."

A few murmurs of agreement followed.

I shook my head quickly at the man in the chair. "I'm in the wrong place, believe me."

"Where are you supposed to be?" he asked curiously.

"I was looking for someone."

"Yeah, who?"

"Nicholas Cooper."

The room went quiet for a few moments, and then laughter erupted from all around. "What crack is this girl smoking?" one asked.

"Just another girl trying to get in bed with an untouchable."

"You're more likely to find the lost world of Atlantis than getting your hands on that one."

The only one that wasn't laughing along was the guy on the chair. "Afraid that can't happen," he told me. "He doesn't like to be seen on such short notice."

"Then I guess I'll come back later," I quickly replied, taking a step back. My back slammed into a hard chest and arms wrapped around me.

"The Prez will like this one," the man gripping me said.

"Like I said," the man on the chair retorted, "she's

too polished."

"Isn't that for him to decide? Look at this bitch. She's so clean, I bet her pussy'll taste like a rainbow."

"I assure you it doesn't," I whimpered.

The man holding me growled, "What floor's Prez on again?"

"In the penthouse suite," someone told him. "The first door."

Stares settled on the man in the chair, waiting for his final say. He leaned back, tearing his eyes off me before gesturing with his hand for me to be taken away.

The man yanked me back and steered me to the door. I tried to resist before he peered down at me just before he opened the door and warned, "We can do this the easy way, or the hard way, and I'm thinking you won't be too fond of the hard way, buttercup."

I stopped resisting.

*

He dragged me into the elevator, and we rode up floor after floor. His grip on my arm was bruising. I stared up at the ceiling, trying to fight the tears in my eyes. Two times the doors opened to let people on, but the second they saw us, they stepped back and let the doors close back on their faces.

This was a very bad place.

People turned the other cheek.

"I really think you should let me go," I said quietly, trembling now.

The biker gripping me let out a scoff. "Why should I do that?"

"If something happens to me, people will know."

He cackled now. That was hilarious, apparently. "And I think you should shut the fuck up. If you wanna live, you'll do as you're told."

"Please, mister, I know you guys aren't all bad."

"Save your breath," he retorted as the doors slid open on the top floor.

He dragged me to a door and began pounding on it. I bent over as we waited for the door to be answered. "The fuck you doing?" he asked me, annoyed.

I sucked in air. "Just having a panic attack."

"Well stand up straight so Prez can see you."

I groaned, forcing myself to stand upright. My head swam. I looked at the biker – another pretty one – as he glared at the door. "I'm going to vomit, mister."

"Shut up," he told me.

"I've been in these situations before, you know, and it doesn't get any easier."

Now he gave me an odd look. I was talking crazy. I felt crazy. I couldn't stop thinking how stupid I was. Did I honestly expect this place to be like the one on the island? That I'd breeze into the room and there the crew would be, cheering as they saw me? That Nixon would fall to his knees and declare how much he missed me? In this fantasy, he had a really great excuse for not telling me he was alive.

Fat tears fell from my eyes. "I'm sort of thinking maybe your Prez isn't home."

Ignoring me, the biker pounded on the door again, calling out, "Prez!"

A loud curse sounded on the other side. I went tense and my knees buckled. He was definitely there, and I was screwed.

The door opened a moment later, and there the

Prez stood, white beard to his chest, fat gut hanging out – definitely *not* the stuff of biker romance.

"I got you a girl." The guy sounded proud.

The Prez swung his old, cataract eyes at me. "She's different."

"Different is good sometimes, Prez."

He made a grunting sound. "She looks a bit too polished for me."

"That was my concern."

I gave him a *what-the-fuck* stare. "No, it wasn't."

He ignored me. "She's got the cleanest skin, Prez. Look at her arms. No track marks, and she's conscious. We don't gotta worry about another OD'er."

Not being a drug addict was supposed to give me an edge?

Prez made another sound before widening the door. "Bring her in."

The biker dragged me into the room. I passed a kitchenette and a small living area that was filled with beer bottles and cocaine. The entire place smelled like really strong pot and body odour – I gagged. The biker deposited me in the large bedroom at the foot of a king-sized bed. Unmade. The covers were half hanging from the bed. I spotted questionable stains as the biker spoke to his overlord before leaving, slamming the door closed behind him.

Just like that, I was trapped in a room with the One Percent's president.

"I kind of let that happen," I whispered to myself.

"What's that, darlin'?" Prez called out to me.

"Nothing."

"You want a fix?"

"What?"

I turned to look at him as he stopped by the doorway, looking me over. "I said you want a fix?"

"What does that mean?"

"A hit. Do you want a *hit*?"

"You mean drugs."

He smiled his yellow teeth at me. He needed a dental plan so badly. "Yeah, I got some coke, some pot, I might even have some pills somewhere."

"No, thank you," I said politely – because you never know, I might *polite* my way out of this.

"I'll be right back. You hang out in here, get comfortable. You can take that sweet little dress off you, or you can wait for me to. Might like doing it with my teeth, actually..." His grumbling trailed off as he left the room and started banging around in the living room.

As he sniffed wildly, I spun around the room, searching for a weapon. Nothing really jumped out except a belt on the floor and the lamp on the nightstand. It was fucking disappointing. You'd think a biker would have some guns hanging around...

I raced to the lamp, picking up the belt along the way and ripped the cord to the lamp out of the wall. Spotting the hotel phone, I quickly grabbed it off its cradle and tried to call 911, but nothing went through (and in a hotel that was frequented by criminals, why on earth would I have expected it would?). Feeling panicked, I dialled the front desk number that was taped to the phone.

"Marx Hotel, how may I help you?" chimed a lady.

"Please, help me," I begged. "I've been forced in a room with a biker. I think he's going to hurt me."

"How would you like me to assist you?"

"Are you fucking serious? Call the fucking cops!"

"I'm sorry, I can't do that. What I can do is send up room service –"

"I don't want room service! I am trapped in a hotel room with the president biker of the One Percent!" I seethed.

There was an awkward silence on the other end. Was this lady for real just sitting on the other end not saying anything?

"Are you fucking ghosting me?" I cried, tears springing to my eyes now.

I heard her breathing. Heard chatter all around her. She muffled the phone and there was some murmuring. I faintly heard, "He will feed us to his dogs. Hang up now."

My heart sank.

She wasn't going to do shit.

"Put the phone down," Prez boomed from behind me.

I spun around. He was in the room, staring at me, his eyes all bright and buzzed. Sniffing, he growled again, "Put the fucking phone down or I'll fucking kill you."

I shakily set the phone down.

Now he glanced at the lamp and belt. "Put those down, too."

"I would really like to hold them," I replied in that polite way again.

He stepped toward me and I stepped back. I gripped the lamp tightly, and he smirked with amusement. When he took another step forward, I jumped on the bed and hurried to the other side, almost tripping over my heels in the process.

"We can do this all night long," he murmured, moving in the other direction now. "It won't make a difference. You're going to wind up under me."

I shook my head, panting now because this panic attack was like a noose tightening around my throat. "Listen, President man, I am not as polished as I look."

"Oh?"

"Yeah, I bite."

He chuckled. "I like it dirty."

"I'm very dirty," I told him. "As in, I'm carrying *a lot* of diseases. You don't want to be up in this."

He kept coming to me, unperturbed. "That's alright, honey. I've got a few surprises of my own."

Oh fuck, ew.

I dry heaved, shaking my head furiously at him, pleading, "I'm not even on birth control."

"I like a bit of risk involved."

"I feel like, perhaps, you should be considerate of what *I* like. This should be very mutual."

"I'm packing a big one, honey. You will be very satisfied –"

"I don't think Nicholas Cooper will be okay with this."

Now he stopped and stared at me. Just when I began to think I was getting through to him, he burst out laughing. The laughs were really over the top and unnecessary. He shook his head; I was *such* a comedian. "Ain't God himself gonna be able to get Nicholas Cooper here in the flesh."

Before I could respond, he lunged at me. This old man could move. His giant body pressed against mine. His hand grabbed at my hand that gripped the belt. On reflex, I swung the lamp at him, crashing it against his head.

It didn't even break.

It just made him really angry.

He growled and ripped the lamp from out of my other hand. He threw both items behind him. I heard the lamp shatter, heard my cries flee my lips as he gripped me harshly around my hair and shoved me down on the bed.

I twisted and turned. I tried crawling away, but he just grabbed at my legs and slid me down the bed effortlessly. I tried kicking at him, but he dodged my feet with such expertise and then ripped my heels off each foot.

"I ain't even hard," he murmured, sounding demonic. "This sorta thing really cramps my libido, but you fucking hit me, and my head hurts, and you know what, bitch? I think you're fun to play with."

His hand wrapped around the back of my head. He pressed my face into the mattress, suffocating me. I jerked, opening my mouth wide to breath, but I could hardly suck a breath in. Pressure built behind my eyes as I struggled to stay conscious, and now as he climbed over the bed, pressing a knee into my spine, I could hardly move either.

I shut my eyes, feeling helpless, feeling like I really did fuck up this time and it was purely my fault.

I just...

I needed to know he was alive.

I needed to see it for myself.

To hear it from his mouth.

For him to admit he let me go, once and for all.

I needed that closure, that final crack in my heart.

"Hey, Prez," a deep voice sounded.

"Yeah?" Prez muttered, easing off my spine.

I twisted around, looked straight at Prez as a bullet cracked through the air.

His head...popped above me.

Blood rained down my body and spurted all over my face.

I didn't scream this time.

51.

VICTORIA...

I slid out from under the body, teeth chattering. I felt pressure in my neck and face as I struggled to breathe. Nothing was coming into my body, though. I started to panic. My hands wrapped around my throat as I tried to suck a breath in.

I was going to die.

My heart hurt so much, I felt like my chest was caving in on itself.

Then...

"Shh, baby," came a tender voice. Arms wrapped around me, hauling me off the mattress and against a solid chest. He held me tightly, sitting on the edge of the bed, rocking me against him. "Shh, baby, baby..."

In my hysteria, I twisted in his arms, fighting him off, but he tightened his grip around me and dropped his head to mine, whispering in my ear, "Breathe, now, breathe. You're alright."

I thrashed some more, trying my hardest until finally I felt a giant surge of oxygen in my lungs. I gasped hard, feeling the weight in my chest ease. He rewarded me with, "Good girl, there it is. Deep breaths, baby."

I breathed in and out, and in and out, but now my stomach was rolling. I could see blood everywhere. I felt it coating my skin. It felt cool against the air. I wiped at my face and stared at my red skin, feeling faint.

Blood, blood, blood. Everywhere. Always. Blood followed me wherever I went.

"Stop that," he admonished, grabbing at my hands and forcing them down into my lap so I wouldn't see. "It's just a bit of blood. We've seen worse, haven't we, baby?"

I didn't respond.

My brain was fried. I was in a state of shock.

Not once did I stop to consider who was holding me.

In the back of my mind, I'd made the connection, but on the surface it hadn't registered. Not until the feel of his stubble brushed against my forehead, and the familiarity of that – the memories that cut through me just by feeling that – hit me with the same velocity as that flying bullet.

I startled in his arms, blinking up at him. At *him*, I repeated.

At Nixon.

He looked down at me as I began to shake my head at him, feeling my lips quiver. He began to frown, reading me and saying, "We'll get to that –"

"Get to what?" I cut in, hysterically. "What will we get to, Nixon?"

"Keep your voice down."

"Or what?"

"We gotta act fast. I only planned to kill this

fucker tonight. Any more guys and we might not make it."

Before I could respond, he pulled a burner cell from his pocket and made a call. "Tyrone," he said, "it's done. Have the footage loop itself while the crew get up here." Narrowing his eyes at me, he added, "There's been a complication."

I heard Tyrone's voice on the other end. "I saw her enter the room. They're going to want to know what happened to her."

"Yeah, yeah." He hung up and slipped the phone back into his pocket. Then he stood up and carried me out of the bedroom and to the lounge.

As he began to settle me on the stain-ridden couch, I shook my head furiously. "Don't, don't, Nixon."

"I gotta put you down."

I dug my bloody fingers into the black sweater he was wearing. "I'll scream, Nixon. I will. I'll fucking scream."

He frowned, opening his mouth to respond when a knock sounded. Gritting his teeth, he picked me back up and carried me to the door of the hotel. He peered through the peephole, telling me, "Bury your head against my chest. I don't want you seeing this."

I buried my face into his chest as he opened the door. Footsteps scurried in. Multiple people by the sounds of it, sounding hushed.

"Take him to the bedroom," Nixon directed, quietly. "Eman, we can't fuck this up, alright?"

"I got this," Eman's voice rang out, cockily. "You hold onto that fine ass girl. Hey, Vixen, it's good to see you, angel face."

"Don't talk to her," Nixon snapped.

Without thinking, I snuck a glance and, sure enough, Eman was there, carrying what looked like an unconscious man over his shoulder.

"Hey," Nixon growled down at me, "don't fucking look."

I buried my face against his chest and shut my eyes, breathing him in.

"You should leave," a familiar voice said. Rowan. "You did enough. We can take care of this."

"I want shots against the chest," Nixon demanded. "I want it to look like Jekyll fired at him first before he got shot through the head. I want Matteo to bleed out. Make it look like he was trying to make a call –"

"Nixon," Rowan interrupted calmly. "We know."

Nixon carried me out of the hotel room and down the hallway. At the very end, he stopped out front of another door and used a key card to enter. The room was dark as we stepped in. He hit a few switches and carried me through an exact copy of the penthouse we were just in.

He took me into the bathroom and set me down on the edge of the tub. This time I let him leave me there as he turned his focus to the shower stall. I looked up at him, feeling brittle.

My memory dulled him. He was bigger than life right now. Bigger than I remembered, and just as gorgeous. I noticed some greys in his stubble that weren't there before, and some lines around his eyes, but other than that, he was perfectly preserved.

My heart beat faster. He turned the water on and then turned to me, pausing as his eyes caught mine for the first time in two years.

It felt heady to look at each other. It was almost hard to maintain that connection.

I wondered if he could see my pain.

I wondered if he sensed how deceived I felt.

His expression was stoic. He barely blinked at me before looking away. He appeared unbothered. It stung so much, I felt hot tears fall from my eyes.

"Get naked," he ordered.

"I'd rather not," I retorted, feeling my nostrils flare as the reality of this – us – hit me.

His jaw tensed. "If you don't get naked in five seconds, I'm going to tear that dress off you. I don't care if I have to do it with my blade. I don't care if you scream when I do it, either, because these walls are soundproof. Decide, Victoria."

"I'm sort of in a state of fucking shock, if you haven't noticed," I seethed, glaring at him now. "I almost got raped. The guy got shot in the head right over me. Oh, and another fucking thing, the man that told me he loved me, that told me he would never let me go, the one that was DYING in front of me on that beach two years ago is kind of fucking alive." I threw my arms up in defeat. "Excuse me for not wanting to get naked right this fucking instant."

His expression cracked. Anger seeped out of him as he bent down and gritted out, "You begged to be let go. You spent two years telling me you were miserable."

"I fell in love with you," I cut in.

"Funny, I never heard you say it once."

"Because I was in denial, you asshole." The veins protruded from my neck as I yelled, "And I don't recall you ever saying it to me, either."

He let out a sardonic chuckle. "I did everything for you, Victoria."

"Victoria," I repeated, rolling my eyes. "You would never say my name before. It's not Vixen anymore, not baby like it was two seconds ago, now it's *Victoria.*"

"Because that's your fucking name, and you begged for me to use it."

I stood, glowering up at him. "I know what's going on. You're punishing me, aren't you?"

"Punishing you how?" he bit back.

"You broke me down until I couldn't be on my own, until I depended on you, and then you set me loose. You wanted me to come crawling back to you –"

"I wanted you to think I was dead," he interrupted, harshly, peering down at me with cold eyes.

"So, you faked it."

"I didn't fake it. I thought I was dying. I almost did, but my spirit wouldn't leave my body. It fought to exist in this fucking wasteland, even if it meant letting you go." He looked me over, that expression hardening by the second. "I gave you what you wanted because I couldn't live with myself knowing you were with me and thinking of what life would be like without me. I loved you more than I loved to breathe. But you? You pushed me away, Victoria. You made it clear every time I took you, every time I begged for you to open up, that I would never have your soul. That your soul belonged to you." With a tense jaw, he gritted out, "I let you go. I did it for the two of us." With a defeated look, he added, "I let you go, and I destroyed myself so you wouldn't."

Tears streamed down my face. I felt so much anger in that moment. "You made me mourn you. You made me think you were dead. I don't think you realize how *FUCKED UP* that is. Who does that?"

"I *was* dead," he told me. "There was nothing left inside me."

"And now?" I prodded frantically. "What's inside you now?"

His face went cold. "Not you."

My lips trembled. I felt like my heart was breaking apart all over again, and he didn't care. "I hate you," I whispered, meaning it with every fibre of my being. "I hate you more than anything, you fucking arrogant asshole."

He had the audacity to smirk. "Good. Hate me all you want."

"I will," I told him, confidently. "I will hate you until my last breath."

His brows shot up. "It takes a lot of energy to hate someone that much, Victoria."

I smiled coldly. "I'll happily spend the rest of my life using every ounce of my energy loathing a fucking jerk like you."

"Okay."

"Yeah, *okay*," I taunted. "That's all you ever did. Use short fucking words –"

"Yeah –"

"—and you do it to piss me off! You always tried to wind me up."

"Sure."

"Yeah, *sure*."

"Get in the fucking shower."

"I'd rather sit in another man's blood than get in

your fucking shower, Nixon."

"Is that right?"

"Yeah, that's fucking right –"

He grabbed me by the arm suddenly and dragged me into the shower stall and under the spray. I tried to get out immediately, but he held me down under the spray until I was screaming at him, telling him I loathed him because I really did. I loathed him. I loathed him so much. He responded by shoving me back against the tile wall of the stall and stepping in. Drenched, he stared down at me, the rage in his eyes pinning me in place.

"Let me go!" I shouted at him. "You're a fucking dickhead. Just go, why don't you. Go and actually be dead and then this time I won't spend every fucking minute missing your asshole face! You abducted me, you forced me to love you, but I know to let you go now! I know I'll never look at your stupid face again –"

"You never cared!" he interrupted, shouting down at me as the water trailed down his face. "You made that clear! You spent every night telling me I didn't matter. I was replaceable! I fought to believe otherwise. But you hopped straight into someone else's bed, proving me wrong. Two years and you were happy to move the fuck on –"

"I was trying to feel something, you ignorant dickhead!"

"I hope he made you feel good –"

"He did!" I lied. "Brian really did, Nixon. He fucked me *so* good –"

"You're a fucking liar."

"But he did! Oh, my god, he fucked me with his big cock –"

"But he didn't play our game, you said so –"

"I didn't need him to!"

"So, he just took you, huh? And you writhed?"

"Yeah, I writhed, but that's not your business! As if you haven't jumped into a million beds by now. Doll made it very fucking clear you were a manwhore –"

"That's right," he cut in, grinning devilishly at me now. "I fucked so many tight pussies, baby. A new girl every night."

"Every night?"

"Every night! They fucking bucked beneath my touch, baby. They groaned in my ear –"

I choked back a sob. "I fucking hate you."

"You've made that clear."

"Well, I'll keep saying it. I hate you."

"I'm starting to think you don't."

"I do. You're a fucking poison, Nixon!"

Now he laughed dryly. "What the fuck do you know about poison? You owned me, Vixen, right from the start. You played me like a fiddle. You coursed through my veins like blood. You ate me on the inside. A fucking tapeworm, that's what you were, growing bigger and bigger. I kept thinking I could keep you. I kept thinking I could make you stay. I was so fucking stupid –"

"I was just a thing to you, Nixon," I argued, feeling my voice break. "You kept me in a box. YOU DIDN'T LET ME GROW!"

His eyes looked bloodshot. "You're right. I didn't."

"I just wanted the fucking sun!" I screamed. "You never gave me the sun."

"No, I didn't." He agreed.

"And it's so fucked!"

"What is?"

"That even if I had the choice, I wouldn't leave just the same."

"Why?" he demanded desperately. "Why wouldn't you leave?"

"Because you were my heart."

I crumbled before him, sobbing. He let me slide down the wall, cradling my knees to my chest. He watched me fall apart, watched me with a raw gaze, and then he dropped down to the floor with me. His arm wrapped around my shoulders. He pulled me to him, resting his forehead against mine. He watched me come undone, and I didn't care that I was so exposed to him. I'd let the bastard have this moment. Let him see how broken he'd left me. I'd pick myself up again, I would.

When the water began to cool, he lifted his arm up and adjusted the water, keeping it so hot, it was barely tolerable.

We sat there, squished together like sardines under the cascading water, still in our clothes, still saying nothing.

I felt him watching me. I didn't have the courage to look back.

I'd exposed myself.

Dressed to the nines, I'd come here for him – he knew this – and he'd just torn me to pieces.

Two seconds back into his world and another head had blown apart over me. More blood, more trauma, this was what it was like, what it would always be like.

Why hadn't I remembered that?

Finally, after what felt like forever, he detached

from me and stood up. I hated that I missed him already. That the space he filled next to me felt too good to want gone.

He threw his clothes off and threw them in a sopping pile on the floor beside the toilet. Then he quickly rinsed himself off, washing his skin like he was desperate to finish.

He stepped out when he was done and left the bathroom, slamming the door behind him. I jumped at the sound, staring dejectedly ahead.

What just happened?

On shaky legs, I stood up and removed the dress. I washed myself with weak movements, hardly able to keep myself steady.

I was so hurt.

It wasn't healthy to feel this sort of pain. To give someone that sort of control over your emotions.

I cleaned myself and stepped out. I wrapped myself in a towel and lingered in the bathroom for a long time. I didn't know if he was out there waiting for me. I didn't want to awkwardly confront him, though part of me itched for another round of seething words because it was a rush in my veins.

I hadn't felt this strongly in so long, and yes, it hurt. It hurt to feel, but it was so much better than not feeling anything at all.

He'd said that to me in the cabin, I recalled.

I hadn't agreed with him at the time, but now... now it made perfect sense.

Opening the door, I took a hesitant step out. The bedroom was empty, but I could hear the sound of a television on in the lounge room.

I tiptoed quietly out of the room, wanting to

catch a peek of him.

I stopped suddenly, feeling stunned at the figure on the couch.

Hearing me, Doll's head snapped in my direction, and she smiled. "Hey, Vix."

A huge wave of emotion slammed into me. I felt tears slide down my cheeks. "Doll."

She appeared concerned. "What's wrong?"

"I'm just...really happy to see you."

She looked sceptical. "And I'm a donkey's uncle."

"No, for real," I told her honestly. "I missed you, Doll."

Her smile softened. "We missed you, too. It hasn't been the same without your pretty face in the meeting room."

Still in my towel, I moved to the couch and sat down next to her. "Really?"

She nodded, studying me. "Really, Vix. As Hobbs said once, you elevated the room."

"You didn't seem to think so at the time."

She let out a hard laugh. "It's alright every now and then for a girl to have a bit of healthy competition."

I shook my head slowly at her, disbelieving. "You're the most beautiful girl I've ever seen."

"I have my moments of insecurity."

"They must be very fleeting."

"They are," she acknowledged, running her fingers through her hair. "Anyway, everyone got used to you around. It was really weird when you weren't." Her brow furrowed as she thought about it quietly. "It was weird to see Nixon without you, actually. It seemed unnatural."

"What happened to him on the island, Doll?" I asked, trying to understand. "How did he survive?"

"That redhead doctor that tended to you –"

"Doctor Sullivan."

"Yeah, she was still kicking around. Hadn't left when she was supposed to."

"Why?"

"Her plane had engine problems, and she said she'd wanted to talk to Nixon about his sister."

I felt a pain in my chest. "Leona."

"Yeah, she tended to her." Doll looked sad now. "She wanted to tell Nixon something about it."

"You knew Leona."

Doll nodded. "She was very lovely."

I wondered what Sullivan had to say to him, but it didn't feel right to pry. "Sullivan saved him?"

"Tyrone said Nixon wanted to die on the island. He'd gone cold, started hallucinating, kept talking to Leona, it was really fucked up, but...Tyrone said he wouldn't die. He just kept hanging in there. It simply wasn't his time. Even Sullivan said it defied logic. She'd never seen someone lose so much blood before. He was airlifted to the hospital in the morning."

My mouth parted. "Morning? He lay there all night?"

"The weather picked up the rest of the night. It wasn't safe to land. The winds were bad. Tyrone was with him. He was real cut up about it."

Tyrone had always cared so much for Nixon. It would have devastated him to watch his good friend slowly pass.

"When he got to the hospital, it was real touch and go," she continued. "Sullivan had tended to him

until he was admitted, and then the staff took responsibility of him. She was also cut up about it. I think...
I think she loved Leona. I never asked Nixon about it personally, but when Leona died, Sullivan grieved hard. Made me real sad for them."

Sullivan, who had been so professional and expressionless with me, may have been hiding her own hurt this whole time. That rattled me.

"Why didn't he send for me?" I asked her just then, fighting back tears. "I would have been there for him, Doll."

"Hobbs said Nixon had decided to let you go the night we were supposed to leave for the job, before Flynn had acted on his fucked up method of revenge."

That made me confused. "Why?"

"I don't know. Hobbs just said it was what he wanted, and when Nixon woke up and realized he wasn't dead, Hobbs said he was still firm about his decision."

I shook my head slowly. "I don't buy it, Doll. He wouldn't have let me go before he'd known about Flynn."

"I disagree," she replied firmly. "Nixon wasn't himself toward the end of your relationship, Vix. He behaved erratically. He was...exhausted all the time. If he left you on a job, he twitched and fumed and lost his shit. He was attached to you in a really fucked up way, and he was starting to realize it. He was...empty, Vix. In a way someone who kept trying and failing would be."

Trying with me and failing when he got nowhere.

Guilt ate away at me.

I thought of so many moments I could have

opened up to him, but I was too proud. Too stuck on our dynamic to ever think it could ever evolve.

At the same time, I tried to reason that our relationship was fucked up.

It was volatility and heavy emotion. When he was tender, I was chaos. He pulled and I pushed.

I could have stopped, but I defied him, fighting him when, in actuality, I was fighting against my own nature.

Levelling her with a solemn stare, I asked her bluntly, "Have there been other women, Doll?"

She appeared sympathetic. With a light shrug, she answered, "I don't know, Vix. He's been really private, especially about that sort of thing."

"You'd tell me if there was, though, right?" I implored.

"I would tell you," she assured me. "I'm being serious, though. If you're asking about a specific girl, then the answer is no. But if you're asking if he's fucked around, I don't know. I haven't seen it personally."

"He told me there's been a new girl every day."

Now her face fell. "Jesus."

Without meeting her eye, I also admitted, "I told him I've been fucking a guy with a big dick."

Her fingers stilled through her hair. "Not sure you should have done that."

"We were angry," I pathetically explained. "It seemed like a good move at the time."

"You've got a hickey the size of a golf ball on your neck, I think he would have figured that out on his own. You didn't have to drive that point home to a guy that literally tore his island apart looking for you."

I felt my face heat with shame, but I was also annoyed. "No one gave me a hickey."

"Well, you have one."

"It's probably a straightener burn." That I never recalled hissing over.

She looked at me dryly. "You should take a hard look in the mirror, Vix."

Yeah, I should.

We sat for a few minutes in silence. I felt utterly shattered. I could hardly keep my eyes open. I needed to get out of here.

Standing up, I made to move to the bedroom when she asked, "Where are you going?"

"I need to go," I told her, unable to hide the panic in my voice. "If he comes back, it'll be awkward, and I really need to be on my own right now."

"You're not allowed to leave," she said, standing up. "You were in the middle of something you shouldn't have been. He told me to keep you right here."

"With all due respect, Doll, I'm not his prisoner anymore."

She let out a shocked laugh, shaking her head at me. "The only person imprisoned in your fucked-up relationship was that cocky asshole, and Vix, freedom isn't looking too good on him."

I should have felt good to hear that, but I didn't. I actually felt bad for the asshole that basically told me he'd fucked a girl a day. I did the math in my head.

That was 730 girls.

I tried to be realistic about it. Because that didn't sound right.

With jobs in between, maybe it was closer to 650, give or take.

No, actually, he would have healed from that bullet wound and that would have taken weeks.

So, it was probably in the 500s.

Want to know the worst bit? Knowing how high his sex drive was, I fucking believed it. The fucker may have realistically banged hundreds of girls in the last two years.

He could fly a kite. I was leaving this place.

I stomped to the bedroom, aware I wasn't really going to make a dramatic exit. I had nothing to wear. I could raid his wardrobe, but if I left, I would have to walk past the penthouse President Fuckwad had died in. I was sure it was being micromanaged, and I was sure the dozens of cameras that were probably on this floor alone would ping my movement.

I sat on the bed instead, and Doll stood in the doorway, blocking it.

"No need to do that," I sighed, defeatedly. "I'm not going anywhere."

52.

NIXON...

He looked out the window of the meeting room, missing the view of the ocean. This cement jungle gnawed at him. The incessant beeping of cars, the constant stream of people and sounds, it was no wonder he was pissed all the time.

"The footage is done," Tyrone said from behind him. "I think you'll be impressed."

Nixon didn't dart his eyes at Tyrone. He simply asked, "You managed to find a girl?"

"Tiger and Eman picked up a hooker. She was pretty wasted. She had the same build as Vixen. Doll had like a thousand dresses lying around. We found a white one, looked very similar."

"How'd she look on the screen?"

"We had her marching in and out of there. Made sure she wasn't showing her face. It's a hard tell, man. You'd have to take the footage to a fucking lab to spot a difference."

"She won't talk?"

"She was drugged out of her mind, Nixon. Eman put her in a motel room. Said he couldn't stand the thought of her being taken advantage of in the state that she was in."

"Typical Eman to have a soft spot for these girls."

"What kind of girls? Hookers?"

Nixon shook his head. "Broken girls."

Patching shit up with Eman had turned out to be a good move. He was extremely useful, and he had many important contacts. He'd given Nixon the best tax specialist you could ask for. Expensive, but necessary. Now, Nixon was capable of finally funnelling his money through various businesses without worrying about putting his trust in the wrong hands. Too many dirty accountants out there. Too many rats.

This wasn't like the island where privacy was respected. In the city, the people bit at the rich, demanding transparency. It was fucking annoying.

There was one more job to complete and then Nixon was finally done.

He'd slaved for two years doing job after job. Burying himself in the need to chase the money. He had believed the more he immersed himself in the underbelly, the less he'd feel for that fucking girl.

She was always such a fucking complication.

Nixon fumed, gritting his teeth, feeling rage he hadn't felt in...*ever*.

It had been building for a while, but tonight was the tipping point. She'd come to find him – but why? Why did she feel the need to confront him? She could have let him be.

She should have let him be.

It was painful to admit that he was a weak fuck. That he'd deluded himself into coming here with the objective of starting anew.

He knew very well that the girl – that toxic fucking girl – existed here. He knew very well she'd been living on her own, had a job, had a beta as fuck boyfriend next door. A beta as fuck boy that left her apartment in the early hours of the morning often. A beta as fuck boy that had put the Christmas tree he'd hand delivered to her door together.

Was it wrong that Nixon had often followed her? That even on the job, with a duffle bag in hand, he'd been so close on the bus from her, he could smell the scent of her hair? That…he'd bought the restaurant, wiped the computers and sent that firm a shit ton of seats, knowing very well that girlfriend of the lawyer boy who worked there would tell him to invite Beta Boy and Vixen? He'd just wanted to see her. God, he'd needed to see her happy for himself.

Was it bad that he watched her from the top floor of that restaurant, feeling like his skin had been submerged in acid, as Beta Boy held her hand and whispered in her ear?

Was it bad that he felt the urge to cry?

That he'd killed for her, he'd shed blood to keep her alive, and in the end, it'd made no difference?

He was such a fucking idiot to think that he might return for her, that after setting her free she might come to him.

Wasn't that the saying these days? If you love something, set it free, and if it was meant to be, it'd come back?

He asked himself how he got to this point, but he knew.

Four months ago, the urges he'd tried to suppress erupted out of the box he'd buried inside him. Overflowing with raw need, incapable of fighting against the voice that warned him he should keep her in the past, that she wanted to be on her own – SHE'D BEGGED FOR IT – he found he simply could not.

He decided he just wanted a little peek.

Just a little taste.

This addiction could be managed with minor doses of the drug – of Vixen. He'd be sane again. He would. As a matter of fact, it would help him; it would reaffirm his decision to leave her be.

Yes, yes, that was what he would do.

He'd tracked her back down, forcing the information out of Hobbs who he'd foolishly made promise never to disclose.

"You told me to not to let you know," Hobbs had yelled. "You said you'd let her go and that was the end of it."

"I want to see her," Nixon had simply said. "I need to."

"You don't *need* to."

"Why won't you just tell me where she is?" Nixon suddenly paused, answering his own question when he realized. "You're afraid of what I'll see, aren't you?"

Hobbs had the worst poker face. He frowned. "Nixon...she's got her own life now."

"I can read between the lines. She's fucking someone."

When Hobbs didn't respond straightaway, Nixon cracked. It was only a little bit. Little bit meaning he trashed Hobbs' office, and Hobbs let it happen. He stared at Nixon pitifully.

"You know where she is," he then said, gravely. "You can easily track her down, Nixon. We took her straight back where you caught her. You're coming to me because you want me to stop you. Well, I can't. Stopping you is like telling a tornado to kindly fuck back off into the sky."

Nixon paced and paced, avoiding Hobbs' eye. "Remind me she doesn't want me."

"That's not true, though. She loved you."

"Remind me that she doesn't fit in our world."

"She shined in it."

"Hobbs –"

"You gave her back her freedom. How about you give her the opportunity to come back to you."

Nixon laughed through his despair. "She would never."

"No?"

"No."

"You think if she saw you across the street, she'd walk on by."

"She would."

Hobbs' face fell. "Then maybe the real issue here is you and your incessant self-loathing."

"Don't tempt me with hope," Nixon retorted. "Don't act like she'd come searching for me."

"Fine, then I won't. Don't go to her, Nixon, because you're too weak for her."

"You think I'm weak for a girl," he snarled.

Hobbs smiled, provoking him. "You are."

Nixon saw straight through the fucker. Knew he was provoking him because he missed Vixen too. He wanted her back just as much.

When Nixon ultimately tracked her down, his sole purpose was to prove to himself, and to Hobbs, that he could walk on by.

He'd waited outside her ugly as fuck apartment building, and when he saw her, with a camera bag, in a pair of jean shorts and badly fitted top, his suffering suddenly made sense.

It made sense why he'd spent this entire time bleeding internally.

It made sense why his heart stopped in its tracks and then beat riotously. Why every inch of him felt seized with a visceral impulse to recapture her.

Watching her, being so close – so far too – was hell and he was burning.

This fucking girl spent her afternoon completely clueless of his presence. What a sight it was. To see her freely walk the streets, in her own element, snapping photos with this dreamy look in her eye.

It was then he realized he'd stifled her.

She was right to want to leave.

Flynn had been correct.

She had been a flower that Nixon had let wilt.

Out here, under the promising sky, she bloomed.

"How's your heart?" Hobbs had later asked him. "Is there anything left of it? Did you walk on by like you said you would?"

Nixon felt a tear escape his eye. "I wish she'd never come into my life. I wish I'd never taken that job. I wish…I wish for hell if it meant this pain would end."

Even dying on that beach, he knew she'd come into his life destined to leave it. Destined to make him feel an emptiness that he'd suffer in silence for, for the rest of his days.

Sometimes…

Sometimes he believed he might see her one day and feel nothing for her. It was an exciting thought to have. To no longer be shackled to another person. To no longer feel that deep pining, soul sucking need to belong to them.

Alas, that was not what fate intended.

The want had never lessened.

Quite the contrary, it grew in secret, multiplying like the strand of a virus.

He'd never tried to let her go. He'd just tried to distract himself from chasing after her, from taking her by the hair and dragging her into his pit so she'd never escape from him again.

After all this time, he still felt she belonged to him.

It unnerved him to feel so vulnerable, even after all the evil he was capable of.

It wasn't the bullet that destroyed him, nor was it watching his island burn, taking with it his money and hopes of the future.

It was a girl.

A girl had obliterated him, flayed his skin, incinerated his veins and all that he was made of, reducing him to blood and bone.

He was a shadow of himself without her.

What a mess.

What a sad way to live.

Hungering for the flesh of a being that may not want you.

Could there be a greater punishment than that?

Love was the greatest shackle of all.

VICTORIA...

I heard him come into the room.

It was completely dark. I was trying to sleep in his bed, wrapped in his covers. I'd raided his closet – his taste in clothing hadn't changed. I'd found a plain tee, it was so big on me, it ended at my thighs. It was a stark reminder how big this guy was. How easily you could overlook it when you stared at his face longer than his body.

Unmoving, I opened my eyes, listening carefully as he walked around the bed. I felt him stopping behind me. Felt his eyes on me. I heard his steady breaths while I'd held my own, waiting.

Waiting for what?

He moved away. I saw his figure move in the dark in the direction of the window. He peered out, his body taut, his profile visible by the glow of the city lights. I moved inaudibly, twisting my body just enough that I could watch him look out.

"How's freedom these days, Victoria?" he suddenly asked, his voice cutting through the stillness.

I winced slightly. Of course, he knew I was awake.

He sounded calm, so I wasn't expecting another throwdown.

Opening my mouth, I softly said, "It's freeing."

He chuckled dryly. "Cute." Glancing briefly at me, he added, "Ambiguous responses usually indicate a level of unhappiness."

"What study is this?"

"Only my own," he replied simply.

"Who were you studying to make that connection?"

"Just you."

I swallowed hard, pretending to feel unaffected as I plainly replied, "Well, you're wrong. I'm quite happy."

"Is it your job that's making you happy?" he wondered, his voice dripping in condescension. "Do you feel good when you help people move from one address to the next?"

"A job's a job."

"Because it takes care of you."

"Exactly."

He glanced at me quickly. My heart jumped. "You live in a shithole. Your fridge is always empty. Your microwave is going to blow up one of these days and everything you possess is going to burn to ash."

I narrowed my eyes at him. "What's your point, Nixon?"

"You say you're happy, I'm trying to find the cause of it."

As he turned to look at me, I flopped to my back and stared up at the blank ceiling. "I'm happy because I'm in charge of my life. I have friends. I have a boyfriend."

"Your friend, the nurse?"

"Yes."

"She's conceited and annoying, and her lawyer fiancé's just another shmuck that gets his ass bought out every time he's taking on a client the mob wants silenced."

My heart slowed. "Have you been watching me, Nixon?"

"Yes."

"So, you've got an opinion about my boyfriend, too."

"Is that a question?"

"No, I already know you have an opinion about him. I stated it so you can tell me what it is. That's how conversations progress, Nixon, I would have hoped you'd have gotten better with this over time."

His voice dropped lower. "Fuck, your mouth, Victoria, it's not changed either."

Just hearing him talk like that, so wantonly, produced a heavy pulse between my legs. "Tell me what you think of Brian."

"I have no issues with your boyfriend," he said. "I think he's a really nice guy."

I turned to look at him. I noticed the way his lips curved up. Fucker was smiling.

I frowned. "You're a liar."

"No, I'm being honest. The guy has the cleanest record I've seen yet. He is Mr Suburbia in the flesh. I can see you with him just fine. He'll provide well, will be passionate about his badge number, will be unflinching in the face of violence because he frequents the gym, has muscles, so he must be tough.

"To ensure you don't ride the bus late at night, he'll upgrade his car to a Honda with the extra safety features. He probably knows how to even change a tire when you break down on the side of the road after coming back from a barbecue one summer night. He'll wear a uniform and maybe one night he'll even cuff you. But that'll be years of comfort in the sack. Years of vanilla sex with oral for really special occasions. I think you two will get along just fine."

I felt heat in my face. I couldn't pinpoint my exact

emotion. I was pissed, but at what exactly? At how blasé he sounded? At how right he was and how much it made me feel dead to think of living that sort of life?

What the fuck was wrong with me?

What the fuck was it about Nixon that drove me to extreme emotion?

I was shaking, clenching my jaw tight, trying not to get worked up. He'd answered and that should have been it, but I detected the amusement in his voice. It was so subtle, anyone else would have missed it.

"Well, then," he continued when I didn't respond, "I'm a little confused, Victoria."

"About what?" I asked, lifelessly.

"If you're so happy, why did you seek me out?"

I let out a breath, feeling shocked. "I've been under the impression you were dead, Nixon."

"Yeah, but why seek me out? You could have continued to live your life and I wouldn't have bothered you."

Ouch.

Like a trigger, my eyes felt raw. "Maybe it was to hear you say that."

"You want closure."

"Yeah."

"You want to know that I'm finished with you."

"You made it clear in the bathroom that you were."

"Does that bother you?"

"No," I lied, heatedly. "I'm relieved. I don't have to worry that you'll come out of the shadows and drag me back into your fucked-up world."

"No part of you desires that?"

"No."

"Well, let me offer you closure," he said coldly, "I don't want you, Victoria. I will not be dragging you into my fucked-up world. You're free to leave whenever you want."

I felt sick to my stomach hearing those words. God, I hated him. "I'd have left already, but I was told I had to stay," I retorted.

"We took care of business," he replied, steadfastly. "You may leave."

I slid out of bed straightaway, feeling so fucking triggered, my body was quaking. I stormed into his closet and grabbed one of his sweatpants from a shelf I'd seen earlier. Then I stomped to the bathroom and slammed the door behind me, locking it.

I was panting hard.

I was unwanted.

Rejected.

He was throwing me out like he seriously didn't give one ounce of fuck.

I bent over to climb into his pants when I looked up at the mirror. My eyes were raw with unshed tears. My cheeks were red, my lips raw from nervously biting the fuck out of them all night waiting for his return.

I glared at myself, wanting to scream.

Why did I love this asshole? Why did the thought of leaving this stupid fucking hotel feel so final?

He hadn't come to the city for me. How foolish of me for hoping.

He'd explicitly told me the amount of tight pussies he'd fucked in my absence, and that should have made me gag with indifference for the asshole.

This was so fucked, and I was almost crying. My legs shuddered as I bent over the sink and splashed water over my face, trying to talk sense into myself. I was so flushed, the cold water didn't do a damn thing to help ease me.

I turned the water off and grabbed the handtowel. I pat my face dry, unable to tear my eyes off my reflection. I muttered curses, reprimanding myself for my fucking stupidity. I wanted to punch a hole in my chest and rip my heart out of it and then squash that muscle in the palm of my hand to stop this fucking pain.

I threw my hair back and dried the water trailing lines down my neck, telling myself not to cry.

Then I paused, my gaze zoned in on the giant red mark on my neck. I leaned over the counter and inspected my skin. My breaths thinned. In my daze to come here, I'd missed it.

Kim and Doll were right.

This was a giant hickey, and it looked bruised.

My mind wandered to Brian when he'd kissed me on the couch. He'd kissed my neck, but I was certain he hadn't sucked it. I would have known – that would have been too kinky for a guy like Brian – and he'd never left marks behind before. Our kisses had been so fucking lame. I winced having to admit that to myself, but it was true. His mouth had done nothing for me.

So, how the fuck...

I paused again and glanced at the door.

Realization hit me.

I felt so *stupid.*

He'd known the layout of my apartment.

Knew how fucking sad my microwave was.

Knew Brian hadn't played our game.

I had completely overlooked it in the midst of my emotion.

Of course.

Mother.

Fucker.

The blood in my veins quickened. I yanked the door open and thundered out of the bathroom, my gaze zoned in on Nixon who was still standing by the window. He turned his head in my direction, his curt eyes lapping at me like I was an insect on the wall.

"You sick fuck," I shrieked, coming to a stop in front of him, "You broke into my apartment. You slid into my bed, and you touched me!"

"Impossible," he replied, smirking devilishly at me. "I did no such thing."

"Liar!"

"Perhaps you were dreaming."

"I was not dreaming it," I retorted. "You fingered me, you sucked at my neck, you told me no one would ever fill the space you did."

He appeared amused now. "That's a vivid dream, Victoria."

"It wasn't a dream."

"Did you like it?"

I gritted my teeth. "No," I lied. "I hated it. I asked you to stop."

"Really?" he replied, raising his brows. "No part of you begged for me to keep going?"

"No."

He took a step toward me. I remained rooted to the floor, refusing to budge as he towered over me.

"You didn't complain that your boyfriend didn't like our game?"

My cheeks burned with embarrassment. "I didn't say that."

"You did."

"You misunderstood."

"So, he fucked you anyway, is that what you're telling me?"

"It is."

His expression cooled. He dismissed me by turning back to the window. "You need to leave," he warned me, edgily. "Before I do something very stupid."

"Like what?" I goaded, standing my ground. "What are you going to do that's stupid?"

"Don't poke the bear, Victoria."

"I want to know what you're going to do."

His composure remained intact. "Something very bad."

"Like what?"

"Victoria, *go*."

"No."

His shoulders tensed as a dark look flashed in his eyes. "I'm not feeling in control of my faculties, Victoria, I will fucking hurt you."

Adrenaline coursed through me. I felt a jolt of excitement. "Why?"

"Why do you think?" he hissed.

"Because of Brian?" I asked, smiling coldly. "Are you jealous, Nixon? Does it piss you off that he touched me –"

My breath ripped out of me as he grabbed me and shoved my back against the window. His hand fisted my hair, forcing my gaze up to meet his. He was so big, his entire body swallowed me whole as he leaned in, his blue gaze wicked, his expression tight with fury.

"I'm going to kill him for watching you writhe beneath him," he told me through clenched teeth. "I'm going to enjoy it, too, Vixen. I'm going to watch the life bleed out of his eyes, and I'm going to smile cruelly at the beta man for thinking it was ever okay to touch what's mine."

His grip in my hair was tight, but not overly so. I feigned pain, hissing, "You're hurting me, Nixon."

His expression lit up as he barked out a dry laugh. "You are unbelievable."

Tears pricked my eyes. "I think you should let me go."

"Why?" he growled. "I warned you not to goad me."

"I regret it."

"Liar," he roared in my face. "You're such a fucking liar."

"I'm really not."

His other hand slid under my shirt and cupped at my sex suddenly, making me gasp. He didn't rub me. He just held it there, palming it, smirking viciously at me. "What is it with you?" he growled, eyes never straying from mine. "What do you like about this, Vixen? Is it that I just take you for my own satisfaction that gets you so wet? Is it that even when I fuck you and you beg for me to stop, that I still pleasure you? Do you like when I prove you wrong? Is that the kink? I never could understand."

Tears spilled from my eyes as I choked out, "It's all of it. It's being reduced to a thing, living under the illusion I have no control over how you make my body feel, but also knowing I have full control. That I can trust someone to push my limits and stop when I tell him to, no matter how on the cusp of pleasure he is."

"Where do you draw the line?" he asked, curiously. "Because it wasn't just in the bedroom you tried to be indifferent to me."

"I didn't draw a line," I answered. "I lived my part, protecting myself from what was happening between us, while also longing for freedom."

"Tell me," he urged, desperately, "is it what you thought it would be?"

More tears fell. "No," I admitted. "It isn't, but I just wanted to have that choice, Nixon."

"You think," he took a deep breath now as he fought to control his emotions, "that if I had given you the choice before, you might have stayed with me on the island?"

"I would have stayed, but it wouldn't have ruined me, and I needed to be ruined."

"Explain."

I smiled sadly. "You needed to let me go. I wouldn't have known otherwise the extent of my feelings. I needed to feel your absence. I needed to have lost you."

He devoured every word I spilled between my lips. He looked wretched. His eyes were raw with unshed tears. It was the first time I ever witnessed him look so utterly broken.

And vulnerable.

I sensed fear in him. I knew it was there when his gaze wandered about my face, the longing, the affection, the desire so fucking thick. When he'd realized what he'd done – when he'd let it slip and knew I'd seen it – it was too late to hide it under his rage.

He knew it, too.

He didn't bother to hide it at all.

His forehead dropped to mine. His gaze was trapped to my lips as he slowly began to trail his finger along my core, sliding it through the wet folds. My eyes drifted shut as sparks flew beneath his touch.

"Did you miss me?" he asked, that cocky edge returning.

"Not really," I forced out between moans.

"You didn't miss my fingers along your cunt?"

"You had them along my cunt very recently," I murmured. "I wasn't so deprived."

I heard the smile in his voice. "What about my mouth?"

I shrugged one shoulder. "What about it?"

"Do you miss my tongue against your clit?"

I opened my eyes, feeling like I was going to come just from the look he was giving me. "Maybe you should remind me what it feels like."

His chest shook with silent laughter. "I'm afraid the days of selfless servitude are over, baby."

"What does that mean?"

His grip along my hair tightened painfully. "Kneel, Vix, because *I* need to be reminded what I've missed about your mouth, and it's not just the utter shit you spew."

Before I could reply, he forced me down to my knees, that hand still fisted in my hair. My fingers trembled as I unzipped his jeans, glancing briefly up at him as he watched my every move.

"I'll fucking bite you if you're rough on me," I

warned, though my lips flickered up.

He smiled back. "Noted."

I purposely took longer than necessary to pull his briefs down. I could see the patience leeching from his eyes, felt my scalp burn from the tense way he was tightening it.

I rolled my eyes when I released his hard dick from his briefs. I'd nearly forgotten how huge he was. He didn't need anymore ego than he already had, so I masked my utter fucking need to devour him by flippantly bringing his tip to my mouth. I sucked him only lightly, hardly giving him what he wanted.

"Baby," he said, threateningly, "I'll throat fuck you if you don't stop this shit right this second."

I bit back a smile and widened my mouth. I played it cool for hardly five seconds before I lost control of myself. I sucked him hard, the way he liked, teased him, the way he liked, making him remember what he missed about me.

"Only *I* know what you like," I told him, watching his expression as it morphed to pleasure. "Isn't that right, Nixon?"

He had a ghost of a smile. "Only you, baby."

My heart soared as I took him in deeper. His breaths came out faster. I could feel his body shuddering above me. Jesus, who was the sensitive one now?

"Oh, Nixon," I murmured, smirking now. "I don't think you're going to last very long."

He barked out a laugh mixed with a tortured groan. "I think you're mistaken."

I took him deeper and he tensed, fighting himself. "Used to take longer than this. What happened?"

"Two years without your sweet fucking lips,

Vixen," he hissed. "That's what happened, but I'm not going to come down your throat. We can do that later."

I wanted to prove him wrong. I sped my movements, determined to feel him come in my mouth. It disturbed me how much I wanted to taste him. How cock hungry I felt for this asshole.

His cock swelled impossibly. Just when he was about to come, he pulled away abruptly and yanked me up to my feet. He dragged me like a fucking ragdoll to the bed and threw me down on it.

"Take your top off," he ordered breathlessly. "Now, Vixen, or I'll fucking tear it off with my blade, and don't think I won't."

I took it off and heard him groan. "Fuck, your body is something else."

"It's really not," I argued.

"Shut up, baby," he retorted, dropping down over me. He dropped his head to my chest and took a nipple into his mouth. My hands grabbed at his shoulders, the tips of my fingers sank into his skin as he moved to the next breast and sucked it. Then his hands came up and palmed them, a soft groan leaving his lips as he pushed my breasts together. "See that," he told me. "See how they fit in my hands just right, Vixen? Tell me your body wasn't moulded for me."

"It is," I admitted, refusing to lie about this. "It really is."

Without letting my tits go, he slid down the bed and buried his face between my legs. His actions were always so abrupt. I jerked at the feel of his tongue as it feverishly worked me. I was going to come already. My hands shot to his head. I grabbed a fistful of that fuckable hair – always that fuckable hair that riled me up – as he devoured me and sent me into a perilous fall.

I chanted his name.

It was all so familiar.

It was everything I missed and more.

I came quickly, the orgasm so big, I shook through it.

He pulled away. "I missed your little sounds," he said. "God, I missed everything about you, baby." Now he paused as he brought his body over me, dropping his head back down to mine. "Why are you crying?"

I was an emotional mess.

The orgasm had left me boneless.

I felt intense whiplash.

"I feel like my soul's being ripped open," I cried. "I spent so many hours thinking about you...I cried myself to sleep, Nixon."

He looked broken. "I never intended to hurt you. I needed you to live for yourself."

"I never moved on," I admitted, breathing harshly. "Nixon, I was never with anyone."

His expression tightened. "That neighbour –"

"We kissed. That was the extent of it."

I watched as he swallowed. "I thought...I thought you'd forgotten me."

I laughed through my shock. "Forgotten you?" Tears streamed down my face. "You were my hero, Nixon. You saved me."

His eyes misted over. He fought to contain himself. "I've not been in a good place, Victoria. I feel... I feel like I've been walking around without a pulse.

Everything works, my body moves, I breathe, and I drink, and I eat, and I sleep...but there's a hollowness in my core. My heart's missing, and I'm okay with living with that void if it means you're happy out here."

I ran my hand over his face, tracing his features. "I'm happiest with you."

The look of vulnerability returned. He sucked in a breath. "It's just been you, baby. Just you."

"No girls?"

He looked at me like I was stupid. "You've ruined me."

"I don't believe you."

He wrapped my leg around his hip, his cock hovering over my entrance. "I don't care. It's true. You've ruined me in this life and the next. It's just you, only you, all you. It's been you since I saw you on that fucking bus, looking so pitiful."

I felt heat in my cheeks. "I was pretty pitiful."

He sank into me slowly, chuckling as I winced. "Go on, baby, say something vile. I know you're waiting for it."

But I was too busy staring into his blue eyes, too busy feeling like I was being healed from a slow death. "I don't think it's one of those times, Nixon. I need you. I need you over me. I need you in me. I need you kissing me, feeling me, whispering in my ear. I need your love and your affection. I need all of it because I've without it for too long and I might die if you don't give me this."

His amusement faded as he nodded solemnly and delivered just that.

He moved in and out of me, bringing his lips to mine, devouring my mouth as he moved slowly in-

side me.
It was intimacy.
It was love.

I'd never felt so peace before.

NIXON...

She was his everything.

He cradled her to his chest, holding her tightly, never wanting to let her go.

He hadn't felt this happy in all his life.

When Jane Sullivan had seen him, had saved him, had tried her hardest to keep the darkness at bay, she'd said something to him.

Something he'd needed to hear.

She'd held his hand and dropped her mouth to his ear, whispering, "Leona's greatest regret was not reaching out to you in time. She loved you, Nixon. She said you protected her. You were her hero. She would want you to hang on. Please, Nixon, hang on."

And he did.

And he'd wondered why when all hanging on had given him was this bleak emptiness.

But as he held Victoria in his arms, smelling her scent, kissing her head, feeling her warmth, he understood why he'd held on.

So he could have this moment.

53.

VICTORIA...

C hatter woke me up from the deepest sleep I'd had in two years.

I rolled over in bed, my arm outstretched, searching for Nixon. When I didn't feel him, I opened my eyes to the sunlight pouring through the window.

I'd slept in. I could feel that the morning had come and gone. Glancing bleary eyed at the clock on the nightstand, I was right. It was noon.

As I slid off the bed and went to the bathroom, I ached everywhere. It was that delicious feeling of being fucked so thoroughly, every inch of my body used and deliciously sore.

The lights in here were oppressive as fuck. I blinked at the mirror and shuddered. I looked like a gargoyle on acid. My hair was everywhere, the bags under my eyes were absolutely criminal. No girl should look so bad in the mornings. Looking away from that negativity, I went to the toilet and then I hunted down some Listerine from the sink cabinet. If there was one thing about living with Nixon had taught me, it was that he was extremely anal about

dental hygiene and the cabinets had always over-
flowed with every bathroom essential.

I washed my hands and face and brushed my teeth
with a new toothbrush.

Feeling a bit better, I wandered out of the room,
still half-asleep, not really paying mind to the fact
that the chatter I'd woken to was still carrying on.

I froze midway to the lounge room, my gaze con-
necting to the couch where Nixon and a biker sat.
They heard me approach and turned their heads to
me.

"I'm sorry," I immediately said, realizing how in-
appropriate I looked. I was still in Nixon's baggy t-
shirt, and while it looked like a tent of a dress on me,
it was white and kind of see-through. I crossed my
arms over my chest in an effort to covertly hide my
boobs.

"It's alright, baby," Nixon replied, smirking at me.
"We were just talking about you."

"Why?" I asked, my tone sounding accusatory.

"Running through what happened last night."

My gaze swept back to the biker. When his eyes
met mine, I realized I'd seen this bastard last night.
"You were the asshole on the chair," I said rudely. "You
sent me to that nasty fucking old man!"

"I didn't want to," he responded. "By the time
everyone was agreeing to send you up, I had no
choice."

I stared at him for a few moments, my eyes narrowed. He sounded familiar, and again, I thought of
Roz when I looked at him. My chest tightened with
emotion as I took another step closer to him, tilting
my head to the side, inspecting him.

566

He didn't *look* familiar, but there was something I recognized in his eyes and in his expression.

"Who the fuck are you?" I asked aloud, more to myself now as I studied him.

When he smiled softly, I felt like the rug had been pulled out from under me. I knew that charming smile. I'd blushed under it furiously once upon a time. Choked up straight away, I questioned in a weak voice, "Flynn?"

"I worried you recognized me last night."

"Oh, my God," I whispered, swinging my eyes back to Nixon. "What the fuck is happening?"

"The powers that be are changing," Nixon replied carefully. "When you see an opportunity, baby, you take it. That's what we're doing."

I shook my head, confused. "I don't understand. Flynn's a biker now?"

"Flynn's climbed the ladder in the most unprecedented way," Nixon explained. "He's revived a dying MC with my help."

I looked between them, shocked. "Why revive the One Percent?"

"They were fading out," Flynn explained. "The club was dying, but the city still feared their name. You can't build that fear without shedding so much blood. I couldn't start a gang up and in such a short amount of time scar the public the way the One Percent have. So, I became part of it. With Nixon's help, I managed to create a new network that ensured they'd rebuild themselves."

"Flynn recruited the crew to intercept the drug supply from the Vipers," Nixon continued. "The Vipers overtook the One Percent when they burnt out.

There was a huge vacuum in the drug market. They began dealing with the cartel themselves, elevating their rank, but they weren't good with their money. They spent it on shit, got the law on their backs, got sloppy with their transport trucks. They were going to cause more harm than good if they weren't stopped. An imbalance in the drug supply would have driven the prices right up, would have created a lot of crime on the streets as people got desperate. This is necessary. A feud, a fight to overtake a sloppy power."

"A resurgence of gang violence," I murmured, remembering what Peter said. "You created another war. The Vipers against the One Percent and their hired rogue contractors."

Nixon nodded. "Yes, baby."

"For what purpose?"

"To evolve," he said. "I don't want to migrate from job to job. I'm tired of cleaning out money houses. It's time for a change. For a new superpower."

"And that's you?"

Nixon glanced at Flynn. "The President of the One Percent is dead, but he got so close to Flynn that Flynn, a spark in the dying embers of that gang, became VP. It was an unparalleled elevation of rank no gang has ever witnessed."

"What did you have to do to get to that?" I asked Flynn, feeling horrified.

Flynn's expression remained blank. "I owe it to Nixon for what he did to help me get there. We shed a lot of blood, Vixen."

"The President was going to die regardless of me being in his room," I said, trying to connect the dots now. "And the unconscious guy on Eman's shoulder –"

"The leader of the Vipers," Nixon cut in. "Sedated on the elevator on his way up, but conscious for the imaginary meeting we orchestrated on his way there. Enough witnesses got to see him. He was just found dead in the Prez's suite in what looked like a shootout between two men."

I felt faint. "This is going to be another blood-bath."

"The Vipers are being cleansed out," Flynn said. "If they're smart, they'll back down. We've intercepted their drug supply, we've made contact with the cartel, we're in the midst of forming a better deal. The Vipers have nothing."

I wasn't looking at Flynn now. My eyes were glued to Nixon's. "Where do you fit into this?"

"I'm buying out businesses," he said. "Hobbs and I will be funnelling the One Percent's earnings through our books."

"Laundering."

"With a cut."

I felt weak now. Like I might collapse. "And Flynn is going to become President?"

"Is that so hard to believe?"

I looked back at Flynn, trying to remember that charming man from two years ago. Any sign of *kid* in him was gone. He was all man. His body had filled out. His facial hair was startling because it made him look older than he was. He seemed...detached but...also self-assured. There were shadows in his eyes. He'd seen and done things he wasn't proud of.

If he hadn't smiled at me, I wouldn't have made the connection. I wouldn't have known it was him. I stared at him for longer than normal. It was downright astonishing how unrecognizable he was.

I felt sad that the man that had reacted purely out of love to avenge his brother was now driven to doing such vile things. Was he so far gone that he could justify wanting to live as a biker of a gang his whole life? And not just any gang, but one that had ravaged the city's streets for so many years, inflicting terror on its citizens and solidifying a reputation in the underbelly.

This was too much to take in all at once. I took a step back, feeling like my head was spinning.

"I need a minute," I whispered, leaving them on the couch to return to the bedroom.

I sat on the bed for a long while, staring bleakly out the window at the skyscrapers and overcast sky.

I couldn't determine what I was feeling. I felt like I was being pulled in all directions. I was infatuated with Nixon, completely consumed in him. I fucking loved him, and being in his arms had felt right last night. I'd spent two years pining for him; I couldn't let him go, no way...

But he wasn't a good man.

He wasn't going to leave the world of crime behind. This was who he was. Did I think for a single moment that he might whisk me back to the island and everything was going to go back to the way it was? Maybe, on that island, I had seen him separate from his corruption. I was detached from it, had only been privy to the information in the meeting room among the crew to know they were up to no good, but he had done the jobs off the island, so it'd never felt all that real.

"You're unhappy."

His voice broke through my thoughts. I twisted my head and found him in the doorway, hands in his pockets, watching me.

"How long have you been there?" I asked.

"Long enough to see the wheels spinning in your head," he answered. "You look frightened."

I turned back to the window and let out a sigh. "I didn't expect any of this. I thought...I thought maybe you'd come here to be with me." I shook my head, feeling stupid. "Instead, you're overthrowing a gang that controls a drug supply."

"You're realizing I'm not all that good," he replied, softly. "That I'm going to be part of the problem, and not part of the solution. It's fucking with your morality."

I didn't answer because he wasn't necessarily wrong.

"I can throw a charity ball every few months if that'll make you feel better," he then said, half-amused, half-serious.

I rolled my eyes. "You're funny, Nixon."

"I care what you think."

"How about caring about everyone else?" I retorted. "How about...*helping* the streets instead of fucking them up?"

Nixon moved across the room, stopping to face me, his back to the wall beside the window. Hands still in his pockets, hair neatly combed back, black sweater, dark jeans, this man had such a simple look, but he seemed to own it in such a way it magnetized the world to him. I hated that when his blue eyes met mine, I felt my pulse weaken, felt my body tighten, felt a million little rockets firing in my body, desperate to be touched by him.

He was such a weakness.

He was already fucking with my head, and he'd re-entered my life for barely a minute.

"The streets will never be clean, Vixen," he told me, trying to help me understand. "No matter what, it'll be rampant with crime, with desperate people after their own selfish needs. That's the human condition, baby, we put ourselves first, even if our needs are volatile and harmful. This isn't the selfless sort of world you keep trying to believe it is."

"You fought to keep the island clean," I replied, stubbornly. "And it was. You did good on that island, Nixon."

"If it were up to me, if it were possible, I'd make the world that way, but micromanaging an island is a completely different beast to micromanaging a city. Out here, it is systematic chaos. Out here, it is mayhem and corruption and the only way to be on top is to become entrenched in the very nature of the beast, until you can't tell yourself apart from it."

He came to me then and knelt in front of me, so I had no choice but to look at him as he continued. "I'm not handing out drugs like it's candy," he said firmly. "I don't care how the money is made. I'm just the method to transferring dirty cash into clean cash."

"And what about Flynn?" I argued, brokenly. "Why is he part of this at all? He was a broken guy, Nixon. He was *good*."

"You're thinking about it all wrong. Stop thinking good and bad. You keep trying to separate this shit into two categories. You're setting yourself up for disaster because the more you try and do that, the more the lines are going to start to blur. There is no good, and there is no bad. There's just us, Vixen. People with their own agendas. And Flynn...he sought me out, baby. He came to me, resolute, with a purpose in mind. The guy had a shit ton of money from his brother before he'd passed. He'd recruited men to sabotage me. He'd done multiple jobs for Toby alone. Whatever his reasons are for progressing to this are his own. I didn't influence him in the slightest. I became his ally."

"But why become his ally?" I implored, staring at him with confusion. "I don't get why you ever let him go. You said...you recognized his rage in yourself, but...it wasn't like you to let him go, Nixon."

His face fell, his eyes grew distant. "When I saw him standing there, holding you against him, pretending he had a weapon on you, I saw the chaos in his eyes. I saw his fear, the weight of the world on his shoulders. He reminded me of you when you ran out of that cabin, falling in the snow, not running from me, but running from yourself. Flynn was at war with himself, not with me. Because Flynn, at the core of it all, still believed there was good and bad. He'd seen his brother be good to him – his brother's goodness was all he knew at the time – and to hear him capable of evil, destroyed him, made him lash out because he couldn't come to grips that you could be two of those things at the same time."

I took a moment to think that over. I recalled the pain in Flynn's eyes when I told him what became of Roz. I felt wretched for him.

And wretched for Nixon because...

My throat swelled with emotion. I blinked tears

at Nixon, whispering, "It reminded you of Leona, too." Nixon's face went tight. I let out a slow breath, adding, "She saw your goodness, and she saw your immorality, and she couldn't understand which of the two outweighed the other."

He didn't respond. His expression was flat, but I knew he was hiding his hurt. I knew it was important for me to also say, "I know your good outweighs it, Nixon."

"How do you know that?" he asked mutely.

I smiled sadly at him. "Because you saved me. You saved me from the bad guys, you saved me from an empty life, you saved me...from myself."

The breath he took was heavy. I could sense his agony. Pulling away, he stood back up and wandered back to the window. With a quiet voice, he said, "You're my greatest weakness, Victoria, and my greatest strength. You gave me purpose in my darkest hour. I knew the light you could bring into my life, had seen it on that mountain, and I selfishly stole that light, stole you, because I wanted to have you to myself. I know what I did was wrong. I know I suffocated you. I was honest when I said I would never steal you again." He turned his head in my direction, staring at me with a look of reverence. "I want you to bloom. I want your light to shine. I also still want *you*."

Tears fell from my eyes. "Nixon—"

"I did come here for you," he cut in. "Even when I saw you with another man, I still felt like you belonged to me. I broke into your apartment, I slept next to you for many nights, holding you in my arms, whispering in your ear. I followed you on the streets. I watched you on the bus. I lured you to the restaurant just so I could watch you eat. It was punishing. It was worse than being away from you and not seeing you do any of these things. The last thing I expected...was for you to ever try and seek me out, dressed the way you were, looking so fucking beautiful in that dress, with your hair down, with the purpose of trying to impress me. I had no expectation you'd come to me, Vixen, but I still had hope you might. That you would see me one day, maybe hear about me from a friend or a co-worker, and maybe...maybe believed what we shared was real."

"It was real," I told him adamantly. "It was real, Nixon. All of it."

"Then stand with me," he told me urgently, the plea in his eyes disarming me. "I can't do this without you. I need your strength and your love. I'm so weak for you, Victoria, I've spent every minute on my knees for you. You've always stood over me, in control of my heart, of my spirit. I need you to need us as much as I do." His gaze grew heavy as he went back to me and dropped to his knees, sliding his arms around me, staring into my eyes. "Be my Queen."

I dropped my forehead to his, studying his face as I rested my hand to his cheek. I lightly kissed him and watched as his eyes closed, as his chest expanded. You'd think I was feeding him a drug.

Whispering, I said, "If I'm your Queen, then you're my King. And that means, we sort of need our own little castle."

"Anything for you, baby," he said.

"I don't want to live in a hotel."

"I'm already building a house for us."

Of course, he was. I smiled. "Is it on a mountain?"

"At the very top."

"Will I have my own horse drawn carriage?"

"Yes," he said. "And you'll leave in it whenever your heart desires."

"Keep going, Nixon," I said, amused. "What else will we have?"

"We'll have each other," he told me, opening his eyes to look at me. "I'll make an entire floor into a library for you. You can have your own arts and crafts room. You can fill our house with your pottery shit –"

"And Christmas lights."

"I don't give a fuck if the lights are on in the summer, baby, you'll have Christmas lights and Christmas trees –"

"Like the one you got me?"

He smiled. "Like the one I got you."

"And my own throne room."

"As long as I get to fuck you in our throne room."

"You may," I consented, smiling devilishly at him. "But don't you think a castle that big is too much space for just the two of us?"

He smiled back, but his eyes were raw with elation. "We can fill it dogs and cats."

"Oh?"

"And farm animals."

"Hmm."

With a tilted head, he added, "And princes and princesses." My heart hammered as he studied my reaction, asking me then, "How do you feel about that?"

Sucking in a breath, I felt a tear leave my eye when I answered. "I feel good, Nixon."

54.

VICTORIA...

I wandered my empty apartment, taking one last look around before I left for good. I didn't expect to feel as sad as I was about leaving it, but...these rooms were filled with sadness, with endless tears spent agonizing over Nixon.

I should have loved to leave it behind.

I didn't.

In these walls, I'd learned to self-soothe, to tell myself that everything was going to be okay.

In these walls, I'd confronted my mother's passing, learned to tell her hello in the mornings and good-bye in the nights.

There was no joy in leaving behind a place that was imprinted with your hardships.

"I think I'll burn this apartment down," said Hobbs, storming out of my bedroom with a filthy glare. "This is oppressive as fuck, Vixen. I want to know the name and number of your landlord."

"Hate him all you want," I replied, amused. "Rent was cheap, Hobbs. People around here sell their organs to the black market just to make rent."

For the first time in a long time, Hobbs actually smiled in response. It was so rare to see that happen.

Ever since I'd gotten back into the picture, Hobbs wouldn't leave me alone. He followed me like a bad smell, determined to make sure I had everything I needed. I figured he might have felt a little guilty for seeing straight through me outside Cabochon, but Hobbs never struck me as the kind of guy that felt guilty about anything. He was so textbook, every step in his life exacted, every decision and action thoroughly thought out.

"And so, ends another chapter," he said as I closed the blinds and set the keys on the counter for the landlord. "What can we expect on our next journey, Vixen?"

With a grin, I said, "What have we endured thus far, Hobbs?"

"Chaos and endless mourning."

"I would have said consistent togetherness, but okay, that's another thing to add to the list."

"If you're referring to the crew, I'd say you're sadly right. I don't know how I wound up with a bunch of idiotic fuckheads."

I laughed. "Ouch."

His nostrils flared. "They never let me talk."

"They get excited."

"I can't ever finish a sentence without one of them saying something utterly meaningless."

I went past him to the kitchen and checked the cupboards one last time, making sure they were completely empty. "It can be infuriating," I agreed. "Tiger's learned to keep it cool, and Eman isn't so temperamental."

"Because Eman is distracted by pussy."

I tossed him a curious look. "And what about you, Hobbs? Any attachments I should know about?"

Leaning against the counter of the kitchen, he gave me a bored look. "I like my privacy."

"Is that a yes?"

"I didn't say that."

"So, there isn't anyone."

"I didn't say that, either."

"Okay, so there *is* someone."

"I know what you're doing. Trying to annoy me into talking. It won't work."

I laughed and, after checking the last cupboard, turned away. "I'm done, I think. The place is empty."

"I found a small present addressed to a Brian outside your door," he mentioned suddenly. "I had one of the movers place it in the car for you."

I cringed so hard. "Brian returned my present after all this time."

Even Hobbs couldn't look me in the eye. "That's awkward."

Ever since *that* night, Brian had taken drastic measures to avoid seeing me. The feelings were mutual. I had to look both ways every time I stepped out of my apartment, which wasn't often because Nixon demanded I be with him every night; he'd finally managed to convince me to move into the hotel until our house was built, though I say the word convince very loosely; it didn't take much effort at all.

My relationship with Nixon had escalated very rapidly, and yet it didn't feel fast enough. One morning, I woke up to a closet full of dresses and a call from the front desk alerting me to dinner reservations at the hotel restaurant downstairs.

I remembered my heart feeling like it had ballooned three sizes.

Nixon was trying to incorporate our old us into the present, and I found solace in that.

Things were different, but also the same, and together it was perfect harmony.

It was weeks of sweet bliss. Weeks of enjoying each other's bodies and company and endless conversation.

As I slid into my heels, smiling softly at the thought of dinner with Nixon, Hobbs took me suddenly by the arm, causing me to look up at him. He looked down at me solemnly, stating, "You can't leave him, Vixen. If you're going to him, if this is what you really want, don't expect he'll let you go. He may tell you it's up to you, but once you cross that line, I think he will snap. You will become his everything."

"What makes you think I want to go?" I asked lightly. "I'm leaving everything behind for us."

"Because I've seen him without you, and it broke me, Vixen." Hobbs looked miserable as he reflected on it. "I never knew what it was like to watch a person live without their soul. I'd never thought it even possible. He proved me wrong, and the dreariness over those two years is not something I can easily forget."

I made sure he saw the stark look in my eye when I leaned to him, stating clearly, "I love him, Hobbs. I am going to look after this heart. I'm not going anywhere. Trust me."

His expression eased as he nodded at me.

We left the apartment and rode the elevator down to the ground floor. As we stepped out of the building, we found Doll by the car, blowing bubble gum as she tried to fit my stuff in the boot of the chauffeur car Nixon had assigned for me.

Hobbs rolled his eyes at her. "Ease it, Doll, you'll break a nail."

"You act like I don't wield a weapon for a living," she retorted. "I think I'm more butch than you at things, Hobbs."

Coming close to her side, he gave her an admonishing look, sternly retorting, "Pull your fucking shorts down, Doll, I'm tired of seeing your ass hang out. I'm also tired of you talking to me in that fucking tone. You reel that fucking attitude in, or I'll really show you how butch I can get."

Their interactions were always so fucking bizarre because Doll, who never listened to anyone or accepted anyone's shit, always obeyed Hobbs. Her cheeks went red as she pulled her shorts down. I didn't know how she was wearing it. It was the end of February now, and the weather was cold and rainy.

I slipped into the car as they talked, not wanting to impede on them. I pulled out my phone – upgraded to the latest version, finally – and checked my messages.

The most recent was from Nixon, telling me in x-rated details how much he looked forward to taking me to bed tonight. I responded that the feeling was so very, *very* mutual.

Under that message were Kim's from a few days ago, but she hadn't messaged me since. Ever since she'd found out I was with *Nicholas Cooper*, she'd taken a step back, but not maliciously. She'd told me over lunch one day that Peter felt uncomfortable with her being around me in light of my connection to Nixon and his criminal affiliations.

I understood her apprehension. I also couldn't blame her, or Peter – even though he was a dirty lawyer. Some lines had to be drawn. We still spoke, we still visited each other in very public places, but she was less nosey this time around, though her curiosity was inescapable.

When their spat ended, Hobbs slid into the front seat next to the driver, and Doll slid into the back with me. She looked like a scolded child, barely meeting my eye as she angrily put her seatbelt on.

The ride back to the hotel was tense. The only sound came from the windshield wipers and the occasional throat clearing from the driver – which annoyed Hobbs because he glared at him every time he did it.

Just when I began to think the ride was going to take forever, a loud BOOM erupted, making me jump in my seat. Traffic slowed down as clouds of heavy smoke emerged from up ahead. I leaned forward, trying to see what had gone wrong, trying to make out what building had just blown up when Hobbs' phone buzzed; and just as his buzzed, Doll's buzzed at the same time.

I watched as they both pulled their phones out, swiping through their screens, eyes transfixed.

In that moment sirens sounded. Police cars zoomed down the streets, their lights flashing, puddles splashing in their wake. Crowds of people ran in the direction of the explosion. I could hear horrified screams and cars honking their horns and doors slamming shut as they fled their vehicles and hurried in that general direction.

Following not far behind were ambulances.

"And so it continues," Hobbs muttered, looking up from his phone. "Another one bites the dust."

"Goodbye, Vipers," Doll whispered, pocketing her phone.

I leaned back in my seat, staring idly ahead, knowing for certain the crew was behind this.

I would later learn just how bloody it got.

In a combined effort, Nixon and Flynn had dismantled the Vipers once and for all.

NIXON...

He looked up from his phone after reading Eman's latest update. The Vipers' main lair of business was currently up in flames. Their vaults had been emptied, their men guarding it wounded; the wiser of them had fled, scurrying from the police as it descended on the nondescript building in light of the explosion.

Nixon stood at the terminal of the Vancouver port, watching a new shipment of storage containers being seized by the authorities. One little mouse told another mouse that the Vipers' last hoorah wouldn't be coming in via trucks, but in shipping containers.

Nixon wondered how much torture Flynn inflicted on the poor Viper that had been kidnapped for such intel. It perturbed Nixon just a little bit how easy Flynn had slid into his role.

"They're done," Tyrone said, coming up to stand beside him. "The city now belongs to the One Percent."

Nixon stiffened a nod. "They've come full circle."

Tyrone looked at Nixon, a bothered look in his expression. "I'm not trying to bring up the past, but I've learned some things very recently, and I'm not sure bringing them to light will matter."

Pocketing his phone, Nixon turned his attention to Tyrone. "What's this about?"

Tyrone rubbed at his jaw, searching for words. "I never liked the kid. I always felt...there was something about him that unsettled me."

"I thought it was the way he looked at Vixen,"

Nixon replied. "Like he wanted her."

"See, that's what I thought at first," he replied, bringing his brows together. "But...the more I thought about it, the more it didn't sense. The look he'd given her that very first day, when she stood by the window, after I'd warned him to look away, he... didn't look at her like he looked at a girl he wanted because, we've been around him now and his behaviour to girls is a lot more loose than he had been with Vixen."

Nixon studied Tyrone carefully. "How did he look at her then?"

"He looked at her like she was a...thing, Nixon. Like...she was a job." He sighed now, seeming disturbed. "When he burned down your island, when he sent his men on a chase around the place, shooting shit up, there was no...method to it. He had the men circle the area long enough for us to get there, to find them and kill them. On top of that, taking Vixen in a car across the island just so she could get on a seaplane made no sense. The seaplanes had a station minutes from the hotel, Nixon. If he wanted her off the island, he would have whisked her away in under twenty minutes. He didn't, though."

Nixon felt the hairs on the back of his neck prickle. "For what purpose?"

"He wanted to get caught," Tyrone told him.

"He would have thought we were going to kill him."

"But you didn't, and he knew it."

"That's too omniscient, Tyrone."

"No, see, it isn't," Tyrone retorted, voice rising. "Think about it. Why did he stir shit with you so much? He wanted to see your reaction. He wanted to know how far he could push you. He made you think he was razor focused on the girl, but Nixon, it was *you* he was working all along. He studied you, the way Roz studied his jobs. He played you, the way Roz used to play around on the job. He was on the island long before he made his presence known. He'd watched you, studied you, found out your strengths...and your weaknesses."

Nixon took a few moments of silent deliberation to respond. "It's a possible theory," he finally said.

Tyrone glowered. "You don't believe it, though."

"No. Flynn didn't know what happened on that mountain—"

"What if he did, though? He worked for Toby for years. He was Toby's best kept secret, Nixon. And then all of a sudden he's galivanting back to San Diego to drive rings around the police? That's bullshit. The kid knew what Hobbs was planning to do through Toby – Toby had informed Hobbs of the fucking job, had told him he might need a driver. Why say that to Hobbs? Hobbs had never needed a driver before that."

"You're saying Toby had something to do with this, too."

"Toby would have looked over every inch of Flynn's life, would have known with absolute certainty that Flynn was related to Roz. It takes some digging, only because their fathers were different, but not so much digging that it becomes impossible to mine out."

"Tyrone—"

"You want to know the clincher?" Tyrone interrupted quickly, looking like a man on a mission now.

"What's the clincher?"

"Okay, here it is." Tyrone leaned closer to Nixon. "Roz had a warrant back in San Diego. Guess what it was for."

Nixon felt his heart plummet. "Rape."

"Rape," Tyrone repeated, nodding. "Roz had a rap sheet longer than my arm. He was a fucking predator. You're telling me Flynn, who he was close to, who he was brothers with, didn't believe his brother was capable of it? He did know. And when Roz died for violating Toby's granddaughter, Flynn disappeared from San Diego almost immediately. I asked around, and once again, not much digging was needed to learn that not only did Flynn go to Toby in light of it, he'd been going to Toby for *years*. He was close to Toby, so close he would have wanted Roz dead just as much for what he did to his granddaughter."

Nixon had to put his hands in his pockets to hide the raging tremors coursing through his fingers. He clenched his jaw, running over the events in his mind, muttering, "Toby said once the One Percent's fall was the greatest mistake. That Hobbs shouldn't have given us that job because of the domino effect."

"It created a rift. Destabilized the drug empire."

"Which hurt Toby's pockets because he was right into the cocaine industry in Seattle."

Tyrone nodded solemnly. "And now Flynn's climbing his way to the top of the One Percent."

"And Toby will be behind it."

"Exactly."

With a weak shrug, he asked, "Where does Vixen fit into this?"

"Vixen was a secret not even Toby knew about.

Flynn wouldn't have known she'd been on that mountain. He would have played his revenge card with her when he snatched her, maybe in an effort to turn her against you, but...I don't think he actually believed she loved you."

"He thought she'd just go with him?"

"Yes, in an effort to hurt you. To make you weak. He knew you loved her. He wanted to see you crumble. A person in despair needs all the support he can get."

"I did need it." Nixon reflected on the moment Flynn had made first contact with him after the events on the island. He'd come to him looking sorrowful, wanting to make amends, wanting to work together.

It may have all been bullshit.

Flynn could have very well needed Nixon and the crew, and their connections, especially Eman's (that man had his hands in everyone's pocket).

And now that Nixon really thought it over, he recognized how easy Flynn drew his emotions out of him. Nixon wasn't so cold. He didn't kill in cold blood. And with Flynn behaving in that kid-like way, it was easy to assume Nixon wouldn't have killed someone so lost and fragile. He played his role so well. Acted so vulnerable, it made Nixon think twice about killing him.

The Flynn that was sitting pretty in the One Percent now was ruthless.

You don't become that ruthless in two years.

Jesus.

"What if I'd died on that island?" he wondered just then, feeling weak with anger. "What then?"

"But you wouldn't have," Tyrone responded. "Flynn's men never shot to kill, and Jane Sullivan was still in town after the seaplane she was supposed to leave on mysteriously suffered engine problems."

Fuck.

Fuck.

Fuck.

Nixon began to pace and Tyrone watched, looking equally betrayed. "What do you want to do, Nixon?"

Nixon laughed emptily. "Nothing."

"Nothing?"

"Don't you get it, Tyrone? There's nothing that can be done here. They've ascended and we *helped* them. I've established myself here, used my real identity to live as clean and transparent as I can. To try and undo this is...impossible. We have a gang that's untouchable now. We have a cartel on the other side of this working to bring their supply in. We have our crew's businesses cleaning the money as it funnels through. The set-up itself is impeccable."

"But we got here under a lie."

"That's right. It was."

"It means we can't trust him."

Nixon nodded, stopping to look up at the cloudy sky with misty eyes. "It means...It means we have to stand our ground at all times. It means...we have to stand on guard always to protect what we love."

It meant an eternity of uncertainty. A lifetime of working to keep the peace, or else everything he built might come shattering down around him.

It meant spending every second cherishing his Queen.

EPILOGUE

VICTORIA...

Nixon opened the door for me and helped me out of the car, planting a soft kiss on my lips. We ignored the eyes darting our way as he took me by the hand and walked me through the hotel doors.

Under the lobby lights, I glanced down at the diamond on my ring finger, loving the way it sparkled in all directions.

"You like it, Mrs Cooper," Nixon stated, smirking at me.

"I love it," I corrected, squeezing his hand tight. "I can't get enough of it."

We had a small ceremony in the backyard of our sprawling new home. Hobbs married us under a blue summer sky. It was strangely emotional for everyone there.

The entire crew looked like they were fighting back tears. I was sure they were mostly happy to see Nixon finally at peace.

I was busy, back in school, still figuring myself out. I had made a few friends, but it was a little hard because everyone knew who I was, and it was sort of off-putting to them. Nixon had made the news repeatedly, throwing hard cash into businesses, even donating to causes. I wasn't sure he gave a true shit about the charities. He did it to make me happy, to see the approval in my eyes. But everyone suspected he had connections to the bikers – they were *always* frequenting his businesses, partying at his club, eating at his restaurants, crashing at his hotel.

"I like what you did to me this morning," he murmured to me. "I could get used to you taking charge more often."

I laughed. "I think I didn't like it as much as you did."

His eyes shined. "No?"

"No."

"So when you rode me, fingers digging into my chest, moaning my name like a prayer until you came around my cock, it wasn't all that good?"

"It was alright," I lied, downplaying it. "I've had better moments."

Just as we arrived at the meeting room, he put his hand on the knob and turned to look at me, that challenge in his eye. "Do you think, if I took you on the table in front of everyone, I could get you to tell me the honest truth?"

I slid closer to him and pressed a kiss full of tongue and heat against his mouth. "I think you can get me to tell you anything you want, Nixon."

His eyes widened. "A truth, for a change."

"Don't get used to it."

"No, I know better not to, baby."

He opened the door and we walked in. The table

was full, the crew were already seated. I glanced around, catching every face.

Tyrone.

Rowan.

Tiger.

Eman.

Doll.

And a few new ones I was slowly getting to know.

My eyes widened when I caught sight of Flynn at the head of one end of the table. He sat there, stoic, his face hard in a way I was still unused to. He wore his cut – PRESIDENT – on proud display.

Nixon took a seat at the other end of the table. He brought me down on his lap, his fingers lightly brushing my inner thigh just under my dress. His gaze was trapped straight ahead, locked onto Flynn. His light expression, his soft smile and amused eyes were gone.

He looked...hard.

And Flynn...looked back with a very similar expression.

I spotted Tyrone's head snapping back and forth, a guarded look on his face. It unnerved me just a little that something felt a little off.

"Who owns me?" I whispered down at Nixon, lightly biting at his ear to catch his attention.

He blinked away from Flynn and turned to look at me. "I do, baby."

I smiled challengingly. "Prove it."

He smashed his mouth to mine, owning my lips, owning my soul. His tongue clashed with my tongue; his lips bruised mine, and I groaned in approval. We kissed with the same passion of two lovers who hadn't seen each other in years.

When I pulled back, satisfied by the wanting look in his eye, I slid off his lap, quickly glancing at Tyrone. Tyrone stiffened a nod to me, grateful I'd broken the ice.

Standing behind Nixon, I slid my fingers through his hair and down his face. I trailed my touch down his throat before sprawling my hand possessively against his chest, right over his heart.

This was my man.

My captor.

My love.

My saviour.

And this crew was my family.

The door slammed open, a glowering Hobbs burst through, mouthing off the traffic, mouthing off the city. "I fucking hate this place," he growled. "Why do you idiots insist on dragging me out of my fucking home and amongst asshole drivers? It doesn't stop raining, and my hair is ruined, and this wind will fucking be the death of me!"

"You should have an umbrella," Tiger said. "Everyone has an umbrella."

"I don't want a fucking umbrella," he retorted.

"You need better hair gel," Doll inserted. "That's why your hair isn't staying in place."

"I think he just needs to cut it," Rowan replied. "It looks a bit long to me."

"I think his hair is beautiful," Eman complimented. "It really is, Hobbs. It's framed around your face just right."

"Fuck you," Hobbs cursed, throwing his briefcase down on the table. "Fuck your bullshit advice and bullshit compliments, I never asked for it."

Everyone laughed. I felt Nixon's chest rumble, saw the way Flynn's face broke from stern to amused.

Hobbs fought the smile on his lips as his gaze swept to mine and lingered just an extra second for me to see the sweetness there.

Then he slammed the briefcase open and growled, "Alright, fuckheads, this is what we're gonna do..."

THE END.

AUTHOR'S NOTE

Thank you so much for taking a chance with Captive and reading! I'm eternally grateful for your support.

I hope you were as consumed with these characters as I was.

If you want to check out more of my releases, or send a message, you can find me here:

www.facebook.com/rj.lewis13

As always, thank you! <3

-RJ

Printed in Great Britain
by Amazon

44476361R00341